Chicagoland

Chicagoland

By Charles McKelvy

The Dunery Press

Chicagoland

By Charles McKelvy

Published in 1988 by
The Dunery Press
P.O. Box 116
Harbert, Michigan
49115-0116

Design and cover illustration by
David Bates Design.

Library of Congress
Catalog Card Number: 88-070418

ISBN 0-944771-00-9

To Natalie

Table of Contents

Rauch and Spiegel

Chapter One

Old Man Harvey kept the heat so low, Mary Margaret Quinn's fingers ached. "Maggie" kicked the space heater but got no warmth for her troubles.

Cursing under her breath, she bent back over the ancient Underwood and continued hacking out copy for the spring plumbing supply catalog.

"Moonlighting," she mumbled. "What a delight!"

The 26-year-old daughter of a steel executive and his professionally Catholic wife, her real job was working the evening shift for Chicago's fabled Municipal News Agency, or Muni News. The agency dished out a steady stream of death and destruction on vintage teletype machines from a dingy 14th floor office.

On warm nights Maggie and her fellows flung open the windows and threw pennies at the elevated trains clattering around the city's "Loop" below. Maggie led the league with a .434 average. Having grown up with four older brothers helped.

Owned by Chicago's three daily papers, Muni News wired its weird stories to most local radio and television stations. None could function without it; none favored it with an on-air credit. Few offered a Muni News "kid" a job. Most of Maggie's colleagues were hoping to report for papers in Little Rock, Peoria or Trenton, New Jersey -- thus graduating to the Chicago "big time" papers after five years in Siberia.

December 1976 wasn't the good old days: then any half-way decent Muni News reporter was practically guaranteed a job at a Chicago daily after a year in the Muni News trenches.

Still, Maggie had her hopes. She was a natural optimist. She was one of the first women Muni News assigned to the mid-watch, or 5 to midnight shift. A South Side Irish-Catholic, Maggie got along with the cops and firemen with whom she spent most of her working hours. She could drink with the best of them.

Overweight and not exactly a raving beauty, she was treated as a kid sister by the younger ones and a favored daughter by sergeants and chiefs. With their tips, she often scooped the dailies' over-paid and underworked police reporters.

Maggie was coming up on two years at Muni News. Except for her first week of training, she had been on nights the whole time. She was accustomed to working 15-day stretches without time off. Only the crippled and lame spent more than two years at Muni News.

She thus applied at all the papers and radio/TV stations.

Nothing.

So one slow news Sunday in September she answered a blind ad in the TRIBUNE: "Growing company seeks intelligent writer to generate bright, lively copy about a wide range of subjects."

Maggie sent her resume and Muni News clippings to the post office box listed, then promptly forgot about it. If nothing came up, she'd start applying out of state.

And that would drive her mother crazy.

Noreen Quinn wanted her only daughter to move back home to their Lace Curtain Irish neighborhood on the city's southwest side. Noreen was forever finding "nice young men" for her at Saint Barnabas Catholic Church.

Her father was always trying to get her to go golfing with him and some of his bright young colleagues. Dad would dearly love his daughter to marry a rising young steel executive, even if the guy wasn't Catholic.

None of Maggie's four brothers had gone into the business. Brian and Bill were school teachers. Terry sold life insurance, and Michael was finding himself somewhere in Southern California. All but Michael were married. Brian and Bill had already produced grandchildren; Terry's wife had one in the oven.

Money had been no object when the boys were in college, especially when Brian and Bill chose Dad's alma mater -- Notre Dame. But when Maggie wanted to go to Northwestern to study journalism, they ordered her to a state school. After all, women needed education for only two reasons: to become school teachers, and/or to provide scintillating dinner conversation when their husbands invited the boss to dinner.

"Why journalism, Maggie?" her father had moaned. "It's a profession for drunks and womanizers."

In solemn tones, he retold the story of his uncle Bertie Quinn. A reporter for a Boston paper, Uncle Bertie had drunk himself to death.

But dad came up with the tuition money for Northern Illinois University. At the beginning of each semester, he invited her to quit school, come home, and work as a secretary at Mid-Con Steel. "You could meet a nice young man," he would say. "Lots of up-and-comers around."

Maggie would feel nauseous and hang up the phone.

After graduation, she did come home. Journalism jobs were scarce, so she actually did work as a secretary for Mid-Con for two years. Finally, she got a job at Muni News.

Over her mother's tears, she and a colleague at Muni News, Norma Jankowski, agreed to share an apartment on north Dearborn Street -- just minutes away from work. Certain Maggie would return, Noreen kept her bed made and room ready.

Maggie shuddered at the memory. She kicked at the space heater again. Her eyes went out of focus as she forced herself to describe a particularly obscene-looking pipe joint. All this talk about "female" and "male" fittings got her thinking about sex. She'd had little of that lately. At least she didn't put out to get stories like Norma.

And working nights certainly didn't give a young woman much time for a normal social life. Mostly it was: beers with the boys at 2 in the morning; six hours of sleep; breakfast at McDonald's; a few freezing hours moonlighting at Harvey Advertising and back to the Muni News grinder.

It was already 3:30 on December 20, and Frank Harvey promised his client final copy by New Year's Eve.

"Shoot," Maggie said, looking at the calendar and her watch. "When am I supposed to do my Christmas shopping?"

Maggie got a pack of Marlboro Lights from her purse and made up for the lack of ashtrays by filling her McDonald's coffee cup with water. She was halfway through her pack and another ream of copy when Frank Harvey announced: "You gotta phone call. And turn that space heater off while you're gone. I'm not made of money."

Maggie took the call outside Mr. Harvey's office.

"Hello," Maggie said.

"Mary? Mary Quinn?" a woman said.

"Yes, this is MAGGIE Quinn."

"You prefer to be called 'Maggie?'"

"Yes." Maggie glanced at Old Man Harvey.

He grimaced and slashed his finger across his throat.

"Well, Maggie, this is Linda Jaffrey. I'm senior vice president for consumer accounts at Rauch & Spiegel."

"If this is one of those surveys or something, you'd better call me at home because I can't . . ."

"Maybe you didn't hear me correctly. I said I'm from Rauch and Spiegel."

Mail order house?

Collection agency?

Front for the mob?

"Yeah, so?"

"You don't remember?"

"No, I don't remember. Look, I really can't talk now. Can I call you later or something?"

"No," Linda Jaffrey said. "I'll be in meetings all afternoon. We've accepted your application for a position as account executive. When can you start? Tomorrow?"

"Application? Tomorrow?!?"

"Maggie, we're swamped here. The sooner you start, the better."

"Get off the goddamned phone," Old Man Harvey hissed, worried that one of his three clients might decide to call.

Maggie nodded at him and said into the phone, "I've got to think this over."

"What's to think over? You want to waste away at Muni News the rest of your life?"

"No, but I didn't expect anything to turn up so fast. What does the job pay?"

"Eighteen five the first year and after that -- well, it depends on you, doesn't it?"

That was double Maggie's combined income from Muni News and Harvey Advertising.

"Rauch and Spiegel -- you're an advertising . . ."

"Strictly public relations. We got out of advertising five years ago."

"Oh. If I take the job, I couldn't start tomorrow. I'd have to give at least two weeks' notice."

"All right," Linda Jaffrey said. "But I want you here on the 3rd -- no later."

"All right. I'll be there on the 3rd. Where are you located? There was no address in your ad."

"You don't know where Rauch and Spiegel is?!?"

"Not exactly."

"You're a reporter, and you don't know where Rauch and Spiegel is?"

"No, I don't know where you are."

"Twenty-sixth floor of the Howers Building. You do know where the Howers Building is, don't you?"

"Three fifty-nine North Michigan, unless they moved it."

"Good. I'll see you on the 3rd. We start work at 8:30, so don't be late. You working at Muni News tonight?"

"Yeah. Why?"

"You mean you don't know?"

"No."

"Mayor Daley: he had a heart attack at his doctor's office. They're saying he might be dead. God, I'd give anything to be in your shoes tonight."

"Mayor Daley? Dead?"

"I've got to run. Remember, don't be late. 'bye."

Maggie was still staring at the phone when she heard Frank Harvey scream, "get back to work! That catalogue has got to be finished by . . ."

"Pardon the French, Mr. Harvey," Maggie said, "but you know where you can stick your goddamn catalog. Now, if you'll excuse me, I've got a story to cover."

She was out the door before he could respond.

Chapter Two

Maggie stepped out on east Adams Street and pulled the hood of her Air Force parka over her head and tugged on her down-filled mittens. She knew she looked like Scott of the Antarctic, but she spent her nights slogging through burning buildings, not cruising Rush Street. She wore a thick wool skirt with two pairs of pantyhose, wool knee socks and her brother Terry's old Boy Scout hiking boots. They were warm and waterproof -- so what if everyone stared?

Maggie stopped at a corner newsstand and asked, "Got the afternoon papers yet?"

"Not yet, lady."

"You hear anything going on this afternoon?"

"Heard lots of sirens about 45 minutes ago. Lots of 'em. But I ain't got no radio; can't afford one sellin' nuthin' but these damn papers."

"Thanks," Maggie said, hurrying west on Adams.

She peered at the passing faces. Something WAS wrong. The general upset clashed with the bright Christmas lights and windows.

Maggie turned north on State Street and overheard two elderly women about to board a bus for the southwest side console one another in whispery Polish. The only discernable sound was "Daley."

The two women looked at one another and crossed themselves.

"What is it?" Maggie asked, reaching for her reporter's notebook and pencil. "What's wrong? What about Mayor Daley?"

"No English," one of them said. The other muttered something in Polish and crossed herself again.

"He can't be dead," Maggie said, rushing on. "No way." Maggie realized as she crossed Monroe Street that she was only five when Daley was first elected in 1955.

Maggie crossed herself.

She had interviewed Mayor Daley that summer after he caught a salmon in Lake Michigan.

"Come on home and have breakfast with us," he said. "You haven't tasted nuthin' until you've had salmon the way Sis cooks it for breakfast."

Maggie made the mistake of calling the city desk first and was ordered to cover an extra-alarm fire in the suburbs.

Now, as she ran through the slush, Maggie wished she had told the city editor to shove it.

Maggie stopped at the bank to cash a check and overheard one customer ask another, "Did you hear the news?"

"No."

"Mayor Daley is dead."

An elderly black man in another line shook his head. His eyes brimming, he said to no one in particular, "He was a good man. A real good man."

"Does anyone know what happened?" Maggie asked.

The black man thought he had heard something about a heart attack. Someone else said the Mayor had apparently collapsed at his doctor's office.

No one knew for sure.

Maggie got her money and ran north on LaSalle Street to Washington Street where City Hall was filled with clusters of whispering politicians and patronage workers.

"Is it true?" Maggie asked a pot-bellied cop idling next to THE elevator that took THE Mayor to THE floor.

The cop shrugged. "Who wants to know?"

"Muni News."

"We don't know for sure, but they've taken him to Northwestern Memorial. If them docs can't save him, nobody can. He looked so good this morning. Top of the world. He even shot a basket at some park this morning."

Maggie patted him on the arm.

As she was turning to go, a raucous argument exploded out of a nearby elevator.

Fifty-first Ward Alderman Vincent "Lightning" Endrijonas shouted: "I was with him this morning at Mann Park. He told me that he wanted me to be . . . hey," he said, noticing that a bystander was recording his remarks in a notebook. "Who the hell are you?"

"Maggie Quinn, Alderman Endrijonas. Muni News. Now what

was it Mayor Daley was telling you this morning at Mann Park?"

"Nothing. He didn't tell me nothing."

"Yeah," Alderman Edward Kluzinski of the 54th ward said. "He didn't tell Alderman Endrijonas nothing."

"You just talked about basketball, right?" Maggie said.

"That's right," Endrijonas said.

"Nothing about successors?"

"What's all this talk about succession? The Mayor's gonna be fine, ain't that right, Alderman Kluzinski?"

"Absolutely. Why . . ."

A pack of reporters burst from another elevator. Muni News's City Hall reporter, Bob Storely, was among them.

"What the hell are you doing here?" he said.

"I always cut through City Hall on my way to work."

"When I need help with my beat, I'll ask the desk for it. Get back to the newsroom where you belong."

"Anything you say, Bobbie."

At the Muni News building, a stranger on the elevator said, "He's dead."

"He was the only mayor I've ever known," Maggie said.

"Me too," another young woman said.

"The best mayor this city'll ever have," an older man said. Maggie got off at 14 and stopped outside Muni News to collect her thoughts and energy. She could hear the city editor, Pete Poulos, roaring over the din of the ancient typewriters and teletype machines: "Copy! I want copy!"

Maggie prayed for strength and walked into the maelstrom.

Chapter Three

Maggie went to Pete Poulos' cluttered desk in the center of the newsroom and waited for the bug-eyed city editor to notice her.

Poulos rolled his sleeves another turn and blue-penciled a page of copy.

"Here," he said, hitting Maggie in the midriff with it, "give this to Art, and take number four over there. Storely's got a story from City Hall to dictate, and I need somebody to start calling Daley's neighbors in Bridgeport."

Maggie nodded and took the copy to the teletype operator.

"Here, Art, just what you need -- another bulletin."

Art stubbed out a Pall Mall and lit another one. "What's it say?"

"Northwestern Memorial is going to have a press conference in 10 minutes."

"For Christ's sake, why don't we just say he's dead?" Art grumbled.

"Because we haven't confirmed it yet," Poulos said. "Now get the damn bulletin out on the wire!"

Maggie went back to Poulos' desk and said, "Look, Pete, I've got to talk to Mr. Shearson. Is he in?"

Poulos continued correcting copy. "I thought I told you to take Storely's story."

"You did, but I really do have to see Mr. Shearson. It's important."

Poulos pounded the metal desk. "Mayor Daley is either dying or dead at this very moment, and you want to talk to Mr. Shearson."

"It'll only take five minutes, Pete. I promise."

"You get an offer, Maggie?" Poulos said without looking up.

"Sort of."

The old Underwoods along the rewrite bank grew still.

"Hey," Poulos said, waving his arm, "this isn't a damn social hour! Back to work!"

Typing resumed, but ears strained.

Maggie glanced at the nearest rewrite desk. Steve Quisenberry bent his boney shoulders over the typewriter and pretended to listen intently into his headset. But he clearly had heard the whole conversation. He brushed his long brown hair out of his eyes and adjusted his glasses.

"So," Poulos said, "where you going -- ROCKFORD STAR? PEORIA JOURNAL? ORLANDO SENTINEL?"

"I'm staying right here in Chicago, Pete."

Steve Quisenberry took off his headset and stared at Maggie.

"You mean the TRIBUNE . . ."

"No, Pete. Not the TRIBUNE, and not the SUN-TIMES or DAILY NEWS either. I got a job with Rauch and Spiegel. I'm going to be a flak."

"What?!?"

"Pete, the sooner I tell Mr. Shearson, the sooner I can start writing Daley stuff. I ran into Alderman Endrijonas on the way to work, and I think he's going to make a power play."

"Storely's on City Hall, not you!" Poulos stormed. "If you're gonna quit and go be a flak, then go tell Mr. Shearson! The rest of us have work to do."

"All right, Pete."

Maggie knocked twice on Mr. Shearson's door and waited.

"Yes?"

"Mr. Shearson, it's Maggie Quinn. Mid-watch police. I need to talk to you."

"Say again."

Maggie repeated herself, louder.

"Quinn? Ah yes. Come in."

David R. Shearson did not rise to greet his employee. Rather, he remained reclined in his wooden swivel chair watching television.

"God," he said, "I'd give anything to be a reporter today. Anything."

Maggie stepped up to the general manager's empty desk and cleared her throat.

Some pretty-boy TV talker was reading the latest Muni News bulletin verbatim.

"Uh, Mr. Shearson, I'm here to give notice. I've accepted a job as an account executive at Rauch and Spiegel, and they want me to start on January 3rd."

Shearson stretched his arms over his head and rearranged his feet on his desk. He was a long, thin man with frail WASP features and silver-rimmed glasses. He had drunk his way out of a promising position on the TRIBUNE's city desk and was awaiting retirement in the backwaters of Muni News.

"Pete says we're beating the pants off the competition. God, I'd give anything to be out there with you kids today."

Maggie caught a wiff of gin and noticed the cabinet was ajar.

"Mr. Shearson, I'm giving notice. I'm leaving in two weeks to take a job at Rauch and Spiegel."

A commercial for laundry detergent broke Shearson's concentration.

"Say again?"

Maggie repeated herself.

Shearson dropped his feet to the floor with a dull thud. "What?!? You mean you're going to promote cat food?"

"Not exactly cat food, but I am going into public relations."

"Why?"

"Because I'm tired of getting the runaround from the papers and TV and radio."

"Do you know anything about Rauch and Spiegel?" Shearson said, glancing thirstily at his cabinet.

"Not really. I've seen a few of their press releases when I've been on rewrite. They can't write to save their lives. I know that."

"Then why work there? Why not stay here and wait for a really good job at a paper or radio station to come along? Pete tells me you've made marvelous progress out there. He says you're one of the best gals we've hired since World War II."

"You mean why don't I take a job at the PEORIA STAR and hope the TRIBUNE'll notice me after a few years?"

"I think you're exaggerating a bit. Surely, it's not . . ."

"Mr. Shearson, stop pretending. You know there's no hope for us in Chicago. We kill the papers every day, and they ignore us when we apply for jobs. All they want are these hotshots with fancy degrees from New York and Los Angeles."

Shearson shrugged and reached for his bottle. "Want some?"

Maggie shook her head.

"Well, help yourself if you change your mind." He poured

himself a glass of straight gin and sipped it thoughtfully.

"No thanks. Not while I'm working."

Shearson smiled. "Yes, but you're leaving journalism. Under the circumstances, I think you can take one small drink on the job." He half-filled a glass and pushed it at her.

"No thanks, Mr. Shearson. I really don't like to drink while I'm working, especially tonight."

"Stubborn, aren't you?"

"Yes."

The news reader reappeared with yet another Muni News bulletin. Shearson propped his feet back on his desk and enjoyed his gin. "Too bad," he said.

"What's too bad, Mr. Shearson?"

"It's too bad the news industry is losing a talented reporter like you. Especially when this city is going to be up for grabs. God, I'd give anything to be a reporter now. There's going to be an amazing power struggle over there at City Hall. Like what goes on in the Kremlin.

"You know, Daley was just like old Papa Joe Stalin. Ruled with an iron fist, and never named a successor. Kept everybody on their toes that way. They all thought the Old Man had given the next alderman the nod, but he didn't give anybody the nod. I suppose he was waiting for one of those idiot sons of his to show some normal intelligence, but he realized he was going to have to live one hell of a long time before that happened."

Shearson was right. There was never going to be a better time to be a reporter in Chicago.

"I don't know, Mr. Shearson, maybe I should . . ."

"Come on, have a drink," Shearson said.

"All right. But just a few sips," she said, taking the glass.

Shearson lifted his. "To your decision to stay at Muni News."

Maggie set the glass back on the desk. "Wait a minute, I haven't . . ."

"Of course you have. Come on, have a drink. Then you can get back in there and scoop the pants off the papers." Shearson smiled and took a sip.

Maggie went to the window and watched a westbound Lake/Dan Ryan train clatter away from the Loop. "Mr. Shearson, I'm going to take the job. I know it doesn't make any sense to you, and I'm not sure it makes any sense to me, but I've got to get out of here."

"But . . ."

"Please hear me out. Okay?"

Shearson settled back in his chair. "Very well. Please continue."

"When you hired me, you said most people worked at Muni News a year, maybe a year and a half and then went on to bigger and better things. I know you didn't promise anything, but you more or less implied that if I did a good job here, I wouldn't have too much trouble moving on to one of the papers or at least a radio news operation."

"I said no such thing. I merely suggested that in the past -- when Chicago was a real newspaper town -- an enterprising Muni News reporter had an excellent chance of moving up."

"Okay. Maybe I just heard what I wanted to hear. Anyway, I'm getting nowhere fast applying for jobs with the papers and radio and TV. I know I should apply in other cities like Peoria and Rockford, but I'm a Chicagoan, Mr. Shearson. I'd rather stay here and drive a bus than take a top reporting job in some place like Peoria."

"You really must love Chicago to take a job in public relations just to stay here."

"That's right, Mr. Shearson. I'd rather be a flak in Chicago any day than a reporter in Peoria. So, I just wanted to tell you that my last day will be the 2nd of January."

Shearson poured Maggie's drink in his glass and took a big gulp. "Why not quit right now? Take a few weeks off and rest up for your exciting new career in public relations?"

"If you think I'm going to miss this story, Mr. Shearson, you're nuts."

Maggie was gone before Shearson could take another sip.

Chapter Four

Maggie had her Underwood smoking within minutes.

She was too late to take Storely's say-nothing story from the Hall, so she suggested a color piece on what she had observed on the way to work. It was the best thing she had ever written for Muni News, and Channels 2, 5 and 7 called as soon as it went out over the broadcast wire, demanding more. THE DAILY NEWS also wanted more for the special edition they were preparing on Daley's life and death.

Maggie had just written two more "takes" when Sal Cipriani, the day police reporter, called with the scoop of the decade: the first official confirmation that Mayor Richard J. Daley was dead of a heart attack at age 74.

Maggie quickly translated Sal's notes into a terse bulletin and shoved it at Poulos.

He glanced at it and said, "Looks good. Give it to Art."

Art's fingers flashed. When he was finished, he jabbed the "bell" key to alert receivers that THE bulletin was on the wire.

Everyone stopped working to observe the historic moment, then they bent back to their typewriters with a vengence.

"Pete, I want to call Alderman Endrijonas and get his reaction. I've got a hunch he's up to something," Maggie said.

"Go for it," Poulos said.

Maggie dialed Endrijonas' ward office on the far southeast side and said, "Alderman Endrijonas please."

"You just missed him," a gruff male voice said.

"You know where he went?"

"Said he was going over to Alderman Mulford's place."

"Alderman Mulford's?!?"

Fifty-third Ward Alderman William "Big Bill" Mulford was the Daley Machine's black lap dog. He was also vice mayor.

"That's what I said. Hey, who is this anyway?"

"A friend of the family," Maggie said, disconnecting. She dialed Alderman Mulford's ward office on south State Street and got the obese alderman himself on the second ring.

"Alderman's office," he answered.

"Alderman Mulford?"

"Yeah, this is him. Who is this?"

"Alderman Mulford, this is Maggie Quinn from Muhi News. Have you heard the news about Mayor Daley?"

"Of course, I've heard the news. You think I live under a rock or something?"

"No, of course not. Since you know that Mayor Daley is dead, I guess you know that that makes you . . ."

"That makes me Mayor of Chicago. That's right. And you're the first to know it."

Maggie banged out a bulletin to that effect and kited it to the city desk.

She put new paper behind the platen and said, "Now then, Mayor Mulford, what are your plans as new mayor?"

"'Mayor Mulford.' I like the sound of that. The Honorable William J. Mulford. Yeah, I like that a lot."

"You'd better get used to it. So, what is your first official act going to be?"

"Well, let's not get too hasty. Our great leader has just passed, and I don't think it's appropriate to take any bold new action at this time. I would like to begin my administration by extending my deepest sympathies to Mrs. Daley and her family."

"Have you given any thought to committee appointments? For example, will you allow to Alderman Endrijonas to remain as chairman of the Finance Committee, or will you appoint someone new to replace him -- perhaps a black, woman or other minority?"

"Well," he said after a pause, "I suppose some changes could be made. I emphasize the word 'could' you understand."

"Yes, I understand," Maggie said, typing his every word.

"But you raise an interesting point Miz Quinn. A very interesting point. Yes, I suppose SOME changes could be made."

"How soon?"

"Well, like I said before, Mayor Daley has just passed. I hardly think it's fitting that . . . oh, would you excuse me just for a moment."

"Sure."

By pressing the headset against her ear, Maggie could hear

Alderman Endrijonas' nasal voice in the background.

"Who's that on the phone?" she heard Endrijonas say.

"Some girl from Muni News," Mulford replied.

"Muni News?!? What the hell you tell her?"

"Nuthin'," Mulford whispered. "Nuthin'."

"Then tell her to get lost. We got to have a us a little talk."

When Alderman Mulford got back on the phone he was all formality. "Miz Quinn, I'm terribly sorry, but I have some ward business to attend to. So if you'll excuse me, I'll have to let you go."

"Is Alderman Endrijonas there? Is that him in the background?"

Mulford disconnected.

Maggie clicked her switch. "Alderman Mulford? Alderman Mulford? Damn, I lost him."

She redialed immediately and got a busy signal. She tried again and got another busy signal. She tore the copy out of her typewriter and flung it at Poulos.

"That's all I could get, Pete. I heard Endrijonas in the background. Something's going on down there. I think we should check it out."

"You stay right here," Poulos said, reaching for his phone. "I'll send Franzon down. He's on south police tonight. Keep trying to get Mulford."

Maggie dialed again and got another busy signal. On the next try she got a recorded message stating "that this number is temporarily out of order."

She flipped through her beat book and found Mulford's unlisted home number. Mrs. Anna Mulford answered on the fourth ring and said her husband was at the ward office.

"Would you please have him call Maggie Quinn at Muni News as soon as he gets home?"

"I want to know how you got this number," Mrs. Mulford said.

Maggie wasn't about to tell her an alcoholic police lieutenant had given it to her in exchange for a bottle of cheap scotch. "A lucky guess. Mrs. Mulford, by law your husband is now Mayor of Chicago. How do you feel about that?"

"You want my opinion?" the woman said, her voice warming a bit.

"Sure."

"If you ask me, it's about time this city had a black mayor. And if anybody deserves to be the first, it's my William. That man has picked up after Daley his whole life. Now it's time he collected. Don't get me wrong. I'm as sorry as the next person about Mayor Daley's passing, but it's our turn now. Whenever Mayor Daley wanted the vote, we gave it to him.

"He wouldn't have been re-elected last year without the black vote. And he wouldn't have had the black vote without my William workin' night and day to get it out," Mrs. Mulford said.

"Mrs. Mulford, does your husband spend a lot of time with Alderman Endrijonas?"

"Look, why don't I have my husband call you when he gets home?"

"Okay. But isn't it true that your husband plays golf with Alderman Endrijonas on a regular basis and that you have both been seen on his boat?"

"I know what you're drivin' at, girl, and I don't like it," she said, slamming down the phone.

Maggie rubbed her ear and grinned at Poulos. "Something is definitely rotten in Denmark tonight, Pete. Mulford's wife about had a coronary when I started asking her about Endrijonas. I'll bet you five dollars that Mulford backs down by the end of the night."

"You're on," Poulos said. "What else you working on?"

"How about a color piece on Daley's love of fishing. Remember that salmon he caught and . . ."

"Give me four takes and then start calling the rest of the City Council for their reaction," Poulos said.

Maggie was halfway into her fish story when every news editor in Chicago called to demand more details on the "Mulford is Mayor" story. Their reporters had been unable to reach either Mulford or Endrijonas by phone and the two men had yet to be found.

Poulos tried to fend them off, but one got through to Maggie.

"This is Dave Klepper at Channel 4. Where the hell did you come up with this shit about Mulford? How do we know this is true? When you'd talk to him?"

"What's wrong, your hotshots can't get a hold of him? I guess you'll just have to give us credit for a change."

Maggie's exclusive survived the night, and they all cheered when every single Muni News customer was forced to attribute the story to the agency.

"Can I buy you a cup of coffee?" Poulos said, accepting Maggie's five dollars.

"No thanks, Pete. But I'll take a rain check."

They were about to leave when a messenger appeared with a one-page press release on Alderman Mulford's letterhead.

It read: "I regret any confusion I may have caused earlier this evening by wrongfully claiming to be mayor of this great city. After further consultation with my colleagues on the City Council, I have agreed that this matter will be best settled by the appropriate committee at such a time after the city has had the proper opportunity to mourn the passing of its great leader."

The messenger was gone before anyone could catch him.

"What are we going to do without you?" Poulos said, handing Maggie her winnings. "You sure you don't want to change your mind, Maggie?"

"You want to put me on City Hall and double my salary?"

"You know Storely's . . ."

". . . old man's an old friend of Mr. Shearson's."

"Well, yeah. But . . ."

"Pete, I've made up my mind. Okay?"

"Okay. But I'm going to miss you."

Maggie swallowed. "Yeah, I'll miss you too, Pete. But I'll be back. Heck, they'll probably have me messenger press releases over here."

He smiled and patted her on the back. "Can I treat you to an elevator ride?"

"Sure."

The Loop was cold and quiet when they left the Spudmeier Building. Workers had already drapped the LaSalle Street entrance to City Hall with black and purple bunting.

"It's something, isn't it?" Poulos said.

"Yeah, sure is."

"Can I walk you to your car?"

"Thanks, Pete, but I'll be all right."

"You sure?"

"Pete, how many times have you sent me out to cover triple homicides on the West Side all by myself?"

"Yeah, I guess you're right."

"Of course, I'm right. I'll see you tomorrow. I've still got two weeks, remember?"

"Right. You take care of yourself, Maggie." He pinched her cheek and trudged across Wells Street to the attended parking garage where he always kept his '76 Olds 88.

Maggie walked half a block north to Wacker Drive and descended the stairs to the lower level where she stashed her rusting '72 VW Beetle amidst the pigeon droppings and empty wine bottles.

Maggie let the engine warm itself against the bitter cold and popped open the ashtray. There were several sizable roaches from which to choose. Plus there was half a lid in the glove box and some rolling papers.

Maggie put a roach between two match heads and was about to snort the night away when she realized what she really wanted to do.

"Not tonight, girl," she said.

She put the roach back in the ashtray, shifted into reverse and backed into the green-lighted lanes of Lower Wacker Drive.

Maggie waited for a SUN-TIMES delivery truck to speed by, and then headed south to pay her respects.

Chapter Five

Knowing that all 3.2 million Chicagoans would want to mourn their mayor, the Daley family began immediate funeral preparations.

By the time Maggie Quinn arrived at Nativity of Our Lord Church on west 37th Street in the wee hours of December 21, police were already corralling mourners behind blue barricades. Enormous network news trucks were in position on the side streets, and for every patrolman there were at least three sergeants, two lieutenants and one captain to tell him what to do.

Maggie pulled up next to a young cop and said, "Officer, can I park around here?"

Police Officer Edward Rigaletti rubbed his hands together and bent into the window to get a better look at this lady. Not half bad, he thought.

"Depends," he said.

"Depends on what?"

"Depends on who's askin'."

Maggie held her press card in front of his frozen face.

"Reporter, huh? Must be a million and a half of 'em here already."

"Look, Officer Rigaletti," Maggie said, reading his name plate, "I was born and raised in this city. I'm not here to do a story. I just want to go in and pay my respects. He was the only mayor I ever knew. I know it sounds funny, but it's like my grandfather died."

Eddie Rigaletti was a short, wirey Italian-American with a big heart. "Yeah, that's kind of the way I feel too. Look, you just park over there behind the funeral home, and I'll watch your car until you come back."

"Thanks."

Officer Rigaletti moved the barricade so Maggie could park next to McKeon Funeral Home where the Mayor had been embalmed.

He's kind of cute, Maggie thought as she mounted the church steps. Looks a little bit like Al Pacino, but he should get a hat that fits.

She slipped into the massive church, instinctively dipped her right fingers in the holy water by the door and crossed herself.

Mrs. Daley and two of her sons were greeting mourners at the altar rail. As she walked up the center aisle, Maggie glimpsed the dead mayor. She stopped and clutched the side of a pew. Her eyes teared over and she had to take several deep breaths.

Maggie composed herself and joined the line. A cross section of Chicago stood before her -- a white steelworker in greasy coveralls; a black professional woman in a tailored dress; an extended Mexican family and a Chinese who smelled deliciously of garlic and oil.

As the line moved forward, Maggie saw that the first professional mourners had already arrived. One was bent over in a front pew with her rosary and lace handkerchief clutched in her fists. She wore a black overcoat, black sweater and skirt and a black plastic rain scarf.

Maggie was speechless when Mrs. Daley took her hand.

Sis Daley smiled bravely and said, "We'll all miss him, won't we, dear?"

Maggie nodded and dabbed at her eyes.

"Thanks for coming on such a cold night," Richard M. Daley said. He wore a deeply wounded expression on his broad Irish face.

His brother Bill was equally devastated. "We're all family tonight," he said.

Maggie filed by the Mayor's coffin wishing that he was just sleeping. Attired in a blue suit with a rosary in his hands, the mayor was arranged in a white-lined mahogany coffin. Another mourner joustled Maggie, and she moved on to an empty pew where she had a good, long cry for her only mayor.

Upon leaving, Maggie again noticed the professional mourner. The woman was still kneading her rosary and weeping. Maggie went to her and touched her shoulder. The woman looked up and Maggie held her sad gaze.

"I feel the same way," Maggie whispered.

The city seemed colder and emptier when Maggie emerged from Nativity of Our Lord Church. Zipping up her coat, she wondered if she should phone in her experience to Muni News but decided this was strictly personal. We're way ahead of the competition, and by this time tomorrow the story's going to be covered to death.

Maybe I will have that joint now, she thought, fussing with her key.

"Problem?"

Startled, Maggie spun around. It was that Italian cop with the big hat.

"Damn lock's frozen. This happens to me all the time."

"Here," Officer Rigaletti said, "let me heat your key with my lighter. Works every time."

"I know, my brother taught me that trick."

"You have a brother?" Eddie Rigaletti said, heating the key.

"Four to be exact."

Eddie let his flame go out and looked at Maggie. "You have any sisters?"

"No."

"God, must have been pretty rough, huh?"

"Hey, it's freezing out here. How about . . ."

"Oh, yeah. Sorry."

Eddie heated the key and turned the lock with it. "There," he said, smiling, "works every time. Well, take care."

Maggie got quickly into her car and started the engine. If the damn Krauts could design an engine that starts in this weather, why couldn't they come up with locks to go with it?

She was going to drive away without a word when the impulse hit her. "Hey," she said, rolling down her window, "think your sergeant would let you go have a quick cup of coffee?"

Eddie Rigaletti's face brightened. "Coffee? Yeah, sure he would! Hang on half a second, okay?"

Maggie watched him run up the block to get permission and wondered what she was doing.

Asking a cute little cop who looks like Al Pacino to have a cup of coffee with me. That's all.

Eddie Rigaletti returned moments later and slid excitedly into the passenger seat. "He said I could take half an hour. God, don't these things have heaters."

Maggie laughed. "I think the Germans are sadomasochists. They like to suffer, and they want everybody else to suffer too."

"Yeah, well maybe you should get an American car. My Buick throws off terrific heat."

"I'm sure it does. So where do you want to go?"

"I don't know -- you decide."

"This is your district. You must know some good restaurants around here."

"It ain't my district. I just got out of the Police Academy. This is temporary duty. I start in the 25th District in January."

Maggie drew a quick breath. The 25th District encompassed all of Alderman Endrijonas' ward and part of Alderman Mulford's ward. Eddie Rigaletti would be a useful person for an enterprising reporter to know in the months ahead. Then Maggie remembered that she had decided to go into PR.

"I say something wrong?" Eddie said, patting his pockets for his smokes.

"No. Not at all. I'm just tired. How about we go to that place at 35th and Halsted? I think they're open all night. I could really go for a big, greasy omelet right about now."

"Yeah, me too. Hey, ah . . ."

"Maggie. Maggie Quinn. Sorry."

"No problem. Call me Eddie."

"Nice to meet you, Eddie." Maggie turned to him and offered her hand.

He took it and grinned. "Yeah, likewise, Maggie. Hey, you got any smokes?"

"Sure, in the glove compartment."

"Oooooh, what do we have here?!?" Eddie exclaimed, examining the bag of reefer.

"So I'm junkie, Officer. Arrest me."

"Only if you don't have any rolling papers."

"They're in there somewhere. You're gonna get high on duty?"

"How's that any worse than all those guys who are drunk on duty? From what I've seen so far, half the force is alcoholic."

"You've got a point."

"Damn right I do."

Eddie found the rolling papers and fashioned a factory-tight joint. Maggie took it from him and inhaled deeply. She took another deep hit and handed it back to Eddie.

"Four brothers, huh?" he said.

Maggie watched him out of the corner of her eye and laughed.
"What's so funny?" he said, self-conscious.
"You."
"What about me?"
"Well, for one thing, you're the first cop I've ever seen smoke a joint while in uniform. And for another thing, can't you find a smaller hat?"
Eddie snatched off his hat and looked at it. "What's the matter with my hat?"
"Don't you think it's a little big?"
Eddie put his hat back on and took another hit. "No. I think it looks just fine." He handed Maggie the joint and sulked.
Maggie turned left on Halsted Street and sadly realized that all the decorations in the world weren't going to brighten Bridgeport's Christmas this year.
"Sad isn't it?" Maggie said.
"What?"
"Mayor Daley dying just before Christmas like this. I mean it's sad that he had to die at all -- but just before Christmas."
"Yeah," Eddie said, still sulking.
They went into the warm, bright restaurant at 35th Street and ordered ham and cheese omelets with hash browns, wheat toast and plenty of coffee.
"You think I look funny in my uniform, don't you?" Eddie said after the waitress poured their coffee.
"Is that why you've been pouting?"
"I haven't been pouting. What makes you say that?"
"Because I grew up with four brothers. If that doesn't make me an expert on male behavior, I don't know what does."
"Okay, so I didn't like what you said about my hat. It was the smallest one they had in stock. What am I supposed to do -- shrink the damn thing?"
Maggie looked across the table at this Eddie Rigaletti and decided he didn't look like Al Pacino after all. He was much cuter.
"You're touchy about your size, aren't you, Eddie?"
Eddie glanced around the busy but subdued restaurant. "Yeah, I guess I am. A little. But what about you; aren't you defensive about anything?"

Maggie smiled and pointed under the table. "My rear end. It's bigger than Brazil."

Eddie laughed so hard, coffee came out his nose. "You're a funny lady, Maggie."

The waitress brought their omelets.

"Could I get some ketchup?" Eddie asked her.

The waitress brought it, and Eddie put it on his omelet.

"What's the matter? You never seen nobody put ketchup on their eggs before?"

Maggie shrugged. "Sure, my brother Terry loves ketchup on his eggs. I just think they taste better with steak sauce." She poured some A-1 on her omelet and pretended to ignore his shocked look.

The marijuana had made them both ravenous, so they ate their eggs with gusto. When they were finished, Maggie said, "hey, why don't you ask the waitress to bring us another order of toast. I'm still hungry."

"Why don't you ask her?"

"Because it's not lady-like to pig-out. Besides, she's got the hots for you."

"How do you know?"

"Because she practically drools every time she walks past you."

"You're somethin' else, Maggie."

"Yeah, and so are you, Eddie. And handsome to boot."

Eddie stopped laughing and looked at the bold Irishwoman across the table. "Yeah?"

"Yeah."

"I think you're cute too."

"Even with an ass the size of Brazil?"

"Even with an ass the size of Brazil."

Eddie ordered more toast and said, "You really haven't told me much about yourself. You a Sox fan or a Cubs fan?"

"Sox fan as long as Bill Veeck owns the team. I grew up on the South Side."

"Yeah? Where?"

"Beverly."

"Beverly!?!"

"You know it?"

"Well, yeah. I went to Ignatius and . . ."

"I know -- all the stuck-up jerks were from Beverly," Maggie said, buttering a piece of toast. "That's what you were going to say, isn't it?"

"Yeah, that's what I was gonna say."

"Well, you're probably right except for my brother Michael. He went to Ignatius and he wasn't a stuck-up jerk."

"What year he graduate?"

"1966."

"Oh, I wouldn't have known him. I graduated in '70. You go to college, Maggie?"

"I went to Northern. Got a B.S. in Journalism. What about you?"

He shrugged and stared at his coffee cup. "I went to Circle for a year, but I hated it. My old man was really pissed when I dropped out -- he's a bigshot professor at Loyola. He didn't want me hanging around the house if I wasn't going to go to school, so I joined the Navy. God, was that a mistake."

"Why? You got to travel didn't you?"

"Oh yeah, but you don't see shit from the engine room of a destroyer."

"Oh. So where'd you grow up?"

"Taylor Street. I know -- how many wise guys do I know, right? Well, for your information, not every Italian is in the Mafia. In fact, most people around Taylor Street are just hard-working people."

Maggie put her hand on Eddie's. "You don't have to tell me. I believe it. You have any brothers and sisters?"

"Just a brother -- Marco. He takes after my old man. Always got his nose in a book. He's got so many damned degrees he doesn't have enough walls to put them on."

"You the black sheep, Eddie?"

Eddie shifted uncomfortably and pulled his hand away to light another cigarette. "If you asked my father -- yeah, he'd say I was. But my mother, well, I'm her baby."

Maggie suddenly wanted to hug Eddie Rigaletti.

"You still living at home, Eddie?"

"No," he said, blushing. "I got my own place now. What about you? You still livin' at home?"

"I've got my own place too. On the North Side."

"On the North Side?!?"

"Yeah," Maggie said, "what's wrong with that?"

"That's where all them faggots and weirdos live. Jeez!"

"So where do you live?"

"Twenty-sixth and Oakley -- with normal people."

"That's not too far, is it?"

"I'm off in another hour. Think you could wait?"

Maggie tried to remember the last time she had spent a night with a man. Certainly not since Muni News had destroyed her social life.

"I think I can wait," she said, smiling in anticipation.

Chapter Six

Maggie realized right away that Eddie Rigaletti was no interior decorator, but his second floor flat was reasonably clean and the stereo still worked.

"What kind of music you like?" Eddie said, throwing his hat on the kitchen counter.

"You have any Rod Stewart?" Maggie said, removing her coat.

"Rod Stewart?!?"

"What's wrong with Rod Stewart?"

"The guy's a faggot. Besides, I don't have any Rod Stewart records."

"Well, what do you have?"

"Rolling Stones and Frank Sinatra. Take your pick."

Some choice, Maggie thought. The lighting was none too subtle and the old, broken-down couch looked as though it could cause spinal damage. "Let's smoke another joint and listen to some Stones," she said.

"Now you're talkin'." Eddie put Mick and his boys on the box and went into the kitchen. "You thirsty?"

"Sure, what do you have?"

"Stroh's. And Stroh's."

"Stroh's is fine," Maggie said.

"How about some chips?"

"Yeah! I've still got the munchies."

Maggie went to sit on the couch and was nearly swallowed up by the thing.

Eddie heard her and raced from the kitchen. "I should've warned you -- that thing is dangerous. You all right?"

"Yeah, but I don't know if I'm ever going to be able to get out of this thing again."

"I got some chairs in the kitchen -- maybe you'd like to sit on one of them."

Maggie bit her lip to keep from laughing. Eddie was too cute for words. "No, I'm okay."

"You sure?"

"Yeah."

Eddie brought two cans of Stroh's, a bag of Jay's Potato Chips, onion dip and half a lid and rolling papers on a plastic tray with the Chicago Bears' logo. When he opened the dip, they had to hold their noses.

"I think I've had that a little too long," he said.

"Maybe you should send it over to the Medical Examiner's Office for an autopsy."

"You know, you got a twisted sense of humor."

"It's from hanging around with cops too much," Maggie said.

"That's the kind of reporter you are?"

"Well, until January 3rd. Then I'm going to start working for this public relations agency."

"Public relations? What's that?"

"Well, it's when you want to be in the newspapers and you hire these public relations companies to get you in the papers."

"Why couldn't you just go to the papers yourself? Why pay some jamoke to do it for you?" Eddie settled next to Maggie and started rolling a joint.

Maggie felt Eddie's muscular thigh against hers. "Good point, Eddie. A lot of people probably would be better off going to the newspapers themselves. But they're afraid or they don't have time, so they hire a PR firm to do it for them."

"It don't sound like you're too excited about going into the business. What's wrong with being a reporter?"

Eddie finished rolling the joint, handed it to Maggie and offered his Zippo lighter.

Maggie accepted and contemplated the question as the marijuana's active ingredients went to work on her central nervous system.

"Nothing," she said, "just that there's no money in it and you work nights forever."

She took another hit and handed the joint to Eddie.

"So you're taking this new job for the money. Is that it?" He inhaled and turned to look at her.

Maggie let Mick Jagger distract her for a moment with his "19th nervous breakdown." Then she looked right at Eddie and said, "You know, this couch is really uncomfortable."

Eddie blanched. "We could sit in the kitchen. Chairs in there are . . ."

"Eddie," Maggie said, petting his knee, "I wasn't thinking about sitting."

"Oh," Eddie said. "Uh, well, we could go in the -- you know."

Maggie bent forward and kissed her Italian gentleman on the cheek.

"Let's."

Chapter Seven

Noreen Quinn surveyed the Christmas table and selected Mary Margaret's new gentleman friend.

"Edward, would you ask the blessing, please?" she said, extending her hands so the family could form a chain around the table.

Eddie gulped, took hands with Maggie on his right and Mr. "Just Call Me Brian" Quinn on his left and bowed his head. "Bless O Lord these thy gifts which we are about to receive through the bounty of Christ. And may we all have a very Merry Christmas. In the name of the Father, the Son and the Holy Spirit, Amen."

Eddie opened his eyes and caught Mrs. Quinn staring at him. She quickly looked away, but he knew she didn't like him. It was obvious the moment he had walked into her brick castle that she thought he had come to collect the garbage. The rest of the tribe had greeted him with the same studied arrogance.

"Dark meat or white meat, Ed?" "Big" Brian said, sharpening his knife.

Never mind that Maggie had introduced her date as "Eddie."

"Uh, a little of both, please," Eddie said, smiling gamely at Maggie.

She pinched his thigh under the table.

Sitting opposite her husband, Noreen Quinn began serving her famous coleslaw. "Mary Margaret tells us you're to be assigned to the 25th District when you complete your studies at the Police Academy, Edward."

Eddie glanced around the table at Maggie's lace curtain family -- counting Maggie there were seven adults and four children. They really thought they were something in their tweeds and pleats, but to Eddie they were nothing but a bunch of stuck-up micks.

"That's right, Mrs. Quinn. It should be quite interesting."

"And damned dangerous," Maggie's father said. He wore a red cardigan that exaggerated his girth. "God, I remember when that area was in its prime -- you could walk along State Street any hour of the day or night without a worry. Remember the old Commodore Theater, Noreen?"

"Oh yes! Those were the days, weren't they dear? Everything was better back then. You didn't have the crime or the congestion. People minded their manners, and you didn't dare go downtown unless you were wearing your finest dress or suit. Now, it's a wonder people wear anything at all when they go downtown," Noreen said. She wore a white silk blouse with pearls and a kilted Stewart tartan skirt.

"I don't know," Eddie said, "I think Chicago's still an okay town. I mean we got our problems an' all, but look at those pictures of New York. That place looks like a pigsty compared to Chicago."

"Have you ever been to New York?" said Maggie's oldest brother, "Little" Brian. He was assistant principal of a high school in an affluent suburb.

Eddie looked at the rosy-cheeked dork in the green sweater. If the guy was going to wear a rug, at least he could get one to match his real hair.

"No, but I've . . ."

Little Brian said, "If you haven't actually been there, how can you say what it really looks like?"

Maggie put her hand on Eddie's leg, but he brushed it away. He had told her it would turn out like this, but she insisted that he would be welcomed like a member of the family.

"All right, I don't know for a fact that there's garbage everywhere in New York. But from what I seen on television and what have you, Chicago's a whole lot cleaner and safer. Okay?"

Little Brian smiled thinly and wondered how low his baby sister was going to reach before she came to her senses and finally married a good Irish boy from Beverly.

"If you say so," he said, after a long pause.

Eddie glared at him and stabbed his turkey.

"So, Margaret," Little Brian said, "what's this Mother says about you selling your soul to PR? I thought no self-respecting reporter ever became a flak."

Eddie was right: this was a big mistake, Maggie realized.

"I'm tired of working nights, and the papers just aren't hiring reporters from Muni News anymore."

"Couldn't you just move to another department, Dear?" Noreen said, ladling out some more coleslaw for one of her mewling grandchildren.

"Mom, like I've told you before, Muni News isn't part of the city government. There's no other department to move to," Maggie said, aware of the angry tic in her left eye.

"Well," Noreen said, with an imperious shake of her head, "if it's not part of the city government, why do they insist on calling it Municipal News? That certainly sounds like the name of a city agency to me."

"You're absolutely right, Mother," Little Brian hastily agreed.

Big Brian drained his scotch and water and said, "What kind of work does your father do, Ed?"

"He's a professor at Loyola. He teaches Italian."

"I see," Big Brian said. That certainly wasn't the answer he was expecting so he lumbered away from the table to refresh his glass.

"Everything is sure delicious, Mrs. Quinn," Eddie said.

"Oh, it's nothing," Noreen said. "But I'm sure you're accustomed to much tastier food at home. If there's one thing Italians know how to do, it's cook."

Maggie was mortified. Two glasses of wine and her mother was already making an ass of herself. And it would only take another drink to get the Old Man going.

"Yeah," Eddie said, "and we've also written a few half-way decent operas in our time, not to mention some pretty good painting and sculpture."

Noreen pursed her lips. "Yes, I suppose one must acknowledge the genius of a Verdi or Puccini, but no one compares to the Irish when it comes to poetry. Take William Butler Yeats for example. You have read Yeats, haven't you?"

Eddie was about to reply when Big Brian lumbered back to the table with his fresh drink. "You can say what you want about that goddamn Mussolini, but he sure as hell made the trains run on time."

"I beg your pardon, Mr. Quinn?" Eddie said.

Big Brian gulped his drink and settled back in his chair for his Christmas address. "I said: that goddamn Mussolini might have been a greasy little dictator, but he sure as hell made the trains run on time in Italy. I'm sure your people thank him for that."

Maggie stroked Eddie's knee to no avail.

"My people are all Americans, Mr. Quinn. Just like yours. I got no more use for Mussolini than the man in the moon. And neither does my family."

Big Brian didn't hear a word of it. "Look at Italy today. How many governments have you had since World War II? Does anybody know? What I'm saying is: some countries just have to have dictatorships, and Italy happens to be one of them. Of course, they're not fighters. Hell, the worst thing that happened to the Germans was having the Italians as their allies in World War II. How's that saying go? If Italy's neutral, it takes three divisions to watch her; if Italy's your enemy it takes four divisions to defeat her; and if Italy's your ally it takes five divisions to save her."

"I think it was 'six divisions to save her,' Dad," Little Brian said.

"Whatever," Big Brian said, waving his hand. "The point is, the Italians are lovers not fighters. Wouldn't you say that's true, Ed?"

Eddie wadded up his linen napkin and was about to throw it on the table when the phone rang.

Maggie broke the tension by bursting out of her chair, and saying, "Oh, I bet it's Michael! He's probably just getting up -- it's almost 10 o'clock in California. I get to talk to him first!"

Watching Maggie make a dingbat of herself, Eddie remembered what his mother always said: stick with your own kind, Eddie.

As the Quinns gathered around the phone to talk to their missing member, Eddie Rigaletti quietly took his mother's advice.

Chapter Eight

After working nights for almost two years, Maggie Quinn was furious when her alarm radio switched on at 6 a.m. on January 3, 1977.

"Shit," she said, swatting at it.

The radio toppled off the nightstand but continued playing.

"Either get up or turn that goddamned thing off," Norma Jankowski called from the other bedroom. Norma was working the evening shift at Muni News and had just rolled in from the 4 o'clock joints an hour earlier.

Maggie tried to get up, but sleep held her fast. Ignoring the motor mouth on the radio who was already ranting about the forthcoming Hall and Oats concert at the Auditorium, Maggie slipped eagerly back into deep sleep.

She was rudely awakened five minutes later when her hulking roommate pulled her out of bed.

"For God's sake, Sweetheart, get your ass out of bed. This is your big day. Come on, move your ass, or you gonna be late. It's already 6:05. Those flaks don't like to be kept waiting -- especially by some Muni News reject. Come on, you maggot, reveille! Reveille!"

"Reject?!?" Maggie yelled, throwing her pillow at Norma's round slavic head. "What do you mean reject?"

Norma caught the pillow and hit Maggie with it in the ribs. "You know what I mean."

Maggie sat up and rubbed her eyes. "Well, I don't see the TRIBUNE or the SUN-TIMES ringing your phone off the hook."

They had had this conversation too many times in the last two weeks.

Norma adjusted her powder-blue robe and started back to her room. "Just get up and go to work," she said.

Maggie turned off the radio and stood up. "All right; all right."

She shaved her legs and arm pits in the shower, twice nicking her knee. She got shampoo in her eyes and nearly scalded herself trying to turn off the water. As she was stepping out of the shower, a gruff male voice said, "Excuse me."

Maggie hastily covered herself with a towel and hopped back into the shower.

One of Norma's infamous "sources" lumbered into the bathroom and urinated copiously. He wore black socks, boxer shorts and a sleeveless "dago" t-shirt. He reeked of stale beer and cigarettes, and there was a wide fold of fat around his middle. Maggie was pretty sure he was an Area Seven Homicide dick, but it was hard to tell without his clothes on.

"Uh, do you mind?" she said. "I have to get to work."

"Huh?" the drunken dick said, splattering urine on the toilet seat and floor. "I didn't know Norma had a roommate."

"Well, now you know. And Norma's roommate has to get to work. Okay?"

The besotted cop finished piddling and turned to face Maggie. He shook his puny penis and leered. "Want some, baby?"

"Look, asshole, I tried to be polite. Now get the fuck out of here before I kick you in the balls," Maggie said, ready to strike.

The cop staggered back a step. He was a big, ugly, black Irishman -- a disgrace to Maggie's race.

"Hey, don't get violent on me, baby. I just want to have a little fun. Know what I mean?"

"Norma," Maggie shouted, "get this asshole out of here now, or I'm going to kick him!"

"You'd have to drop your towel to do that, baby," the detective said, grinning wickedly.

Shit, just what I need on my first day.

"Norma! Goddamn it, would you . . ."

"All right already," Norma said, walking buck-naked into the bathroom and grabbing her man by the crotch. "Come on, lover boy, leave Princess Margaret here alone. Today is her big debut in the land of flakdom. She needs all the time she can get to make herself presentable."

Pawing at Norma's pendulous breasts, the big cop obediently followed her out of the bathroom.

Maggie took a deep breath and stepped out of the shower. She slammed the door shut and locked it. Then she faced her mop of unruly hair and set to work. When she was finally satisified at 6:45, she realized that her period had started.

"Of all days," Maggie said, rummaging under the sink for a Tampax. As usual, she was unprepared for the monthly onslaught.

She opened the door a crack and called, "Norma!"

For a long moment there was nothing but drunken moans and wet, slurpy sounds. Then Norma emerged from the depths of some demented delight to say: "Now what do you want?"

"Uh, could you come here for a minute?" Maggie said, certain there was no God.

"No, I'm busy. What the hell do you want?"

"Uh, you know."

"No, I don't know. Oooh, Tommie. Lower. Ooooh, that's it."

The big cop sounded like a bear going for grubs.

Maggie shrugged. "My period started, and I'm out of Tampax. Do you have any?"

All slurping stopped, and then there was sustained laughter.

Finally, Norma came forth with an industrial-size box of Kotex. Her old Polish mother had taught her that good girls didn't put foreign objects in their "pocketbooks," and Norma was not one to defy her old Polish mother.

"Here," Norma said, handing Maggie the box, "help yourself."

Maggie wanted to be sick. "Thanks, Norma. Thanks a million." She resolved to buy a box of Tampax on her way to work.

"Don't mention it, Sweetheart," Norma said. She winked and stumbled back to her dick.

When Maggie was finally dressed in a blue skirt and ruffled white blouse, it was 7:15. She allowed herself a glass of orange juice and a Dannon Blueberry Yogurt, threw on her coat and pumps and dashed out the door.

She had to bend into the biting northeast wind off the lake to get to Michigan Avenue where she waited in vain for a southbound bus. The few that stopped were so packed that she didn't even try to get on. Finally, she figured that Rauch & Spiegel was within walking distance and set out at a healthy cadence.

She was just getting warmed up four blocks later when she crossed the Michigan Avenue Bridge. The cold had turned the Chicago River an emerald green and there were even blocks of ice floating on the surface of the chemical soup. Angry blue-gray clouds scrolled overhead, occasionally allowing the sun to peak through. Maggie glanced up at the clock on the Wrigley Building.

8:15 -- 10 minutes to spare.

She considered running down the steps to Lower Michigan Avenue and having a quick joint to fortify herself, but figured it would be best to report with a clear head. On the first day at least.

Maggie looked up at the Howers Building at the south foot of the bridge where Fort Dearborn used to be. The Indiana limestone needed a good sandblasting and the windows were filthy, but the old girl was certainly preferable to the black boxes that were popping up everywhere. And the view of north Michigan Avenue and the lake was certainly better than the elevated tracks she had seen from Muni News.

Still, Maggie wanted to keep walking. Maybe spend the morning at the Art Institute and have lunch at the Walnut Room at Field's. The tree was probably still up, and she had finally gotten a Field's card. Having only taken one day off between jobs, Maggie needed some time to herself. But she also had to pay her north Dearborn rent.

So she pushed resolutely into the Howers Building but stopped at the cigarette stand before catching an elevator for the 26th floor.

The woman ahead of Maggie bought the last box of Tampax, so she settled for a pack of Marlboro Lights and the possibility of bumming a tampon upstairs.

Elevators serving the 26th floor stopped at every intermediate floor, and Maggie's car was crowded with local traffic, so it was 8:29 when she finally walked into the lobby of Rauch & Spiegel.

It was dimly lighted and done up in tired '50's furniture. There was a two-year-old issue of TIME on the coffee table and a autographed photograph of Dwight Eisenhower on the wall. The late President had inscribed: "To my good friend Bernie Spiegel -- all the best. Ike."

Hoping the stale smell was temporary, Maggie went to the reception desk and announced: "I'm Margaret Quinn. I'm supposed to see Linda Jaffrey."

The big woman with black hair looked up from Robert

Ludlum's latest thriller and said, "Do you have an appointment?"

"Yes. I'm a new employee. This is my first day."

The receptionist smiled, flashing two gold teeth. "Welcome to Rauch and Spiegel." She pronounced it "Rowk and Speegull" and spoke mostly through her nose. "I'm Florence Ziskey, but just call me Flo."

Flo extended a professionally manicured hand that had at least one gold ring on every finger and a wrist-full of silver bracelets.

"Pleased to meet you, Flo. And just call me Maggie."

"Maggie. That's a pretty name. I wish I had a pretty name like Maggie."

"What's wrong with Flo?"

Flo Ziskey rolled her raven eyes. "Who're you tryin' to kid?"

"Uh, maybe you should tell Linda Jaffrey that I'm here."

"She's in a meeting until 10. Can't be disturbed. Big powwow with some new client," Flo Ziskey said. A red light blinked on the phone set at her fingertips. "Half a sec. Good morning, Rauch and Spiegel. I'll check. Whom may I say is calling?"

Flo punched another button and said, "Bernie, do you want to talk to Dr. Fischbein?"

Flo smiled at his answer. "I didn't think so."

She punched another button. "Dr. Fischbein, Mr. Spiegel seems to have stepped away from his desk. Could I have him return your call as soon as he returns?"

Flo rolled her eyes at Maggie.

"I certainly will, Dr. Fischbein. Have a nice day."

She stabbed the button and shook her head. "Fischbein is Esther Spiegel's shrink. He says he can't cure Esther's neurosis unless Bernie comes in too, but Bernie wouldn't get within 50 feet of a psychiatrist if his life depended on it. I tell you, Maggie, you could write a book about this place."

Maggie wondered if she had smoked a joint after all.

"I guess. What am I supposed to do until 10? Linda Jaffrey insisted that I be here at 8:30 sharp."

Flo Ziskey shrugged her huge shoulders. "I'm almost done with this book. Be happy to lend it to you in about 10 minutes as long as that damned phone stays quiet." Flo opened her book and started reading.

"You mean I should wait out here?"

Annoyed, Flo said, "Where else are you going to wait?"

"In my office," Maggie said, wondering if Pete Poulos would take her back.

"Unless Linda's planning to put you in the supply room, there isn't an empty office for you."

"There isn't?"

"Look, why don't you make yourself comfortable, and I'll lend you this book as soon as I'm finished with it."

"Shouldn't you tell Linda Jaffrey that I'm here?"

"Why? If she told you to start work today, then she knows you're here. Now, if you don't mind, I want to see how this ends."

Maggie settled on the musty orange couch and thumbed the old TIME. She grimaced at Jimmy Carter's cheesy smile and was glad she voted for Gerald Ford. Even if he did bump into things.

Messengers came and went; Flo answered the phone occasionally, and the cheap wall clock finally found its way to 9:30.

Maggie stood up and stretched. "Where's the ladies' room?"

Only two paragraphs away from denouement, Flo was perspiring. "What!?!" she said, startled.

"I'm sorry to bother you, but where's the ladies' room?"

Flo wiped her forehead. "Down that hall, then left, then right. You can't miss it." Flo returned eagerly to her book.

"Uh, could I ask you a favor?"

Flo looked up. "Now what?"

"You have a spare Tampax? I'll pay you back as soon as I get a chance to . . ."

Flo Ziskey closed her book and smiled. "Sweetheart, this hasn't been your day has it?"

Maggie shook her head.

"Of course you can have a Tampax. Here," she said, fishing in her enormous black handbag, "have four."

Maggie thanked her a little too effusively and made her way to the ladies' room. Enroute, she noted the threadbare carpeting, washed-out the walls, and cheap hotel art. No one greeted her as she passed, but several of her new colleagues looked furtively up from their cluttered desks. Maggie was surprised how small the offices were, even those facing north Michigan Avenue.

And the typewriters! Even Muni News wouldn't have them.

Maggie was finishing her business in the ladies' room when a woman entered the next stall and commenced to cry and sob.

The woman tore great gobs of cheap toilet paper to dry her tears, but her ducts would not be stopped.

Obviously the woman had just been informed of the death of a close relative. Maggie was pondering the proper etiquette for expressing condolences in the WC, when another woman entered the third stall and also began crying.

Maggie flushed and retreated quickly to the reception area.

Having finished her book, Flo Ziskey was now available for conversation.

"Flo, was it my imagination, or did I just hear two women crying in the john?"

Flo rolled her eyes conspiratorily. "Just between you and me, Sweetie, this place is a real snake pit. You've got to have skin like an elephant to survive here."

Maggie edged closer on the couch to Flo's desk. "What do you mean?"

"Well, for one thing -- oh, damn. Half a sec. Good morning, Rauch and Spiegel." Flo's eyes widened. "Why, yes, she's right here." She gave Maggie a lewd wink and handed her the phone. "Sounds like your boyfriend."

Maggie gasped. If it was that no-good Eddie Rigaletti she was going to slam the phone in his ear.

But the caller was one of her colleagues from Muni News, Steve Quisenberry.

"Steve? I, ah . . ."

"I know, you're sure I'm not calling to wish you good luck at your new job," he said, dryly.

"I am a little surprised."

"Yeah, well, I'm sure you're real busy, so I won't keep you. Look, the reason I'm calling is because I'm leaving Muni News too."

"You are? Where're you going -- The TRIBUNE? SUN-TIMES?"

"Yeah, right. Actually, I'm going to be an associate editor at the WORKERS' WEEKLY."

"THE WORKERS' WEEKLY?!?"

What had begun in the late '60s as a free street paper "for all the people," was now a highly profitable shill for Chicago's real estate hustlers and massage parlor operators.

"Yeah, what's wrong with that?" Quisenberry said, stung.

"Steve, you've got to be kidding. That thing is . . ."

"You're gonna tell me being a flak is any better?"

"All right." Maggie glanced at Flo who was busy pretending not to eavesdrop.

"Look, I've got to go. Knowing you, you didn't call just to tell me you got a new job. What do you want, Steve?"

"To find out if it's true that Rauch and Spiegel is going to represent Alderman Endrijonas."

"What?!?"

"You heard me."

"That's the craziest thing I've ever heard. Why would . . ."

"Because they'd represent Adolph Hitler and Attila the Hun if they were still alive. Plus, Endrijonas is planning to . . ."

Alderman Vincent Endrijonas himself suddenly emerged from the inner office into the reception area. He wore a tailored, gray wool suit, gold cufflinks and his inevitable Palm Springs tan. He was followed by a tiny woman in beige with a towering mane of frosted hair.

"I'll talk to you later, Steve," Maggie said, trying not to stare.

"Wait. Are they representing Lightning Vince or aren't they? The WEEKLY's planning to do a big investigation of Endrijonas, and you could be a big help to us."

Despite her spiky heels, the little woman with big hair had to stare up at the unctuously handsome alderman. Her eyes sparkled girlishly as she said in pure Brooklynese, "Well, it's been a real pleasure, Alderman Endrijonas. We look forward to working with you."

"I heard that," Steve Quisenberry said.

"Goodbye, Steve," Maggie said, quickly cradling the phone. She knew from her first syllable that this woman was her new boss, Linda Jaffrey.

Alderman Endrijonas took Linda Jaffrey's hand and kissed it gallantly. "With your help, Linda, we'll get our message to the people of Chicago."

people of Chicago."

As he turned to leave, two gorillas in dark suits materialized and escorted him to a waiting elevator.

Maggie waited until Linda Jaffrey stopped being moonstruck and said, "Hi, I'm Maggie Quinn. You must be Linda Jaffrey."

Little Linda blinked her big, brown lashes. "Maggie Quinn? Are you with American Cyanide? I'm not scheduled to meet with you until 1 o'clock."

"No, I'm the reporter from Muni News you hired. Remember?"

Linda Jaffrey cocked her hip and puckered her glossy lip. "No. Refresh my memory."

Maggie glanced at Flo who was rolling her eyes and trying not to laugh. Maggie decided Flo was all right.

"You called me the day Mayor Daley died. You said you wanted me to report for work on January 3rd at 8:30. It's January 3rd, and I've been here since 8:30."

Linda Jaffrey turned on Flo. "Well, if she's been here since 8:30, why didn't I know about it?"

Flo Ziskey calmly inspected her manicure. "Because, Linda, you left your usual strict instructions that you were absolutely not to be disturbed under any circumstances."

Linda Jaffrey backed up half a step and snagged her heel on the carpeting. Maggie had to catch her to keep her from falling on her tight little ass.

Linda Jaffrey wrestled out of Maggie's grasp and said, "Well, I don't remember telling you to report today. And I certainly don't have time to talk to you, because I'm in meetings all day. Flo, give her the stylebook and some press kits to read and put her in that office back by the mailroom. You can spend the day getting acquainted with us, and I'll talk to you first thing tomorrow morning and get you working on some accounts."

She rotated on a heel and was gone.

"Dr. Fischbein would have a field day with her," Flo said. "Well, I guess you're here to stay, Maggie old girl. Come on, we'll roust out Mark Roberts and get you settled."

"Who's Mark Roberts?"

"He's just a free-lancer. Come on, I don't want to be away from the phone too long."

Flo took Maggie to a pie-shaped cubicle at the end of the

farthest corridor. It had an ancient gun-metal gray desk, the oldest operating Underwood typewriter, a window with a view of the U-shaped building's inner court and a chain-smoking young man in a coffee-stained white shirt.

"Sorry, Markie," Flo said, bursting in unannounced, "but you're gonna have to move again."

Chapter Nine

"Where?" Mark Roberts said. His voice was deeper and richer than Maggie expected from such a small man.

Flo shrugged. "I think Shirley Berquist's sick today. Try her office."

Mark Roberts nodded grimly. "Or maybe I should just work out on the sidewalk." He looked at Maggie for the first time and smiled wryly. "If you're going to work here full-time you have my condolences."

Maggie watched him pack up his things, noting that he certainly had been busy. It appeared that he had written drafts for at least 30 press releases.

"Thanks, but I'm sure I'll love it here. By the way, I'm Maggie Quinn," she said, extending her hand.

Mark Roberts merely nodded. "Flo's probably already told you who I am, so there's no need for formal introductions. Well, I'll get out of your way so you can start your dazzling career in PR."

He loaded his arms with papers and pencils and left.

"I've seen people treat dogs better than they treat him around here," Flo whispered. "But without Mark to clean up everybody's messes, this place would collapse in a second. He's the only decent writer here, and he's not even full-time."

"Why doesn't he want to work full-time?"

"Because he thinks he's some great writer or something. Says he needs time for this novel he's writing. Still, he's here at least four days a week, sometimes five."

"Hmm. Let's see, I think Linda wanted you to get me . . ."

"Oh, that's right. Be right back."

While Flo was gone, Maggie gazed across the court at the opposite windows. In one, a stunning blonde suddenly got up from her desk and went to her door. A swarthy man with bowed legs entered quickly and they locked in an instant embrace. They had their hands all over one another when one of them doused the light.

Maggie was peering into the dark when Flo returned with her reading material.

"This stuff'll bore you to tears, Sweetie, so I brought you my Ludlum book too," Flo said. "Just give me a call on 14 if you need anything."

"Thanks."

Maggie could not make herself comfortable in the rickety chair, so she settled for a cigarette. She thumbed through the Rauch & Spiegel stylebook noting at least 20 typos and glaring grammatical errors in the first pass. In the back, under "local media," they still listed CHICAGO TODAY even though it had been defunct for more than two years.

Maggie turned to the press releases. Every lead was buried, and the one about some second-home development in southwestern Michigan didn't even include the values of the homes or how to get there. Just lots of self-serving quotes like: "These quality residences are built with the quality-conscious corporate professional in mind and feature the highest quality amenities including . . ."

". . . indoor plumbing and wood-burning floors," Maggie said, letting her eyes go out of focus.

She was about to turn to Robert Ludlum when she saw the light come on in the blonde's office across the way. The Zorba the Greek character was actually zipping up his fly, and the blonde was applying fresh lipstick.

This isn't a PR agency, it's a B movie, she thought.

Maggie started a fresh cigarette and wished she HAD smoked a joint before coming to work. She lingered with Ludlum until 11:50 and decided to head out for lunch. As she made her way to the elevators, she noticed that she was alone in the idea.

In the few cases where there was an open door, she saw the same sorry sight -- the young PR professional bent over his/her typewriter, with a half-eaten ham sandwich in his/her hand.

"Is it okay if I go to lunch?" Maggie said when she reached reception.

Flo looked up from the latest VOGUE. "Sure. Enjoy." She looked down at the latest VOGUE.

The elevator doors were just closing when Maggie heard someone running and yelling, "Hold it! Hold it!"

She punched the "open" button, and Mark Roberts leapt aboard.

"Thanks," he said, panting.

"Sure," Maggie said. "Should I hold it for anyone else?"

"Are you kidding?!?"

"No."

"Nobody goes to lunch at this place. They're all chained to their desks."

"So I gathered," Maggie said, pushing the "close" button.

"Hey, you want to have lunch with me?"

"Okay. Where?"

"There's this little place on Lake Street I like. Good burgers, and the beers are only 50 cents."

"You're on."

MacGregor's was full of smoke and noisy people. The burgers came in wicker baskets with "cottage fries," a dill pickle and a dab of coleslaw.

But before serving them a plastic pitcher full of beer, the waitress carded Mark.

He turned bright red as he fished in his pocket for his wallet.

"What kind of license is this?" the waitress said, squinting in the dim lighting.

"Michigan," Mark said, curtly.

"It looks kind of flimsy to me. Are you . . ."

"I can vouch for him waitress," Maggie said.

The waitress looked at the lady with the tough voice and nodded. "All right. But I still say that license looks flimsy to me."

Mark plucked it out of her hand and said, "Just bring us a pitcher, okay?"

"How about something to eat too?" Maggie said.

Mark just wanted the waitress to go. "Yeah, and two burger baskets too."

The waitress gave Mark a withering look and left.

"What if I wanted the shrimp basket?" Maggie said, teasing.

"Well you didn't, did you?"

"Mark, I was joking. Lighten up."

He forced a smile. "All right. You got any smokes? I must have left mine in the office."

Maggie handed him her pack. "So where're you from in Michigan?"

"Grosse Pointe Shores. It's a suburb of Detroit. What about you?"

"Chicago. South Side. So how'd you end up here?"

"Unless you want to write press releases for Ford, Chrysler or GM, there's nothing in Detroit. My father was in the Army with Bernie Spiegel, so he gave him a call when I moved down here. I'd rather be a reporter, but nobody's hiring."

"Tell me about it. That's why I took the job at Rauch and Spiegel."

The waitress brought their pitcher, and Mark poured them each a glass.

"Here's to your brilliant career in PR," he said.

Maggie klinked his glass. "May it be short and sweet." She took a long drink and studied Mark Roberts.

"What's wrong, I have a zit on my forehead?"

"No, I was just thinking that . . ."

"What?"

Maggie could hardly say that she thought Mark was cuddly cute, so she said, "I hear you're writing a novel."

"Who told you that?"

"I never reveal my sources. You are, aren't you?"

"Yeah," Mark said, taking another cigarette from Maggie's pack, "I'm writing a novel. What about you?"

"No. I've tried a few short stories, but not a novel. God, you're talking hundreds of pages, plot twists, character development -- all that stuff. How do you do it?"

"If you write a page a day, you've got 365 pages in a year." Mark waved his finger at a passing waitress. "Another pitcher when you get a chance."

"I never thought of it that way before."

"It works for me. On the days I work at Rauch and Spiegel, I get up at 5 and put in an hour at the typewriter. On the other day, I write maybe three hours and spend the rest of the day doing whatever research I need. I even sneak in a little writing at Rauch and Spiegel."

"Tsk tsk."

"Look, the stuff they give me to write is so simple-minded I have to work on my book, or I'll go crazy."

"Mark, I was just kidding. I don't care if you build model

airplanes on their time."

"So you're really not there because you're having some brilliant career in public relations?"

"No way, Jose."

"Good. I was worried."

"So what's your book about?"

Mark shrugged. "This guy from a small town in Michigan. He makes it into the major leagues without playing in college or for a Triple A team. He does it completely on his own."

"Sounds interesting. Is it autobiographical?"

"Do I look like a baseball player to you?"

"I don't think Luis Aparicio is much bigger than you, and he was one of the best shortstops of all time."

"How do you know about 'Little Looie'?"

"I got his autograph the day the Sox won the pennant in '59. God, what a day -- the fire commissioner turned on all the air raid sirens and freaked out the entire city. It was great!"

The waitress brought their burgers and another pitcher.

Mark waited until she was gone and said, "So if you're not going to have a brilliant career at Rauch and Spiegel, what are you doing there?"

Maggie took a big swig of beer and said, "How old are you, Mark?"

"What?"

"I said: how old are you?"

"Twenty-two. How old are you?"

"Twenty-six, and by the time you're my age, maybe you'll realize that life doesn't always work out the way you want."

"That's why you're working at Rauch and Spiegel?"

"I'm there because I couldn't get a job at the papers. I spent the last two years at Muni News busting my . . ."

"You worked at Muni News?"

"Well, yeah, but . . ."

"Why didn't you tell me that in the first place," Mark said, his face all aglow.

"Because it's no big deal."

"No big deal! People kill to get jobs at Muni News. God, I'd give my left arm to work there."

"Save it. I could probably get you an interview this week if anybody to replace me."

"Would you call him now?" Mark Roberts said, grabbing Maggie's hand.

"Do you know anything about Muni News, Mark?"

"I know that all of the big names in journalism in this country worked there at one time. If you want to work at a good paper, it's the best place to start. One of my Journalism professors at Michigan State even told me that a year at Muni News was better than a Masters in Journalism."

"Maybe, but I worked there almost two years, and look where it got me."

"Yeah, but you didn't try hard enough. If you waited long enough, you would have gotten a job at one of the papers. Now you're stuck in PR."

Maggie's heart sank. "You really think so?"

The waitress tried to clear their table, but Mark waved her away saying, "I'm not done with my french fries yet." He ate a few to make his point and looked at Maggie. "I can't figure you out -- you actually go from Muni News to the sleaziest PR firm in town. Are you nuts or what?"

"You really want a job at Muni News?" Maggie said, grabbing her cigarettes.

"Yeah!"

"Then get your little ass over there and apply. But don't tell them I sent you. Now, if you'll excuse me, I'm going back to work."

She slapped a $5 bill on the table and left.

Chapter Ten

Maggie was still so mad she didn't notice the demonstrators until she was about to enter the Howers Building.

They were mostly white women, and they were mad. They blocked the entrance with a tight oval and carried signs reading: "Rauch & Spiegel is killing Third World children!"

"Excuse me," Maggie said, trying to break their circle.

"Do you work for those pigs?" a woman demanded.

"I beg your pardon?" Maggie said, trying not to laugh.

"I said: do you work for Rauch and Spiegel?"

"What difference does it make?"

"What difference does it make?!? They represent American Cyanide -- a company that dumps known carcinogens in the Third World. They represent BabyForm -- a company that brainwashes Third World mothers into using their artificial infant formula instead of nursing their babies at their breasts. They represent . . ."

". . . Papa Doc and Idi Amin," Maggie said, joking.

"They do?" the woman said, aghast. "You hear that, everybody? This lady says those pigs represent Papa Doc and Idi Amin!"

Maggie slipped into the revolving door during the ensuing hubbub and boarded the first available elevator.

She laughed all the way to the 26th floor and was still chuckling when she returned to Rauch & Spiegel.

"What's so funny?" Flo said, looking up from a COSMOPOLITAN article on more meaningful orgasms.

Maggie caught her breath. "There were these demonstrators downstairs picketing against us for representing American Cyanide and . . ."

". . . BabyForm. I know, they're there every other week. So what's so funny about that?"

"Well, for fun, I told them we also represented Papa Doc and Idi Amin."

Flo's expectant smile disappeared. "You weren't joking -- we DO represent the Haitian Tourist Board AND the Ugandan

Ministry of Tourism."

Maggie blanched.

"Oh," Flo added, "here's a message for you."

Flo handed Maggie a pink slip that read: "See me ASAP!! Linda Jaffrey."

"What time did she leave this?"

"Almost an hour ago. A word to the wise, Sweetheart, don't take more than a half hour for lunch if you want to keep your job here. And, go easy on the booze." Flo said, pinching her nostrils.

"I'll keep that in mind, Flo."

Linda Jaffrey was on the phone but motioned for her subordinate to take a seat in front of her teak desk. She had a commanding view of North Michigan Avenue and a wall full of art only a gynecologist could love. Her designer "In" and "Out" baskets bulged with papers and there were piles all over her desk. She shuffled through one stack as she spoke on the phone.

"Certainly, Mr. Barrington, we'll get you in the WALL STREET JOURNAL. No problem. Yes, Mr. Barrington. I understand. Of, course. Yes. Goodbye, Mr. Barrington," Linda Jaffrey said, sounding as sweet as a hand-kissed maiden.

For Maggie she reverted to her normal voice: "Where the hell have you been all afternoon? We're not paying you to do restaurant reviews."

Maggie was about to tell her how far she could shove it when Zorba the Greek himself walked unannounced into Linda's office.

Switching on the sweetness again, Linda said, "Hi, Gil. What's up?"

"We've got to talk about American Cyanide when you get a chance," he said, his voice a deep Mediterranean blue.

"Sure," Linda said. "I'll be finished here in a minute."

"Well," Gil Dayette said, looking through Maggie's blouse, "I'll leave you girls to your little coffee klatsch. But see me as soon as you're finished."

When he was gone, Maggie laughed. "God, who was that guy?"

Linda Jaffrey's face hardened. "He just happens to be president of this agency."

"Oh," Maggie said. "Is he married?"

"He happens to be divorced. Now get out your pencil and pad so I can give you your assignment."

"Uh, I didn't . . ."

"Damn it! When I call you in here, you bring a pencil and pad! Do you understand?"

"Yes. I'm sorry. I won't let it happen again."

"Good. Now then, I need you to rewrite a press release -- if I can just find it."

Linda Jaffrey fished through three piles before she found what she wanted. Then she handed Maggie the red-penciled remains.

"I need this ASAP so we can get it on the six o'clock news. Think you can do it?"

Maggie studied the story. "Sure, but there's just one problem."

"What?!?" Linda Jaffrey said, looking up from another pile that had caught her attention.

"There's no news here. Alderman Endrijonas starting a 'Beautify Your Block' contest isn't news. Everybody's going to cheap it out."

"Cheap it out?"

"They won't run it unless there's a news angle. I can tell you right now that . . ."

"I don't care what you think," Linda Jaffrey said, shrieking. "I didn't hire you to think. I hired you to get publicity for our clients. If that's too complicated, you can go back where you came from."

Maggie swallowed. "Sorry. I just . . ."

"Just rewrite the press release and have it on my desk by 3:30. Okay?"

"Okay."

Hurrying back to her office, Maggie nearly knocked over a man in a rumpled gray suit.

"I'm sorry," she said, "are you all right?"

He righted his glasses and peered at the young woman. "Nothing seems to be broken. What about you?"

"I'm okay."

"Good," he said, smiling. "Say, you're new here, aren't you?"

Wondering where they had found such a run-down relic, Maggie nodded. "I'm Maggie Quinn. I'm working for Linda Jaffrey."

"Pleasure to meet you, Margie. I'm Bernie Spiegel. Are you a Bears fan?"

Maggie took a second look at the balding man with the bad posture. "Yeah. Sure."

"What'd you think of the game Sunday?"

"The offensive line let them down."

"Exactly what I thought. Say, would you like to join me for a cup of coffee?"

"Sure."

Bernie Spiegel ushered Maggie into his corner office and seated her before his vast, empty desk.

"Do you take cream and sugar?" he said, lifting the phone.

"Just black," Maggie said, surveying the man's photo gallery. He was in every picture posing with the likes of Eisenhower, Nixon, Ford, Carter, Mayor Daley, all three Kennedys, and a little black man in a starched uniform.

"Peggy, would you bring in two coffees -- one black and one with cream and sugar. Quite a collection, wouldn't you say?"

"Yes, it certainly is. Who's that?"

"Oh. That's me with President Duvalier of Haiti. A real gentleman. Tragically misunderstood, I'm afraid. It hasn't been easy getting him good publicity, but we've succeeded when other shops wouldn't even try. That's what sets us apart, Margie. We're willing to take risks here at Rauch and Spiegel."

He went to the far wall and pointed to a picture of himself with two women with enormous hairdos. "This was our best campaign -- I really put the 'Curly Twins' on the map. Our first big account really. Took it on spec. Nobody thought American women would want to wear their hair like that, but I traveled those girls all over the country and got them in every newspaper you can name.

"Television was a lot easier nut to crack in those days because they were desperate for programming ideas. So I'd just show up in the studio with the Twins and next thing you know, there they'd be explaining how the Curly Corporation had saved them from a life of poverty in Tennessee. Oh, those were the days. Of course, I was young then. Full of energy. Had to be. With the schedule we were on, we were lucky to get three hours of sleep some nights."

Bernie Spiegel's secretary appeared with two paper cups of vending machine coffee and departed.

Maggie took a sip and said, "What's Idi Amin like?"

"He's one of the funniest men I've ever met," Bernie Spiegel said, settling behind his desk. "But you should see that country of his. They say that's where the original Garden of Eden was. I wouldn't be at all surprised, because Uganda's a real peach."

"I'm sure it is, Mr. Spiegel. Well, I'd better be going because Linda Jaffrey wants me to . . ."

"Hell of a nice kid, that Linda Jaffrey. Knew her father back in Brooklyn, you know. That Sy Jaffrey was some kind of card. Made his money in real estate. Always tried to get me to invest in some shopping center somewhere. Poor bastard keeled over on the golf course. Heart attack. He was dead before he hit the ground." Bernie Spiegel gazed out the window.

"I'm very sorry to hear that," Maggie said, glancing at her watch. It was 2:55.

"Don't be. That was five years ago. Plus, he smoked like a chimney. Me, I haven't had a cigarette in years. Oh, I enjoy a cigar or two on weekends -- drives Esther up the wall, but I always say: if you can't enjoy life, what the hell's the reason for living? Don't you agree, Margie?"

"Definitely, Mr. Spiegel. Look, I really have to get this press release . . ."

"I remember my first press release. I still have it here somewhere," he said, opening and closing a drawer. "Oh well. Anyway, it was a dandy. Makes me want to cry just thinking about it -- how these poor Tennessee girls got their big chance when they saw that the Curly Corporation was having a contest to find the perfect twins for this new fangled hairspray of theirs. The contest, by the way, was my idea. And you wouldn't have believed all the pictures that poured in. From everywhere. Eskimos in Alaska, black, white, brown -- you name it. Everybody wanted to be the Curly Twins," Bernie Spiegel said, settling into the memory.

"What became of the Curly Twins, Mr. Spiegel?"

Bernie Spiegel grimaced. "Shirley became an alcoholic and died of cirrhosis. Edna ran off with some musician. Haven't heard a hoot from her since. Look, don't you have some work to do or something?"

Maggie blushed. "Yes, Mr. Spiegel. I was just . . ."

"Then get to it! I'm not paying you to sit around and chat all afternoon," he said, dismissing her with a wave.

Maggie was in such a rush to get back to her office that she collided with the woman coming out of the next office.

"Oh, I'm sorry --- oh, Linda. I . . ."

"God, you're clumsy," Linda Jaffrey said, brushing herself off. "Do you have that press release for me?"

"Not yet. I was talking to Mr. Spiegel and . . ."

"I'm not paying you to talk to Mr. Spiegel," Linda Jaffrey said in a harsh whisper. "Now get the damn thing rewritten. You've got less than 30 minutes. Get moving!"

As she turned to go, Maggie glanced into the office Linda Jaffrey had just visited. Gil Dayette was zipping up his fly and grinning enormously.

*   *   *

Maggie had more trouble finding a new ribbon for her typewriter than rewriting the press release.

She finally found the former on a back shelf in the supply room and the lead for the latter buried on the second page. She was hurrying out of her office at 3:24 to deliver the goods when the blonde from across the way intercepted her.

"Let me see that!" the blonde demanded.

"Sorry, but I've got to get this to Linda Jaffrey."

The blonde tried to grab the release out of Maggie's hand, but Maggie backed out of reach.

"That bitch had you rewrite my press release on the 'Beautify Your Block' contest, didn't she?"

"Look, I've got to have this on Linda's desk by 3:30. So if you'll excuse me, I'll . . ."

"She's sleeping with Gil Dayette, isn't she?"

"I don't know, and I don't care. All I care about is getting this press release to her by 3:30," Maggie said, pushing past the smaller woman.

"She's going to tear your press release apart too. You'll see," the blonde said, rushing to the ladies' room for a good cry.

Linda Jaffrey was on the phone again when Maggie appeared, but she motioned for the press release. She continued her conversation as she read the release with her red pencil posed to strike at the least error.

"Could I put you on hold for half a sec, Mr. Gagney? Thanks," Linda said.

"This is fine," she said to Maggie. "Have Louise type it and get it over to that broadcast place of yours ASAP."

Maggie was halfway out the door when Linda added, "Oh, and take it by Alderman Endrijonas' office for his approval."

Maggie found Alderman Endrijonas' office in a remote corner of the fifth floor of City Hall. The Alderman wasn't in, but his special assistant Tom King agreed to review the release. "Looks fine to me," he said, appraising Maggie.

"It'd be a lot better if there was some hard news in it," Maggie said, wondering how the young hotshot got his hair to lie so flat.

"You sayin' that this contest ain't newsworthy?"

"Yeah."

"Look, Sweetheart, we ain't payin' you to tell us what's newsworthy. We're payin' you to get us on TV. Now if you can't do it, we'll get somebody else. You understand?"

"Got you," she said, taking the release and turning to leave.

"Me and the Alderman'll be watching the six o'clock news. We better be on it, or I'll be on the phone to your boss."

What an asshole, Maggie thought, heading down the hall to the elevator bank. The Office of the Mayor was still draped with black and blue bunting. A secretary guarded the darkened inner office where Richard J. Daley had ruled his city state.

For a moment Maggie imagined she saw Mayor Daley seated behind his desk. Then she realized someone WAS seated behind the mayor's desk. The corridor was empty and the secretary was preoccupied with paperwork, so Maggie pressed her face against the glass and peered into the mayor's office.

In the dim light, the person behind the mayor's desk appeared to be Alderman Vincent "Lightning" Endrijonas.

Chapter Eleven

Pete Poulos shook his head. "If your client wants this stuff publicized, then he can pay $40 to put it on the PR Wire like everybody else."

"Pete, they don't even give their employees free coffee. They're too cheap to shell out forty bucks for something they think they can get for nothing. Come on, Pete, just one favor. Please," Maggie said.

"You bring me some news, Maggie, and I'll put it on the wire. This isn't news, and you know it. Now if you don't mind, I have to . ."

"Thanks, Pete," Maggie said, turning away from his desk. Thanks for nothing.

She was wondering which wrist to slit first when she saw Steve Quisenberry bent over the broadcast desk editing the 5:30 news summary.

Maggie hailed the Blessed Virgin Mary and asked for one small favor. "Just one," she whispered.

"Hi, Steve. They have you on broadcast until you leave?" she said, smiling sweetly.

"Oh, hi," Steve Quisenberry said, hardly looking up. "You already trying to pedal some puff over here?"

Maggie waited until Pete Poulos got busy on the phone before continuing. "Look, I need a little favor."

Quisenberry kept editing. "What?"

"Add this to the evening news summary," Maggie said, slipping Steve the press release.

"Are you kidding?" he said, glancing at it. "Endrijonas wants this on our wire, he's going to have to pay to . . ."

"I know," Maggie said, whispering. "That's what Pete said. But if you put this in your news summary, and there's no reason Pete has to know, I'll feed you stuff on Endrijonas when you go to the WORKERS' WEEKLY."

Steve Quisenberry's eyes widened. "Yeah?!? Like what kind of stuff?"

Maggie came all the way into the broadcast cubicle. "Like I

just happened to see a certain alderman sitting behind Daley's desk in the dark."

"BS!"

"Cross my heart and hope to die."

Steve Quisenberry looked at Maggie. "Serious?"

"Yep."

"Aren't you worried about jeopardizing your big PR career?"

"Yeah, but I'll be careful. Nobody'll ever suspect me. So, do we have a deal?" Maggie said, holding her breath.

Steve sneered at the release. "'Alderman Vincent Endrijonas today announced the creation of a *Beautify Your Block* competition aimed at . . .' -- God, how can you write this crap?"

"Steve, are you going to use it or not?"

"You'll really be a source? A good source?"

"Yes!"

"It could get dangerous. Endrijonas is no Boy Scout, you know."

"I know."

"All right. I'll put this in the summary, but I'm counting on you for some really good stuff."

"You got it."

"And one other thing."

"What?"

"You have to buy me a drink when I get off."

"Sure, Steve, that'd be great," Maggie said, just wanting to go home and soak in the tub.

*   *   *

They went to a bar with a TV and raised their glasses when the anchorcreature mentioned Endrijonas' contest before the first commercial break.

"Thanks, Steve," Maggie said.

"You mean they would have fired you if that didn't get on the news?"

"Probably. This woman I work for is a real bitch. God, they're all crazy."

"So why work there? Why didn't you just stay at Muni News until a real job came along?"

"Steve, we've been through this before. The real jobs weren't coming along, and you can't tell me that WORKERS' WEEKLY is really a step up from Muni News."

Steve Quisenberry brooded over his beer. "You hungry?"

"Yeah."

They ended up at a Chinese place on Division Street that laced everything with MSG. They were both sweating profusely by the time they finished the pork-fried rice.

"Can I walk you home?"

"Sure," Maggie said. It was a Monday and she was exhausted, but she needed some male companionship, and Steve had always been a good listener. Plus Norma Jankowski was working tonight. "Would you like to come up for a drink?"

Tired of only being a good listener, Steve agreed.

They walked without touching past the Rush Street singles bars and then Steve looped his arm through Maggie's. "I don't know about you," he said, "but I'm freezing."

"Me too," Maggie said, pressing closer.

Norma had left her usual mess in the kitchen, and there was a bowl of melted chocolate ice cream on the counter, but Maggie was just glad to have her gone.

"Beers are in the fridge, Steve. Help yourself. I'm going to clean up some of Norma's mess, and I'll be right with you."

"God, how can you live with that pig?"

"To tell you the truth, now that I'm making real money I'm thinking of getting my own apartment."

"Good idea," Steve said, rummaging in the refrigerator.

They were soon settled on the couch with cold cans of Old Style, Jay's Potato Chips, a cigar box full of pot paraphenalia and Donna Summer on the stereo. Steve cleaned Maggie's marijuana and rolled three perfect joints. Summer's steamy music liberated their libidos before they finished the first one.

Reaching for the ashtray, Steve moved his thigh against Maggie's. When he leaned back, Maggie was ready for his kiss. Steve retreated once to remove his glasses, and then they embraced in earnest.

They were each wondering who should make the first move to the bedroom when the buzzer interrupted.

"Probably some drunk from Rush Street pushing the wrong

button again," Maggie said, reluctantly going to answer. She pressed the speaker and said, "Who is it?"

"Maggie, it's Eddie. Eddie Rigaletti. I want to apologize for Christmas. Can I come up for a minute?"

Maggie was mortified. "Eddie? I . . ."

"I just want to apologize. Okay?"

"Just a minute, Eddie," Maggie said, smiling gamely at Steve. "Steve, uh, it's this cop I know. Uh . . ."

Steve shrugged. "Hey, it's your place."

Maggie was so flustered she missed the "talk" button on the first try. "Okay Eddie," she said, "you can come up. But just for a minute."

Eddie Rigaletti had found a police hat that fit and an "extra" issue leather jacket that made him mildly menacing. He and Steve locked eyes as soon as he walked through the door.

"Uh, Eddie, this is Steve Quisenberry," Maggie said, "Steve, this is Eddie Rigaletti."

Eddie sized up the situation and removed his hat. "Nice to meet you, Steve. Well, I won't keep you two. I just wanted to stop by and apologize for running out on you at Christmas like that. I just . . ."

"Don't apologize, Eddie. I'm sorry my family was so rude to you. I just told everybody you had an emergency call," Maggie said, wondering if her face looked as red as it felt.

"Yeah, well, I'm real sorry. It was a real immature thing to do. I was in the neighborhood, and it was bothering me, so I figured I'd just stop by and apologize for being such an idiot," Eddie said, extending his hand to Maggie. "Will you accept my apology?"

Maggie took his hand and smiled. "Sure, Eddie."

Eddie released Maggie's hand and put on his hat. "Well, that's all I wanted. I'll be seeing you. Nice to meet you, Steve."

"Hey," Steve said, glimpsing the district number on Eddie's sleeve, "you work in the 25th?"

"Yeah," Eddie said.

"Is it true that on-duty cops are assigned to take Alderman Endrijonas' wife shopping and deliver her groceries?" Steve asked.

Eddie shifted on his feet. "This guy a reporter, Maggie?"

"He works at Muni News, but he's . . ."

" . . . going to be associate editor of THE WORKERS' WEEKLY. Look, man, you're not on the air or anything. I'm thinking about doing a story on Endrijonas when I go to the WEEKLY, and I want to get all the background I can. I'm not going to quote you or anything. I just want to know if the cops in your district are ordered to do favors for Endrijonas and his family."

"I've got to be going," Eddie said.

"Hey," Steve said, springing up, "the night is young. You're off duty, right?"

"Yeah."

"Then have a beer. Or," Steve said, pointing at the pot, "a little wacky tobacky."

Eddie eyed the pot. It HAD been a long day. He handed his hat and jacket to Maggie and settled on the couch. "All right, but I'm just staying for one joint."

Steve Quisenberry was practically panting. "Hey, Maggie, why don't you get Eddie a beer? And another for me while you're at it." Steve lit the joint and handed it to Eddie. "Here you go, man. This is dynamite reefer."

"Yeah, I know," Eddie said, glaring at his rival, "I've smoked Maggie's pot before."

Maggie fled to the kitchen and stuck her head in the refrigerator. She considered hiding behind the celery until they both left.

When she finally returned to the living room with a tray full of beer, Eddie and Steve were on the second joint, and Eddie was looking considerably more relaxed.

"So," Steve said, giving him a friendly swat on the arm, "you really think the Sox are better than the Cubs?"

"Hell, yes," Eddie said. "Man, the Cubs are nuthin' but a bunch of commie faggots. Ain't that right, Maggie?"

Maggie took a seat opposite Eddie and Steve and said, "I know it's against the law in this city, but I actually like both teams."

That satisfied neither man; they each took a generous gulp of beer.

Steve moved in for the kill. "So, you never did tell me - is it true you guys run errands for Endrijonas on city time?"

"Can I trust this guy?" Eddie said, looking at Maggie.

Despite his uniform, Eddie seemed so young and innocent. "You promise not to reveal him as a source, Steve?"

Steve gave Maggie a hurt look. "Of course. You know me better than that."

Maggie gave Steve a hard look and then turned to Eddie. "All right, Eddie, you can trust him."

"Okay, Steve. But if it ever gets out that I told you this, I'll break your fuckin' face. You hear me?"

Steve nodded.

"Good. You wanted to know if guys in the 25th are ordered to be nursemaids to Endrijonas and his family, right?"

"Yeah," Steve said, flushed with the thrill of THE STORY.

"It's all true. In fact, I had to deliver their groceries my first day on the beat. I mean, it's like some private kingdom down there. There's always some kind of city vehicle in front of Endrijonas' place. You ever seen his house?"

"No," Steve said.

"Go down and have a look. It's a mansion. I mean the rest of the people in that ward live in dumps. They all work in the mills, so they can't afford big places. But their fearless leader, who claims he lives entirely on his salary as an alderman, has a goddamned palace. The lot alone's gotta be an acre. Guy's got a lighted tennis court. Man, you really should check it out," Eddie said.

"I will. So what else goes on in the 51st Ward?"

"You want somethin' really juicy?"

"Yeah," Steve said.

"Well, dig this. That dude actually has Streets and Sanitation trucks and crews building a road for him up on his farm in Michigan. People in the 51st Ward don't even have curbs, and Alderman Endrijonas is pulling that shit. Can you believe it?"

"Yeah. So tell me more, Eddie."

"Okay, but how about firing up another joint? It's been a long day."

Now that it was turning into boys' night, Maggie slipped unnoticed into the bathroom and began preparing for bed. When she retired at 11, Eddie Rigaletti and Steve Quisenberry had exhausted all her pot, beer and potato chips but not their interest in Alderman Endrijonas.

"Why don't you guys continue this conversation on Rush Street?" Maggie said, appearing in her red flannel robe. "I've got to get up early tomorrow."

Steve and Eddie were surprised to see her.

"Jeez, Maggie," Eddie said, "we got a little carried away. Can we help you clean up this mess?"

"No," Maggie said, ushering them to the door, "I'll take care of it in the morning. Good night."

Steve and Eddie each kissed her on the cheek and left Maggie to sleep alone.

Chapter Twelve

By the end of January, the Endrijonas faction arranged to have
56th Ward Alderman Michael Blandings serve out the remaining
two years of Daley's term as mayor. A confirmed bachelor, the
bookish Blandings lived next door to his mother in Bridgeport
and was an obedient 54-year-old boy.

Big Bill Mulford never again asserted his right to succeed
Daley, repeatedly denying that he had ever made such a claim to
Muni News.

After one month at Rauch & Spiegel, Maggie Quinn came
through for more clients than she cared to remember. With three
hours notice, she convinced 14 reporters to attend a reception for
the Ugandan minister of tourism. For the American Swine
Growers Association, she chased a piglet around Pioneer Plaza
as delighted school children and minicam operators looked on.

She wrote and placed press releases for American Cyanide,
BabyForm and the Plastics Institute, and now she was
organizing a press trip to The Banyon Development
Corporation's new Harbor Cove Community in southwestern
Michigan.

"You really expect all 40 of them to show up?" Linda Jaffrey
said, opening her mail as she spoke to Maggie.

"If they don't, I'm going to have their kneecaps broken,"
Maggie said.

Linda allowed herself a tight smile.

"Whatever it takes, but that bus had better be full, or we lose
the Banyon account."

"No sweat, Linda."

"I'll take your word for it. Everything else taken care of? Press
kits, name tags, room assignments . . ."

"Everything but the booze, and I'll get that at Fleischmann's as
soon as we're done."

"Okay. But remember, I don't want you getting drunk on that
bus. Let them have all they want, but you stay sober."

"I'm an old hand at this, Linda. Trust me."

* * *

Maggie pushed a shopping cart through Fleischmann's Wholesale Liquor Store snatching half-gallon bottles of scotch, bourbon, vodka and gin off the shelves. She selected four liters of good French wine and a gallon of "dago red." She bought: vermouth, tomato juice, worcestershire sauce, tonic, soda, ginger ale, olives, cherries, miniature onions, cocktail picks, a case of beer, bags of ice and plastic cups.

The man in the cowboy hat at the checkout counter was impressed. "A little late for New Year's, aren't you, sweetheart?"

Maggie laughed. "Don't I wish. This is for a bunch of reporters. Think they'll be able to drink it all?"

"Reporters? Maybe you should buy another cart full."

The old sots beamed as they boarded the bus and saw the bar Maggie had set up at the back.

"I hope you didn't forget the olives," said Ted Luthey, editor and publisher of GOLD COAST NEWS.

Real estate writer Terry McNally brought half the newsroom from the SUN-TIMES.

"I'd better get a story from one of you guys, or I'm going to throw you in the river with cement overshoes on," Maggie said.

"No problem," Terry said, leading the charge to the booze.

Maggie had checked off 39 of the 40 names by the 11 a.m. departure time and didn't have to look to see who was left.

"You want to be there by one o'clock, lady, we'd better roll," the driver said.

"Five more minutes."

Maggie cupped her eyes against the sun and stared down Wacker Drive. "Damn it, Steve," she whispered.

Maggie waited, then boarded the bus.

"Let's go," she said.

The driver was pulling away from the curb when Steve Quisenberry pounded on the door.

"I was on deadline," he said.

She glared at him.

When they were flying down the Dan Ryan Expressway, Steve said, "Were you really going to leave without me?"

"Yes."

She went to the back of the bus where she made herself a bloody Mary.

"Damn," she mumbled under her breath, "I forgot the celery."

"Don't worry, dear, I have some in my purse," said Gladys Honeycutt, editor of THE CHICAGO REAL ESTATE GUIDE. She muffled a burp. "Be prepared, I always say."

By the time they reached the Michigan state line, Maggie was leading everyone in the Notre Dame fight song.

When the singing dissolved into several conversations, Steve Quisenberry took Maggie's arm and whispered in her ear, "Eddie Rigaletti gave me a tour of the 51st Ward the other day."

"That's nice."

Steve took the last beer. "When are you going to give me some stuff on Endrijonas?"

"What do you need me for when you've got a source like Eddie? Between the two of you, you ought to win a Pulitzer."

"Very funny." He sipped his beer. "I ran into Norma the other day. Said you're getting another apartment in a week."

"Yeah."

"Where?"

"Near DePaul. So how are things at the WEEKLY?"

"They'd be a lot better if you'd start giving me some stuff on Endrijonas like you promised."

"There's no stuff to give right now."

"Bull shit!"

"All right. Alderman Endrijonas is really a double agent for the KGB, and he's going to be commissar of Chicago when the Russians take over."

"You've changed, Maggie. You really have," Steve said, studying her.

"Fuck you, Steve," Maggie said, moving to another conversation.

They left the interstate just over the Michigan line and took a two-lane highway deep into the Michigan woods. Suddenly a hand-carved wooden sign welcomed them to Harbor Cove. The sun, snow and lake made a fine scene. Cross-country skiiers kicked across the golf course, and a flock of Canada geese swam in the lake.

"What they'd do, put anti-freeze in there?" Ted Luthey said.

David O'Banyon himself greeted them at the lodge. Banyon Development's 35-year-old president and chief executive officer wore a charcoal suit with a fresh rose in the lapel.

"Nice job," he said to Maggie after his minions had taken the reporters to their rooms. "These people going to write some good stories about Harbor Cove?"

"For sure, Mr. O'Banyon."

"Good. Oh by the way, a couple of local reporters will be joining us for dinner. Mike Long of the HARBOR HERALD is no problem. He thinks Harbor Cove's the greatest thing since sliced bread. But this kid from the STAR is a pain in the ass. I want you to run interference on him tonight."

"Sure. What's his name?"

"I don't know. Jewish. Ask one of my people. Little bastard's been snooping all over this place."

"Mr. O'Banyon, is there a reason this guy's snooping around?"

"Do your job, or I'll find a PR firm that will," he snapped.

Maggie found her room and went straight to the bathroom.

"Surprise," she said, pulling back the shower curtain.

Steve Quisenberry covered himself with a wash cloth. "Jesus, Maggie, what the hell are you doing?"

Maggie threw her coat on the bed and unbuttoned her blouse.

"Help me with this zipper and move over."

"You're drunk."

"I'll get the zipper myself." Maggie finished undressing and stepped into the shower. "I don't think Eddie'll interrupt us here, do you?"

"Maggie, this is MY room!"

"OUR room, Steve. Shut up and wash my back."

* * *

Maggie intercepted Les Stern at the dining room door and lead him to the bar.

"I'm Maggie Quinn. Let me get you a drink."

Stern wore wash pants, a knit tie and a worn corduroy jacket. He had Maggie by an inch, but she outweighed him by at least 10 pounds.

"You're with the PR firm, aren't you?" he said.

"You've done your homework. What are you drinking?"

"Beer."

Maggie got their drinks and handed him his bottle.

"I hear you went to Michigan State," she said. "They've got a pretty good journalism program from what I hear."

"You know why that lake out there never freezes?" he said.

"Very funny." She spotted Steve and pulled him next to her. "I'd like you to meet Steve Quisenberry. Steve's associate editor of THE WORKERS' WEEKLY in Chicago."

"You hiring?" Stern asked.

Steve laughed and got himself a beer. "Where'd you say you were from?"

"I'm writing for the BRIDGETOWN STAR until something better comes along. Could I send you my resume and some clips?"

"I'd better go look after my client," Maggie said.

She went to O'Banyon and said, "We've got our friend from the STAR just where we want him. My friend Steve Quisenberry's associate editor of . . ."

"Fine. Let's get this show on the road. I've got a flight to catch after dinner," O'Banyon said.

Maggie wanted to sit with Steve, but he was too engrossed in coversation with Stern to notice her. So she sat with the SUN-TIMES crowd and swapped lies as young waitresses in colonial costumes served roast duck and Michigan wine by candlelight. After the deep-dish apple pie, the reporters retired to a conference room and watched the requisite slide show.

At Maggie's coaxing, Terry McNally of the SUN-TIMES asked a few questions about future plans for development.

When Stern tried to interrupt, Maggie stood up and said, "I'm afraid Mr. O'Banyon has to leave. But drinks are on the house at the Cove Lounge."

Stern was nearly trampled in the stampede.

"Nicely done," O'Banyon said. "I'll be looking forward to some good press when I get back."

Maggie blocked Stern from pursuing her client. "Come on, Les, let's go have a drink."

"I know -- you're just doing your job."

"Les, look . . ."

"Save your booze for these schmucks. I've got a newspaper to write," he said, leaving.

"You sure took care of him," Steve said.

"Wasn't hard. You want a drink? The price is right."

"I'd rather take a walk."

They got their coats and headed for the lake.

"That Stern guy isn't as dumb as you think, Maggie," Steve said.

"What do you mean?"

Steve pointed at the lake.

"What -- midget Russian subs?"

"Maggie, it's 15 degrees and that lake's not frozen."

"O'Banyon says . . ."

"O'Banyon built that lake over a toxic waste dump, and now he's trying to sell off all the condominiums here and get out before anyone finds out."

"I don't believe it. There's a spring under there, that's why the lake's not . . ."

"There are thousands of barrels of dioxin, PCBs, Mirex, DDT, phosphorous -- you name it -- down there, and it's all oozing together into a chemical soup."

"But the government wouldn't . . ."

"You think the politicians in Chicago are corrupt? You should have heard what Stern said about the ones around here. O'Banyon's a big-time developer. They're not going to let a little pollution problem deprive them of all that new tax money."

"Yeah, but the EPA and the State of Michigan aren't going to let somebody build a resort on a toxic waste dump."

"The EPA can't begin to keep up with all the shit that's going on in this country, and the state depends on local prosecutors to enforce their laws. Stern says O'Banyon gave the local state's attorney a piece of the action. Guy never peeped after that. O'Banyon got this land for practically nothing, he slapped the place together for practically nothing, and now he's unloading it for a bundle. When the suckers who buy out here finally realize they're sitting on a time bomb, your client will be long gone."

"I'm cold. You coming?"

Steve stared at the lake. "No. I want to have a look around."

*   *   *

Maggie awakened from a nightmare at 3 a.m.

"What a dream," she said, reaching for Steve.

He wasn't there.

He wasn't in the bathroom either.

"Must be having a nightcap," Maggie mumbled. Then she looked at her watch.

She dressed quickly and went to the desk.

A sleepy high school student in a three-cornered hat looked up from his Stephen King novel.

"You seen a guy about 6'1" with long brown hair? Kind of stooped. Skinny."

"Haven't seen anybody."

"The bar still open?"

"Closed at 1:30. You want me to call the sheriff's patrol?"

Maggie chewed her lip. "Yes. And give me a flashlight."

Ten minutes later, Maggie found Steve Quisenberry's body floating face-up near the shore of the unfrozen lake.

Chapter Thirteen

"I'm very sorry, Mrs. Quisenberry," Maggie said.

"Were you a friend of Steve's?"

"I worked with him at Muni News."

"It's nice that so many of you could come."

Maggie made small talk with the rest of the family and went to the open casket. She collapsed to her knees and crossed herself.

"Steve, I'm sorry," she whispered.

Steve wore a navy suit and too much pancake makeup.

Maggie touched his forehead and was going to join her Muni News friends when Eddie Rigaletti intercepted her.

Eddie removed his police hat and studied Steve. "Wasn't no accident if you ask me," he said.

"Eddie!"

"What, you think he went for a midnight swim?"

"Eddie, his parents are right over there. This isn't the time for us to. . ."

"Let's go outside then. I need to talk to you."

Maggie caught Pete Poulos' eye and waved. "I want to talk to my friends from Muni News. You've got a telephone, why don't you . . ."

"Just give me five minutes," Eddie insisted.

"All right."

Eddie took Maggie to the parking lot and told her that Steve had been threatened by an anonymous caller just before the trip to Michigan.

"Why didn't he tell me?" Maggie said.

"Probably didn't want to worry you. Plus, he was pissed that you weren't feeding him stuff on Endrijonas like you promised."

"If he was so mad at me, why did he go up to Michigan with me?"

"Because he was on to something about Endrijonas and that O'Banyon guy."

"What?!?""

"He called me the night before you went up there. Said Endrijonas was a silent partner for Harbor Cave or whatever you call it. Had city crews and equipment dredge the lake and build the roads. He bought the land originally from American Cyanide for practically nothing. They had dumped all their nasty chemicals there and wanted to unload it fast before the public found out.

"Then Endrijonas turned around and sold it to O'Banyon for triple what he paid for it, but he's still got a piece of the action. Steve went on that silly-ass trip of yours, because he wanted to check it out."

"Got a cigarette?"

"Sure."

Maggie lost herself in the cigarette for a moment. Then she said, "I'm sorry I ever said I'd help him with this Endrijonas business."

"Maggie, you're a reporter."

"I WAS a reporter. I'm a flak now. I . . ."

"That's bullshit, and you know it. You knew Steve didn't go up there just to write some cute little story about duck ponds. You knew something was going on up there, and you wanted Steve to know about it."

"Eddie, I invited Steve on that trip because --- because I wanted to."

Eddie caught the look in her eye. "All right, you were horny. But there's more to it than that, isn't there, Maggie?"

"I'm making good money for the first time in my life, Eddie. Okay, my company represents some low-lifes. But what company doesn't? And don't tell me the Chicago Police Department's full of saints."

"Maggie, we're not talking about money. Our friend's lying in a coffin in there. He's dead because some scumbags wanted him out of the way. Accidental drowning my ass!"

"How do you know? He could have slipped."

"Yeah, and Hitler accidentally invaded Poland. Come on, Maggie, we're dealing with some hardball dudes here."

"Then why did Steve . . ."

"Because he was a reporter. And so are you."

Maggie finally looked at Eddie. "So what am I supposed to do?"

Eddie smiled. "I was hoping you'd say that. Now, I've got this plan, see, and . . ."

Chapter Fourteen

"Catching up on your beauty rest?" Flo Ziskey said, looking up from her bodice ripper.

"Give me a break," Maggie said, "it's only 9:15."

"Hot date last night, sweetheart?"

"Flo!"

"Okay, be that way. But I know THE look when I see it. Was he -- you know?"

"Do I have any messages?"

Flo smirked and handed Maggie a pink slip reading: "See me ASAP! Linda."

"What time did she . . ."

"An hour ago, lover girl. And she's called twice looking for you."

Maggie mumbled and went to her office where she leisurely prepared for the day. Then she bought a cup of vending machine coffee and strolled to Linda Jaffrey's office.

"You wanted to see me?" she said.

Linda and Gil Dayette were listening to David O'Banyon scream through a speaker phone.

Linda gave Maggie a murderous look and pushed a copy of the BRIDGETOWN STAR at her.

Maggie unfolded the paper and whistled at the 16-point headline: "HARBOR COVE COVER-UP UNCOVERED!"

She grimaced at the fuzzy photograph of the lake and scanned Les Stern's copyrighted story while O'Banyon said: "If you people can't get them to print a retraction, I'll get someone who will!"

Maggie refolded the paper and nodded at her superiors. They were only too glad to let her talk.

"Mr. O'Banyon, this is Maggie Quinn. The situation isn't as bad as you think, presuming that none of the allegations in this story are true."

"Of course they're not true."

"Good. Then it's just a matter of responding to each point with facts and figures," Maggie said.

"Sounds reasonable," O'Banyon said. "Why didn't you think of that, Dayette?"

"Miss Quinn used to be a reporter. That's why we hired her," Linda said, silencing Gil with her finger.

"That's right," Maggie said. "I know exactly what this Stern guy is doing, too. Probably got some disgruntled employee to feed him all this crap. He doesn't quote anyone by name in the whole story. It's the biggest cheap shot I've ever seen. He's using this to get a job at a big paper. All we have to do is go to the owner of the STAR with a point-by-point rebuttal, and we can nail his ass to the wall."

O'Banyon laughed. "What part of Ireland your people from, Maggie?"

"County Mayo."

"Mine too. See what happens when you finally hire the Irish, Dayette?"

Gil grunted and grimaced at Maggie.

Maggie smiled at her bosses and said, "The sooner we get working on this, Mr. O'Banyon, the . . ."

"Dave. Please."

"All right -- Dave, why don't I drive up this morning and we can have something ready by the end of the day."

"Terrific. I'll have an office ready for you, and the entire staff will be at your disposal." He was whistling the Notre Dame fight song when he switched off.

"I'd better hit the road," Maggie said, heading for the door.

"Wait a minute!" Linda said. "What about the press kit for the Haitian Tourist Board? And those media calls for American Cyanide? And . . ."

"You do it, Linda," Gil said. "We blow this, and we'll both be out on the street. You drive to work today, Maggie?"

"No."

"Rent a car from Hertz and put it on my expense account. The biggest, fastest thing they've got. We're counting on you."

Maggie was so giddy she almost gave the Girl Scout salute.

*   *   *

"Eddie, the speed limit's 55!"

"This baby don't know how to go 55," Eddie said, delighting in the Continental.

"Okay -- you get a ticket; you pay for it."

"I'm a cop, remember?"

"You're also a lousy driver. Now slow down!"

Eddie reluctantly let the big car slow to 65. "Our plan's not going to work if I don't have enough daylight, and it's already past noon."

"We've got plenty of time."

Maggie stared at the stark Michigan landscape.

"You worried?" Eddie said.

"Yeah. You?"

"Yeah. Maybe we should smoke a joint."

"That would just make me more nervous."

"Yeah, me too."

They looked straight ahead for a moment, mesmerized by the snow-dampened pavement.

"Maggie?"

"Hmm?"

"You miss Steve?"

"Mmm huh."

"If he was alive, I bet you would have ended up marrying him."

"Why do you say that?"

"You're both college types. You read books and watch educational television and all that good stuff. I just figure you…"

"… liked Steve better than you?" Maggie said, turning to look at Eddie.

"Well, yeah. Especially after that little stunt I pulled on Christmas. You must have thought I . . ."

"Eddie, I love you."

"What?!?"

"The speed limit's 55; slow down."

Chapter Fifteen

O'Banyon himself met Maggie at the main lodge.

"You made good time," he said.

"Traffic was light."

"I've set up a conference room for you. Ted Blankenship from legal and Jerry Danvers from operations are at your disposal. You need anything just holler. Okay?"

"You bet, Dave."

Maggie introduced herself to the laconic lawyer and the oblivious operations manager and set to work.

"All right, let's start with this business about the lake. What proof do we have that it's not built on a toxic waste dump?" she said, brandishing her Bic.

Danvers loosened his tie. "Uh, Ted, do you still have that permit from the Department of Natural Resources? I can't seem to find . . ."

"I'll have my secretary get it," Blankenship said. "What else?"

"Stern says . . ."

"Alleges. Stern alleges," Blankenship the lawyer said.

"Right," Maggie said. "Stern alleges there were pay-offs -- that local and state officials knew it was a toxic waste dump but issued a permit for the lake anyway. Can we prove there were no bribes?"

Blankenship thumbed through a file folder. "Here -- a letter from the president of the Bridgetown Chamber of Commerce welcoming us to the area."

Maggie looked at the letter and at Blankenship. "Got anything else?"

"Yes. Our word," Blankenship said, staring back at Maggie.

Maggie doodled in the margin and looked out the window at the lake. She could just barely see Eddie on the far shore.

"Then the STAR will just have to take our word. What about his claim that Banyon Development never came through on its promise to pave the roads and put in curbs and storm sewers?"

Danvers reddened and rifled his papers.

Blankenship patted his arm and said, "We never made such a

promise."

"Do we have proof -- a contract?"

"They'll just have to take our . . ."

". . . word," Maggie said, doodling again in the margin.

And so it went with each of the 29 allegations in Stern's story.

O'Banyon reviewed Maggie's notes, saying, "Looks good to me. Have one of the girls type it up and get it over to the STAR. And tell those bastards they'd better put this in their paper just like it is, or there's going to be -- look, just get this over there. I've got a plane to catch."

"Leave it to me, Dave," Maggie said.

*   *   *

Les Stern looked up from his typewriter at the character in the black leather jacket and grabbed his letter opener.

"He doesn't bite," Maggie said, stepping into view.

"What do YOU want?!?" Stern said.

Maggie motioned for Eddie to take a seat and did likewise. "Just a few minutes of your time."

"We're not printing a retraction, so you can just . . ."

"Who said anything about a retraction? My friend Eddie has been doing some research today, Les, and I thought you might be interested in what he found out."

Stern glanced uncertainly at Eddie. "Look, I'm on deadline, can you . . ."

"Fuck your deadline, pal," Eddie said. "The lady said she has something to say to you, now shut up and listen."

Stern put down his letter opener and folded his arms around his chest. "All right, I'll give you five minutes."

"First of all," Maggie said, "everything in your article was true."

Stern dropped his arms. "What!?!"

"You heard me."

"But you're O'Banyon's flak; you . . ."

"Steve Quisenberry was a good friend of mine, and Eddie has proof that O'Banyon had him killed."

"What proof? The coroner ruled it an accidental drowning. He was snooping around out there in the dark and fell in and drowned. It's slippery out there."

"Steve was an excellent swimmer," Maggie said.

"And unless you got some gigantic ducks around here, I found some interesting footprints at the far end of the lake."

"You mean . . ."

"That O'Banyon had his goons in scuba gear under the lake. When Steve was alone, they grabbed him and held him under. No witnesses, and the cause of death was clearly drowning. Except they didn't cover their tracks and one of the dumb fucks lost this," Eddie said, reaching in his pocket.

Stern examined the diving mask strap and shrugged. "Doesn't prove anything. Might have been lost by somebody snorkling in there last summer."

Eddie smiled patiently. "You're right: people come from all over to snorkle in that cesspool."

"All right, but what makes you such an authority?"

"He's a Chicago cop, Les. And he works in Alderman Endrijonas' district."

"Endrijonas?!? Is he . . ."

"Put some fresh paper in your typewriter, Les." Maggie lit the first of many cigarettes and started dictating THE STORY.

Chapter Sixteen

"I think it's time you and me had a little talk, Miss Quinn."

"We're having a little talk right now, Alderman Endrijonas."

"No, I mean a face-to-face. Just you and me."

"Alderman, if you have something to say to me, just say it right now -- on the phone."

"Face-to-face, Miss Quinn. In my ward office. Monday morning -- 9 o'clock. I'll see you then," Endrijonas said, disconnecting.

Maggie looked at the phone and then at Eddie. "What do you think?"

Eddie chewed his lip. "He knows you wrote that article. I just know it."

"But who would have told him?"

"Any number of people. Hell, Endrijonas owns that damn county up there. One of his flunkies probably saw us going into the STAR. He's probably got snitches there too."

"So what do I do?" Maggie said.

"Go see him."

"Alone?"

Eddie put his arm around Maggie and kissed her. "No. But he'll think you're alone."

*   *   *

Maggie was three blocks from Endrijonas' office when gates blocked the 106th Street bridge over the Calumet River.

"Shit!" she said, looking at her watch. It was 8:50.

There was no way around the gates, so Maggie had to watch an endless ore boat get tugged down the river. It was 8:57 when the bridge finally descended.

A kid in a Camero tried to muscle in ahead of Maggie, but she gunned her Beetle, beating him across. Enraged, the kid honked and flashed his lights.

Maggie turned in her seat and gave him the finger. "Asshole!" she screamed.

The kid tailgated her to Torrence and flipped her the bird as he entered the Wisconsin Steel Works.

"I hope you're late and they lay you off," Maggie muttered.

She looked at herself in the rearview mirror and took a deep breath. Then she eased the Beetle to the curb, got out and looked up at an enormous purple-on-yellow sign that read: "Alderman Endrijonas welcomes you to the Fightin' 51st Ward."

Maggie stepped into a long, dimly lighted room and told a woman stuffing envelopes that she had an appointment with the alderman. It was 9:00.

"Alderman Endrijonas ain't here," the woman said, still licking.

"When do you expect him."

The woman shrugged and kept licking. "I don't know. I'm not his secretary -- he don't tell me where he's going. You want to wait; you can help me stuff these envelopes."

Maggie went to the window and scanned the street. Where the hell was Eddie?

Maggie turned back to the woman and said, "Can I use your phone?"

"As long as it's a local call."

Maggie stepped toward the phone, stopped and instinctively ran for the door. She was halfway out when the explosion welled up from the basement and tore the two-flat from its foundation.

Chapter Seventeen

Rollcall ended promptly at 8:30 a.m., and Eddie rushed for the door.

"Not so fast, Rigaletti," Sergeant McInerny said. "The lieutenant wants to see you."

"Can it wait, Sarge? I got to . . ."

"No."

Eddie sighed and went to Lieutenant Durkin's office. He rapped on the door and waited for the inevitable, "Whaddye want?"

Eddie cracked the door and said, "Lieutenant, it's Officer Rigaletti. You wanted to see me?"

The big Irishman motioned for the little Italian to enter his office and be seated. Hearing no police radio, Eddie figured silence was a lieutenant's perquisite.

"So," Durkin continued saying into the phone, "I'll talk to the wife and set something up. Yeah, that'd be great. Good talking to you, Hank. Yeah, you too."

Durkin cradled the phone and pursed his lips. "Be right with you, Rigaletti." He went to his private bathroom and, without bothering to close the door, pissed long and powerfully.

What an asshole, Eddie thought.

Durkin emerged zipping up his fly and smiling. "Damn coffee around here goes through you as fast as the booze," he said.

"Yes, sir," Eddie said.

Durkin settled heavily in his wooden chair and arranged some files. "So what did you want to see me about, Rigaletti?"

"Sergeant McInerny said you wanted to see ME, Lieutenant."

Peeking at his watch, Eddie saw that it was already 8:40. He knew he could be at Endrijonas' office by 9:00 if he left immediately.

Durkin ran his hand through his thick salt-and-pepper hair. "Oh, now I remember. Do you speak Spanish?"

"No, sir."

"You don't?"

"Rigaletti's Italian, Lieutenant. I speak a little Italian, but that's really about it."

"Well anyway, the pastor over at Saint Ida's asked us to help him start an indoor soccer league for the Mexican kids over there, and I figured you'd be the man for the job what with you being, uh, you know -- "

"Yes, sir. I know," Eddie said, wanting to punch the fat mick.

"You do play soccer; don't you, Rigaletti?"

"A little, and I know the rules."

"Good. Well, why don't you go over to Saint Ida's and introduce yourself," Durkin said, leafing through his papers. "Ah, here it is -- pastor's name is Father Mendez. Seems okay, but you never know with the Mexicans. Sons-of-bitches are your best amigos one day, and they're sneak-attacking the Alamo the next. Of course, I'd rather have them any day than the shines, but the beaners can be a real pain in the ass. Especially since we don't have anybody who speaks Spanish in the district.

"So you go over there, Rigaletti, and lay a little of that Latin charm on him. Italian, Spanish -- practically the same, right? Smooth his feathers. Show him that the police aren't all a bunch of big fat micks like me," Durkin said.

Eddie was leaving when an explosion reported from the middle distance.

"Must be demolishing more of that old mill on 106th Street," Durkin said. "Way it's goin' around here, Endrijonas is gonna have to put the whole damn ward on the city payroll. Just be grateful you got a city job, Rigaletti."

"Yes, sir."

When he was past sight of the district, Eddie flashed his blue lights and sped toward Torrence Avenue. His sense of disaster was confirmed when he saw the size of the firefighting force arrayed against the blazing cavity that had housed Alderman Endrijonas' ward office.

"Situation's under control. Bomb and Arson is here," the field sergeant told Eddie. "Get back to your beat."

The explosion had caused the brick building to collapse on itself, and the resulting fire had devoured both adjacent apartment buildings.

"Anybody hurt, Sergeant?" Eddie said, standing on his toes to survey the scene.

"Rigaletti, this ain't your beat, and I don't remember puttin' out no call for district-wide assistance. Now take off before I write you up."

Eddie disappeared into the crowd of firefighters and asked the first paramedic if there were any injuries.

"We got one fatality so far," the paramedic said.

"Any identification?"

"Female. That's it so far. She must have been in the office on the first floor when it hit. Probably killed instantly by falling debris. Just as well because she would have burned to death otherwise. Fire department got everybody out of the other buildings in time. Oh yeah, a couple of firemen had to be treated for smoke inhalation. Idiots didn't put their masks on tight enough. That's about it. Hey, you all right?"

Feeling light-headed, Eddie slumped against the ambulance. "The body -- that lady you found -- she still here?"

"Paddy wagon took it to the morgue already. What's wrong -- she a friend of yours or something?"

Eddie was about to reply when television lights temporarily blinded him. Blinking, he saw that a professionally concerned Alderman Endrijonas had come to survey the damage for the six o'clock news.

Enraged, Eddie seized the alderman's trenchcoat and screamed in his face: "You killed her, you slimey bastard!"

The television reporter, a thin-faced young man with no hat, boots or gloves, motioned for the minicam operator to switch off.

"Officer, can't you see I'm trying to conduct an interview with Alderman Endrijonas?" he said, fussing with his hair.

Ignoring Eddie, Endrijonas nodded curtly at the nearby sergeant, and burly cops were soon escorting their comrad away from the scene.

"I warned you, Rigaletti," the sergeant said. "Now I'm gonna have to write you up. Get the hell out of here!"

"But, Sergeant, Endrijonas set this up. He was supposed to meet a friend of mine in his office at nine -- when the place blew up. He killed her for Christ's sake!"

Eddie struggled to free himself.

"That's enough, Rigaletti. You get your ass out of here right now, or I'm arresting you. You understand?"

The mini-cam operator had flicked his lights back on, and Endrijonas was looking duly concerned. Eddie watched him for a moment and took a deep breath. "I understand, Sergeant."

The sergeant nodded, and the beat men released Eddie.

One of them whispered, "You're steppin' on some pretty big toes, Rigaletti. Cool it."

Eddie nodded grimly and walked away. He was almost to his car when he heard a woman across the street scream: "Somebody help! There's a body over here!"

Eddie got there first and saw through the blood and blisters that it was Maggie. Finding a raspy breath and a weak pulse, he shouted for the paramedics.

They were assisting Maggie in an instant.

"How the hell did she end up over here?" one of them said.

"She was in the building when it blew up," Eddie said, hysterical. "She got blown all the way across the street! God, why didn't anybody find her sooner?"

Eddie touched Maggie's forehead, and in defiance of the sergeant's orders, followed her to the hospital.

Chapter Eighteen

Eddie sat in the police room at Saint Agnes Hospital and chewed his knuckles. Ignoring the dispatcher's umpteenth radio summons, he tried to pray. But his anger and anguish got in the way.

So he crushed his half-smoked cigarette underfoot and went to the bay where they were treating Maggie.

"How's she doing?" he said.

The bearded intern finished inserting the trach tube and looked up. "In plain English?"

"Yeah."

"She's lucky to be alive."

"Is she going to . . ."

"Do I look like God to you, Officer?"

Looking at the mess that was Maggie, Eddie said, "You save her. Understand!?!"

The intern shrugged and began suturing a deep cut on Maggie's forehead. "Do you mind -- you're blocking the light," he said.

Eddie back-stepped. "Is there anything I can . . ."

"Yeah, go have a cup of coffee. I'll let you know as soon as we're finished with her."

"Hey, if she needs blood or anything, I'm right here. Okay?"

"We'll let you know. Now let us work on her. All right?"

"All right."

Eddie contemplated the corridor for a moment and then charged to the pay phone.

"Give me the head guy," he said when he reached Muni News.

"Who is this?" Pete Poulos said, taking the call.

"A friend of Maggie Quinn's. Alderman Endrijonas just tried to kill her. They got her in the emergency room at St. Agnes Hospital. She was in Endrijonas' office when it blew up. She got blown all the way across the street. He was supposed to meet her there at nine see, and . . ."

"Who are you? How do you know all this?"

"Look, pal, one of your old reporters is down here lookin' like she got run over by a fuckin' beer truck. If you're not interested, maybe I'll . . ."

"All right -- I'll give you somebody on rewrite."

"No. You take the story. And just like I give it to you. And for your information, my name is Edward J. Rigaletti. I'm a patrolman in the 25th District. Check it out if you don't believe me."

"We will. Now what's your story, Officer Rigaletti?"

Ignoring the "no smoking" signs posted over his nose, Eddie lit a Marlboro and, in a manner that impressed even Pete Poulos, recounted the the events that had lead to Steve Quisenberry's death and Maggie's grievous injury.

"Well, what do you think?" Eddie said, lighting his fourth cigarette.

"It's already going out on both wires," Poulos said. "And you tell Maggie for me to hang in there. You hear?!?"

"I hear you," Eddie said.

*   *   *

Eddie waved his arms and shouted: "Over here, fellas!"

The "News You Need at Nine" van stopped where Eddie directed, and the crew quickly assembled their equipment.

"You Officer Edward J. Rigaletti?" the reporter said, consulting his Muni News wire copy.

Eddie was about to answer when news vans from the three network affiliates arrived. While they were setting up, reporters and photographers from the three dailies appeared. Eddie was so excited he had to go in and take a leak. Then he poked his head in Maggie's bay and asked, "How's she doin', doc?"

"She's doin'."

"Good."

Eddie went to the media and began telling THE STORY. He was just getting to Alderman Endrijonas when someone called from one of the television trucks: "Hey, there's been a big El crash in Loop! Lake/Dan Ryan train rear-ended a Ravenswood. At least two cars derailed and fell on Wabash Avenue. Let's go!"

Ignoring Eddie's protests, the reporters rushed away to cover what was now THE STORY.

Eddie kicked the concrete and went back inside to check on

Maggie. A black kid with a knife wound was in her bay. Eddie tore around until he found Maggie's intern. He was now disinfecting an old woman's gangrenous foot.

"Where is she?"

"Where's who?" the intern said, not looking up.

"Maggie Quinn! The woman you were just working on!"

"Oh, yeah. We stablized her and sent her to intensive care. You know, you're not supposed to be in here."

"Where's intensive care?"

"They don't allow visitor in intensive . . ."

"Where the fuck is it?"

"Fifth floor. Take that elevator over there. But don't tell them I told you."

Maggie was in the last bed by the window. She was on a respirator and connected to a tangle of plastic tubes.

"You look like a spaghetti factory," Eddie said, leaning over to kiss Maggie's forehead.

Except for the artificial breathing, she appeared dead.

"You're gonna be okay, kiddo. I know it."

"Officer, what are you doing up here?"

Eddie gave the nurse his altar boy look. "I'm going. But you take good care of her. You hear me?"

The nurse nodded and sent him on his way.

Eddie was astounded to see Lieutenant Durkin waiting for him as he got off the elevator. Lieutenants rarely left their desks.

"Lieutenant!?! What are you . . ."

"I thought I told you to go see that priest at Saint Ida's."

"You did, Lieutenant, but . . ."

"But nothing, Rigaletti. Give me your badge."

"Lieutenant, you can't . . ."

"Try and stop me, Rigaletti," Durkin said, ripping the star off Eddie's leather jacket.

Chapter Nineteen

The Sister of Mary's Joy said Eddie could see the patient for five minutes.

"Yes, Sister," Eddie said.

He checked the roses again and stepped into the room.

"Hi," he said.

"Hi," Maggie said.

They smiled bravely at one another for a long moment, then Eddie fumbled with the flowers.

"Here, I got these for you. But it looks like I'm not the only one who's been here."

Maggie lifted what was left of her left hand and pointed. "They're lovely, Eddie. Just lovely. Why don't you put them over there by the window? Sister'll get a vase for them later."

Eddie found a place for the flowers and seated himself next to Maggie's bed. Now he could not help but stare.

"My hair's starting to grow back -- at least in places," Maggie said, rolling her eyes. In so doing, she accentuated the total absence of eyebrows and eyelashes.

Eddie leaned forward in his chair. "Maggie, I'm so sorry this happened to you. It should have been me, not you."

"Eddie, I don't want to hear that kind of talk."

Maggie extended her right hand. Eddie took it.

"Yeah, okay. How's the food here?"

"I just started eating solid food on Monday. That was the most wonderful cheeseburger I ever ate."

They laughed.

Then Eddie got up and kissed Maggie's disfigured lips. "There," he said, "I should have done that as soon as I walked in."

"Eddie, you don't have to . . ."

"Maggie, I love you. You hear me -- I love you."

"I know," Maggie said.

"Maybe when you get a little better I can take you outside. They have a beautiful garden."

"So I've heard. But you don't have to. It's such a long way to come, and . . ."

"I want to. Besides, I've got a lot of free time on my hands. Department shit-canned me."

"What?!?"

"Union's fighting it for me, but I don't think I have a chance. Endrijonas controls the whole damn police department. God, he controls everything. Did you know that Bomb and Arson said the fire was caused by a faulty boiler? Can you believe it? And the press has been treating Endrijonas like he was the real mayor. Mayor Blandings doesn't get out of bed unless Endrijonas tells him to. And Endrijonas has absolute control of the City Council. Can you believe it?"

"Yeah. Rauch and Spiegel fired me too. And my father had to sic his whole legal department on them to get their insurance company to pay for this. But you know what?"

"What?"

"I don't care. We're both alive -- that's what I care about, Eddie."

Eddie looked through the gauze and scars at the most beautiful woman in the world.

"Me too," he said.

The End

Stormin' Norman

Book One:
Then

Chapter One

"Hey, Blake, you're finally gonna have a roommate."

I looked up from my PLAYBOY. "What? Who?"

Chief Harvey said, "Soul brother, Blake. From Chicago. Your lucky day, boy."

"What's his name, Chief?"

The big Georgia cracker grinned. "James. Norman James. Yeoman Third. Made Second Class but got busted back to Third on accounta he don't cotton much to authority. Maybe you can be a good influence on him. You know, teach him some of your high-society ways. Now put down that damn beat-off book and get this place squared away for your new shipmate."

"Aye aye, Chief."

It was August 26, 1969, and the moist heat was creeping in from the South China Sea. I looked out my window at the Naval Recreational & Communications Center, Kaohsiung and wondered if I'd have time for a swim before this James character showed up. Taiwan was miserable in August, but we had our wonderful pool. However, first things first.

I turned back to my work and was chasing the last dust mote when someone rapped heavily on the door and stepped into my room.

"You must be . . ."

"Yeah, Norman James." He dropped his duffel bag and surveyed the tight quarters. "Least you got an air conditioner."

"Yeah."

At 6'1", I had him by a good inch or two, but he was broader in the shoulders and more solid all around. I didn't realize he was wearing a cap until he plucked it out of his fertile 'fro.

"Hey," I said, offering my hand, "where are my manners? I'm Terry Blake. Yeoman Second Class. Welcome to the rock."

Norman took my soul shake with a sly grin. "The rock?"

"Yeah, as in Republic of China. But we call it the rock, because it looks like a rock. At least around here."

"Man, this is a damn country club compared to my last duty station." Norman kicked off his shoes and sprawled out on my bunk.

"Where was that?"

"Okinawa. Most fucked up place on earth. Somethin' wrong, man?"

I realized I had been staring at him. "No. No, not at all. Hey, you all checked in?"

"Yeah." Norman folded his hands behind his head and farted. "Don't have to report for duty until tomorrow morning. Man, I sure could go for some pussy. How about you, ah . . ."

"Terry. Terry Blake."

"Yeah. Well how about you, man? You gonna sit around this dump and play with your dick all night, or do you want to go out with Stormin' Norman and party?"

"Well I was going to take a swim, and then . . ."

"Wake me up in an hour and we'll go get us some of that sideways pussy I been hearin' about."

Norman James closed his eyes and went to sleep before I could tell him that this uptight, white, suburban virgin didn't have the faintest idea where to find pussy in Kaohsiung.

Chapter Two

"Where you say you were from again?"

Norman and I were riding the number 51 bus into Kaohsiung.

"Flossmoor. It's next to Homewood."

"Flossmoor! Sounds like somethin' the damn dentist would tell you to do. Flossmoor, or your damn teeth'll rot out you mouth. They let black people live there?"

I smiled nervously at an elderly Chinese woman who was leaning against my elbow.

"Well, yeah, I suppose, uh . . ."

Norman rolled his eyes. "Niggers need not apply. I understand."

The driver swerved to avoid a farmer and his water buffalo, and we toppled against one another. Norman reeked of Aqua Velva.

"Crazy mother fucker!" Norman said.

Everyone stared at him, and he laughed until his eyes watered. "Look at all these little people, Jerry."

"Terry. It's Terry."

"Yeah. Like little monkeys. Damn!"

Norman laughed some more; the Chinese kept staring, and I wondered what I was getting myself into.

The thick aroma of raw sewage suddenly filled the bus.

"What the hell is that?" Norman said, looking out the open window.

"Believe it or not, they call it the Love River. One of Kaohsiung's major tourist attractions."

"Man, that thing makes the Chicago River look like a damn swimming pool."

When we got into the center of town, Norman pulled me off the bus and told me to stay close as he headed down Hsin Le Street.

"What about that place?" I said, pointing at a brightly lighted bar named the China Dollhouse.

"Hell no. Too many damn sailors. I like my pussy fresh, man. What about you?"

"Yeah. Me too."

Norman took a left at the next side street and walked headlong into throngs of Chinese. I caught up with him next to an open-air restaurant.

"You hungry, man?" he said.

I watched as the cook grabbed a black snake out of a box, beheaded it with a cleaver and quickly rendered its slithering carcass into bite-sized morsels.

"Uh, actually I had a burger and some fries while you were taking your nap. But if you're hungry, I'll have a beer or something."

Norman claimed a table next to the cook and nodded. "Gimme one of them bad things," he said.

The cook grinned and fetched a snake for Norman. When he looked at me, I said, "Just a beer, thanks."

Norman ate that entire snake, licked his chopsticks and ordered another one.

"Man, you don't know what you're missin'."

I swigged my Taiwan Beer from the bottle. "I'm not into real food. I guess that's why I haven't really come into town much. When I got my orders for Taiwan, I was real excited about eating all this great Chinese food. But then when I got here, I realized that the food they eat in China is a lot different than the Chinese food we eat back home."

Norman gulped his beer and regarded me.

"What's wrong?" I said, fidgeting.

"Man, you is the whitest white dude I ever met. The absolute whitest."

I gulped some more warm beer. A Chinese businessman approached our table and said in careful English: "Are you gentlemens Americans?"

"We sure as hell ain't Chinese," Norman said, grinning.

The man smiled and shook our hands. "I want to congratulate you for fine achievement of landing man on moon. America very great country to do such a thing." He nodded and disappeared into the pedestrian traffic.

"Yeah, America's a real great country. Wastin' all that money to put some asshole on the moon while half the people on the South Side don't got no heat in the winter time. Great country, my ass!"

"I don't know, I kind of think it was a good thing to do. You know for . . ."

"For what, man? So some honky golfer can take his big step for mankind? That's bullshit. Just bullshit. With all the money Nixon spent for that, he coulda bought decent housing for people that ain't got none. What the hell good is it havin' some dude walkin' around on the moon when people are unemployed and hungry and cold and bein' hassled by the pigs all the damn time? Huh?"

I shrugged. "Hey, why don't you hurry up and finish, and we'll go get us some pussy?"

"What's the matter, you don't like politics?"

"It's not that, I'd just rather get me some pussy. That's all."

Norman gulped the last of his beer. "All right, let's go get us some pussy."

We walked four miles or more before Norman was satisfied.

"No honky ass sailors around here."

I surveyed the dense, dimly lighted neighborhood. Chinese in white sleeveless t-shirts and khaki pants regarded us from doorways. "No, you're right about that."

"Except for you, of course. But you don't count, because you're really a blue-eyed soul brother, right, Jerry?"

"Terry, not Jerry."

"Suit yourself. Come on, let's get us some pussy."

"Where? There's nothing but apartments around here."

"Jus' follow me."

Norman walked boldly up to the nearest doorway and said to the man there: "Where can we get us some poontang around here?"

The man shrugged and said something in Chinese.

Norman made a graphic gesture with his fingers and leered.

"Ah," the man said. He smiled and pointed to a storefront down the street.

The man there knew enough English to know what we wanted.

He ushered us into a drab room with a ceiling fan and clapped his hands. An ancient woman appeared with two glasses of cool jasmine tea.

"You wait. I bring girls. Plenty clean. Plenty beauty. I right back. You wait here."

We sipped our tea and smiled at the old woman. Smiling back, she reached in her dress pocket and produced an amazing assortment of colored condoms.

"Japan. Number one. Forty dollar. You buy."

"Forty dollars!" Norman said. "That bitch is crazy."

"That's forty New Taiwan dollars. In other words, a buck."

"Shit, I still ain't puttin' one of them damn things on my dick. Them things is for sissies. Be like takin' a shower with boots on. No way, mamma san, no way."

"You buy," the old woman said, shaking her wares at us.

"Maybe we should, Norman. You never know about these girls here."

"You sound like you got yourself a case of the clap from one of these slanted pussies."

"No, but . . ."

"Well, then ride bareback, man."

"You buy," the old woman repeated. "Must buy."

"What's wrong, your girls dirty?" Norman said.

The woman shook her head vigorously. "Girls velly clean. You buy. Must buy."

"All right," I said, reaching in my pocket. "Give me two: a red one and a blue one."

The old woman took my money, gave me two rubbers and disappeared.

"I told you, man, I ain't usin' one of them damn things. And I mean it. You want to put two bags over your dick, that's your problem. But there's two things I NEVER do -- wear rubbers and eat pussy." Norman gulped his tea and slammed the glass on a table. "I wish that mutha fucka would hurry up. My dick is so hard it's gonna break."

I took a deep breath and watched a chameleon, or "wall tiger," stalk a resting mosquito. Got her, but there were millions more to pester me that horribly humid night.

"What's wrong with eating pussy?"

"Are you serious?" Norman said, rolling his eyes.

I shrugged. Closest I had ever gotten was Frannie Kopler's belly button at the beach party after the senior prom. That's when she decided she really didn't want to go all the way.

"Yeah, I'm serious."

"That's nasty shit down there. Tastes like old dead fish. You eat pussy, Jerry?"

"Terry."

"Whatever."

"Well . . ." I was saved by the approach of two motorcycles.

"'Bout time, man. I thought my dick was gonna melt down or somethin'."

Our smiling Chinese pimp entered the room and said: "I got two number one girls. Clean. Beautiful. $6.50 American. Blow and fuck."

"Let's have a look, Hop Sing," Norman said, lighting a cigarette.

"Sure, G.I.," the pimp said.

He clapped his hands and two blushing little Chinese woman appeared. They wore white silk blouses, black skirts slit up the side and three-inch heels. The prettier one wore a pink flower in her hair.

"A-number-one. All clean," the pimp said.

"Ugly. Ugly. Ugly." Norman said. "Come on, Jerry, let's go find us some good-lookin' pussy."

I looked at the hookers. They weren't that bad. Not bad at all. And one of them could be my first fuck. Right here in this building. Right now.

"They're fine. Just fine," I blurted. And before I knew it, I had seized the one with the flower in her hair.

"Good," the pimp said, pushing the other one at Norman. "You pay now, then all you want. $6.50 each. Pay now."

Norman gave me a murderous look. "Hey, dude, if you ain't no cherry, you sure is actin' like one."

"All right, I'm a goddamn cherry. I want to get laid. And the sooner the better. Okay?"

Norman smiled. "All right, Terry. We'll go fuck these little monkies right now." He reached in his pocket. "And it's on me. And don't you ever forget who paid for your first fuck."

How could I, especially after he had finally gotten my name right.

The pimp lead us into an adjoining room and switched on the light, a naked bulb. The rectangular room contained two parallel beds and a wash basin. Olive paint peeled from the walls and a ceiling fan spun listlessly overhead.

"No rough stuff, G.I. You understand?" the pimp said.

Norman snorted, and I nodded. The hookers giggled.

When the pimp was gone, my date lead me to the far bed, perched on the edge and peeled off my pants and skivvies with alarming speed. She examined my equipment with a jeweler's eye.

"Oh," she said, "you so big. So velly big."

Norman laughed, and his date stared at my half erection.

"Now you," Norman's date said.

"Sure," Norman said, stripping down. "You want to see some real cock, bitch. Take a look at this."

The three of us simply gawked.

Finally, Norman's hooker said: "Too big. Too big. You hurt me with that."

Norman just laughed. "Damn, bitch, ain't you never seen a real dick before? I guess not. Hell, all these little chinks around here probably gots dicks the size of worms. All right, quit starin' and take your damn clothes off."

Norman's hooker tried to run, but he grabbed her and threw her on the bed.

"All right, I'll take your clothes off for you."

He wrestled her clothes off, spread her legs and forced himself in. She howled and cursed him in Chinese. Norman humped her all the harder. She pounded his back with her fists and screamed in his ear.

"You love it, bitch. I know you do."

My companion and I were mesmerized. When the screams became moans and whimpers, we decided to get down to business.

I turned off the light, peeled off the rest of my clothes and fumbled in the dark for my first real encounter with the opposite sex. She guided me with an off-key rendition of: "If you go San Francisco be sure you wear flower in your hair . . . ."

She repeated that refrain four times as I petted her private parts. When I went to kiss her she pushed my head away.

Then she unrolled the red condom over my root and guided me in. No bells or whistles, just Norman James muttering: "You love it, bitch, I know you do . . ." in the near darkness.

I ejaculated before the first cycle of pelvic thrusts and felt myself go swiftly soft.

My guide was distressed. I wanted to sleep, but she wanted more out of me. She planted my hand on her pussy and stroked my limp dick. She rubbed her breasts against my chest and kept singing about San Francisco.

When I finally got hard again, she replaced the red rubber with the blue one and had me back in for seconds. This time I had more staying power and held back long enough for her to fake an orgasm. At least she stopped singing that damned song long enough to hoot and holler a little.

"That's the way, Terry," Norman said. "Give that little chink some real fuckin'."

"Yeah," I said.

I came a second time and settled next to my serenading sweetheart.

"Hey, Terry, tell that bitch to quit that damn singing. Drivin' me crazy."

"Shuuussh," I said, putting my finger to her lips.

"No like?" she said, pouting.

"I like quiet right now. Okay?"

"More fuck?" she said, trying to resuscitate my dead dong.

"Please. No. Let me rest. Okay?"

She muttered something in Chinese and left the bed. I lay there and listened to Norman's litany of sexual bravado as long as I could. Then I got up.

As part of her service, my date lead me to the wash basin and soaped and watered my privates. She put a basin on the floor, squatted over it and gave herself a damned good washing. She dressed, kissed me on the cheek and was gone.

Norman, meanwhile, was still planking away.

"Hey, Norman, I'll wait outside, okay?" I said.

"Yeah, sure," he said without missing a stroke.

Chapter Three

When Norman was finally finished, we bought a bottle of Taiwan rum and climbed the steep and winding road to Shou-Shan Park.

"Pretty isn't it?" I said, pointing at the twinkling harbor below. "And it even smells good up here."

Norman swigged the rum. "Still smells like gook shit. Whole damn place smells like gook shit."

"Yeah, well."

"Here, have some of this nasty shit."

I swallowed a mouthful and leaned back. A few unfamiliar constellations poked through the smog cover.

"Well you can say what you want about how bad it smells here, but I'll take this any day over Vietnam. Can you imagine what those poor suckers are doing over there tonight?"

Norman grabbed the bottle back and killed it. "Their own damn fault for bein' so stupid. That's what I think."

"Yeah, I suppose. Still, it could just as easily been us instead of them. Of course, I think the Navy's got it a little easier over there, at least from what I hear. Unless you're on one of those river patrol boats in the Mekong. Then I guess you could get your ass shot off as fast as any grunt."

"My uncle was in Korea, man. Said them fuckin' gooks was like ants. They fired their machine gun until the barrel melted off, and them little monkeys still kept comin'. You can have that shit, man."

"You know, I've talked to some Chinese here, real gung-ho Nationalists, who're chomping at the bit to send troops over to Vietnam. They want to start marching north until they hit Peking and flush Mao's fat ass down the can. Can you believe it?"

"Yeah," Norman said. "Nothin' gooks like better than killin' other gooks. Man, life don't mean shit over here. Not a damn thing. Well, if they want to go over to Vietnam, I say let 'em. Put the little monkey-ass mother fuckers on the first ship outta this sewer and let 'em loose. But get all the Americans out first. Then let the little yellow bastards shoot the shit of out each other."

"I get the impression you don't like Orientals."

Norman laughed. "Shit, man, where'd you get that idea?"

"Well, you being from the South Side of Chicago and all, I'd think you'd hate white people more."

"I do, man. I do. It's just there ain't a lot of you honkies around to hate right now."

"I see."

"Yeah, I bet you do. Man, how you feel if all the police in Flushmore be black. Be big, mean-ass black pigs what come down on your shit every night an' day. Roust you ass every time you step out on the street. Call you momma and yo sister a 'ho' and tell you you ain't nuthin' but a lazy-ass white boy what ain't gonna amount to nuthin' on accounta you brain the size of a damn pea. How you like that, Terry?"

"Not too much I guess."

"Yeah, not too much. Come on, let's get us another bottle of rum."

We were halfway down the road to Kaohsiung when we saw the motorcycle. It was a red Honda 350 cc.

"Dude's probably fuckin' his neighbor's old lady back there," Norman said, pointing at the dense foliage lining the road.

We listened for a moment and heard a woman giggle.

"Yeah. Well that dude don't need his motorcycle do he?"

"Norman, I don't think . . ."

"Man, you is one negative mother fucker. Didn't I get us some pussy tonight?"

"Yeah."

"And didn't you enjoy it?"

"Yeah."

"Well, then trust old Norman."

"But what if we get caught?"

"Man, we ain't gonna get caught. This is Taiwan, man. Not Flushmore."

The hookers were one thing, but stealing a motorcycle. "How are we going to start it? I don't know how to hot-wire anything. Do you?"

"No need to. Wait here." Norman disappeared into the darkness and returned five minutes later laughing. "Stupid mother fucker left his keys in his pocket, and he left his pants hangin' on a bush. Come on!"

Norman started the bike with one solid kick and aimed it down hill. He was rolling when I hopped on back.

"If we get caught, we're gonna . . ."

"You rather walk, Terry?"

"No."

"Then shut up and enjoy the ride."

Norman gunned the bike down the steep road, laughing through the turns. I lightened up and laughed with him. Hell, I was half in the bag.

I was all the way in the bag after we finished another bottle of rum.

It was well past 10, and most of the evening strollers had gone home. Norman raced us around the empty streets, screaming: "Power to the people! Mao up in here!"

I yelled, "Charlie Manson for President" and sang a medley of protest songs.

Finally we were racing out of the city on a road I didn't recognize.

"Where're you goin'?" I screamed in Norman's ear.

"Shit if I know. Jus' hang on, man."

"There's nothing to hang on to."

"Then put your arms around my waist and hang on to me."

"All right."

I clung drunkenly to a black man I had just met that afternoon and watched Taiwan tear by. We crossed the stinking Love River again, and then we were riding in darkness on a two- lane road.

Norman gunned the bike as fast as it would go and howled into the wind. My feet came loose and flopped dangerously close to the spokes.

"What the fuck you doin' back there, man?"

"My feet!"

In struggling to regain my footing, I upset our balance. Norman fought to get it back but couldn't. The bike shot across the narrow shoulder and arced us into oblivion.

The sensation of flight was so exhilarating, neither of us said anything until gravity drew us back to earth.

"Damn!"

"Oh shit!"

We landed in a rice paddy. The mud arrested the bike, flinging Norman and me free. Momentum took us another ten yards and then we lay there unharmed but laughing very seriously.

So seriously that we weren't aware of the chrome-helmeted Chinese military police until they were shining flashlights in our faces.

"Get up," the one who spoke English said. "Get up now!"

"Fuck you, Charley Chan!" Norman said, rolling over on his back.

"Norm," I whispered, "I don't think you want to be messin' with these guys."

Norman sat up and flipped his middle finger at the flashlight.

I tried to sit up too but my head was spinning too fast. I was too drunk to do much of anything but listen.

"We want see military ID. And registration for bike."

"Ain't got none," Norman said. "Hey, man, aren't you gonna ask if we hurt? We had us a nasty damn accident on accounta you chink-ass roads bein' so ridiculous, and all you can do is do some pig routine about IDs. Fuck you!"

"Norm, I think . . ."

"I'll handle this, Terry. All right?"

"Sure, but . . ."

I was dragged to my feet and frisked. The man in pressed khaki found my green military ID and held it in front of his flashlight. He matched it against my face and nodded.

"Now you," he said to Norman.

They tried to pull Norman up, but he shoved them away.

"I ain't got no ID on me," he said, wiping himself off.

"What?!?"

"I said I ain't got no ID on me. These mother fuckers want to know who I am they can call up Commander Fishhead or whatever his damn name is."

"Holy Shit, Norm. You really didn't bring your ID?"

The cops spoke in Chinese and then came at Norman from both sides. When he swung at one, the other chopped him in the kidneys with his truncheon. Norman gasped and dropped.

"Mother fuckers!" Norman said. "Mother fuckers!"

"Now you show us ID," the Chinese MP said.

Norman glared up at them. "I done told you man, I ain't got it on me. Call up Commander Fishhead . . ."

"Fishbone," I said.

"Yeah, call up Commander Fishbone at the Naval Recreational and Communications Center, and he'll tell you who I am. And then go fuck your bad self."

When the cops attacked Norman again, I lunged at them and was met with a truncheon. The darkness then became absolute.

Book Two:
Now

Chapter Four

"Terry, you were over there, weren't you?"

I looked over my Compaq Deskpro. "Over where, Marlene?"

My young colleague pointed out the window at LaSalle Street. "In Vietnam."

I followed her finger. The leading elements of the Vietnam veterans parade I had been hearing so much about where just crossing the Chicago River into the heart of Chicago's financial district. Computer-paper confetti snowed on the bright June day. General William Westmoreland and a vet in a wheelchair lead the multitude.

"Well, I wasn't actually in Vietnam."

"But you were in the military then, right?" Marlene O'Grady was right out of college with a B.S. in Public Relations. She was five when Norman Davis and I were keeping Taiwan safe for Democracy.

"Yeah, I was in the military then, Marlene."

"Then why don't you go march in the parade. I'll finish the Maplewood press kit for you. Go on, enjoy yourself."

"You sure?"

"Sure, I'm sure. If Karla asks where you are, I'll just say you went to Dawson Design to approve some layouts."

"I bet they didn't teach you that at Northwestern."

"I'm learning," Marlene said. "Now go on before Karla comes back from lunch."

"All right."

I soon found myself standing along LaSalle Street with major misgivings and private doubts. What right did I have to march with guys who had actually served in Vietnam? Hell, the closest to combat I had ever gotten was that night Norman and I ended up in the rice paddy.

Still, I had volunteered for military service with the full knowledge that I could be sent to Vietnam. Not my fault that the Navy's Bureau of Personnel, or BUPERS, had seen fit to station me in Taiwan.

The crowd was getting bigger by the moment. Women rushed

into the street and kissed bearded vets. Everyone was crying and waving. The vets were marching with their old units, many wearing remnants of their uniforms. Colorful guidons and American flags snapped in the breeze.

No one bothered to march in step, not even General Westmoreland. They just strolled and waved and wondered at the warm reception they were receiving. After more than ten years, they were finally getting their parade.

And still they came. There was a unit from Australia. Another from the Philippines. And, of course, Army of the Republic of Vietnam veterans. Many of them owned popular restaurants in a once-seedy section of Uptown. Vietnam's loss was Chicago's gain.

The Great Lakes Naval Training Center band lead a contingent of Navy veterans. When they struck up "Anchors Aweigh," I automatically saluted.

A number of Navy veterans returned my salute. The sharpest by far was a trim black man in a full set of dress blues. I blinked. It was Norman James.

He blinked back. "Terry?!? Terry Blake?!? That you, man?"

"Yeah, Norm. It's me."

"Well, get your ass in the parade!"

I froze.

Norman James ran over and pulled me into the parade.

"Come on, man. We've got just as much right to march as anybody else."

"I guess."

None of the other vets seemed to mind or notice, so I fell in with my old shipmate.

"Terry Blake," Norman said, inspecting me. "Damn! You lookin' real good for yourself, dude. You some high-priced LaSalle Street lawyer now, or what?"

"Naw. I'm an account supervisor at Mandel & Simpson Public Relations. That's our building on the corner. What about you, you old salt? God, you look terrific."

He did indeed. Narrow waist, broad shoulders, and biceps that bulged under the blue cloth. A dash of gray in his short Afro for distinction.

"I couldn't get in my uniform if I tried. My mother finally gave it to Goodwill," I said.

"Your momma? You livin' with your momma? A little old for that aren't you, man?"

"I lived at home for a while after I got back. I live in Old Town now."

"Got a wife? Kids?"

"No, still looking. What about you?"

"My old lady split with the kids. Went to California with some dude. I don't care about her, but I miss my little girls. Damn I miss 'em."

I put my hand on his shoulder, and before I knew it we were locked in a tearful embrace. Other vets patted us on the backs as they passed.

"I've been meaning to call you for the longest time, Norm. I just . . ."

"Yeah, I know. Got too damn busy. I know."

We hugged one another tight and then continued the parade arm-in-arm.

"So what are you up to these days?" I asked.

"A lot of shit, man. Right now I'm working at Northwestern Memorial as a psychiatric nurse. But I've got some big plans, Brother Terry. Real big plans. And I think it's more than a coincidence that we finally got together today after all these years."

Plans? What kind of plans? Norman was sounding just the way he had that night we ended up in the rice paddy.

We were approaching the reviewing stand at LaSalle and Randolph.

"Hey, come over here," Norm said, pulling me toward the red-white-and-blue bunting. "I want you to meet a friend of mine."

"You know General Westmoreland?!?"

Norman laughed. "No, man."

As we approached the stand, Mayor Hamilton Jefferson leaned forward and said: "My, my Norman, aren't we looking sartorially elegant today."

"Mr. Mayor, this is my old shipmate Terry Blake. He's going to be my PR man."

Chicago's first black mayor took my limp hand and squeezed heartily. "Glad to hear it, Terry. Glad to hear it. We're going to give Norman all the help we can in beating those scurrilous scoundrels in the 51st Ward. But he needs a good PR man. Especially one who was with him over there in Southeast Asia."

Dumfounded, I looked at Norman and then up at the mayor.

The two of them just grinned.

Chapter Five

"Are you for real, Norm?"

Norman looked up from his hot and sour soup. "Yeah, I'm for real. I aim to become alderman of the 51st Ward, but I can't do it without you. Nobody wins without media exposure. You know that. Hell, you guys run the damn country now. Look at Reagan. Man ain't nothin' but a PR pipe dream. Wind him up and he performs.

"But it works. Dude could take a dump on the White House lawn and the country would still love him. You guys are incredible. Now give me one good reason why you couldn't do that for me?"

I wiped at my mouth and smiled at the waitress. A cute little number in a red Mandarin jacket. Norman was noticing her too.

"Well, I could talk to Karla Kemper. She's my boss back at Mandel & Simpson. We don't normally take political accounts, but since you're an old friend of mine, I'm sure she'd consider making an exception."

Norman shook his head. "I don't want your damn agency, man. I want you. Just you. Quit and work for me full time."

"Could I have some more water?"

"Sure," the pretty waitress said. "Were you guys in the parade?"

"Yeah," Norman said. "As a matter of fact we were."

The waitress poured our water and put the pitcher on the table. We were the last of the lunch crowd so she could take her time.

"So you guys were over there, huh?" She had a Chicago accent that would have done old Mayor Daley proud.

Norman winked at me. If I was going to be his mouthpiece, it was time to practice.

"Yeah, we were over there. Hey, you're not from Taiwan by any chance. We spent some time there," I said.

"I was born in Hong Kong, but my family moved here when I was three. I'm as American as you guys."

Norman grinned. "What's your name?"

"Vikki. Vikki Chang. And yours?"

"Norman James. And this is my old shipmate Terry Blake. He's going to be my PR man."

"Your PR man? What, are you famous or something?" Her eyes were wide with excitement.

"He's running for alderman of the 51st Ward," I said. Vikki's enthusiasm was getting to me.

"That's right here! God, would you give me a job if you win? I'm tired of working in this dump." Vikki looked contempuously at the woman behind the counter. "My mother never gives me a day off. All I ever do is work in this crumby restaurant."

"Well, Vikki, I think I might have some work for you even before I'm elected. How are you at public speaking?"

"Public speaking. You mean like getting up in front of groups and . . ."

". . .and telling them how Norman Davis is going to bring good government back to the 51st Ward. Yeah, that's what I mean. You don't speak Chinese by any chance?"

"Some Cantonese. But that's what most of the people around here speak. Why?"

"Because I might just be looking for a good precinct captain here. That's why."

Vikki scowled at her mother. Then she smiled at Norman and me. "Well, you've got her," she said.

*   *   *

"Uh, Karla, can I have a word with you for a second?"

Karla Kemper swiveled her chair and hit me with her hard green eyes. "Only if you've got the Maplewood press kit to show me."

"Actually, I wanted to introduce you to an old Navy buddy of mine -- Norman James."

Karla glowered. "I told you this morning I wanted that Maplewood press kit on my desk by one o'clock. Now it's practically three, and all you have is some old friend of yours. Jesus, Terry, this is a business not a goddamn social club. You were out drinking all afternoon, weren't you? I didn't believe that bullshit Marlene fed me for a second."

"Karla, Norman's running for alderman in the 51st Ward. He

knows Mayor Jefferson personally. In fact, I just saw the mayor seek him out during the parade."

"Parade? What parade?" Karla Kemper's world began and ended with Mandel & Simpson.

"The Vietnam veterans' parade. You must have heard it."

"Oh, that's what that was. God, it took me ten minutes to get a goddamn cab."

"Anyway, Norman needs PR for his campaign. He wants me to be his PR man, but I thought I'd better clear it with you before I really. . ."

"You say he's connected to Mayor Jefferson?" Karla ran a hand through her red mane.

"That's right."

"Well, set up a meeting with him and Jim Michaelson."

"Karla, he's right here. I thought maybe you'd like to meet him."

Karla exploded. "You don't bring people in off the street to meet me, Terry. What the hell do you think this is? You've been here long enough to know how we go after new accounts. We make presentations; we run credit checks; we get references -- we DO NOT bring people in off the street. Do you understand?"

I was about to reply in kind when Norman pushed past me.

"The bitch does have a point, Terry," he said, sneering at Karla's bad taste in expensive art. "Come on, let's go out and have a drink. I told you this would be a waste of time. And I told you: I want you to be my PR man, not some overpriced agency with bogus art."

"Wait a minute," Karla said, getting up. Dollar signs danced in her eyes. "You said you're a friend of the mayor's?"

"That's right," Norman said, eyeing my buxom boss.

"Well, why don't we go in the conference room and talk?"

"How much is it going to cost me to do business with you people?"

Karla stopped at the edge of her desk. "Well, we can talk particulars later, but we normally bill at $3,000 per month minimum, plus expenses. And we insist on a one-year contract, minimum."

"And what do I get for my $36 grand plus expenses?"

"The best public relations consulting money can buy."

"Can you get me on the six o'clock news?"

Karla didn't seem so collected now. "Public relations isn't an exact science, Mr. James. Just like medicine or denistry, we can't guarantee results, but we certainly can give you the very best . . ."

"Shit! Thirty-six grand and you can't get me on the six o'clock news. See you later, Terry." Norman did an about-face and quick-marched toward the door.

I stood at the turning point.

Karla decided it for me by screeching: "Goddamn it, Terry, don't just stand there! The man's connected to Mayor Jefferson. We need an in with the administration. Go after him, you idiot!"

I caught Norman at the elevator.

"You know what I could buy with $36,000?" Norman said. He punched the "Down" button again.

"Norm, I said I'd be your PR man, and I meant it."

The elevator arrived empty, and Norman stepped in without hesitation. He punched "Lobby" and waited for the doors to close.

I batted them open and stepped in with him.

"This means you quit that fancy-ass dump?"

"That's what it means," I said.

Norman smiled. "Well, you won't regret it. After all, I'm the one who bought you your first pussy. Right?"

"Right."

"What do you say we go celebrate? Then we can start planning. Damn, we're gonna turn this town upside down!"

"Umm, Norm, what about, uh, you know, money? I'm not exactly rich or anything, but I was making $32 grand a year up there, and I . . ."

Norman squeezed my shoulder. "And you've got a yuppie lifestyle to maintain. I know, man, I know. Don't worry about a thing, Terry. You won't even have to quit your membership at the East Bank Club."

"Actually, I belong to Lake Shore."

"Lake Shore!?! Well, if you're going to be my PR man, you'd better switch to East Bank. That's where all those heavy media dudes hang out."

"Right. Hey, I've been meanin' to ask you -- what, uh, happened that night in the rice paddy? You know, after that

Chinese MP knocked me out."

"You mean, how you ended up safe and sound back in your rack while they threw my black ass in jail?"

"Yeah."

"Real simple. Them gooks hate niggers. Just like here."

Chapter Six

"Why can't we just talk to Mr. Petrilli on the phone," I said.

"Because Alderman Petrilli don't respect nobody unless he's had a sit-down with him. You un'erstand?" The party to whom I was speaking was Anthony Scambino, committeeman of the 51st Ward.

I understood that I was already afraid of the Italian-American gentleman the newspapers had dubbed "Funny Face." I had hoped to get his blessings for Norman's candidacy over the phone and leave it at that.

"Uh, well, Mr. James really has a busy schedule, you see, and well. . ."

"You want our endorsement; you come out and have a sit-down with the alderman and me. We don't do business with people we don't know. Is that so hard to un'erstand?"

I knew he was trying to be reasonable and pleasant, but something in his voice suggested bodies in car trunks.

"No," I said, trying to sound reasonable and pleasant. "I guess it isn't. When, ah, would you like to meet?"

"This afternoon. Three sharp. You know where we are?"

"On Blue Island near Western?"

"You got it. Three sharp."

"Three sharp."

Perspiration had glued my hand to the phone.

* * *

"You know why they call him 'Funny Face'?" Norman said as he turned his pewter Toyota Camry southwest on Blue Island Avenue.

"Because he's got a funny-looking face?"

Norman laughed. "No, because when Scambino first started out in the mob, he was a collector. Most collectors would go for a dude's kneecaps if he was late paying off a loan. Not Scambino. He'd put their heads in a vise and then he'd say: 'Look at the funny face the guy's makin'.' That's why they call him Funny Face."

"Where'd you hear that?"

Norman gave me a knowing look. "Man, I was born and raised in this city. Remember?"

"So was I."

"Yeah, but you spent too much time in the suburbs. Hey, is that the place?"

"That's it."

Norman parked in front of Dominick Petrilli's aged funeral home. He turned to me and said: "I'm countin' on you, Terry. I really am, dude. I need this guy's endorsement, even if he doesn't have the power he once did."

"I'll do my best," I said, wondering how my face would look in a vise.

An ancient Italian woman in black greeted us at the door and lead us through a darkened parlor to Petrilli's paneled office adjacent to the unoccupied embalming room.

The oldest member of the Chicago City Council wore a black suit, tinted bifocals on tortoise frames and a bemused smile. He sat with his gnarled hands folded on a polished walnut desk. Funny Face Scambino stood to the alderman's right and wore a beige linen sports jacket and white-on-white shirt. The latter was opened at the collar to display a large gold snaggle tooth. The committeeman had a Palm Springs tan, a modest gut and a mop of curly coiffeured black hair that was probably graying under the Grecian Formula.

After the introductions, Alderman Petrilli said: "So you want to take my place in the City Council?"

"That's right, Alderman Petrilli. I not only want to take your place; I'm going to take your place."

The ancient alderman allowed himself a soft chuckle. "That's good, Mr. James. That's very good. You remind me of the young Dominick Petrilli when he first came to America. Not afraid of nobody." Then his face darkened, and he pounded his fist on the table. "Who the hell do you think you are comin' in here and tellin' me you're gonna take my place?

"I been alderman of dis ward for more than 30 years. I was gettin' out de vote and servin' de people of dis ward when you was shittin' in yer goddamned diapers. An' yose got de nerve to come in here and tell me you're gonna take my place when I retire. Who the hell are you to tell me a goddamned thing?"

I adjusted my tie and wondered where they kept the vise.

Norman just kept his cool.

"For one thing," he said after a long pause, "I am assured of the mayor's full endorsement and support."

I could almost hear Scambino and Petrilli thinking: that fat nigger faggot.

Alderman Petrilli shifted his gaze to me. "And you my friend, what's in this for you?"

I shrugged. "Norman and I were in the Navy together overseas. We got to be good buddies over there, and so when we ran into each other at the Vietnam veterans' parade the other day, he didn't have to twist my arm too hard to get me to be his PR man."

"You say Navy?" Alderman Petrilli said, his face brightening.

"That's right," I said. "You were in the Navy during World War II, weren't you, Alderman Petrilli?"

"Damn right I was. Spent two goddamned years floatin' around the South Pacific in a tin can. It weren't no pleasure cruise, I can tell you that."

"I can imagine," I said, leaning back to listen. I tapped Norman on the arm, and he did likewise. "Your ship ever get attacked by kamikazes?"

Petrilli's rheumy eyes rolled. "Them crazy little nips always went after the carriers, but we was awful damn close to them flattops. We couldn't a been more than a half mile away when the 'Intrepid' got it off the Philippines in '44. I was a gunner's mate, so I was up where I could see all the action. Man oh man! Made the 4th of July look like kid stuff. Kah boom!!! Things blowin' every which way. You'd a thought the goddamned sky was fallin' in the way it sounded.

"And them sorry sons-a-bitches what was on them flattops. God Almighty! We'd be pickin' 'em outta the drink half the night. Unless the sharks got to 'em first. Some of 'em was so burnt up they looked like bacon. Goddamned Japs! And now everybody's drivin' a goddamned Jap car and watchin' goddamned Jap TVs."

"Yeah," Norm said with a straight face, "it's a damn shame,

isn't it?"

Alderman Petrilli nodded. "Yeah, it sure as hell is. So you two jamokes was in the Navy, huh?"

"That's right," Norman said.

"You wasn't officers, was you?"

"No way," Norman said. "We were deck abes just like you, Alderman."

Alderman Petrilli beamed. "I like you boys. I like yose a lot. Now tell me, what are you gonna do for the 51st Ward if you're elected?"

"We're working out a detailed platform right now," I said. "I'd be happy to send you a copy when I finish it."

"All I wanna know is -- are you gonna take good care of my people?" Petrilli said.

"Alderman," Norman said, "if I'm elected, the people of the 51st Ward will continue to get all the services they've come to expect under your fine leadership."

Petrilli smiled and waved his hand. "Tony, get our friends here some coffee, okay?"

It was clear from his set expression that Funny Face did not share his patron's high opinion of us. "Yes sir, Alderman," he said.

"Ah," Norman said when he returned, "just the way I like my women -- hot, strong and black."

Alderman Petrilli elbowed Funny Face. "Hey, Tony, that's what you always say."

We all laughed, but I still couldn't help thinking about heads in vises and bodies in car trunks. As we sipped our coffee, the ancient alderman studied me.

Then he said, "What parish you from?"

I wondered if I should tell him that I was really an apostate Presbyterian who only went to church on Christmas and Easter to please his mother. This being politics, I said: "Saint Barnabas originally. But now I live in Saint Clement's."

"You one of dem North Side faggots?" Funny Face said.

"No. I like women as well as the next guy."

"He ain't no faggot," Norman said. "He had them little gook broads all shook up when we was over there. If ever there was a ladies' man, it's Terry Blake here."

"Dat's good," Alderman Petrilli said. "'Cause we ain't got no sissies in de 51st Ward. Got just about evert'ing else, but we ain't got no sissies. One time, dis ward was mostly Eye-talian and Greek. And some Bohunks and Polacks. Now me and Tony here is about de only paisans left. Yose got a big Chinese population here -- mostly in Chinatown, but dem people is bustin' out all over. And more of 'em comin' over all the time.

"Not that I mind 'em, you un'erstand. They're hard workin' little sons-a-bitches, but it's hard to get 'em organized. Stick to themselves is what they do, God bless 'em. Run their own affairs. Police their own neighborhoods. That's all well an' good, but you can't count on 'em come election day. Nobody can."

"We can," Norman said. "In fact, we've already got somebody working on that for us."

I stared at Norman. If he meant that waitress at the Chinese restaurant -- the Dragon Palace or something like that -- we'd better get over there right quick and tell her.

"Chinese?" Petrilli said.

"And damned pretty," Norman said, leering.

"It true their pussies are sideways?" Funny Face said.

"You'd better ask Terry here about that. He was the big cocksman over there."

I shrugged. "What can I say?"

Everyone chuckled, then Alderman Petrilli rose and shook our hands. "Gentlemen, I thank yose for comin' out an' havin' dis little sit-down with me and Tony this afternoon. I gotta say that I'm very impressed with the way you present yourselves, and I like to see our veterans represented in the City Council.

"But as you know, yose ain't the only declared candidate. After we've interviewed 'em all, we'll get back to you one way or another. Oh, yeah, dere's one more t'ing."

"And what might that be?" Norman said.

"Tony here remains as committeeman, and I, uh, well, I act as your advisor. Help you serve the ward better. Provide continuity. Dem is the conditions for our endorsement. And some other minor t'ings that we'll discuss at the appropriate time."

"What minor things?" Norman said, sitting down again.

Petrilli shrugged. "Minor t'ings. Nothin' to worry about." Petrilli nodded at Funny Face who pulled his wad from his pocket. "Give 'em some lunch money, Tony. They're nice boys. I think we might be able to work somet'in' out with 'em."

My mouth watered as Funny Face offered me a crisp $50, but Norman rudely pushed the money aside.

"We don't need your money, and we don't need your endorsement. When I'm elected next spring, I'll decide who's committeeman. And I don't need advisors. The Machine is broke, old man. Broke. Come on, Terry, we got us a pile of work to do."

A furious Funny Face tried to block our exit, but Alderman Petrilli serenely said: "Let 'em go, Tony. They'll learn. Believe me, they'll learn."

* * *

When we were a safe distance from the Petrilli Funeral Home, I said: "Shit, Norm, you don't mess with guys like that. Are you crazy or what?"

Norman threw his head back and howled. Tears rolled down his cheeks. "You tellin' me you're afraid of those old spaghetti benders?"

"What about you? You were the one who was telling me how Funny Face got his nickname. They seem like scary guys to me, Norm. I don't think it's such a good idea to . . ."

"Terry, it's a new day in this city. Old mob guys like that don't run things anymore, and they know it. Despite all their Al Capone bullshit. You know what that old fart was telling me?"

"No. What?"

"He wants me to be the nigger in the window while he runs the store. That's what he's telling me. Well, Dickhead Daley's been dead for almost ten years. Plantation politics are long gone in this city: Mayor Jefferson's seein' to that. And there's nothing those guys can do about it. Fuck their endorsement!"

"Yeah, I suppose you're right."

"I know I'm right. And look at this ward. Damn sidewalks are cavin' in everywhere you look. Half the curbs are gone, and there's garbage everywhere. If that's what the Machine can do for you, you can have it."

We drove in silence for a while observing the ward's

dilapidated conditions.

Then I said: "But those guys were gonna offer us money, and the mayor's people haven't exactly been too loose with their purse strings. And, well, I've got the small matter of rent and groceries and car payments to deal with and . . ."

Norman took a hard left on Racine and accelerated through a predominantly Mexican neighborhood with a Bohemian name.

"You're right, we got to do something about your money situation. I've been thinkin' about it long and hard, and I think I have just the solution. How much you say you need to live on?"

"Well, I suppose I could get by on 15 hundred, but two grand or better would be real nice."

"How about three grand a month?"

"Three grand?!? God . . ."

".I figured you'd like that. Then we'll go get the check right now."

Norman drove downtown to Northwestern Memorial Hospital and took me to the psych unit where he worked evenings as a nurse.

"I don't get it," I said. "One of these patients rich or something?"

"They're all rich, or they wouldn't be in this nuthouse," Norman said. He went to the duty supervisor and asked: "Is Jimmy Morgenstern around?"

"Yeah, he was in the rec room last time I saw him. As long as you're here early for a change, James, you can start passing meds."

"In a minute." Norman lead me into a brightly painted rec room with ping pong tables and a stunning view of Lake Michigan.

"Anybody seen Jimmy?" he said.

"In the bathroom," a fat neurotic said.

"Probably playin' with himself," another patient said, giggling.

We found Jimmy Morgenstern in the bathroom, but he wasn't playing with himself. He was looking for his spine.

Chapter Seven

"Jimmy my man. You got to get a hold of yourself," Norman said, gently leading the emaciated young man out of the bathroom.

"They took my spine; they took my spine; they took my spine; they took my spine . . ." Jimmy said, swatting at his back. His thin black hair was a greasy mess and his fly was open. He wore a wild, frightened expression under his cracked glasses.

"We'll find it, Jimmy. We'll find it. Now let's go back to your room, okay?"

Jimmy looked at me. "Do you have my spine? Did you take my spine?"

I looked helplessly at Norman. "What's his problem?" I whispered.

"His old man's a heavyweight shrink. Runs the Morgenstern Psychiatric Clinic in Rogers Park. When Jimmy here was growing up, old Doc Morgenstern figured he was some kind of nut for playin' with his dick. So he went in there and disconnected a few wires. Been fuckin' with the boy's brain ever since," Norman said.

"You're kidding!"

"I wish I was."

Jimmy suddenly grabbed my arm. "What did you do with my spine?" he said, spraying me with spittle.

"Let go of the man, Jimmy," Norman said, firmly and gently.

Jimmy instantly obeyed.

"But how could he get away with it? I mean wouldn't the AMA or the city or somebody stop him? The man turned his own son into a vegetable!"

"Yeah, and he's in the society pages every day. Dude is probably the number one or two shrink in the Chicago area. Gets all the big research grants -- whatever he wants."

"But . . ."

"But nothin'. You wouldn't believe the bullshit doctors get away with. Ain't no profession like it. They cover each other's asses like you can't believe."

"Even when they turn their own sons into vegetables?"

"Even when they turn their own sons into vegetables."

We got the unfortunate Jimmy Morgenstern back into his room and shut the door.

"Now, Jimmy, I want you to call your daddy and tell him he's got to come right over here," Norman said.

"No, he'll hurt me."

"He's not going to lay a hand on you. Now just give Daddy a call, and tell him he's got to come by right away to discuss something important. You got that?"

Jimmy watched Norman's lips and nodded.

"Oh, and tell him to bring his checkbook."

Jimmy did exactly as he was told and reported that his father would be over in half an hour.

"Good," Norman said. "Well, I've got some work to do. Terry, why don't you go grab yourself some food and watch the tube. I think the Cubs are playing St. Louis tonight, aren't they?"

"I thought you were a Sox fan."

"I am, but I keep an eye on the Cubs every now and then."

"You only do that because you recognize superior talent."

"Superior talent, my ass. They win their candy ass division one year, and everybody's actin' like they're world champions."

"Sox fans should talk."

"Yeah, yeah. Go on. I'll be with you in a minute."

I settled in front of the 27-inch floor model and tuned in the boys in blue. They were losing 2-1 in the top of the seventh. Three up three down. Figures. The Cardinals got a run off two hits and a base on balls in their half of the inning.

But the Cubs came alive in the top of the eighth. Dernier singled to left and stole second before Sandberg took his second pitch. Then Sandberg hit a long fly ball to left center that looked like it was going to be caught. But Vince Coleman somehow misjudged it, and Dernier scored and Sandberg scampered safely to second.

Leon Durham got his big black bat off his shoulder and hit a solid stand-up double, scoring Sandberg.

"Way to go, Leon!" I shouted. "Way to go!"

Some seven or eight patients echoed: "Way to go, Leon! Way to go, Leon!"

When I sat down, they sat down. When Keith Moreland singled to left driving in the tying runs, they rose and cheered when I rose and cheered.

I looked at them and smiled. "Exciting game, huh?"

They all stared blankly at me, waiting for my next attack.

It came when Jody "the Georgia cracker" Davis hit into a double play. I was about to throw my shoe at the screen, when Norman restrained me.

"You're not setting a good example, Terry." He turned off the television. "Come on, old Doc Morgenstern is here. Time to collect your paycheck."

Nathan R. Morgenstern, M.D. was a little man with a big cigar in his puss and bulging green eyes. There were gravy stains on his silk tie and his suit needed pressing. Despite the warm June weather, his wife Barbara wore a mink stole. She also wore impenetrable black sunglasses and a blonde wig held on with beautician's tape. The two of the them had to be each pushing 70.

Jimmy tried to climb the walls when he saw them.

"He's not going to hurt you, Jimmy," Norman said.

Jimmy pointed wildly at his father. "He took my spine! He took my spine!"

Dr. Morgenstern adjusted his bifocals and considered his son. "Delusional. Definitely delusional. Well, James, what is so urgent that you called your mother and me over here tonight? You know we have to be at the opening of that new art gallery on Michigan Avenue by 8." Dr. Morgenstern looked at his two-bit Timex. "It's already 7:30. Now what do you want?"

Barbara Morgenstern adjusted her stole and moved her lips without talking.

Jimmy backed away from his father and pointed at Norman. "He-he-he wanted to talk to you."

Dr. Morgenstern noticed Norman and me for the first time. "You? A nurse? You want to talk to me?"

Barbara Morgenstern was fiddling with her wig, causing clumps of matted gray hair to appear around the fringe.

"Actually, he wants to talk to you," Norman said, gesturing at me. "This is Terry Blake. He's my campaign manager."

Now I was campaign manager. News to me.

"What the hell are you talking about?" Dr. Morgenstern's cigar had gone out. He felt in his pockets for fire. "Goddamn it, Barbara, what the hell did you do with my lighter?"

"I didn't touch your stupid lighter," Barbara said, still fiddling with her wig.

"Here, doc, let me," Norman said, holding his flaming Zippo under the dead cigar.

Dr. Morgenstern puffed gratefully. "Thanks. Now what the Sam Hill are you talking about? Campaign? What campaign?"

Norman smiled. "I'm running for alderman in the 51st Ward. Terry here is my campaign manager. But it's going to be an uphill battle, isn't it, Terry?"

"Yeah. Yeah, that's right," I said.

Norman nudged me. If I wanted money, it was up to me to get it.

"You called me all the way over here to tell me about your stupid campaign? And what difference would it make to me anyway? We live in Glencoe for God's sake," Dr. Morgenstern said.

I swallowed. "It's not your vote we need."

Dr. Morgenstern fondled his cigar. "Wait a minute. If you're suggesting what I think you're suggesting, I . . ."

"Terry here used to be reporter for the CHICAGO TRIBUNE, and he still has lots of friends in the newsroom who would just love a nice juicy story about a North Shore shrink who rewired his own kid. Wouldn't they, Terry?"

Actually, I had worked for the TRIBUNE'S suburban supplement and had little clout in the newsroom. But that didn't stop me from saying: "Yeah, Norm, they'd be real interested."

Dr. Morgenstern shifted his eyes between us. "You think I'm gonna let a couple of two-bit punks like you scare me?"

Barbara moved her lips again without talking.

"Your cigar went out again, Doc," Norman said.

"Gimme that lighter."

"Your hands are shaking, Doc," Norman said.

"I've got important friends in this town. The TRIBUNE wouldn't dare run a story like that. They wouldn't dare!"

"Don't shout, Doc. You'll upset the patients. You, of all people, should know that."

Dr. Morgenstern backed into the corner. "I don't believe you. I don't believe you could do it."

"You still have your press card, Terry?"

"Yeah, I think so." I found it in my wallet and showed it to the good doctor.

"The kid was sick. He was exhibiting abnormal tendencies. I'm the most respected . . ."

"Call the newsroom, Terry."

I picked up Jimmy's phone and started to dial.

"Hold on. Hold on a minute." Dr. Morgenstern wiped his brow with a soiled handkerchief. "What, ah, what kind of money ah ..."

"Three grand a month through next April," Norman said.

"Three grand? Until April? Why that's . . ."

"Thirty-three grand even," Norman said, offering his lighter. "But you don't have to pay it all at once. In fact, you can just make low monthly payments of three grand. Starting right now."

Dr. Morgenstern accepted Norman's light and puffed distractedly. "Jesus H. Christ! Three grand. I'm not a rich man, fellas. I got . . ."

"You got your checkbook?" Norman said.

"Well, yeah, but . . ."

"Then write the goddamn check or Terry calls the TRIBUNE."

Nathan R. Morgenstern, M.D. wrote the goddamn check.

Chapter Eight

A week passed; Dr. Morgenstern's check cleared, and Funny Face Scambino didn't put our heads in vises.

Even though the February primary was still eight months away, four others had already announced their candidacy for alderman of the 51st Ward.

A follower of Lyndon LaRouch, Shirley Boyle wanted mandatory testing for the AIDS virus and quarantine for anyone who had it. Although she was a black woman, her views were right of Atilla the Hun. She didn't have a chance.

Nor did Allen Straub, a self-made mope whose sole issue seemed to be fountain pens. If elected, Straub said he would get Mont Blanc, Waterman, Parker, and Pelikan to create a fountain pen free-trade zone in the 51st Ward. Straub also wanted to start a pen repair school in the ward and require the Chicago Board of Education to put inkwells back in student desks. Straub was unfortunately fat and terminally single.

But the third contendor had us worried. Oscar Fuentes was an articulate third-generation Mexican-American attorney who had the full backing of 13th Ward alderman Ivan Kovar and his opposition faction. That of course meant Alderman Petrilli and Funny Face Scambino

Fuentes was handsome, well-spoken, bilingual, a decorated Vietnam combat veteran, married to a beautiful but dutiful wife and the father of three adorable children.

"This Fuentes guy is gonna kill us," I said. It was a bright Sunday morning in July, and we were settled in temporary campaign headquarters -- Norman's lakefront apartment.

Norman was engrossed in the Sunday comics. "What?"

"I said this Fuentes guy is gonna clobber us if we don't get our asses in gear."

Norman finished reading Dick Tracy and dropped the funnies on the floor. He was still in his sweats from his morning lakefront jog.

"You hungry?" he said stretching.

"Yeah. But .. "

"But let me take a shower, and we'll go over to Chinatown and mix a little business and pleasure."

* * *

"Vikki, right?" Norman said, smiling.

Our waitress Vikki Chang beamed. She was wearing her red mandarin jacket and her hair in a tight pony tail. "That's right. Hey, how's your campaign coming along? I haven't heard much about you in the media."

Norman gave me a look. "I've got a lazy PR man. What can I say?"

"Hey, look, I can't really talk now. My mom'll kill me if I don't get to these other tables."

"What time you get off?" Norman said.

Vikki glanced at her mother behind the cash register. "I'm supposed to work ' til ten, but I'll talk my mom into letting me off early."

"Then why don't we go out and have a drink? We need to talk to you about joining my staff. We've got to have somebody work Chinatown. And I figure you're perfect."

"Maybe. But then that's what you said last time you were here. I thought you were going to call me. What happened -- lose the number?" Vikki Chang was adorable when she pouted.

"We got busy. What can I say? Anyway, here we are now. Ain't that right, Terry?"

"Yeah, here we are." I gazed fondly at our gorgeous waitress and realized Norman was doing likewise.

Vikki Chang smiled at each of us in turn, starting with Norman. "I'm glad. Real glad."

After we finished eating a whole, steamed pike and other assorted goodies, Vikki talked her mother into letting her go early. We went to a brass and fern bar near her South Loop apartment to talk.

"Your momma doesn't like us, does she?" Norman said, sipping his rob roy.

"My mother wants me to marry a nice, rich doctor from Hong Kong," Vikki said. "She's so square I can't believe it. but she doesn't run my life anymore. Thank God. So tell me what you want me to do for your campaign. God, I'm so excited. I thought you guys were just bullshitting me that day."

"No, we're for real," I said, trying not to gawk at Vikki. She was wearing a tailored white blouse and bedroom eye make-up.

"We had to get our act together, and now we're ready. And we really need your help, because we've got a challenger who could really give us trouble."

"That Oscar Fuentes guy?"

"Yeah. He's gonna get most of the Hispanic vote unless we get lucky, and I'll get all of the black vote. So the Chinese vote is crucial. That's where you come in."

"How much are you going to pay me?"

"How about $15 hundred a month?"

"How about $16 hundred a month?" Vikki said.

Norman grinned. "You got yourself a deal."

I scratched my ear. "Uh, Norm, where uh . . . "

"Terry here'll pay you, Vikki. He handles all the money. Now how about another one of those silly drinks you're having."

Vikki said "Sure," and I got a stomach ache realizing that I would have to part with more than half of my monthly $3,000 windfall.

But Vikki Chang soon made me forget all my financial worries by inviting us up to her apartment to "smoke some really excellent pot."

"You guys like U2?" she said, bringing some munchies from the kitchen.

"Yeah, I dig 'em," Norman said.

News to me.

He took another toke and handed me the joint.

I was so blasted I could see my blood circulating. I took another hit anyway. "Damn! This stuff is powerful! Where'd you get it?"

"From my cousin in Hawaii. Can you believe it? She just sends me joints in her letters. God!"

I handed Vikki the joint, and she sat cross-legged on the floor between us. Norman was on the love seat, and I was sinking into the black bean-bag chair.

"So how did you guys meet again?"

Norman laughed. " In a Chinese whorehouse."

"I though you were in Vietnam."

"Uh," I said, "actually . . . "

"We were in Taiwan TOO, " Norman said. "If it wasn't for me, Terry here'd probably still be a cherry. Ain't that right, Terry?"

I looked at Norman. He was trying to block me out of the play, and I didn't like it. But I was too stoned to do much about it. The man had an unfair advantage -- he had a limitless capacity for booze and drugs.

"How old were you?" Vikki asked.

"Twenty."

"Really? I was 16 when I lost my virginity," Vikki said. "What about you, Norman?"

Norman just laughed.

Vikki went to her stereo and turned up the volume. "God, aren't these guys great?" She swayed sensuously with the adenoidal music.

Norman was up and dancing with her before the thought occurred to me. Then they were in one another's arms and moving toward her bedroom.

I clouded my burning jealousy with a fresh joint. I was awfully tempted to walk out and find another line of work, but Vikki winked at me before she closed the door. I'm sure she did.

Chapter Nine

Public Relations is not an exact science. You write the ultimate press release, and it never gets above the bottom of the slush pile. Then you write some schlock about your candidate declaring the 51st Ward a nuclear-free zone, and the switchboard lights up.

Actually, I got a call Saturday evening from the producer of the Dave Byrd Show at WCGO-AM. They had booked a man who had made three trips to Mars for their show at 11:30 p.m., but he had apparently been called away from the planet at the last minute.

"So could your people make it?" the producer said.

"Sure. Sure they could make it." Vikki and Norman were going to go dancing at the Limelight, and I was going to tag along, but this sounded more entertaining.

"Good. Have them here by 11 at the latest. You know where we are?"

"Yeah. No problem."

"One more thing: this nuclear-free crap is old hat. Your guy have anything else? Any dirt on Jefferson or Kovar?"

"No, but if Norman David is elected he's going to see that the Chinese-American community finally has a voice in City Hall.

"And he's got a plan for an enterprise zone next to Chinatown. It's only logical because Chinatown's overcrowded, and there are all those abandoned railroad yards right next door."

"How come you didn't say anything about that in your press release?"

Because I just thought of it. "Because I was saving it for next week."

"You mean we get the exclusive?"

"Yeah. You get the exclusive."

"Great?! See you at 11."

"Norman wasn't too nuts about my idea, but Vikki thought it had merit.

"Run it by me again," Norman said, as he steered us north on Michigan Avenue.

"You've got all these people crammed into a couple of square blocks of Chinatown. People are leaving Hong Kong every day because they're scared shitless about what Bejing is going to do when they take over. But most of them are going to Canada or San Francisco because there's more room there."

"And because they like the weather better. Hong Kong has a mild climate compared Chicago. That's why most people don't come here," Vikki said.

"Maybe I should come out in favor of changing the climate," Norman said. "Hey, how many people listen to this fool ass show anyway?"

"I forgot to ask. But what difference does it make? It's radio, Norm. This could be our big break. And this Chinatown thing could be the issue that really gets noticed. Other reporters listen to these shows. You guys come off good, and we should be on easy street the rest of the way in."

Vikki rubbed Norman's neck. "Maybe he's right."

Norman swatted her hand away. "We'll see."

Dave Byrd certainly saw what he liked. "Welcome to the Dave Byrd Show," he said, rising to take Vikki's hand. He was a balding little butterball with bifocals and a pretentious pipe.

Nobody looked better than Vikki Chang on a Saturday night. She accepted David Byrd's hand, flashed a demure smile and said: "I'm Vikki Chang. This is Norman James, the next alderman of the 51st Ward. And our campaign manager -- Terry Blake."

Dave Byrd nodded at Norman and me. "I didn't expect the world of politics to produce such beauty." He clung to Vikki's hand.

"Yeah, well it's time for a change, isn't it?" Norman said, glaring at Vikki.

Ignoring Norman, she said, "I'm going to be Ward Committeeperson when Norman's elected. And there's not going to be any more patronage when we're in office."

This was news to me, and from Norman's reaction it was news to him.

"Well it would appear that the voters of the 51st Ward will be getting both beauty and brains," Dave Byrd said, still clinging to Vikki's hand.

To keep Norman from killing the little creep, I wondered if we could get some coffee before we went on the air.

"Actually we just have room for two of you in the studio," Dave Byrd said. "So, Jerry, if you don't mind, you can sit with Arnie over there in the producer's booth." He smiled at Vikki and reluctantly released her hand.

"No problem," I said.

Norman and Vikki masterfully described my eleventh-hour scheme for a Chinatown enterprise zone, and anytime Dave Byrd tried to play probing reporter, Vikki fluttered him with her bedroom eyes.

"So what you're saying is you do have Mayor Jefferson's full support."

"What we're saying, Dave, is that we have the support of the people of Chicago," Vikki said, flashing her eyes at the old jock.

"Well," Dave Byrd said, "it certainly sounds as though you two are on your way, and I must say I was pleasantly surprised when you walked into the studio. When you've been interviewing Chicago politicians as long as I have, you come to expect a certain, shall we say, appearance. Let me assure you dear listeners that Miss Chang and Mr. James do not fit that picture. Well, you've heard them outline their plan for an enterprise zone next to Chinatown and call for better services in the 51st Ward. Now, as we do every night, let's open the phone lines and take your calls."

I watched the producer key in the first call on a display that could be read in both rooms. Shirley Boyle wanted to know why Norman wasn't demanding the immediate quarantining of all AIDS patients.

I nudged Arnie the producer. He disconnected Shirley Boyle.

I approved the next caller -- Allen Straub the pen nut.

"Where do you guys get off saying you're first with this enterprise zone business?" Straub fumed into the phone.

Norman said: "Mr. Straub we're talking about a mixed-use development that will provide not only jobs BUT housing for thousands of enterprising people. Correct me if I'm wrong, but your proposal only seems to deal with fountain pens. I'm sure I don't have to remind our listeners that we've been in the computer age for a few years now."

Arnie disconnected Allen Straub in mid-squawk and connected Mr. Wayne Li, president of the Chinese-American Business Association.

"My wife woke me up when she heard what you were talking about. Let me be the first to say your idea is wonderful. The Chinese-American Business Association has been trying to get City Hall interested in such a plan for years. But we've never had a voice before. Now apparently we do. We are most eager to meet with you Mr. James," Mr. Li said.

"Likewise, Mr. Li," Norman said, smiling at me.

Dave Byrd looked at the wall clock and said, "We've got time for one more call."

One anonymous caller wanted to know about Norman's war record. It had to be Oscar Fuentes or one of his operatives. Another unidentified caller wanted to know why Mr. James wasn't crediting Alderman Petrilli for his "fine efforts in helping the fine people of Chinatown." Had to be Funny Face Scambino.

I was about to elbow the producer when Norman said: "I don't mean to be rude, Dave, but we've got a full day of campaigning tomorrow. So, if you don't mind, we'd probably better be going."

"I'll let you go, but only on one condition."

"What's that?" Norman said.

"That you and your lovely assistant here promise to come back real soon."

Vikki smiled. "You've got it, Dave."

Chapter Ten

Mom didn't get wind of what I was up to until Norman and Vikki appeared on a public service television program on the following Sunday morning. A golf widow most of her adult life, Mom often sought televised companionship after returning from the 7 o'clock service at church.

There was also the telephone.

". . . and I was so proud when they mentioned your name, Dear," Mom said. As always, she was holding the transmitter too close to her mouth.

"Yeah, I guess I'm really in the big time now, huh?" The Cubs were down 5-1 with one out in the top of the ninth, and Lee Smith was throwing nothing but balls and wild pitches.

"Evelyn Hunt -- you remember her daughter Janet -- said she heard your friends on the radio last week. but she said the announcer identified you as Jerry Blake. Why didn't you correct him?"

"Because I wasn't on the air." Lee Smith walked another Dodger, loading the bases.

"That doesn't seem fair. If you're the campaign manager, shouldn't you be on the air too?"

"That's not the way it works in politics, Mom. The campaign manager is behind the scenes. We do all the work, but we don't get any of the glory."

"That young woman you've got is quite attractive for an Oriental. Don't you think so?"

"You mean Vikki? Yeah, she's something else."

"I always thought you might end up with an Oriental girl. In high school you dated every Jewish and Catholic girl you could find. I don't think you ever brought home a nice Protestant girl. They say those Oriental girls make good wives and mothers. Edith Glover's son Eddie married a Korean girl. They live in Alsip. He's with the state police or something. You remember Eddie, don't you?"

Steve Sax hit into a double-play to retire the side. The fans were on their feet. God, why hadn't I gone to the game?

"Uh, no. I mean yeah. Sort of. He was two years ahead of me."

"Am I catching you at a bad moment. You seem distracted."

"No, I'm just watching the Cubs game."

"Your little Oriental friend isn't there, is she, Dear?"

"No, it's just me and the Cubs, Mom."

"Oh. Well, the reason I called was to invite you and your friends down for dinner next Saturday."

"Mom, I'm sure you couldn't help but notice the color of Norman's skin. That's not a deep tan you saw."

"Dear, this is 1986. There's a nice black family on Cherry Hill now. He's a professor at the University of Chicago, and his wife teaches somewhere too."

"What about, Dad?"

"You leave your father to me."

"You sure you want to do this?"

"I'm sure," Mom said. "I'll call Susie too and invite her."

Oh no, not my dingbat sister. "All right, we'll see you next Saturday."

The Cubs got five runs in the bottom of the ninth to beat the Dodgers by one. I should have gone to the game.

*   *   *

"Where do I pull over for the strip search?" Norman said.

"Very funny. My mother said there's a black family just a block away from them now."

"Yeah and in the South they used to have darkies living in the backyard. Only they called them slaves."

Vikki was enraptured by the big houses and massive, manicured lawns. "What was it like growing up out here?"

"Actually I spent most of my childhood on the South Side of Chicago."

"When his high school got too dark, his parents moved his white ass out here. Ain't that right, Terry?"

I looked at Norman. "Do you want to have dinner at my parents' house or don't you? We can turn around right now and forget the whole thing if this offends you too much."

"No way, man. I been looking forward to this. It's like old

Margaret Mead going off to study some strange tribe. Hey, do your parents have indoor plumbing?"

"That's it! Come on, let's turn around."

Vikki sidled up next to Norman. "Be good," she cooed.

Norman worked his jaw a while. Then he half-smiled. "All right. But I want you to promise me, man, that your daddy won't have me turned into one of those little black lawn ornaments."

What could I do but laugh?

Mom greeted me at the from door with a kiss on the cheek.

"Mom, this is Vikki Chang. Vikki, my mother . . ."

"Call me Max, dear. We're not big on formality around here."

I was about to introduce Norman when I realized he had disappeared. "Ah, just a minute, Mom. Norman was here a second ago." I stepped back into the front yard and found him bent over the rose bushes. "What the hell are you doing?" I whispered.

"Trying to find where your parents hid their little black jockey," he said.

"For Pete's sake, Norm, they don't have a little black jockey. Now would you please come inside and meet my parents?"

"You sure you don't want me to go around back through the servants' quarters."

"My parents don't have a servants' quarters. They don't even have any servants. Well . . "

"Well, what?"

"Well, my mother has a lady come in and clean every other week, but . . ."

"But she's some black lady, ain't she?"

"Yeah, but . . ."

"I knew it. I knew it."

"All right, so we're racist honkies who've enslaved half the black race. If our food isn't good enough for you, I can take you over to Robbins for some chitterlings and collard greens."

Norman straighted suddenly, pressing his face against mine. "Don't you be makin' fun of my people."

"And don't you be makin' fun of my people," I said.

Our staring contest resulted in backslapping laughter.

When I finally got Norman to the door, Mom said: "I was

going to send the Mounties out to find you two."

"Sorry, Mom. This is Norman James."

"Pleased to meet you, Mrs. Blake," Norman said, a picture of politeness.

"Oh please; call me Max."

"Okay. Pleased to meet you, Max."

As Mom shepherded us through her empty nest to meet Dad and Susie, Norman whispered, "Terry, your momma's a knock-out."

Mom was holding up remarkably well for a woman of 62. Her hair was still mostly auburn, her face was fresh from all the walking she did, and the summery silk blouse, pearls and navy skirt did her slim figure justice.

"Yeah, she takes good care of herself," I whispered, wondering what Norman was going to think when he saw Susie.

When we walked into the den where Dad and Susie were watching the White Sox, my little sister practically had an orgasm at the sight of Norman. She was wearing a racy red jogging outfit which meant she was currently overweight, but she was as much the blue-eyed, blonde bombshell as ever.

The ever-lean lord of the manor was tan and fitted in lime green pants, a pima cotton shirt and loafers. He was nursing a gin and tonic and an "I broke par" grin. Sixty-three going on sixteen.

"Dad, Susie, these are my friends Norman James and Vikki Chang."

Dad sprang out of his leather recliner and gave Norman a manly handshake. "Heard a lot about you, Norman. About time the city got somebody of your caliber in office."

Norman nodded.

Dad turned to Vikki, grinning widely. "I knew there had to be some brains behind these two. Pleased to meet you, Vikki."

Vikki fluttered her eyes and offered her hand. She was wearing a black and red pants suit that highlighted her hair and figure. I could hear Dad's hormones.

"It's a pleasure to meet you, Mr. Blake," she said.

"Please, please -- it's Phil."

"All right -- Phil."

Susie stepped forward and took Norman's had. "I guess I'll

have to introduce myself. I'm Terry's kid sister, Susan."

Oh, it was Susan now.

"Nice to meet you, Susan," Norman said, smiling.

Vikki glanced disapprovingly at Susie and nodded. "Yeah, nice to meet you, Susan."

"Likewise," Susie said, cat-eying Vikki.

"Well, what's everybody drinking?" Dad said.

" He makes a mean gin and tonic," I volunteered.

"Sounds good to me," Norman said.

"Do you think you could make a sloe gin fizz?" Vikki said.

Norman gave her a murderous look, but Dad was already looking for the sloe gin.

"Well, here's to your election," Dad said, when we all had our drinks.

Norman caught Susie's eye as we all clinked glasses. "What do you do for a living, Susan?"

Susie blushed. " I'm a field sales supervisor for Xerox. Actually, it's a new job, because I just got a promotion."

"Congratulations. It must be fascinating work," Norman said.

Susie blushed redder and backed up a step. Norman followed her.

"Well, she said, "it's never dull -- I'll tell you that. Why just the other day, Shirley Rousch -- she's one of my reps -- Shirley had this copier practically blow up in her face while she was on an installation call at this big law firm on LaSalle Street, and all the lawyers. . ."

As Susie blithered, Dad closed in on Vikki. "So what do you think of the world of politics, Vikki?"

"I love it, Phil. Norman and Terry here rescued me from a fate worse than death -- waitressing in my parents' restaurant."

"What restaurant is that?"

"The Dragon Palace. It's in Chinatown."

"Really? Where?"

Jeez, Dad, if you're going to put the move on her at least ask her interesting questions.

"On Cermak near Wentworth."

"I always get those two streets mixed up. Is Cermak the one that runs east/west or is it Wentworth?"

I went to the kitchen to hurry Mom along.

"I hope your friends like Cajun cooking," she said, peering into her microwave.

"I'm sure they'll love it, Mom. Anything I can do to help?"

"No. I'm all set. Why don't you light the candles and call everyone to the table."

Dad sat at one end and Mom at the other with Vikki and me on one side and Norman and Susie on the other.

"Would anyone like to ask the blessing?" Mom said.

"I'd be happy to, Max," Norman said. "Dear Lord, bless this food which we are about to eat and bless these fine people gathered around this table. Bless us in all our endeavors, Lord, that we may strive to achieve a more perfect world. A world free of hunger and hate. A world free of war and evil. As we sit at this fine table, may we be mindful of those less fortunate than ourselves. May we also resolve to ease their pain and suffering. We ask all this through your son, Jesus Christ our Lord. Amen."

"Amen," we chorused.

Mom was no Cajun cook, but we all pretended to like everything, especially the key lime pie.

"Mmmm, this is good," Norman said, wolfing it down.

"There's plenty more," Mom said, smiling.

"Don't mind if I do."

"I wish I could eat like that," Susie said. "God, I look at food, and I gain weight."

"You don't look like you need to lose weight to me."

"REALLY?"

"Really. You look like you take real good care of yourself."

"Well I just joined this health club in Oak Park where I live, but I don't get over there enough. It's usually so late by the time I get home from work that I just don't feel like doing anything. You know?"

"Yeah, I know. But you've really go to discipline yourself. Say, maybe you'd like to come over to the East Bank Club and work out with me sometime.?"

"You belong to the East Bank Club?!?"

"Yeah."

"Wow! I'd love to."

As Norman and my twice-divorced sister slid into an intimate conversation about exercise, I offered to help Mom with the dishes in her oak-cabinetted kitchen.

"Your father will do that. Won't you, Phil?"

Dad was caught off guard. "What? Well, sure, Max. Sure."

"You kids go and make yourselves comfortable. We'll be with you in a minute."

We went to the den and flipped on the Sox game.

"God," I said after half an inning, "how can you watch these jerks?"

There was no deterring Norman and Susie so I suggested to Vikki that I give her a tour of the house.

"That'd be great," she said, sneering at Susie. "Come on, I want to see how the other half lives."

"Okay."

Vikki was awed by Max and Phil's rambling split-level ranch house. "God, wouldn't you just love to live in a place like this?"

"I did live in a place like this, and it drives you crazy after a while."

"It wouldn't drive me crazy. No way."

Mom had turned my old room into a combination storage bin/guest room/office/sewing room so that didn't hold our interest. The master bedroom did.

"Would you look at that bed? God, an entire family could sleep on that," Vikki said.

"You could make an entire family on this bed," I said, surrendering to my long-thwarted libido.

"Terry! What the hell are you doing?!" Vikki said, pounding my back with her fists.

I wrestled her to the bed and kissed her on the mouth. She shook her head nearly breaking my nose.

"Would you let go of me?!"

I relaxed my grip. "All right."

"What the hell do you think you're doing?" Vikki ran a hand through her hair.

"I just got carried away. I . . ."

"If you want to make love to me, just ask like a normal adult."

"Really?!?"

"Really."

"Well, do you want to make love with me?"

Vikki touched my cheek. "Terry, this is your parents' bed."

"So?"

"So, they're right downstairs. Doesn't that bother you?"

"No. I'm 37 years old. My sex life is none of their business. Besides, it'll make it more exciting. God, you don't know how long I've been waiting for this."

Vikki's cheeks became blood red, and her breathing quickened. I ran my fingers through her hair and offered her a gentle kiss. She returned a ferocious one.

We were fumbling with one another's clothing when Norman kick open the door and said: "I hate to interrupt this little love-in, but that Fuentes mother fucker is on the news sayin' my war record is a made-up piece of shit."

Chapter Eleven

Norman stared unblinking into the cameras and said: "I'd like to read a short statement, and then I'll be happy to answer your questions."

Vikki and I were seated behind the candidate at the Cinco de Mayo Elementary School in the heart of the Mexican barrio. An enormous portrait of Benito Juarez was suspended behind us; Mexican and American flags flanked the stage.

Norman surprised me by putting on a pair of tortoise-shell reading glasses.

"Where the hell did he get those?" I whispered.

"I picked them out for him. They make him look distinguished. Don't you think?"

"But he's got 20/20 vision in both eyes."

"So?"

"So what the hell does he need glasses for?"

Norman turned and gave me an angry look.

"Because they make him look sexy," Vikki whispered.

Norman turned back to the press and read the statement I had written for him: "Rather than respond to my opponent's nefarious allegations about my record of service to my country, I'd like to ask a few questions of my own. Why, for example, are his workers going door-to-door in white neighborhoods of this ward saying that a vote for me is a vote for the 'niggers?'

"Ladies and gentlemen of the media, all you have to do is look behind me to see that my campaign is truly a rainbow coalition. My campaign manager Terry Blake is a white male, and my special assistant and the next committeeman of the 51st Ward -- Vikki Chang -- is a first-generation Chinese-American. And if you'll look at the volunteers around you, you'll see that every ethnic group in this ward is equally represented."

Norman nodded, and his carefully integrated supporters shook their placards and shouted, "Viva Norman! Viva Norman!"

The mini-cams caught it all.

Norman smiled. "To date, I am the only one to propose a serious plan of economic renewal for the 51st Ward. My proposal to create a mixed-use development adjacent to Chinatown has already won the full support of the Chinese-American Business Association. Mayor Jefferson is studying the plan and is expected to endorse it.

"And all my honorable opponent can do is stoop to petty racism and innuendo about my national service. If that's the way he wants to run his campaign -- fine. But I choose to take the high road. I'm running on the issues not on slander and libel. I'm running for Alderman of the 51st Ward because I believe in the 51st Ward. It's already a great ward, but it can be better. And it will be when I'm elected. Thank you. Now I'll be happy to answer your questions."

It was a slow news day so the press had come out in force. They waved notebooks, tape recorders and microphones in Norman's face, shouting their multi-parted questions in cacophonous chorus.

Norman pointed to the reporter from the black-owned DAILY DEFENDER. "I'll take your question first, Brother John."

"You've made a serious allegation about racism, Mr. James. What do you intend to do about it?"

Norman calmed the restive reporters with his hands and said, "Well, my first concern is the safety of my staff and volunteers. I therefore have alerted the Chicago Police Department, the State's Attorney, the Board of Elections and the U.S. Attorney. I would like to remind my honorable opponent that this is America, not Nazi Germany. We have a right and a duty to hold free and open elections in this country."

Norman pointed at the SUN-TIMES reporter.

"Fuentes says he has documentation that you never set foot in Vietnam. Furthermore, he says . . ."

"One question at a time. Please," Norman said, smiling calmly at the minicams.

"Well, what about it, Mr. James? Were you in Vietnam or weren't you?"

The press pushed close for the answer.

Still smiling calmly at the minicams, Norman replied: "I will soon produce documentation proving that the money my opponent collected for the relief of the earthquake victims in Mexico City never got anywhere near Mexico City. In fact, I will soon demonstrate that hardly a dime of that money -- more than $250,000 in cash collected from the fine working class people of this neighborhood -- never left Mr. Fuentes' pocket. Now if you'll excuse me, ladies and gentlemen, I have a rather full day of campaigning ahead of me."

Norman nodded, and we quickly exited stage right.

When we were a safe distance away, I said, "Norm, where the hell are you going to come up with something like that?"

"You'll think of a way," Norman said. "You were an ace reporter, right?"

"Well . . ."

"Well, that's what I'm payin' you for."

You mean that's what Dr. Morgenstern is paying me for.

"It's not going to be easy. Where the hell did you hear that anyway? Fuentes looks clean as a whistle as far as I can tell."

"Just a hunch. Hey, let's go to the Dragon Palace. Man, I could eat a damn horse."

Vikki had been brooding since we got in the car. Now she looked intently at Norman and said: "Will you answer me once and for all -- were you or were you not in Vietnam?"

Norman glanced at her. "I'll answer your question if you answer mine first."

"What's that?" Vikki said, slumping in her seat.

"Were you really going to let Terry fuck you on his momma and daddy's bed?"

Checkmate.

Chapter Twelve

I didn't have to be fluent in Spanish to recognize a death threat, and I heard plenty as I snooped my way along 18th Street.

Word spread that a nosey gringo was asking embarrassing questions about Oscar Fuentes, and everyone either clammed up or threatened me with bodily harm. The Latin Hawks street gang would have beaten me with baseball bats at Loomis if a squad car hadn't serendipitously appeared.

After four solid days of frustration, I was ready to call the Vatican and nominate Fuentes for sainthood. Then an old lady in a bakery said she had a niece who had a friend who might know something.

I arranged a meeting, and Fuentes' facade quickly fell away.

We sat in the back of a Greek restaurant on Halsted Street sipping egg-lemon soup. She had identified herself only as "Maria" and had not removed her dark sunglasses despite the dim lighting.

"You know Oscar was a big Jefferson backer in '83," Maria said. Her accent was more South Side Chicago than Mexico, and her features were more Spanish than Aztec. Her dark beauty excited me.

"Yeah, so I've heard. So what happened?" I slid my hand into my side pocket and activated my tape recorder.

Maria's brown eyes widened. "Nothing -- that's what happened. Oscar worked his rearend off for Jefferson -- delivered the 51st Ward on a silver platter. And what does he get? Nothing. Oh, Jefferson was full of big talk about appointing more Hispanics to key positions and all that crap, but he didn't do a damn thing. And he wouldn't even answer Oscar's phone calls after he was in office a few months."

I frowned. "That's not the way . . ."

"Of course it's not the way your candidate's going to tell it. Hamilton Jefferson has him eating out of his hand."

"That's not true. Norman James is . . ."

". . . the biggest bullshit artist I've ever seen. All I want to know is: what's a nice guy like you working for a crook like that? Huh?"

Realizing I hadn't given it a good thought since I agreed to work for Norman, I turned off my tape recorder. The story of my life -- dull suburban boy always ready to fall in behind the fast talkers.

"Well, that's a good question. I was tired of my job at this PR agency downtown. I ran into Norm at the Vietnam veterans parade, and he kind of sweet-talked me. I don't know. I guess that's not much of an answer, is it?"

Maria removed her sunglasses and smiled at me with her soft, brown eyes. "No, it's not. Like I said, you're too nice a guy to be working for a creep like him. God, he's a black version of Ivan Kovar."

"I like excitement -- what can I say? And what about you? Why did you agree to come here and spill the beans on Fuentes? You must have been pretty close to him at one time or something."

"Or something." Maria drank some wine and wiped her lips. "All right, I was his mistress. He threw me over when he found out I was also sleeping with this Puerto Rican guy. Oscar hates Puerto Ricans more than he hates blacks."

"No wonder Scambino and Petrilli like him so much."

"Three peas in a pod."

"So is it true he pocketed the earthquake money?" I put my hand on my tape recorder and then withdrew it.

"Let's just say they didn't use approved bookkeeping procedures. We had people coming in and literally giving us the shirts off their backs. Their entire paychecks. It was unbelievable. In the beginning Oscar really wanted every last dime to go to Mexico. But you have to understand Mexican politics. Makes Chicago look like Disney World. Every official we talked to wanted his cut.

"Oscar was born and raised up here so he had no idea things were like that. He got discouraged after a while and figured screw it -- I'll put the money to better use up here helping my own people. So it's not a black-and-white issue like your friend thinks. Or is he really your friend?"

Good question, considering I feared Norman James more than I liked him.

"Sure he's my friend. Forgive me for being gross, but if it wasn't for him, I'd probably still be a virgin."

"You mean you two are . . ."

"No. We were in the Navy together in Taiwan. We went to a whorehouse -- well, it wasn't actually a whorehouse -- and Norman paid for it. It was my first time."

"How sweet. So you weren't in Vietnam. Were you?"

Infected by Maria's honesty, I said, "No, we weren't in Vietnam. Taiwan is the closest we ever got."

Maria poured us some more wine. "You know what we are?" she said.

"No. What?"

"A couple of suckers."

I raised my glass. "A toast."

"To what?"

"To a couple of suckers."

We klinked glasses and finished our meal in the best of company.

I had completely forgotten about my tape recorder by the time we finished our Greek coffee.

"So tell me," Maria said, "who's sleeping with the little Chinese girl?"

"You know you're not what I expected at all." We were both a little giddy from wine and liqueur.

"What were you expecting -- some barefoot campasina with three babies at her breast?"

"Well . . ."

"The 20th Century is finally filtering down to 18th Street. You didn't answer my question."

"You mean . . ."

"Who's screwing Susie Wong -- you or that Neanderthal you're working for?"

"Her name's Vikki Chang, and, well Norm's kind of . . ."

"The loyal lacky's still waiting his turn. How long have you been waiting, Terry?"

"Too long."

"Well guess what?"

"What?"

"If you take me back to my place, you won't have to wait any

longer. How's that?"
"What are we waiting for?" I said.

*   *   *

"You know I don't even know your last name."
Maria rolled over and caressed my back. "Sandoval. And
Maria is really my first name. I'm a paralegal for a law firm in
the IBM building. I was born in Monterey, Mexico and brought
here when I was ten. I have four brothers and three sisters. I'll be
28 on October 5th, and . . ."
"All right, all right."
Maria had the window open in hopes that the murderously
muggy August afternoon would yield a breeze. Kids were
having a bilingual laser battle on Throop Street, and some punk
was racing his muscle car around the neighborhood. The
Douglas El rattled by on its ancient tracks, and the ice cream
man called: "Helados deliciosos; helados deliciosos . . ."
Maria's small, neat apartment was freshly painted in white and
peach, and her table fan was providing some comfort. I trailed
my fingers along the lovely curve of her spine and surrendered
to an inner peace I hadn't know in a long time.
"This is really nice. Really nice."
"Mmmm. Could you scratch my back. Ooooh. Lower. That's it.
Aaah."
"Maria Sandoval. That's a pretty name."
"So's Terry Blake."
"You think so?"
"I wouldn't have brought you here if I didn't. I don't go out
with guys with ugly names."
We laughed. Then we kissed, hugged and made love again.
When we were spent, Maria said, "Are you really going to
smear Oscar?"
"I thought you hated him."
"On a personal level, yeah, I think he's a real two-timing, racist
son-of-a-bitch. But I know he loves the people of this
neighborhood. If he's elected, he'll work his ass off for them."
"Hmmm."
"What's that supposed to mean?"

"I was just thinking about this whole thing. About what a snake pit politics is. It's gotten to the point where I don't even know when I'm lying or telling the truth."

"Didn't you tell me at the restaurant that your background's in journalism?"

"Yeah. More or less."

"Well, you know, they're starting this newsletter at the law firm where I work. It's for all their big-shot clients and everything. And they're looking for an editor."

"I don't know squat about law. I'm sure they're looking for somebody with a background in legal writing."

"Not necessarily. They're looking for a good writer. I could help you with all the legal jargon."

"Really?"

"Sure. No sweat. The people they've interviewed so far have barely been able to walk and chew gum at the same time."

"You know, I did cover some trials when I was at the TRIBUNE. You really think . . ."

"I know you'd do an excellent job. Now shut up and scratch my back again."

Chapter Thirteen

I accepted the job at Maria's law firm before I said a word to Norman. Fear. Plain and simple.

Plus he was busy. Extremely busy. He had finally been accepted into the Reverend Jesse Jackson's inner circle and was forever fawning for the press and jetting off to conferences on the coasts. Vikki often accompanied him.

I had planned to give Norman two weeks notice, but the time and Norman got away from me. So it finally came down to the Saturday before the Monday I was due to begin working for Maria's law firm.

I called Vikki, and she said Norman was at Operation PUSH Headquarters on Martin Luther King Junior Memorial Drive to hear Daniel Ortega gush about Gucci communism in Nicaragua.

"Why aren't you there?" I said.

"Because I've got to get our place organized."

"What place?"

"If you'd bother to come around once in a while, you'd know that we rented a campaign office on Wentworth just south of Cermak -- right in the middle of Chinatown. Where have you been anyway? Norman's really pissed."

Did I detect hurt in Vikki's voice, or was it just my imagination?

"Well, I might as well tell you first -- I accepted another job. I'm leaving the campaign."

"What!?!"

"Yeah. I'm going to edit a newsletter for this law firm in the IBM building."

"Terry, are you crazy? You can't abandon Norman now. He'll be furious. You know how he is."

"Yeah, I know."

"So why are you doing this?"

"Vikki, I just . . ."

"You just what?" I certainly had her attention.

"I'm just not cut out for politics. I didn't know that until I gave it a try. Now I know."

"But you were doing such a great job." She really sounded upset.

"Come on, Vikki. Norm won't be happy until he's on the cover of TIME Magazine. And now that he's hooked up with Jesse Jackson, he doesn't need me to get publicity."

"Did you meet another woman, Terry?"

"What?"

"You heard me."

"What difference does that make?"

"It would certainly explain why we haven't seen you. Is she pretty?"

"Yeah, she is as a matter of fact."

"What's her name?"

"Maria. Maria Sandoval."

"Mexican? You're going out with a Mexican?"

"Mexican-American. What's wrong with that?"

"Is she as pretty as me?" Vikki sounded absolutely petulant.

"Well . . ."

"If you say 'yes' I'll break your arm."

I smiled. Vikki Chang WAS jealous. "She's pretty, but in a different sort of way."

"What sort of way? It's her hair, isn't it? Those Mexican girls have beautiful hair. Not like this curly mop I have."

"Vikki, your hair's beautiful."

"You think so?"

"Yes, definitely. I've always thought that."

"So why are you running around with this Maria creature?"

"She's not a creature, and I'm not running around with her. I just . . ."

"You just what?"

"Well, you know."

"No, I don't know. Where'd you meet this woman anyway?"

"While I was trying to dig up some dirt on Fuentes."

"Oh yeah, we were wondering whatever happened to that project. We thought you got kidnapped by banditos or something."

"Very funny."

"So what did you find out about Fuentes? Did he pocket that earthquake money? I bet he did."

"Well, it's not as cut-and-dried as you think."

"Terry, whose side are you on?"

"You sure you don't want to go with me to PUSH Headquarters?" I said.

"No, I told you I've got to get this place cleaned up. Besides, Norman is really going to be pissed. I'd think it over if I were you."

"Yeah, well. Maybe I'll see you later, huh?"

"Maria. I think that's an ugly name."

"Vikki!"

She hung up without further comment.

*   *   *

Operation PUSH Headquarters was crawling with cops, mini-cams and creepy guys in black suits. King Drive was lined with stretch limos with tinted windows. So much for the simple Sandinista life.

I parked my Ford Escort two blocks south and walked briskly toward the imposing old church that served as Jesse Jackson's window to the world. A group of black teenagers eyed me from the porch of a two-flat. I stared at the sidewalk.

A burly black man in a dark suit stopped me at the door and asked to see a press pass. Another black man appeared from behind and patted me down.

"He's clean."

I looked at the first man and stammered.

"What you sayin', man?"

I took a deep breath and tried again: "I'm not a reporter."

"Then who the hell are you?"

"I'm Norman James's campaign manager. He's running for alderman in the 51st Ward. I need to talk to him."

"You got some kind of I.D.?"

"I.D.? For being a campaign manager?" I peeked over the security man's shoulder. Daniel Ortega was at the podium wearing his designer glasses and a tailored suit. Jesse Jackson was just as well dressed and sat behind the commie clothes horse, and behind him -- the dapper Norman James.

"You ain't gettin' in without an I.D. or an invitation. That clear, you nut-case dude?"

I exhaled. "Can I wait out here? I've really got to talk to Mr. James."

"No way, dude. We've got a world leader in there today. You want to talk to your man, you call him on the telephone. Now, I suggest you move along."

I stepped back into the other security guy. "Sorry."

He pushed me aside, saying: "Do like the man says, dude, and move along."

The black teens on the porch watched with interest; inside, Daniel Ortega denounced Yankee imperialism.

"Could I at least leave a message for Mr. James?" I said. The other security guard jabbed me in the sternum with his forefinger. "Dude, the man told you to move along. Now move along."

Remembering where I was, I moved along. I was still shaking when I got to my apartment. I had a cold beer, then I phoned Norman's answering machine.

After the beep, I said: "Norm, this is Terry Blake calling Saturday morning at 11:30. I tried to see you at Operation PUSH this morning, but I couldn't get in. Look, I'm leaving the campaign. I took a job as the editor of a newsletter for this law firm in the IBM building, and . . ."

Beep.

I cradled the phone and gulped my beer. Then I got another bottle and awaited Norman's response.

* * *

I killed the six pack without a call from Norman. I tried his number again and hung up before the beep.

It was too nice a day to be sitting in my "garden" apartment waiting for his Lordship to return my call, so I called Maria. She agreed that the zoo would be lovely, and off we went. We had dinner at a Vietnamese place on North Broadway and went to a show.

It was some comedy with Jackie Gleason, but I don't remember too much because we made out through most of the movie.

"My place this time?" I said as we left the theater arm-in- arm.

"Only if you have air conditioning."

"Well, it's earth-sheltered."

"Earth-sheltered?"

"Yeah -- it's underground -- your basic basement apartment. First to flood, last to get heat -- but it does stay pretty cool in summer."

Maria smiled wickedly. "Well, it better be pretty cool, because I'm hot for your bod tonight."

"Don't you worry -- it'll be cool."

It was until the phone rang. We had half finished undressing one another, and Maria was all for letting it ring.

But I was sure it was Norman.

"If it's him and I don't tell him tonight, he's really going to be pissed. Besides, he's a hard man to get a hold of."

Maria grabbed me where it counts and said, "So are you. Now hurry up."

"Okay." I kissed her on the lips and went reluctantly to the insistent telephone.

"Hello."

It was Vikki, and she was pissed. "Terry, you've really got to get an answering machine. I've been calling you all afternoon. Where the hell have you been?"

"Vikki it's Saturday for Pete's sake. I do have a personal life you know."

"You've been with that Mexican, haven't you?"

"Vikki . . ."

"I bet she's there right now, isn't she?"

"Vikki . . ."

"I knew it."

"Vikki, why are you calling? I was expecting Norm. Have you talked to him today?"

"No. I haven't seen or heard from him all day."

"Then why are you calling at this hour? You sound upset."

"I am upset. You'd be too if you kept getting calls all day from some creep who keeps threatening to kill you."

"What?!?"

"You heard me -- I've been getting death threats all afternoon from some creep who says he's going to kill me if Norman doesn't stop attacking Oscar Fuentes."

My heart raced. "Did he say who he was?"

"No."

"Have you called the police?"

"No, he said he'd know right away if I did. I've been trying to get a hold of you and Norman all afternoon and evening and I just . . ." Vikki burst into tears.

"Did he have a deep voice? With a real South Side accent?"

Vikki blew her nose. "Yeah. I think so."

Funny Face, it had to be Funny Face Scambino. The guy wouldn't hesitate to use violence if his interests were threatened, and my little investigation would certainly appear to do that. "Vikki, I'm coming. You hear me, I'll be right there."

"Oh, Terry, hurry! Please!"

"I will. Now where's this place again?"

"On Wentworth -- just south of Cermak on the east side of the street. You can't miss it. Please hurry, Terry. Please. I'm so scared."

"I'll be right there. Don't let anyone in until I get there -- you hear."

"Okay, but hurry, Terry. Please hurry!"

"I will."

Maria was dressed and at my side. "I'm coming with you," she said, handing me my pants.

"You sure? Sounds like it could be dangerous. Some guy has been threatening Vikki over the phone. Says he's going to kill her if we don't lay off Oscar Fuentes."

"That's BS. Oscar wouldn't do anything like that," Maria said.

"Maybe, but Vikki's really upset. And I do know somebody who would."

"Who?"

"Petrilli's committeeman -- Scambino. The guy they call 'Funny Face.'"

"Oh yeah. Yeah, he would do something like that, wouldn't he?"

"Yeah. You sure you want to come?"

"Yes."

I dressed, and we went quickly through the night to Chinatown. It was still packed with patrons, so we had to park two blocks away in a lot. We ran all the way to Norman's campaign headquarters.

The door was unlocked, and Vikki did not answer my call.

"Maybe we should call the police first," Maria said, restraining me.

"Let me take a look first."

"Terry, I really think . . ."

"Maria, she could be hurt."

"All right, but I'm coming with you."

"All right."

Book Three:
Later

Chapter Fourteen

No, this isn't Terry Blake.

It's me -- Norman James. Alderman of the 51st Ward. That's right, I won. Won big, in fact. In the February 24th election, not in no run-off.

I got 61 percent of the vote. Fuentes got less than 30 percent, and that pen nut and that crazy LaRouche bitch got the rest. Before I forget -- Mayor Jefferson got re-elected. Big. Beat old Ivan Kovar clean out of his britches.

I'll be sworn in tomorrow, and that means we're running this show now. No more Council Wars. No more of that block of 29 shit. The brothers run it. We've got 32 out of 51 council seats and all of the big committees. Mayor Jefferson's going to appoint me head of the Aviation Committee. That means I get to run O'Hare. Why not: I'm a frequent flier.

I'm backing Vikki Chang for committeeman, and I think she'll get it. Scambino and Petrilli have been laying low lately, but I'll tell you more about that in a minute.

But first I want to clear up something that's been botherin' me for a long damn time. That business in Taiwan. Remember?

Accordin' to Terry Blake, I acted like some crazy nigger from the South Side who had it all comin'. You know, when them crazy ass Chinese police beat the livin' shit out of me.

Terry said I sassed them dudes. That's why they jumped on my shit like that. Terry also said that he was too drunk to do much of anything. Said he fell out after they beat him on the head.

Well that last part is true. The dude did fall out, but not before he got my black ass in deep shit. Here's what really happened that night back in '69:

We went out looking for pussy just like Terry said. Oh, and speakin' of pussy, I got to say at this point that Terry's sister Susie was the worst piece of ass I ever had. Had the fattest thighs I ever seen and just lay there like some big old cow goin' -- "Ain't you done yet?"

Anyway, her brother weren't much better. When we was with them whores in Kaohsiung, he acted like some little kid or somethin'. Stared at my dick like he was some goddamn queer. Man, I met all kinds of crazy white dudes in the Navy, but that Terry Blake was the strangest of 'em all. By far.

I mean the dude was still a virgin that night when went to the whore house. Didn't even know how to put on a damn rubber. I practically had to tell him where to put his damn dick. And then he shoots his load in two seconds flat. He finally gets it up for a second shot, and while he's humpin' away, he's watchin' me. Watchin' me, you understand. I figure this dude is some stone faggot.

Not that I got anything against faggots, mind you. Just as long as they're open about it. I don't care if you do it with farm animals, as long as you're open about it. I just can't abide sneaky people. I mean if you decide that you like doin' it with men, then be proud of it. Be open about it. Don't be like that damn Terry Blake. All sneaky and shit. Givin' me them snide little looks while we was in that whorehouse.

Maybe it wasn't his fault. I mean when I was comin' up on the South Side, sex wasn't that big a deal. I got me my first pussy when I was 13, or was it 12. Twelve. And I got it regular ever since. No big deal. It wasn't wrong, and wasn't right -- it was just there. A natural part of life. Not some big mystery like it musta been for Terry Blake. Poor dude had to beat off half his life before he had the guts to go out and get laid. And then I practically had to take him by the hand. Pathetic, man. Just pathetic.

Anyway, after we left the whorehouse, Terry insisted that we buy some more booze. I mean, the dude was on some kind of rampage or somethin'. Like a damn kid away from home the first time. I kept tellin' him he didn't need no more booze, but he wouldn't listen.

And that business about stealin' the motorcycle. That was his idea. He done that. Not me. No way. I ain't no thief. Never have been and never will be.

So Terry goes and grabs this dude's motorcycle, push-starts it and tells me to hop on. That's right -- he was drivin' the damn thing, not the other way around like he told you.

And he was doin' the worst job of drivin' you can imagine. Kept poppin' the damn clutch and stallin' us out. We fell over at least three times. I told him I'd be happy to drive, but he says no, he's got everything under control.

My own damn fault for listenin' to him, I suppose, but I was young then too. But a hell of a lot wiser than him.

Next thing I know we're out in the countryside and he's speedin' away like he's Mario Andretti. I'm tellin' him to slow down, but he don't listen. I was sure we was gonna be killed. Just sure of it.

So I'm tryin' to talk him down, then all of sudden the dude just passes out. We're goin' 60, 70 miles an hour on an unlit road out in the middle of Taiwan on a stolen motorcycle, and the dude falls out. Before I could do anything, the bike flies off the road and we're in this damn rice paddy up to our eyeballs in mud and shit.

I thought Terry was dead, but then the dude is laughin' his fool ass off like this was some kind of big joke. He was still laughin' when them Chinese MPs showed up.

I told him to let me do all the talkin', but no, he says he out-ranks me so he's in charge.

So what does he say?

He tells them mother fuckers that I stole the bike. That I put him up to it. Got him drunk and made him come along for the ride. Lied his ever-lovin' white ass off. And them Chinese bastards believed every damn word of it. Every damn word of it.

I mean we're talkin' Taiwan in 1969. They wasn't no dummies. They knew who was givin' 'em all that aid. Uncle Sugar. And they was more than happy to keep Uncle Sugar's nigger boys in line. Yes, sir.

Well, them Chinese pigs sure kept me in line. Beat the livin' crap out of me with their nightsticks. I'm screamin' for Terry to help, and he's just standin' there watchin'. Like it was some spectator sport. I guess for him it was -- watch the nigger get his ass beat.

Anyway, they let Terry go, but they hauled my black ass off to the nastiest little jail cell you ever want to see. I don't want to ruin your supper, but, man, it was nasty. I mean real nasty. Hot. Bugs. And just a little hole in the floor for doin' your natural functions.

Kept me up in there for three weeks. That's right, three weeks!

Navy took its damn sweet time gettin' me out. And I'm sure old Terry was out there singin' some tune to save his own ass. Hang the nigger. Why not?

When they finally did get me out, they busted me down to E-2 and sent me straight off to an ammunition ship stationed off Vietnam. Okay, so I never set foot in the 'nam, but I seen it. And I coulda had my ass blown to kingdom come any time. It wasn't them gooks we was afraid of so much as our own goofy pilots and ships.

Everybody high on somethin' out there. Sooner or later we figured some damn fool was gonna use us for target practice. When we made a port call in Hong Kong, they stuck us so far back in the harbor, it practically took us three days to get ashore for liberty.

Anyway, I never seen Terry Blake again until that parade. But I never stopped thinkin' about that night in the rice paddy. Never. I said, Norman, if you ever see that white mother fucker again, you're gettin' even. And I mean even.

Well, I got even all right.

When I seen him standin' by that parade, I knew. I knew. I had him. And by the way, I had every right in the world to march in that parade. I risked my ass for the war effort. You sit on an ammunition ship off Vietnam for six months and see if you don't lose a few pounds worryin'.

Anyway, I led that white boy right along. Made him think he had a right to march in that Vietnam parade even though he never got close to the 'nam. That's why I never said anything about bein' on the ammunition ship when Fuentes raised all that ruckus about my war record. I coulda come clean and told everybody what I was doin' off the coast of Vietnam. Hell, as far as I'm concerned I'm just as much a war hero as that damn Mexican.

But I wanted Terry to think I was jus' like him -- sittin' out the war in same safe duty station. You know, he never asked me what happened to me after that night in the rice paddy. He knew I was in the slammer, but he didn't know what happened to me after that. He didn't want to know. The dude hung my ass, and he didn't want to know.

Never asked me in all the time we've just been together. Not once. You figure.

Anyway, I sweet talked him into bein' my campaign manager. Rubbed his little ego and got old Doc Morgenstern to pay his salary.

I've got to admit, he wasn't too bad. Got me on the radio and TV. Of course, I could have done all that myself, but I wanted to set him up. Get him nice and comfortable, and then get even for what he done to me on the ROCk -- in Taiwan.

Well, with Miss Vikki's help and cooperation, I done avenged myself just fine. Got that fool white boy and his Mexican girlfriend to come runnin' over that night last August to campaign headquarters. Thinkin' that old Scambino was up to no good.

And, as far as the police and the FBI are concerned, he was. I expect they're gonna indict Scambino anyday now for the arson deaths of Terry Blake and Maria Sandoval. Maybe indict Petrilli too. They been talkin' to old Oscar Fuentes too, but I don't think they're gonna get him. That's okay -- he couldn't get elected sewer commissioner now.

The main thing is I won. And I won big on accounta Terry Blake. Findin' him and his Mexican girlfriend in the smokin' ruins of my campaign headquarters was the best thing that could have happened to me.

I played the shocked and outraged candidate of the people. My white campaign manager and his Mexican assistant had been blown to kingdom come by the forces of repression and plantation politics. My Chinese assistant had received death threats over the phone.

Me too, or so I said.

Terry would have been happy with all the coverage his funeral got. And he would have been pleased with my performance. I mean, I just cried my eyes out. And them wasn't fake tears. I was cryin' because I couldn't help thinkin' we could have been really good friends.

If he just wasn't the whitest white dude I ever met.

The End

Viking Funeral

"The kin of the dead Wyglif now drew near and, taking a piece of lighted wood, walked backward toward the ship and ignited the ship without ever looking at it. The funeral pyre was soon aflame, and the ship, the tent, the man and the girl, and everything else blew up in a blazing storm of fire."

Eaters of the Dead
(The Manuscript of Ibn Fadlan, Relating His Experiences with the Northmen in A.D. 922)
by Michael Crichton
Alfred A. Knopf, New York, 1976

Chapter One

It became known in 1976 as the Morris Fishbein Institute of Forensic Medicine, but Mark Anderson called it the county morgue.

It was a vibrant September 1978 afternoon in Chicago, and Mark didn't mind the traffic. His rented Miller-Meteor hearse was air-conditioned and equipped with stereo AM-FM. Mark had it tuned to a blaring rock station.

The Bee Gees started "stayin' alive, stayin' alive," so Mark punched the button and got something more to his liking: Jim Morrison howling about his L.A. Woman.

Mark Anderson was a lanky 28-year-old who wore his thin blonde hair long enough to hide his receding hairline. His blue eyes and broad forehead betrayed his Swedish ancestry, but his fine nose suggested a relationship with Rome. Mark thought his body was too long and boney, but women found him instantly attractive, often thinking at first glance that he was European.

Mark snuffed out a Marlboro and backed the hearse into the loading bay next to a blue-and-white paddy wagon. The wagonmen brought fresh bodies to the morgue for autopsies and identification, and funeral directors took them away to be buried or cremated. There was a constant exchange.

Mark nodded at the cop, and the cop touched his cap. Mark thought of all the $20s he had put in the man's back pocket in exchange for one of the county's unclaimed dead. It was usually worth the effort provided he could get the state welfare people to pay him for the case.

Mark watched the cop turn back to his hip flask and figured the guy had a right to drink on the job. Wagonmen got the stinkers, and the police department provided them with nothing more than a flimsy cot that usually fell apart if the stiff weighed more than 225 lbs. Mark always gave the guys free surgical gloves and profusely thanked them for performing such a vital public service.

Didn't people know that without the wagonmen cholera and dysentery would be as common as the cold?

Mark locked the hearse and bolted up the loading bay steps.

Avoiding a fresh bloodstain, he walked briskly to the front desk where he impatiently made his presence known.

A fat patronage worker sat behind the formica counter sipping stale coffee and smoking a non-filter cigarette.

"I know you're real busy," Mark said, "but maybe you could give me a second or two."

The clerk grunted and glanced at the intruder. The damn kid wasn't even wearing a suit, and he expected some kind of respect. If he had any kind of clout he'd be wearing a dark suit and acting like he owned the place.

Mark pulled the paperwork out of his back pocket.

"I'm here for Raymond Zimowski."

The clerk struggled to his feet and shuffled to the counter. "Where're you from, bub?"

"Anderson Funeral Home. On South Canal. It's in the book."

"What was the name again?"

"Zimowski. Raymond Zimowski. Z-i-m-o-w-s-k-i. Died a week ago today."

"I don't care when he died," the clerk said. "When they bring him in?"

"Day before yesterday."

"Now we're gettin' somewhere. What did you say: day before yesterday?"

"Yeah."

The clerk ran his finger down the page. "Here it is. Zimowski. Raymond F. Case number 267. You got some ID?"

Mark held his funeral director's licence under the clerk's nose. "You know where to go?" he said.

"Yeah."

Mark walked past a frightened black family and stabbed the elevator button. He listened to the creaking elevator mechanism and wished he had smoked a joint. The tarnished steel door finally opened with a shudder, and Mark took a last breath of fresh air before entering the world of the dead. As the elevator filled with the bittersweet smell of decay, Mark instinctively breathed through his mouth.

He closed his eyes and listened for the door to creak open. Then he blinked at rows of yellow feet protruding from black plastic body bags.

A muscular black man wearing a Southern Illinois University T-shirt and green surgical pants hurried by with a sheet of plywood.

"Say man," he yelled at a mate, "gimme that hammer."

Other black men lifted the county's unclaimed dead into pine boxes for burial in mass, unmarked graves next to the forest preserves.

Mark watched two attendants pull the plastic off a body and use it to line a nearby casket. Then they lifted the naked remains of a jaundiced wino into the box and quickly nailed a lid over it. One shoved the empty cart into a corner and the other went for another to repeat the procedure. Mark understood their haste: once removed from the refrigerators, the unembalmed bodies rapidly decomposed.

"Come on," a supervisor shouted over the din, "we've got to get 26 of these out of here in an hour. Let's get a move on."

An attendant pushed Mark aside so he could get another cart through the cluttered corridor.

Mark folded a $20 in his palm and waited for his main man, Tyrone.

Tyrone soon appeared wearing a Cubs T-shirt and blood-stained green surgical pants. He carried a sack lunch in one hand.

"Say man," he said, "I be right with you. I just want to put my lunch in the fridge."

Tyrone returned shortly with an extended palm. Attendants were forbidden from assisting funeral directors, hence the "fee."

Mark gave Tyrone the $20, saying: "Number 267, Tyrone. Name's Zimowski. Raymond F."

"Wait here, my man. I know where this dude is."

Mark backed into a cot containing the remains of a young Mexican who had been shot in the head and stabbed repeatedly in the torso. Clumps of dried blood caked the youth's nose and ears. His eyes were rolled up in a final look of terror. Police evidence tags adorned his body.

The other wagonman and an attendant appeared with a cot bearing the body of a young black man who had been shotgunned in the chest.

Seeing Mark, the cop said: "You believe it, this jamoke tried to rip off a Mexican gin mill with a knife."

"Fool nigger," the black attendant said.

Mark shook his head. The smell was starting to get to him. What's keeping Tyrone, he wondered, craning his neck. Tyrone finally appeared with Mark's client.

"Here's your man," he said, pulling a wire tag off an exposed toe. "Where's your cot?"

"Oh shit, I knew I forgot something. Can you wait a minute?"

"Yeah, but hurry, man, I gots lots to do."

Tyrone was waiting impatiently when Mark returned. "Where'd you park, man, in Detroit?"

"Sorry," Mark said, setting up his collapsible cot. "I, ah . . ."

"All right, give me a hand with this dude, he's heavy. Real heavy."

They pulled the plastic off Raymond F. Zimowski's huge white body, took deep breaths and heaved him onto Mark's cot. Mark quickly sealed the shroud over the naked corpse and wheeled him to the elevator.

"Thanks, Tyrone, I appreciate it."

"Your money always good here, brother," Tyrone said.

Chapter Two

"Comfortable back there, Raymond?" Mark said, accelerating down the entrance ramp. "Good. You need anything, you just holler, okay?"

Raymond Zimowski was silent.

"Mind if I smoke, Raymond?" Mark looked in the rearview mirror at the shrouded giant. "No, I guess you don't."

Mark opened the glove compartment and selected a joint from the perfect dozen he had put there. He punched the lighter and savored the illicit cigarette.

"Too bad you don't smoke anymore, Raymond. This is really dy-no-mite shit, man. Dy-no-mite!"

Mark made a happy sound when the lighter popped back and fired up the joint. He took a deep hit, turned up the radio and sped through the afternoon rush hour traffic toward Chicago's Loop.

"I don't know about you, Raymond, but this shit always makes me hornier 'n' hell. And look at all these ladies. Damn!"

Two stunning businesswomen crossed in front of Mark's hearse and did a double take when the realized that the hunk behind the wheel was young and smoking a very strange cigarette.

Mark gave them a friendly wave and powered the window down, but they walked quickly out of earshot.

"Story of my life, Raymond. You have to be a rich lawyer or accountant to have any luck with the ladies in this town. But then I guess you know all about bad luck, don't you?"

Mark glanced in the rearview mirror and took another deep hit.

He drove north on Dearborn and then dipped down a steep ramp into the bowels of the Richard J. Daley Civic Center. Mark gave an old black man a $5 bill and the keys to the hearse, saying, "Be back in 10 minutes, Billy."

Billy nodded.

Ignoring the long lines at the Burial & Birth Certificates office, Mark slipped through a side door and sought his connection -- Larry.

Larry took the crisp $10 with a slight nod and processed the death certificate in no time.

"Goin' to the Sox game tonight?" Larry said.

"Are you kiddin'. I wouldn't walk across the street to see those jerks."

"But I thought you were from the South Side."

"Yeah, but that doesn't mean I have bad taste."

"Don't tell me you're a Cubs fan."

"Yep. Have a good weekend."

"Yeah, you too. Even if you are a Cubs fan."

Mark and Raymond Zimowski were soon speeding north on Lake Shore Drive.

"Would you look at those waves, Raymond. Got a real good northeaster' goin' today. Real nice. Of course, that means the fish are going to be running deeper, but that's cool. You do much fishin', Raymond?

"No, huh. Well, let me tell you, God doesn't count the time you spent fishin' against your allotted time on earth. Maybe you should have done some fishin' Raymond. You'd be sittin' up here with me instead of bein' a stiff back there."

Mark glided around a Mercedes convertible and waved at the woman behind the wheel. She lifted her designer sunglasses in amazement at the speeding hearse.

Mark laughed.

He exited at Irving Park and locked his door with his elbow. Uptown -- home of the dispossessed, depressed and deranged. A mental patient shuffled listlessly past the hearse at Broadway.

Mark snuffed the remnant of the joint in the ashtray and wheeled through Graceland Cemetery's stone gateway at Clark Street.

"Hi," Mark said to the secretary at the window, "I'm from Anderson Funeral Home. I called yesterday. Cremation -- Raymond F. Zimowski." Mark handed her the death certificate.

"Oh yes. We're expecting you, Mr. Anderson."

The woman produced a partially completed cremation authorization and handed it to Mark.

"I believe you said the cremains were to be surrendered to you."

"Right -- at the family's request."

Mark completed the paperwork, got back in the hearse and rolled down the window.

"Well, Raymond, this is it, buddy. Your last ride, but what a ride, huh? Couldn't ask for a better day, and you've got to admit, this place is first-class."

Mark took Raymond on a long ride around the perimeter of the graceful old cemetery, pointing out his favorite headstones along the way. Then he turned a corner and backed the hearse up to the chapel doors. The crematorium attendant was waiting. "Better give me a hand with him; he's heavy," Mark said.

The attendant nodded and they soon had Raymond F. Zimowski in a corrugated cardboard cremation container and on his way down the freight elevator to his final appointment.

"Say, just out of curiosity, what do these things cost?"

"Not much," the attendant said. "You're a young fella, you should give some thought to doing more cremations. You ask me, it's the way to go. You saw how crowded it is out there."

Mark nodded.

"Well, it's the same everywhere. And I don't think you're going to see too many new cemeteries going in, not with the price of land the way it is now. No sir. Well, here we are. Help me wheel him over to the second oven. She's up and ready."

They pushed the cart to what looked like a kiln and inserted Raymond F. Zimowski. The attendant secured the heavy, cast-iron door and led Mark back behind the unit.

"Care to say anything?" he said.

"How about a moment of silence? He committed suicide, but he still deserves a moment of silence."

They bowed their heads and prayed silently.

"Amen."

"Amen. Well, here goes. You can watch through that little window, if you want."

Mark went to the window and watched the blue flames engulf the cardboard casket and its contents. It was hard to distinguish much, and the noise made him think he had stuck his head in a jet engine.

The attendant tapped Mark on the shoulder, led him to his office and offered him a cup of coffee.

"You say he did himself in. I don't mean to be nosey, but I

just am interested . . ."

"He wanted to be a professional baseball player. Actually he wanted to play for the Cubs. He was all-city in high school and played some college ball. But then he started partying too much and was too fat for one of those try-outs the Cubs have. He didn't make it, so he ate more and got fatter. When he didn't make it this last time, he went in the basement and drank a half gallon of paint thinner."

"Poor kid. Say, I don't think I've seen you around before. You new in the business?"

"More or less. I graduated from Worsham in June. I own Anderson Funeral Home at 21st and Canal."

"Can't say I ever heard of it. That's all Mexican down there, isn't it?"

"Pretty much. But there're still a few Lithuanians and Poles around from the old days."

"Anderson? Don't sound Lithuanian or Polish to me."

"It's Swedish."

"Well, if you don't mind my askin', what's a Swede operatin' a funeral home in a neighborhood like that for? Your old man crazy?"

"My father's not in the business. He's an insurance broker in the Loop," Mark said.

"What?!? Your old man ain't in the business? You mean you started . . ."

". . . my own funeral home? Yeah. I know it's crazy, but so am I. Anyway, I was an intensive-care nurse at Presbyterian St. Luke's. One day I realized that I was spending a lot of time doing what you might call grief counselling. I was good at it. Better than the doctors and even most of the chaplains. I don't know what it was; I just had this knack for helping people get their grief out. I was willing to spend time with them and let them cry.

"Then one of my best buddies was killed in a car wreck a week before he was supposed to get married. I was going to be his best man. His fiancee flipped out. I mean totally flipped out. I went with her and my friend's mother to make the arrangements for the funeral. There we were, all upset and everything, and this fat old funeral director acted like he was selling us a used car.

"Didn't even have a box of Kleenex on his desk. He couldn't wait to get us into his casket showroom. You know the routine."

"Oh yeah," the attendant said.

"Well, that experience got me to thinking. The only way I could move up in nursing was to go back to school and take more chemistry classes, but I hate chemistry. So just for a joke, I called up Worsham and checked out their requirements. Didn't sound hard at all compared to nursing school, and next thing I know I'm in there having an interview with one of the counsellors. "Well, I went to Worsham, did my apprenticeship at Weinmann & Sons on the Gold Coast and the rest is history."

"Weinmann? The Jewish place?"

"Yeah, it was a real trip. But I'll tell you, I really respect the Jewish burial customs. No messin' around with the body. Especially those old Orthodox rabbis. In the ground by sundown if possible. No embalming, a simple wooden casket. I learned a lot from those people -- an awful lot."

"You don't have any family in the business? You're completely on your own?" the attendant said.

"Yeah, I know that sounds crazy, but it's true. Anyway, you were saying earlier that I should think about doing more cremations."

"You bet. You could get in on the ground floor here. I just read the other day that almost 30 percent of all California cases are cremated. And it's up around 25 percent in Florida. Just a matter of time before it catches on here. You payed $135 to have him cremated, right?"

"Yeah."

"And you would have payed about $600 for a burial here, plus the grave marker, and a vault and all the rest."

"Well, it was an unusual situation. His parents are both dead, and his sister really didn't have much time or money."

"Well, there you are. The way things are going, I don't think that's going to be so unusual. And like I said earlier, cemeteries are filling up fast."

Mark contemplated the weathered monuments.

"Look, I've got an idea, see, and maybe . . . "

They talked until the flames had reduced Raymond to three pounds of gray minerals. Then the attendant pulverized the "cremains" and swept them into what could have passed for a cookie tin.

"Here you are," he said. "Think it over. What have you got to lose? Like I say, we've got a lovely little chapel up there that's hardly ever used."

"I will."

Mark shook the man's hand and left humming a happy note.

He drove south on Clark Street to Wrigley Field and parked across from the right-field gate.

Raymond's sister Rita was waiting. She had black hair and better things to do.

"That's it?"

"Yeah," Mark said, hefting the tin. "All taken care of. How're you doin'?"

"Fine," she said, crushing a cigarette on the walk. "Let's get this over with, all right? I've got to pick up the kids and get dinner ready before the old man comes home."

"Right."

They went to the gate, and Mark asked the usher to summon Don from the ground crew. The Cubs had just lost to the Cardinals in the first of a three-game series. They had to win either Saturday or Sunday to clinch third place in the National League East. For their long-suffering fans, a third place finish was equivalent to winning three consecutive World Series.

Don came to the gate and told the usher to admit Mark and Rita.

"All right," the kid said, "but no food."

"It's not food," Mark said.

"Well, what is it?"

"Minerals. For the grass."

"Let me see."

"All right." Mark opened the tin and let the kid have a good look. "Okay?"

The kid shrugged. "Okay, go ahead. But stay with him."

Mark slipped Don a $50, and they walked through a tunnel that ended along the ivy-covered right-field wall. The sun cast a gridwork of shadows on the groundskeepers.

"Any place in particular?" Don asked.

"He wanted to play right field," Rita said. "So how about right over there?"

"All right. You wanna say anything first?"

"No," Rita said. "Just do it, all right? I've got to pick up my kids in 15 minutes."

"Okay. You two stay right there." Don took the tin and a rake and strolled into right field where he nonchalantly spread Raymond's cremains into the thick grass.

He handed the empty tin to Mark and rolled his eyes.

"Anybody see me?"

"Nope. Thanks a million, man."

"Any time."

Mark turned to give his condolences to Rita, but she had already gone to pick up her kids.

Chapter Three

"Catchin' anything, Mister?"

Mark glanced at the skinny Puerto Rican kid. "Na. Coupla perch -- salmon must be out deep today. You want this spot, you can have it."

"Thanks, Mister." The kid pulled a coil of string out of his pocket. "You got an extra hook?"

"Sure. In fact, you can have this lure. Lotta good it did me."

The kid beamed. "Really?"

"Yeah. Here, take it."

Mark turned into the northeast wind and walked away from the mouth of Montrose Harbor. The cold Canadian air refreshed his face. A lone sailboat ran with the wind, crashing through the mountainous swells. Mark went to the hearse, stowed his gear and started the engine. He was just pulling away when he saw a commotion at the breakwater. The Puerto Rican kid was hauling in a huge salmon with his string and Mark's lure.

The other fishermen egged him on, and one guy had his net ready.

Heaving with all his strength, the kid finally wrenched the great fish from the lake and into the net.

Damn, Mark thought. That's gotta be at least a 25-pounder. At least. Where the hell was that fish five minutes ago? Mark got a fresh joint out of the glove compartment, cranked up the radio and followed the wind south along Lake Shore Drive.

He got off at North Avenue and cruised through the Rush Street area thinking he might pop into one of the pick-up joints for a beer and a leer, but he wasn't in a bullshitting mood. So he took Clark Street south through the nearly deserted Loop and cut right at Archer.

He hadn't eaten since breakfast, so he went to his favorite restaurant in Chinatown and demolished two orders of steamed dumplings, an entire steamed pike in garlic sauce and a large bowl of hot-and-sour soup.

Mark burped appreciatively, got change back on his $10 and headed for Metro Livery on west Adams Street.

He was half a block away when he remembered to fill the tank. Fuck it, he thought, needle's practically on full.

"Where do you want it, Mike?"

"Leave it here with the keys in it," the old man said, struggling off his stool. "You fill it up?"

"Sure," Mark said, "I always do. What do you think I am?"

Mike poked his head in the window and peered suspiciously at the gas gauge. "Next time top it off."

He turned and shouted something in Greek. A skinny D.P. with shiny black hair appeared from nowhere and drove the hearse deep into the gloom.

"Wanna do a wedding tonight? We need one more driver."

"No thanks, Mike. I'm beat. Been a long day."

"How about tomorrow night? We got a big job -- bunch of stockbrokers or somethin' -- three limos. Could be big tips."

"All right, Mike. What time should I be here?"

"5:30 sharp. And shine yer shoes this time. Hear?"

"Yeah, sure, Mike."

Mark got in his '74 Dodge Dart and took Ashland to 18th. Then he headed east through the Mexican barrio that abutted his Eastern European enclave.

His two-flat building needed a lot more work than he could do or afford, and the local gangs often exchanged gunfire under his window at night.

But it's a start, Mark thought, passing under the Dan Ryan Expressway and turning south on Canal Street. It's a start, and the most important thing is I'm on my own.

Mark parked on the street and surveyed the swatches of yellowed siding that were peeling off his ancient two-flat. The Latin Whoevers had left their mark in black spraypaint. Together with the pigeon shit and soot, it had a pleasing postmodern look to it.

"Hey," Mark yelled to three Mexican kids sitting on the curb. "I thought you guys were gonna keep an eye on my place for me?"

"They bigger than us," one said. "What we gonna do, get killed for a coupla bucks?"

"Well, here's six bucks. How about keepin' an eye on my car for about 10 minutes. Think you can do that?"

The kids nodded and reached greedily for the money.

Mark let himself in the back way and bounded up the winding staircase.

"Goddamn it!" he screamed, tripping over a furry object on the top step.

The gray kitten mewled.

Mark grabbed it by the thick of its neck and shook it. "You guys are supposed to be killin' rats, not sleepin' on the stairs. I coulda broken my neck."

The kitten mewled again.

"All right. I know. You're hungry. I haven't been home all day. I missed you too. Where's you brother? You don't know? Come on, let's go find him."

Mark entered his apartment through the kitchen and called: "Rat patrol! Chow time!"

The other kitten bounded out of the living room.

"There you are."

Mark picked them both up and rubbed them against his face. "What about you, huh? You kill any rats today? Hmmm? I'm gonna inspect this place, and I'd better find some dead rats, or I'm gonna start cuttin' your rations."

The kittens purred and licked Mark's face.

"All right. Full rations tonight, but . . . "

The phone rang.

"Half a sec," he said, setting them down. "Anderson Funeral Home, may I help you?"

"Mark, it's Mom."

Helen Anderson sounded so distraught her son sat down.

"Hi, Mom. How're you doin?" Mark wiped his forehead and reached for a fresh pack of Marlboros.

"I've been trying to reach you all day, Dear," she said. "Didn't they tell you?"

Mark glanced at the beeper on his belt. "Those idiots. I'll have to call the service again. Sorry. I was out on a case. You sound upset. What's wrong?"

Helen Anderson's voice broke. Then she cried and said, "It's your father. He's got cancer."

Mark crushed the crush-proof pack in his hand.

Chapter Four

Mark could hear them before he turned the corner. He took a deep breath two doors away from his father's private room and plunged in.

Wearing his Marshall Field's bathrobe and slippers, Karl Anderson was seated on the edge of his hospital bed watching the University of Illinois football game with his oldest son, Jonathan.

Ever the good grandmother, Helen Anderson was coloring in the corner with her reasons for being -- cute little Kristin and even cuter little Erika. Jonathan's wife Judy was in the bathroom.

Hating to interrupt such bliss, Mark entered quietly and raised his right hand in a limp greeting.

The big man on the bed was too intent on watching his alma mater beat Iowa to respond. Jonathan waved at his little brother and motioned him away from his line of vision. He too was an Illini.

Mark had gone to the University of Illinois' Chicago campus, or "Circle." Everyone, especially Karl and Jonathan Anderson, knew that Circle was vastly inferior to the Champaign-Urbana campus.

Seeing her "baby," Helen Anderson rushed to Mark and gave him a hug and a kiss. At 57, she was still a striking woman, albeit a few pounds overweight.

"It's been so long, dear," she said, looking up at her son. "Don't be a stranger next time."

Mark swallowed. "Right. Well, anyway, uh, here I am." He turned to his father and waited for the commercial. "So what's the doctor say, Dad?"

Mom put her finger to her lips, and Jonathan shook his head.

Karl Anderson was an inch taller than Jonathan and about even with Mark, but he had his youngest son by 20 pounds.

At least he had had Mark by 20 pounds.

"What do you expect the doctor to say?" Karl said. His voice was drawn and raspy. "You bring any cigarettes, Mark? Your mother won't let me smoke." He gave her a withering look.

"No, in fact, I just quit."

"Oh, Mark, that's wonderful," Mom said.

The commercial ended, and the Fighting Illini returned the punt to the Iowa 15. Karl and his oldest boy lost themselves in the game.

Judy Anderson came out of the bathroom and greeted her brother-in-law with a wave and a smile.

"Hi, Judy. How's everything?"

"These two are running me ragged," she said, nodding at her daughters, five and three. "Just wait until you have kids."

"Sure."

"Have you called Elaine Donaldson's daughter, Wendy?" Helen asked, looking hopefully at Mark. "I promised Elaine you'd give Wendy a call. She's such a nice girl, Mark, and she's a good Lutheran."

"Mom, please."

The Fighting Illini drove to the Iowa five, making it first and goal.

"Goddamn it!" Karl said, coughing. "Would you two quit yacking over there? Can't you see we're about to score?"

"Sorry," Mark said. "Go Illini! Beat Iowa!"

"I'd like to see Circle beat Iowa," Jonathan said. "They couldn't even beat Mother MacAuley in tiddleywinks."

"No, but we're favored by six points against Our Lady of Perpetual Motion."

Horrified, Helen pushed Mark into the hall saying, "Not today, Mark, your father is very upset."

"Could have fooled me."

"That's enough."

"All right." He took her hand. "I'm sorry. But what about you? How're you doin?"

Helen Anderson gave her son her best brave look. "You know Mom."

Mark nodded. "Yeah. I'll go get some ice or something. Be right back."

Mark took the long way to the ice machine. On the way back to his father's room, he stopped at the nursing station and asked, "Who's the attending for room 273?"

"Who wants to know?" the nursing supervisor said.

"The patient's son."

The supervisor flipped through her charts. "Doctor Tiefenbach. Michael J."

"Is he here today?"

"No," the nurse said, "he's attending a conference in Baltimore."

"Great. Thanks."

"Young man?"

"Yes," Mark said, turning.

"Your father is being a little ah . . ."

"Stubborn?"

She nodded sadly.

"That figures."

"Would you try to reason with him? If he doesn't have surgery, well, I'm afraid . . ."

"I'll try. But I doubt it'll do any good."

"He practically threw the poor chaplain out of his room, and he won't discuss it with any of us. Dr. Tiefenbach wants an answer by the time he returns from Baltimore, so maybe you could . . ."

"I'll see what I can do."

"Thank you."

Mark smiled and returned to his father's room where Iowa not only had stopped the Illini drive but was now threatening to tie the game. Karl and Jonathan were pissed.

"Coffee, tea or ice," Mark said, shaking the pitcher.

"Would you shut up!" Jonathan said. "Can't you see we're in trouble?"

"Au contraire, Johnny Boy, WE'RE beating the pants off our Lady of Perpetual Motion in straight sets of tiddly. . . "

"Goddamn it!" Karl yelled. "If you're going to talk, go out in the parking lot. The Illini have to . . ." His voice broke into a long, bloody cough.

Helen scooted Judy and the little ones out of the room and went for the nurse. Jonathan shifted uneasily in his chair, and Mark went automatically to his father's side.

"You'll get more of it up, Dad, if you lean forward like this," Mark said, showing him how.

Karl was too weak to push his son away. He gestured furiously at a box of tissues on the night table. Mark handed his father a big wad and watched in horror as his father quickly filled it with bloody sputum. Karl had only switched to filter cigarettes last year.

Helen returned with the nurse, and Karl waved them away.

"I'm all right," he said between coughs.

"Are you sure?" Mark said. "The nurse is here. Why don't you let her . . ."

"Goddamn it, didn't you hear me? I said I'm . . ." He coughed uncontrollably.

"Mr. Anderson, I can give you something for that cough. I told you that before. Your doctor entered an order on your chart for it. What do you say, Mr. Anderson?"

Karl finally stopped coughing and pointed at the screen. "After the game's over," he whispered, hoarsely.

Iowa chose that moment to tie it up. Then Kristin and Erika careened back into the room wanting to play with Grandpa.

Mark stepped back and watched the ice bucket fly, seemingly in slow motion, at the television screen. For a moment he thought his father had broken the set.

"Hey," Mark said, "I've got a great idea, let's watch the Cubs game for a while? They win today, and they've got third place in the bag."

Karl stomped off to the bathroom to cough in peace, so Mark switched to Channel 9. It was bottom of the 9th, one out and the Cubs were leading 4-3. But the Cardinals had two men on and Keith Hernandez at the plate.

"Holy shit," Mark said, settling into a chair. "Come on, Reuschel, you gotta stop 'em, big guy."

"How can you root for those losers," Jonathan said. "Come on, let's turn back to the Illinois game."

Mark glared at his brother, and Jonathan backed down.

Rick Reuschel tried an inside curve that didn't break, and Hernandez smacked it toward the right-field wall. Normally it would have bounced off Sheffield Avenue, but there was a brisk northeast wind, so the ball floated high over right fielder Bobby Murcer's head.

Murcer popped down his sunglasses, shielded his eyes with his mitt, and frantically adjusted his position. He backpedaled until he was on the warning track. He caught the ball in the webbing, crashed into the vines, recovered and hurled it to first base, trapping Simmons for the double play.

The announcer Jack Brickhouse could only say, "Hey, hey, hey, hey . . ."

"Atta boy, Raymond. Way to go!" Mark shouted, appreciating that the game-winning play had occured over his client's ashes.

Chapter Five

"Hey, Pedro, pick up the pace. We've gotta be in Aurora before the end of the century," the nasal commodity broker said.

The young commodity groupie on his lap giggled and added, "Yeah, Pedro, hit the gas!"

Mark adjusted the silly black cap Metro insisted he wear and looked in the rearview mirror. There were four of them back there: the nasal jerk, the little jerk, the big jerk and Debby the Dingbat.

For five cents, I'd dump the lot of them on the Eisenhower and let them fight their way home through the West Side. Four stupid honkies against half of Africa. Bunch of . . . ah, forget it. Mark bit his lip and concentrated on the traffic. Unfortunately it was light and didn't hold his attention for long.

"Wanna snort a line, Pedro?" the little jerk said, laying a trail of white powder on Dolly's hand mirror.

"No thanks."

"You sure? This shit is 99.9 percent pure, Pedro."

"I'm sure."

The little jerk leaned forward and patted Mark's shoulder.

"I know how it is, man. Get in trouble with the company, and you're out on the street looking for a job. But, hey, relax, we're not gonna tell anybody. Are we?"

"No way," the others chorused.

Mark shook his head. "I'll take a pass. I've got a bad cold."

The commodity clowns chortled.

"Yeah sure," Dolly said. "Well, if you're not gonna party with us, turn on some tunes."

"I already told you, the radio doesn't work back there."

"Well, Pedro, I got a great idea," the nasal one said. "Why don't you crank up your radio?"

Mark bit his lip and did as he was told. Anything for a tip.

"Can't you get better reception than that?" the little one said.

"Like I said before, the antenna's broken."

The little one, who was leader because his daddy owned the firm, shook his head and said: "What kind of company are you working for anyway, Pedro? Radio doesn't work back here; antenna's broken; this thing rides like a tank; and it looks like it hasn't been washed in four months."

"Look, I just drive what they give me. Maybe if you'd write a letter to . . ."

"Back up, Pedro," the little one said, patting Mark on the shoulder, "you're getting it backwards. Service starts at the bottom -- with you. You're the company's representative, so why don't YOU tell your people to get their act together, or they're not going to get any more of our business. Hate to disappoint you, Pedro, but that's the way it works in the real world."

Mark felt his digestive enzymes sour. He took a deep breath and nodded.

"Good boy, Pedro. And so you don't forget, we're not going to give you a tip tonight," the little jerk said, smiling smugly.

The others laughed hysterically. They were soon mixing pot and a bottle of champagne with their coke.

Mark caught a whiff of the dope smoke and craved it. He cracked his window and took a hit of cool evening air instead.

"Hey, Pedro, shut the damn window. We'll tell you when we want some air-conditioning," the leader said.

Mark closed his window, cranked up the radio to full volume and drove sullenly to Aurora.

"Okay," he said, exiting the Tollway, "I need some directions now."

"Directions?!? You're a professional driver, Pedro. We're paying you good money to get us where we want to go, and you're asking us for directions? Jeez," the little one said.

"Look, pal," Mark said as calmly as he could, "nobody bothered to tell me where this place is. You said you'd show me when we got to Aurora, now you're giving me a bunch of grief. As far as I'm concerned, we can sit here all night."

The little jerk looked to his friends for support. They weren't so sure now. This Pedro guy was pretty big, and now he looked pissed.

"Well," the little one said, "why didn't you follow those other limos? You were supposed to follow them."

"As you might recall, we had to go back for your friend's purse."

Debby the Dingbat curled her lip.

The little jerk exhaled impatiently. The big galoot in the driver's seat was spoiling his fun. "All right, pull in here -- by the hotel. I'll call and find out."

While the little jerk was making his phone call, the others smoked dope, drank champagne, snorted coke and gave Debby the Dingbat a good feel. She thought it was wonderful. All she had to do was marry one of these geniuses, and she'd be set for life. It was worth having hot hands up her shorts.

The little jerk got the directions all screwed up, and it took them forever to get to their client's house in a remote subdivision.

"Wait in the car, Pedro," the little one said. "We'll let you know when we want to go."

It was cold, so Mark left the motor running and the heat on. He tipped his cap over his eyes and slumped in his seat. The other two drivers were in one of the other limos snorting coke or smoking dope or both. They waved at Mark, inviting him to join them.

Mark ignored them. He tried to sleep, but he kept seeing his stricken father behind his eyelids. Mark let the motor run until the tank was half-empty and then switched off the ignition. There was no telling where those yo-yos would want to go next, and he was in no mood for more of their complaints.

When his bladder was too full to ignore, Mark tiptoed into a sideyard and began to relieve himself. He was only down a half cup when a ferocious German shepherd bounded out of the darkness and bit his ankle.

Stuffing his dripping dingus back in his pants, Mark hissed at the snapping dog and retreated to the limo. A light went on in the living room, and an armed and frightened suburbanite peered out the window.

"Nice doggie," Mark said, backstepping into the limo. He kicked the dog away and slammed the door.

This is nuts. I'm still full, the tank is half empty, and some maniac and his killer dog want my hide. Mark was in a deep funk two hours later when the coke-crazed commodity creeps emerged from the party.

"Come on, Pedro," the little jerk said, slapping Mark's

shoulder, "let's get a move on. The night's young, and Rush Street awaits."

"Anywhere in particular on Rush Street?" Mark asked.

"We'll let you know when we get there. Just drive -- if you can."

They smoked and joked while Mark drove in silence. His bladder was full again so he stopped at the first gas station.

"Hey, Pedro," the little jerk said, "what do you think you're doing? I told you to head for Rush Street. I'm not paying you to stop for gas."

"I've gotta take a leak."

He counted to twenty after he had gone to the bathroom and got back in the limo without comment.

"If you had to take a leak, Pedro, you should have gone on somebody's bushes while you were waiting. We're the customers, remember?" the little one said.

"Right."

Mark entered the Tollway, accelerated the big, clumsy car to 60 and settled back for the long ride to Chicago.

"Hey, I thought I told you to get a move on. We want to get to Rush Street this year, Pedro. Now put the metal to the pedal. All right?" It was the little one again.

"I'll lose my chauffeur's license if I get a speeding ticket," Mark said.

"Fuck your license, Pedro. There aren't any cops out here. Now get your ass in gear, or I'll make sure you never drive another limo again. You understand?" The little twerp was full of scotch and false courage.

Mark pounded the gas pedal and had the big, black boat up to 75 before he caught sight of himself in the rearview mirror.

"Hey," the little jerk said, sensing the sudden deceleration. "I thought I told you to . . ."

Mark ignored him until they were in the heart of the West Side ghetto on the Eisenhower Expressway. Known locally as Little Africa, it was a place where the cops never slept on the job.

Mark abruptly pulled over to the shoulder at Kedzie Avenue, turned in his seat and said firmly: "Party's over, fellas. This is where you get out."

Debby the Dingbat giggled, and the commodity clowns gaped.

Finally, their fearless leader said, "Real funny, Pedro."

"Yeah, I'm a real comedian," Mark said. "You guys want to party all night, this is the place, man. The action never stops out here. And, if you get scared, there's a police station right over there. Run fast enough, and you just might make it."

Before they could respond, Mark pulled the besotted fools out of the limo and left the three terrified white boys on the asphalt.

Debby the Dingdat was so stunned she barely peeped when Mark asked her where she lived.

"With my mother, on the South Side," she said, wondering what the maniac in the front seat was going to do next. He surprised her by driving her straight home.

Mark was ready for the fat, greasy dispatcher when he pulled into the Metro garage.

"Save your breath, Jerry -- I quit," he said.

"But," Jerry sputtered, "that's a criminal offense leavin' customers on the Eisenhower like that."

"Did they make it to the police station okay?"

"Yeah, but . . ."

"Yeah, but nuthin'. And they probably got a cab from there and went to Rush Street. Nobody was hurt, and as long as we're talking about criminal offenses, what about promising customers full-service livery and giving them . . ."

"All right, all right," Jerry said, waving his beefy hand. "Just take off, and I'll think of something to tell Mike in the morning."

Mark went off whistling into the night.

Chapter Six

Mark reluctantly fed the Rat Patrol, warning them, "One more can of this crap, and then you're gonna have to start catching your own food. You guys understand?"

The kittens mewled and hungrily attacked the cat food.

Mark laughed and resolved to get some rat traps.

He went downstairs to his cramped office just inside the entrance and sorted through his bills. With the mortgage payment, phone, gas, electric, and embalming supplies, he owed $605.28. He had $143.25 in his checking account. The State of Illinois owed him $550 for three cases he had done three months ago, and Raymond's sister promised she would pay him soon. But he knew it was going to be a long time before he saw any of that money.

And after last night, he'd be damn lucky if that Greek prick at Metro ever settled up.

Mark sighed and rubbed his forehead. The bar across the street was open and already filling with aging Eastern Europeans who had just made their token appearances at Mass. Mark was halfway out the door before he caught himself.

He forced himself back to his desk and took inventory of himself and his business. It didn't take long, and the results were sobering.

I'm operating a small, unknown funeral home in a changing neighborhood; my parents think I'm nuts; I don't have any money in the bank to speak of, and those jerks won't even talk to me about another loan. The Association of Independent Funeral Directors is helpful, but they don't have any money.

Mark thought about going back to Weinmann & Sons. Old Man Weinmann liked him and said there was always work for him, but Mark wasn't going to admit defeat. Not yet.

Forgetting it was Sunday morning, Mark called information and asked for the CHICAGO SUN-TRIBUNE's number.

"Yeah, could you connect me with advertising?"

"The advertising office is closed on Sunday. If you want to place an ad, call back tomorrow morning," the switchboard operator said.

"Oh yeah, it is Sunday, isn't it. Look, uh, wait a minute, how about connecting me with one of those reporters? You know, the guys who write the paper."

"I'll ring the newsroom," the operator said.

"Newsroom," a high-pitched but husky female voice said.

Mark hadn't counted on a woman.

"Uh, hi, this is Mark Anderson. I run the Anderson Funeral Home, er, the Anderson Funeral Home AND Cremation Service at 21st and Canal, and I was . . . "

"You got an obit, call back tomorrow. You want the direct number, I'll give it to you. What's with you guys, anyway?"

There was no hiding such a strong Brooklyn accent.

"I don't have an obituary. I'm calling because I have a news story."

There was a long pause.

"A funeral director with a news story? What is this, some kind of joke? Who is this really? You one of Alderman Petrilli's creeps?"

"No. I'm Mark Anderson, and I own the Anderson Funeral Home and Cremation Service at 21st and Canal. I've got a story for you."

"You're serious, aren't you?"

"Yes."

She softened her voice. "Hey, look I'm sorry. You wouldn't believe the calls we get here. I'm Diane Roth. Nice to meet you, Mark."

"My pleasure."

"So what's your story, aside from the fact you run a funeral home at 21st and Canal? God, where is that?"

"Practically under the expressway. You know that church with the two spires you pass on the Dan Ryan just after the Loop?"

"You work there?!?"

"And live there too."

"That's a story in itself. Funeral director lives under expressway. What -- you bury 'em in the pylons?"

"Very funny. No. I'm legit, ah, Mrs. . . . ."

"Diane'll do. Sorry to be the wiesenheimer. I'm right in the middle of a big story. In fact, I thought you were somebody from

. . . look, what's your angle?"

Mark took a deep breath. "Well, first of all, when was the last time you got a call from a funeral director who was willing to talk prices over the phone?"

Diane lighted a fresh cigarette and scrolled a fresh sheet into her typewriter. "Yeah, and . . ."

Chapter Seven

Karl Anderson sat on the side of his bed fighting the cough.

Just have to control the damn thing. That's all. Can't be as bad as they say.

He saw the wastebasket full of bloody tissues.

All right, all right, I'll cut back. Half a pack a day. Maybe I'll even try those low tars. Helen'd love that. Hell, she won't be happy until I quit.

The big man got out of bed and walked to the window. He could see the run-down neighborhood where that idiot kid of his had his funeral home. Thinking about Mark made him mad. Mad enough to cough up more blood.

He was doubled over when the visitor tapped him on the back.

"Jesus Christ! You scared the shit outta . . ."

A bloody cough cut him off, and his visitor, a man every bit as big as he, helped him to the bed.

Then the visitor took a cylindrical device out of his pocket and held it against his neck.

"Having a rough time of it, aren't you, Karl?"

Karl Anderson stared at the man and his mechanical voice. He coughed some more and stared some more.

Finally, he said, "Who the . . ."

"Name's Charley Collins. I'm a volunteer from the American Cancer Society. Didn't your doctor tell you I was coming? He was the one who asked for a visit."

Collins wore gray slacks, a navy blazer and a white turtleneck. He had a friendly, weathered face that reminded Karl of Jack Hawkins.

"If you've talked to my doctor, you're doing a lot better than I am. It's nice of you to come, but I really don't think it's necessary."

Collins nodded and settled in the chair opposite Karl. "You sure? I don't have another appointment for an hour."

"Wait a minute. I don't get it. What's your angle, Mr. . ."

"Charley. Please."

"All right, Charley, what's in this for you? You get a

percentage on every one of those gizmos you sell? Or my doctor going to give you a kickback if you talk me into going through with this bunk?"

Charley Collins laughed so hard his big shoulders shook. "The wife would like that one. She's been after me for years to get some money out of the outfit that makes these things. She says I'm the best salesman they've ever had."

"Well, you are pretty good with that thing. Although it does, well . . ."

"Sound like a robot? Go ahead, it's all right. I've heard worse. Between you, me and the lamppost, it can be damned embarrassing -- walking into a restaurant and having everybody stare at you when you order. But believe me, Karl, it's a hell of a lot better than not being heard."

Karl was amazed at the feeling and inflection in his visitor's artificial voice. He almost asked to give it a try himself.

"You didn't answer my question, Charley. What's in this for you?"

Collins smiled. "Certainly not money. Although I like your idea. But can you imagine trying to get money out of a doctor? Good luck. I don't know, I feel better when I do this. And it gets me out of the house."

"I take it you're retired," Karl said.

"Going on two years. And it was driving me crazy until I started doing this."

"What kind of work did you do?"

"Believe it or not, I sold refractory bricks to steel mills. They designed a special device for me -- had extra volume. Worked great. And, I used it at home whenever I wanted to let the kids have it. Scared the daylights out of them for a while."

"Speaking of kids, ah . . ."

"Karl, the surgery is all in your neck. As a matter of fact, we had our third almost nine months to the day after I got home from the hospital. Boy, did that surprise the hell out of the neighbors. People have all kinds of crazy ideas about laryngectomees. Your doctor tells me you're in insurance."

"That's right. I'm a broker."

"You do a lot of phone work?"

"Yeah," Karl said.

"Well, there's no reason you can't continue after your surgery. In fact, there's almost no limit to what a laryngectomee can do. Except maybe swimming, but I've heard of a guy in Florida who rigged up some kind of snorkel. Anyway, the reason I'm here this afternoon is to tell you that there's life after a laryngectomy."

Karl shifted on his bed. His throat hurt like the devil, and he felt another bloody cough coming on, but it could wait. It would have to wait.

"Well, I appreciate your time. But I'm not so sure I'm going to need the whole sheebang. My doctor's been talking about this new treatment they're trying with -- I don't quite understand it, but it's something with neutrons or something. Anyway, it means I wouldn't have to lose my larynx."

"I understand, Karl. Believe me, Karl, I understand. You've got to do what you think is best. And nobody -- not me, not your doctor, no, not even your wife -- can tell you otherwise. Well, I'll just . . ."

"No, wait, Charley. I didn't mean to give you the bum's rush. In fact, if you can hang on a second, I'll get us both some real medicine."

Collins's eyes twinkled. "How'd you get away with it? They always found mine."

"Necessity is the mother of invention," Karl said, going to the bathroom. He returned with a plastic bottle. "Looks like an innocent jug of hand lotion, doesn't it?"

"Sure does," Charley said.

"Well," Karl said, filling two paper cups with scotch, "it's lotion all right, but not for your hands. Skol."

"Skol."

They sipped their scotch appreciatively. Karl was ready to offer his new friend some more, when Charley Collins had a coughing spell.

When a laryngectomee coughs, everyone listens. And watches.

Charley Collins bent forward and brought up gobs of viscous phlegm through the breathing hole in his neck, or stoma. He grabbed a handful of tissue and managed to get most of it, but some of it dripped through his fingers.

Then his face contorted and his body convulsed as another wet

Then his face contorted and his body convulsed as another wet cough coursed up his trachea.

Karl was flummoxed. Good God, he thought.

When the coughing was finished, and Collins had regained his amiable composure, Karl said, "That happen often?"

Collins nodded and reached for his electro-larynx. "Has to, or you'd choke on the stuff."

Karl downed the rest of his scotch, went to the bathroom and slammed the door.

Chapter Eight

"Mr. Anderson, what a pleasant surprise."

"The usual, John," Karl said, settling on a stool. He looked morosely at the mural behind the bar and wondered what his Viking ancestors Fritjof and Ingeborg would do.

"Live life to the fullest, goddamn it," he said.

"Beg your pardon, Mr. Anderson?" the bartender said, returning with Karl's extra-dry martini.

Karl looked fondly at the man in the gold vest. "Nothin', John. Nothin' at all. Just keep 'em coming."

The good bartender nodded and moved down the bar to tend to other members of the Swedish Athletic Association of Chicago.

At one time, the North Side club was full of vigorous Swedish-Americans. Now the most strenuous activity occured at the bar where Loop businessmen like Karl Anderson came to exercise their elbows.

Karl's inflammed throat wanted nothing to do with the martini, but Karl didn't care. He closed his eyes and forced it down. After a few sips, he got the golden glow and it wasn't so bad.

He was soon ready for another. And then another. And then another.

And then he was ready to talk.

John hovered nearby.

"Son-of-a-bitch wants to cut my goddamn throat out," Karl said.

John set a full one on the bar and said, "Why's that, Mr. Anderson?"

"Damned cigarettes finally caught up with me, John."

"I noticed you weren't smoking, Mr. Anderson."

"Don't think I'm not dying for a smoke right now. God, I'd give my right arm for one of those little bastards. Nah. Damn throat's killing me. You remember all that coughing last time I was here?"

John nodded.

"Well, the wife got on me about it, and I went in for a check-up. The family doc sent me to this specialist -- guy practically

crawled down my throat. Anyway, the long and short of it is --
I've got cancer of the larynx."

Karl hoisted the fresh drink and took a long, reflective sip.

"Son-of-a-bitch says the cigarettes did it. The cigarettes and
this stuff. Biggest bunch of bullshit I ever heard in my life.
Anyway, all these medical geniuses put their noggins together
and came up with the brilliant idea that I have to have my
goddamn larynx cut out."

Karl's throat was hurting from the booze and bitter talk, so he
paused.

John brought him a glass of water, and he downed half of it.

"Well, I don't know if you ever seen any of those sorry sons-
of-bitches, but they sound like a bunch of goddamn robots. They
cut a hole in your neck, and a couple of times a day you have to
cough through the damn thing. Most disgusting thing I've ever
seen."

John wiped the bar and coolly contemplated his customer. "So
what choice do you have, Mr. Anderson? I mean if you don't
have the surgery."

"Well, the wife threatened to leave me if I didn't have the
surgery. Can you imagine that? After all these years."

John adjusted his black-rimmed glasses.

"Well, the wife's not going to have to leave, because I'm going
to get this damn thing fixed. But I'm sure as hell not going to
have a damn hole cut in my neck!"

Karl took a swig of martini with a water chaser. That seemed
to work, so he took another.

Karl slid a $5 across the bar. "Here, John, fix yourself a fresh
one."

John nodded and went to his "special" whiskey bottle and
poured himself a shot of colored water.

The two men clinked glasses and sipped their drinks.

"Where was I, John?"

"You were saying that you had a solution, Mr. Anderson. One
that wouldn't require surgery."

"Oh yeah. That's right. Well, you see, I'm not one of these guys
who sits back and lets those damn doctors push him around. So I
did some checking around, and I found out that there's this new
procedure -- something to do with neutrons. Anyway, they do it

out at Argonne or one of those places out west. It's all still experimental, but apparently they've had some results with it. From what I hear, it's better than radiation because these little things are smarter than X-rays.

"I don't really understand it, but that's what this one doctor told me. Anyway, I asked my doctor about it, and he said it was an option. He's not pushing it because he wants all the money for himself. Says it's still in the experimental stage, but he's just saying that because he hasn't figured out a way to get a piece of the action yet.

"So the long and the short of it is, John, I told the doctor today that I'm not going to have the surgery. Told him to get me in on this neutron deal as fast as he can. I'll be good as new in no time, and I won't sound like some goddamn robot," Karl said.

Feeling a cough clawing up his throat, he swigged the water and motioned John for more. When he had the cough in check, Karl killed his martini and struggled off his barstool.

Although John had already put a generous gratuity on Karl's tab, he readily accepted the $10 tip.

"Want me to get you a table upstairs, Mr. Anderson?"

"Huh?"

"Are you dining here tonight, Mr. Anderson? I'll get a table for you, if you are."

Karl couldn't remember if he had called the wife.

"They have the smorgasbord tonight?"

"They sure do, Mr. Anderson."

"Well, then I'm staying for dinner. Nothing the wife cooks compares to that."

Karl was plodding toward the exit, when Nels Langren, the loudmouthed lawyer, brushed past him.

"Hey, Anderson," Langren said, "you see the article about your kid in the paper this afternoon?"

"No," Karl said, wondering what Langren was up to. Ever since the son-of-a-bitch moved to the North Shore, he loved to lord it over the rest of the membership.

"Well, take a look," Langren said, handing Karl the afternoon edition of the SUN-TRIBUNE.

"I don't have my glasses. Must have left 'em somewhere. Here, you read it. They probably made Johnny principal, right?"

"No," Langren said, flipping through the paper. "It's about your other kid -- the tall one."

"Mark!?!"

"Yeah," Langren said, "he got himself a nice write-up in the business section."

"Mark?!? In the business section?"

"Like me to read it for you, Anderson?"

"Sure."

Langren adjusted his bifocals and read: "Headline reads: 'Funeral home to offer prearranged cremation plan.' Then it says: 'A South Side funeral director soon will begin marketing a prearranged cremation plan for $450. Mark Anderson, owner and operator of the Anderson Funeral Home & Cremation Service, is convinced he has a viable concept because of the growing popularity of cremations.' Then it goes on to quote some cremation association about the growing popularity of cremation, and there are some nice quotes from your kid. And it's on the first page of the business section."

Langren clapped Karl on the back and extended his hand in congratulations.

Karl was stunned.

"You ought to be proud of that kid, Anderson," Langren said.

Karl looked the lawyer right in the eye. "Damn right, I am," he said. Then he turned to John the bartender and proclaimed, "Set 'em up, John. Drinks are on me."

This was met with a Viking yell and much drinking in Mark Anderson's honor.

Chapter Nine

"Anderson Funeral Home & Cremation Service. May I help you?"

"Oh my, aren't we fancy? May I speak with THE Mr. Mark Anderson?"

"Just a minute, I'll see if he's free. Whom may I say is calling?"

"Oh, just tell him it's a secret admirer who read about him in the paper the other day."

"Just a moment, please." Mark put the phone down and said, "Mr. Anderson, call on line one."

Then he picked up the phone and said, "This is Mr. Anderson. May I help you?"

"Ooooh," Diane Roth said. "THE Mr. Mark Anderson?"

"The one and only. So how's it goin', Diane?"

"I was just going to ask you the same thing."

"Well, I've had three prearrangements over the phone already. One guy's a widower -- dying of cancer. Wants to get everything taken care of now so his deadbeat relatives don't screw it up after he dies. And, I've had an invitation from a church in Hyde Park to speak to one of their adult groups. Unitarians or something. Apparently, they're real big on cremation. I was out at Graceland yesterday and got everything set up there, so things are really cooking. No pun intended."

"Sure. You sound a lot better than you did the other day when you called."

"I feel terrific. That article really did it. I don't know how to thank you, Diane."

"I bet your family's real proud of you."

"Oh yeah. They're jumpin' for joy."

"Well that's terrific, Mark. I'm really happy for you."

"Yeah. Like I said, I really appreciate what you did. If there's any way I can . . ."

"As a matter of fact there is. My Sanitary District investigation is winding down this week, so I'm looking for something new. I was thinking, maybe you could help me go after the funeral industry. What do you say?"

"You mean like point out the shysters and all that?"

"Yeah. You'd be my consultant. Sort of. But you'll be an unnamed source. You've got my word on that. You told me the other day the funeral industry is ripe for reform. You said you're one of the few funeral directors in town willing to quote prices over the phone."

"Well, I'm not the only one. My association is on the up-and-up, and Weinmann & Sons, and . . ."

"Sure," Diane said, grabbing a fresh reporter's notebook. "Look, why don't we have lunch and talk about it. I'll pick you up."

"When?"

"Half an hour?"

"Sure."

Mark looked at his faded funeral home. Half a century would be better.

"Good. So I'll see you in half an hour. You can give me the grand tour, and then we'll go have lunch in some exotic South Side restaurant. Any good places down there?"

"Chinatown's right nearby. We can pop over there. I know a place that has terrific steamed dumplings."

"Great, I'm starved."

Mark was beginning to think the Latin Beagles or somebody had abducted her when a tiny lady in spiky heels, designer sunglasses and a fox jacket rang his bell.

"Diane?" he said, staring.

Diane Roth looked up at the hunk in the doorway. "That's me," she said, pushing up her sunglasses so Mark could see her dancing green eyes.

Mark was mesmerized.

"We going to stand out here all afternoon, or you going to invite me in off the street?"

"Oh, yeah. Sorry. Come on in. Place is kind of a mess right now. I was having some remodelling done, but I ran out of money. Maybe when things pick up . . ."

"It's cute," Diane said.

"This is my office. Apartment's upstairs, and parlor's back here through these doors." Mark flicked the lights. "Not much to look at. But someday . . ."

"Mm hm. Where do you, you know, prepare the bodies?"

"Back here. Follow me. It's not very big actually."

Diane grabbed Mark's elbow. "Is there . . ."

"No customers today. Sorry."

Mark led her through the parlor and an adjacent lounge and unlocked a side door.

"You sure you want to see this?"

Diane nodded.

Mark opened the door, revealing a small, rectangular room that was dominated by a slanted stainless steel table. A stainless steel table with a sleeping kitten on it.

"Hey, you bum," Mark said, grabbing the creature by the scruff of its neck. "You're supposed to be killing rats, not sleeping in here. How'd you get in here, anyway?"

The kitten mewled. He just wanted to go back to sleep.

"Mark, you're hurting him."

"Am I hurting you?" Mark said, petting the kitten and kissing it. "Huh? You have a gripe for this reporter here?"

The kitten licked Mark's cheek and purred.

Diane smiled.

Mark set the kitten on the floor, saying, "Go find your brother, and terrorize some rats. I call them the Rat Patrol, but they're really the Snooze Patrol."

"I see you like to listen to music while you work."

"Yeah. The only way to fly."

She went to a shelf and examined a gallon bottle. "Cavity King? God, what a name. What's it for?"

"You really want to know?"

"You bet. The works."

"All right. Let's assume a case just came in. I put him or her on the table like this -- with the head on this block at the high end."

"But why embalm them in the first place? Isn't that a big rip-off. I mean you're going to rot eventually, right?"

"Absolutely. That's the whole point of my simple cremation. If the body is cremated within 24 hours after death, there's absolutely no need for embalming. Take the Orthodox Jews for example . . ."

"Tell me about them," Diane said, rolling her eyes.

"Oh, I didn't . . ."

"With an accent like mine? Come on. Actually, my family was Conservative, but my cousins were Orthodox."

"So where was I?"

"You were saying that embalming isn't necessary. But still you've got this room full of Cavity King."

"Right. If people are enlightened, then there's no reason for embalming. But you'd be surprised how many people insist on a wake. Got to see grandma off. A lot of people, like the Mexicans around here for example, like to kiss the corpse. On the lips. Can you imagine what it would be like if we didn't have embalming? You don't hear about cholera or dysentery epidemics anymore do you?"

Diane shrugged.

"Well, that's because funeral directors are providing a real public service. Plus, a lot of people die away from home. There are strict federal requirements for shipping a body interstate. And you wouldn't believe the requirements for shipping a body to Mexico."

"All right, already. So how do you do it?"

Mark walked her through the whole procedure, finishing with, ". . . so basically it's a matter of draining the body's fluids and replacing them with preservatives. On that appetizing note, how about some lunch?"

Diane clicked her pen and patted her tummy. "God, I thought you'd never ask."

*   *   *

"What do you call these again?" Diane said, wiping her mouth.

"I don't know the Chinese name, but I just call them pot stickers, because they stick to the pot."

Mark lifted a pork-filled dumpling from the steaming metal pot with his chopsticks. He dipped it in a vinegar and ginger sauce and popped it in his mouth.

"Mmmm, mighty good, eh?"

"Delicious. I was beginning to think the only thing you could eat in this town were half-pound hamburgers, pan pizza and gyros."

"Spoken like a true New Yorker."

"You think so?"

"Yeah. I could take you to some places in this town that'd really knock your socks off."

"Really?"

"Yeah."

"Yeah, but a handsome guy like you probably has all kinds of women to go out with," Diane said.

"Not really."

"You gotta be kidding. I'd think girls'd be crawling all over you."

"You want to know the truth, Diane?"

"Yeah."

"You're the first lady who's shown any real interest in what I do. Believe me, it's the ultimate turn-off."

"Well, that's their problem. Actually, I think it's fascinating. And you're so open about the whole thing. You're definitely not what I expected."

"What did you expect -- some old guy with clammy hands and a black-polyester suit?"

"Something like that."

They ate in silence for a while, enjoying the food and one another's company.

Finally, Mark said: "Look, I've been thinking about this story you want to do about the funeral industry, and I've got an idea."

"So tell me," she said.

"Well, I got this letter a couple of weeks ago, see, and . . ."

Chapter Ten

The black Electra edged to the curb at 20th and Canal.

Two figures, both in black leather jackets and dark sunglasses, emerged and walked briskly toward the funeral home at 21st Street. One man carried a black Samonsite briefcase. Both wore Smith & Wesson Model 19s on their hips. Big men with big guns.

"I think this is them," Mark said, closing the curtain. "Ready?"

His companion nodded.

"Okay, here we go."

The bell rang.

Mark's heart raced at the sight of the two heavies.

"Can I help you, gentlemen?" he said, swallowing.

The one with the briefcase nodded. "Yeah, we're from Imperial Limited. You called, remember?"

"Oh yeah. Come on in." Mark admitted them. "Excuse the mess. We're doing a little decorating. This is my wife, Bonnie, and I'm Mark Anderson."

Mark extended his hand.

The man with the briefcase gripped it tightly. "John Jurzak. This is my partner, Joe Christopher. Nice to meet you. Ma'am."

They couldn't get their eyes off the missus, a shapely blonde in a tight T-shirt and jeans with a bandanna around her forehead.

"I'd shake your hands," Mark's "wife" said in a pleasing Virginia accent, "but as y'all can see, I've got paint all over myself. Well, it's a pleasure to meet you gentlemen. If y'all excuse me, I'd like to finish this here wall."

"How about we talk right here? Make yourselves comfortable." Mark settled behind his desk. "You guys like some coffee?"

"No thanks," Jurzak said, still leering at the lady of the home, "we don't drink on the job."

His partner laughed.

"Okay," Mark said, folding his hands, "so let's get down to business."

"Excuse me, ya'll," Bonnie said, poking her head in the office.

"What?" Mark said, pretending to be annoyed.

Jurzak and Christopher didn't mind the interruption at all.

"Would ya'll mind if I put on a little music? I just can't seem to paint without it."

"Not at all," Jurzak said, removing his sunglasses. "Yeah, put on some tunes."

"Bonnie" perched an oversized portable radio on the stepladder and fiddled with the dials. Every station seemed to be playing the soundtrack from GREASE. She grimaced and kept searching until she got "Mountain Jam" by the Allman Brothers.

"That's better," she said, humming along.

Jurzak watched her paint for a while and then turned to Mark. "You said you had something for us. Let's have a look." He put his briefcase on his lap and flipped it open.

Mark nodded and opened his top drawer. He handed Jurzak a small manila envelope.

Jurzak removed his sunglasses and emptied the envelope into his hand. It contained four teeth with gold fillings. Jurzak examined each in turn with a practiced eye and various jeweler's tools.

"Eighteen karat -- all of 'em. God bless those old D.P.s. Walkin' around with goldmines in their mouths. Well, let me weigh 'em, and we'll settle up. You want cash or travellers checks?"

"Let me think for a minute," Mark said. He watched Jurzak pry the fillings out of the teeth with interest. "After I got your letter, I got to thinking. You know, we wire their jaws shut, so it's not like somebody's going to pry grandma's mouth open at the wake and notice that her fillings are missing. Besides, what does she need them for anyway?"

"That's what we figure," Joe Christopher said.

"You guys get much response from other funeral directors?" Jurzak gave him a sharp look. "Yeah, we do all right. Why?"

"Just curious. That's all. I just wondered if I was the only one, or if . . ."

"No," Joe Christopher said, "we just got a big sale from Amery and Cartwright. Can you . . ."

His partner elbowed him.

"Yeah, well, looks like you got just under 8 ounces here," Jurzak said. "If you want, we can put the money in a Swiss bank account for you."

"Nah. Actually, I would like travellers checks. If you don't mind."

Jurzak grimaced. Something wasn't right. He could smell it.

"Little trouble making up your mind, today?" he said.

Mark tried to laugh. He was about to reply when the phone rang.

"I'll get it, honey," Bonnie said. "Hello, Anderson Funeral Home & Cremation Service. Oh hi, Mrs. Anderson. Mmmm hmmm. Just fine. Sure, he's right here. Mark, it's your mother."

Mark wanted to groan. My mother. He took the phone. "Hi Mom. What's up?"

Helen Anderson was in the kitchen having coffee and cake. "Mark, who was that young lady? She acted as though she knew me. I don't believe I've met her, have I?"

"You know how Bonnie is, Mom. Look, I've got some clients in the office; can I call you back?"

"No need, dear. I just called to invite you to dinner on Sunday. I'm doing your favorite -- meatloaf and baked potatoes. Maybe you'd like to bring your, ah, lady friend?"

"Bonnie," Mark said, cupping the phone, "we have any plans on Sunday?"

Bonnie stopped painting and pursed her lips. "Why no, Sweetie, I don't believe we do."

"My mother wants us to come for dinner. That okay?"

Bonnie smiled sweetly. "That's just fine. Tell her I'll bring my famous cornbread."

"Fine, Mom," Mark said. "Bonnie's going to bring her cornbread. What time do you want us?"

"Mark," Helen said, "who's Bonnie? I've never . . ."

"Fine. We'll see you at one. Bye."

That boy is getting crazier all the time, Helen thought, staring at the phone.

The performance worked, and Jurzak handed Mark a stack of signed travellers checks, totalling $4,000.

"Five hundred an ounce sound fair to you?" he said. "That's what they were paying in New York yesterday."

"Fine. Well, gentlemen, it's been a pleasure doing business with you."

Jurzak handed him a business card. "Stay in touch. You get

some more of those old D.P.s -- and you must get a lot of 'em around here -- give us a call. Like I say, the gold ain't doin' them any good."

Jurzak and his partner smiled brightly at the missus and let themselves out. Mark went to the window and waited until their car was gone.

"Well, Sugar Pie, you get it all?"

Diane pulled off her wig and grinned. "Every last word and sneer," she said, patting the radio that concealed a taperecorder and camera. "Plus, we had two photographers across the street getting them coming and going. This is terrific!"

Mark shrugged. "Yeah, I guess."

"Hey, don't worry. I told you I'm not going to mention your name or funeral home."

"Yeah, but it's not gonna be too hard for them to put two and two together."

"Mark, you've got the press behind you. Nothing's going to happen, believe me. Besides, you've got something else to be happy about."

Mark looked up at the redhead on the ladder. "What's that -- you're going to give me a free subscription?"

"No, little old Bonnie and her world-famous cornbread are goin' with you Sunday to your momma's house."

Chapter Eleven

"Shit!" Karl said, rummaging through HIS drawer. "Goddamn it, Helen, where the hell is my lemon squeezer?"

Helen was in the dining room setting the table.

"What, Dear?"

"I said: where's my lemon squeezer? I've told you a thousand times it belongs in the front part of my drawer." Karl felt another cough coming on and rubbed his throat. When he had it under control, he said, "Would you come in here, please?!?"

Helen took one more look at her table and answered Karl's call.

Karl was in his corner, under the sign that read: "I only drink when I'm alone, or when I'm with someone." He pulled his drawer all the way out and pointed.

"Goddamn it, Helen, how many times have I told you to stay the hell out of my drawer?"

Helen took a deep breath and went to the sacred drawer. "There it is," she said, "it's right there under the screwdriver. In the back."

"What the hell's it doing there?"

He had started drinking when she went to church and was spoiling for a fight.

"How should I know? I've learned my lesson about going near your drawer. Now if you'll excuse me, I've got to make my coleslaw. The kids will be here in 20 minutes."

Karl grabbed his lemon squeezer, slammed his drawer and stomped off to his bar in the nook between the kitchen and dining room. It was afternoon now, so he made himself a scotch and water with three parts scotch and one part water.

Karl fitted half a lemon into his squeezer and juiced his drink to taste. Then he lumbered off to the den and fired up the RCA.

He was engrossed in the Bears game a half hour later when Mark and his guest let themselves in the front door.

"Mom," Mark called, "we're here."

Karl scowled and swore under his breath. Just when the Bears were starting to look like they might do something. He struggled out of his Fighting Illini chair and headed for the bar.

In her haste to greet Mark, Helen collided with her husband, spilling the remnants of his drink.

Karl was responding with murderous rage when a bloody cough choked his words. Utterly frustrated, he thrust the empty glass into his wife's hands, stomped into the powder room, and slammed the door.

Mark was showing his lady friend the portraits of grandfather and grandmother Anderson when Helen made her graceful appearance.

Helen took one look at her baby's latest infatuation and didn't like her. Too much perfume, and that red hair. Good heavens, poor dear must pay an awful lot to look that bad.

And who in her right mind would be caught dead in a clingy dress like that? Not that she doesn't have something to show, but for goodness sake, this is Beverly not some North Side bar.

"Hi, honey, I'm so glad you could come. This must be Bon . . ."

"Actually, Mom, this is Diane. Diane Roth. Diane, this is my mother, Helen Anderson."

"Oh," Helen said, taking Diane's hand.

"Pleased to meet you, Mrs. Anderson. You were right: I was Bonnie the other day when you called. And," she said, affecting her Southern accent, "little old Bonnie did bring her cornbread, just like she promised."

"Diane is a reporter for the SUN-TRIBUNE, Mom. If you can promise to keep a secret, I'm helping her do an investigation for the paper. She was at the funeral home the other day pretending to be my wife so we could fool these guys who . . ."

"That's nice, Dear. Well, let's not stand here in the living room when Dad can fix you both something to drink. Here, let me take that, Dear."

Diane handed Helen her cornbread.

Helen peaked under the foil. It was real all right.

"Why don't I pop this in the oven and warm it up for dinner. We're going to eat as soon as Jonathan and Judy and the kids get here."

"Anything we can do to help, Mom?"

"Not a thing," Helen said, leading them into the kitchen. "I don't see Dad, Mark, so why don't you fix Darlene a drink.

Everything's right there."

"It's Diane, Mom. Diane."

Helen glanced over her shoulder. "Oh, did I get it wrong? I'm sorry, Dear. You know me and names."

"Don't mention it, Mrs. Anderson," Diane said. "You should see me when I'm writing about aldermen. I can never get them straight."

"See, Mark. I'm not the only one."

Helen put the cornbread in the oven.

Mark sniffed his mother's meatloaf and rubbed his stomach.

"Smells mighty good. Wait until you get a bite of Mom's meatloaf. It's the best."

Diane wondered if she was getting involved with another momma's boy. Nobody could be as bad as Jeffrey, but she was beginning to have her doubts.

"I'm sure it'll be delicious," she said.

"Oh it will, Diane. How about a drink?"

Diane nodded.

"Bloody Mary sound okay?"

Mark had vowed to go easy on the booze today, but what was Sunday without a good bloody Mary?

Mark was just adding the celery to Diane's drink when Karl emerged from the nearby powder room, startling them both.

"Hi, Dad," Mark said, looking up from his work. "How are ya?"

"You put the vodka in first?" he said, ignoring Mark's guest.

"Dad, I'd like you to meet Diane Roth. Diane, this is my father, Karl Anderson."

Karl grunted.

"Here," he said, pushing Mark aside, "let me make the drinks. Go help your mother. She's been slaving away in the kitchen all morning."

This time Helen had some bowls to carry to the table, and he dutifully did so. Diane helped in spite of herself.

"Hey," Mark said, "want to see the backyard?"

Diane wanted to see the North Side.

"Sure, why not?"

As Mark led her through the den to the back door, Diane noticed a strange object atop the television.

noticed a strange object atop the television.

"What's that? Something you made when you were a little boy?"

"Oh, that. It's my father's. Better not let him see you playing with it. We caught hell if we even touched it when we were kids."

Diane hefted the flat-bottom model ship. "It's heavy, like it's made of wood or something. Did he make this?"

"No, it's one of those models they used in the Pentagon during World War II to plot ship movements and all that. You know, like in SINK THE BISMARK."

Diane carefully returned the cruiser to its place. "I must have missed that one, Mark. Say, didn't you want to show me the backyard?"

"Yeah. Come on."

"Oh there you are." It was Karl, and he was bearing a tray with three bloody Marys. "Now," he said, handing one to Diane, "this is a proper bloody Mary."

Diane took a sip. "Oh you're right. That's delicious." She took a second, bigger sip. "Best bloody Mary I've ever had." She raised her glass. "A toast. To the bartender."

Karl smiled, surprising his son.

Mark accepted his drink with a polite nod and took a sip. Diane was right -- it was delicious. Of course.

Karl took his drink and clinked their glasses.

"Skol."

"Skol."

"Skol."

"You like football, ah . . ."

"Get me a ticket to a Bears game, and I'll follow you anywhere," Diane said, her eyes glued to the instant replay.

They sat on the sofa, and the three of them watched the Bears blow the field goal attempt.

Then Helen appeared with bowls of pretzels and potato chips. "How are the Bears doing?"

"Lousy," Karl said, like it was Helen's fault.

"Oh. Well don't eat too many snacks. It'll ruin your appetites. I'm going to call the kids and see what's keeping them."

There was an official time out, and the screen was filled with true-life radial tire testimonials.

"Mark tells me you've got throat cancer, Mr. Anderson. How's it going?"

Mark gulped his drink swallowing an ice cube whole.

But Karl Anderson didn't mind. "Well," he said, "the damn doctor wanted to cut half my throat out, but I got him to do a little checking and he came up with this experimental program out at Fermilab."

"Really?" Diane said.

Mark pretended he had known about this bit of news all along.

"Yeah," Karl said, "something to do with neutrons or some damn thing. I don't really understand it, but then I was a business major in college. Anyway, they've got some of the best damn scientists in the country running this deal. And, there's no surgery. They get the cancer cells with these neutron things. Apparently, they're a hell of a lot more accurate than regular X-rays."

"When do you start, Dad?"

Helen stepped into the room.

"Actually, Mark, I was kind of hoping you could take Dad for his first session on Wednesday. Jonathan, of course, can't get away from school, and I'm chairman of the church rummage sale this year and . . ."

"Sure. I'll be happy to, Mom."

Karl looked tentatively at his son. "Maybe we could have lunch at the club afterwards. I'm sure I'll be ready for one of John's good stiff drinks."

Remembering that he had a business to run, Mark was about to beg off when his brother and his family burst through the front door.

Chapter Twelve

Karl ate little and drank much as the noisome dinner unfolded around him.

Helen and Judy prattled endlessly about all the young women they knew who were having babies. Diane chafed to change the subject, but there was no detering the fertile females from matters of maternity.

When they had utterly exhausted the subject, Judy asked Diane for her cornbread recipe. When Diane finished reciting it, their interest in the childless woman ended.

Jonathan followed with an endless explanation of the new teacher evaluation program he was designing.

Then it was time for Kristin to talk about her new tooth and for Erika to bring everyone up-to-date on Sesamee Street.

Bored beyond belief, Diane wondered why Mark wasn't asserting himself. The guy had just had a big write-up in the paper, and no one had said one word about it. Not one word. No one had asked him about his business. Nothing. Like he was invisible or something. She glanced at him. He had been drinking steadily since they arrived, and now he was on his third glass of wine. The booze had given him a glazed look and a forced smile.

"Say," Diane said, "anyone see the write-up Mark got in the SUN-TRIBUNE?"

Silence. Then everyone stared at Mark as though he had just materialized.

Karl shifted in his chair and gulped the last of his scotch and water.

Oh good, Diane thought, somebody read the article.

"Goddamn Japs got just what they deserved," Karl said, staring into his drink.

"I beg your pardon, Mr. Anderson."

"I said those goddamn dirty little yellow bastards got just what they deserved!"

Even Kristin and Erika stopped fidgeting and fighting. "Mr. Anderson, I don't see what . . ."

Mark grabbed her arm and shook his head.

Karl continued: "All these goddamn liberals running around saying we shouldn't have dropped the A-bomb on those dirty little Jap bastards. Christ Almighty, do you have any idea how many American boys would have been killed if we had had to go through with the invasion?"

"Didn't you say that they didn't expect the first five waves to make it past the beachhead, Dad?" Jonathan said.

"Damn right. And for what? So a bunch of goddamn dirty little yellow Jap bastards wouldn't get blown up. You think they gave a goddamn about us when they bombed Pearl Harbor? You think they gave a goddamn when they forced those poor bastards on the Bataan death march. Goddamn dirty little Jap bastards got just what they deserved. I'd do it again in a second. In a goddamn second!"

"Mr. Anderson, I happen to be one of those liberals you were talking about. And I don't think it was necessary to vaporize Hiroshima and Nagasaki. The Japanese were putting out peace feelers to . . ."

"Bullshit," Karl said, slamming the table so hard the dishes jumped. "That's the biggest bunch of bullshit I ever heard. Those dirty little bastards would have fought to the last man, woman and child to defend that goddamn island of theirs. Look what happened on Okinawa."

"I assume you were there, Mr. Anderson. In the Pacific I mean."

"I would have been. I had orders . . ."

"I see. But you never actually served in the Pacific."

"He served in the Pentagon during the war, Dear," Helen said. "He was what you might call a desk pilot."

But Karl wasn't down for the count. He faked with a half-real cough and said, "The reason I didn't serve in either the Atlantic or the Pacific wasn't because I didn't want to, it was because of those goddamn kikes who ran the Bureau of Personnel."

Mark dropped his fork. "For your information, Dad, Diane is Jewish."

"It's all right, Mark," Diane whispered.

"No, it's not all right," Mark said, standing. "Apologize! Now!"

Karl waved his empty glass at his wife. "Get me another drink, goddamn it."

"Let's go," Mark said, taking Diane's arm. "Thanks, Mom. It was a wonderful dinner. Judy, Johnny. Kristin, Erika."

Mark walked past his father without word.

When they were gone, Karl had a real coughing attack and stormed off to the upstairs bathroom where he remained for a long time.

Chapter Thirteen

"I'm really sorry," Mark said as they sped away from his parents' house.

"You should apologize to yourself for not standing up to him sooner. Why did you . . . ."

"Diane, he practically called you a dirty Jew. You mean that didn't bother you? It sure as hell bothered me," Mark said.

"Of course it bothered me. But I can fight my own battles, Mark. It may surprise you, but anti-semitism is nothing new to me. But what does bother me is how you could sit there and let him go on like that. I don't know if I should be saying this. I mean, I hardly know you, and . . ."

"No, go ahead. I want to hear what you have to say."

Mark turned right on Longwood Drive and pointed to the mansions lining the ridge. "Nice, huh?"

"Yeah, real nice," Diane said. "You want to hear what I have to say, or you want to give me a guided tour?"

"I want to hear what you have to say."

Diane took his hand. "I like you, Mark. I like you because you're for real. You're not one of those empty suits I always seem to find. You know what you want, and you try to get it.

"At least that's what I thought until you got in front of your family. It's like you were an entirely different person when you walked into that house."

Mark chewed his lip and drove.

"Mark, I liked you from the minute you phoned that first time. You were so cute I wanted to reach through the phone and give you a big hug. I wouldn't have come down here today if I didn't like you. If I wasn't interested."

"I'm glad, because the feeling's mutual."

"Good. So I can tell you what I think?"

"Of course," Mark said.

"All right, here goes. Mark, you haven't left home. You're . . ."

"Bullshit!" Mark said, gripping the wheel. "I live at 21st and Canal for Christ's sake. I've got my own business.

"I've done it all. . ."

"I'm not your mother, Mark. And you're not your father. You don't have to talk to me like that." Diane withdrew her hand and looked out the window.

"I'm sorry, Diane. You did't deserve that."

"No, I did't. You know, you sound just like your father when you're mad. Just like him."

Mark accelerated down the entrance ramp, deftly working the three-speed manual transmission.

"So what makes you such an authority on all this, Diane?"

"You really want to know?"

"Yeah."

"Years of psychotherapy."

"You went to a therapist?" Mark said.

"I still do on occasion. The woman saved my life. After Jeffrey and I split up, I was a real mess. I was all set to move back in with my mother until I started seeing Elaine."

"Elaine?"

"My therapist. She absolutely forbid me from moving in with Mother. She's helped me through a lot of difficult stuff. I'd be happy to give you her . . ."

"Nah. I can take care of my own problems. Anyway, what am I supposed to do, Diane? Never see my parents again or what?"

"That's not what I'm saying, and you know it. All I'm saying is there's a wonderful, talented guy in there, and I didn't see him once while we were at your parent's house. It was like you weren't even there, Mark."

"I was there when my father said . . ."

"Yeah, you were there then, but where were you the rest of the time?"

Mark chewed his lip.

"Ground control to Mark. Hey, it's me, Diane. Friend."

"Sorry. I don't know. I think you're right, Diane. I don't know. I've never really talked to anyone about this before."

Diane took his hand. "Talk to ME about it. I'm a good listener."

"OK. But let's go to the zoo or something. It's a such beautiful day."

"How about if we go to my apartment and talk?"

Chapter Fourteen

"About Sunday," Karl Anderson said, staring at the East-West Tollway.

Mark glanced at his father.

"It was the booze talking. 'Nuf said." Karl squeezed Mark's knee. "All right?"

"All right, Dad. All right."

"Good," Karl said, "good."

They didn't say another word until Mark was exiting at Illinois 59.

"What the hell are you doing?"

"Taking you to Fermilab," Mark said.

"Then why are you getting off here?" Karl put on his bifocals and opened his briefcase. "Says right here to get off the Tollway at Farnsworth Avenue. That's the next exit."

"Dad, I've been here before. Believe me . . ."

"What were you doing here?"

"I wanted to look at the buffalos."

"Buffalos? What the hell are you talking about?!?"

"You'll see. That's why I want to get off here. You can see them when you come in the front way."

"All right, but if we're late, I'll . . ."

"Dad, we're a half-hour early. Don't worry. Trust me."

There was a herd of bison, but Karl Anderson was not impressed. Nor was he impressed when he was not immediately treated.

"Goddamn it, they said I'd be in and out of here like that. What the hell kind of three-ring circus are they running out here anyway?"

"Dad it takes them time to set up. It's not like they . . ."

"How the hell do you know?" Karl said, getting up and pacing.

"Dad, this is one of the top research facilities in the world. It takes time to set up precision equipment."

Karl found an old SPORTS ILLUSTRATED and gave it his divided attention.

The treatment room was finally ready, and an aide took Karl

away for his subatomic bombardment.

"How long's he going to be?" Mark asked her when she returned.

"Since this is his first time -- probably 40 minutes. Maybe 50. Next time it'll only take between 20 and 30 minutes."

"Do you really think this is going to help him? His doctor wanted him to have surgery, but he got freaked out. He's really counting on this."

"Are you his son?"

"Yeah, how'd you guess?"

She smiled. "It's pretty obvious."

"I'm Mark. Nice to meet you, Hazel," he said, reading her badge.

"Well, Mark, I'd love to tell you that he's going to be cured when he walks out of that room, but I can't say that. We're dealing with cancer, and I . . ."

"Look, I don't want to keep you from your work. I think I will take that walk after all. I'll be back by 11:30. Thanks, Hazel."

Hazel nodded. When the patient's son was gone, she dried her eyes.

Chapter Fifteen

"Mr. Anderson, what a pleasant surprise. And I see you've got one of the boys with you today."

"Yeah," Karl said settling on a stool. "You remember John don't you, Mark?"

"How are you?" Mark said, sitting next to his father.

"Very good, sir."

It had been a long, silent ride in from Fermilab, and the Anderson men were in need of drink.

"Well, now that we've dispensed with the formalities, let's get down to business. What'll you have, Mark? This is on me."

For a crazy moment, Mark wanted to say just a Coke, or a tonic and lime or even a glass of water.

"Got any Jameson's today, John?"

"Jameson's," Karl said, making a face. "You're going to drink that Irish crap when you can have anything you want?"

"I like it, Dad. All right?"

Karl shook his head. "All right. John, give the boy what he wants. I'll have the usual."

"You want yours neat or on the rocks?"

"On the rocks," Mark said. "With a splash."

"I don't get it? Irish whiskey? Where in God's name did you develop a taste for Irish whiskey? Damn stuff tastes like pine tar."

"It's an acquired taste, Dad. What can I say -- I like it. All right?"

John soon returned with Karl's extra-dry martini and Mark's Irish and water.

Karl inhaled the intoxicating aroma. "Ahhh. I've been looking forward to this all day. Well," he said, clinking Mark's glass, "here's looking at you."

Mark lifted his glass and contemplated the golden mist rising around the ice cubes. One drink, remember. One drink.

"To your health, Dad."

"Skol."

It wasn't long before John served them another round. And

another. And another.

"They have the smorgasbord tonight, John?" Karl said.

"They sure do, Mr. Anderson. Would you like me to reserve a table for you?"

"Like to join me for dinner, Mark?"

"Huh?"

"I said: would you like to have dinner here? They have the smorgasbord tonight."

"The smorgasbord, huh? I kind of wanted to get back and take care of some things, but I suppose they can wait until tomorrow. Twist my arm."

"They've got fresh salmon tonight," John said.

"Sold," Mark said. "Dad, can you excuse me for half a second."

Mark went to the phone booth and dialed his service.

The young woman said: "All clear. Ooops, wait a minute. Yes, you did have a call at 2:30 from, um, another girl took it. Let's see, I can't read her writing very well. Imperial something or other. That ring a bell?"

"What? Imperial who?"

Then it hit him. Imperial Limited -- those creeps who bought dental gold from funeral directors. What the hell did they want? Diane had promised that he wasn't going to be mentioned in the story. Besides, she said the damn thing wasn't going to run for another couple of weeks.

"They leave a message?"

"Uh, yeah. Let's see: 'Nice article, kid.' I think that's it. Does that make sense?"

Mark staggered. "Yeah. Yeah, that makes a lot of sense. They leave a number?"

"No."

"That was the only call?"

"The only one."

"Look, I'm going to be out for the rest of the evening. If they call again, tell them I'm out of town, okay?"

"Yes, sir."

Mark cradled the phone and started to dial Diane's direct number at the SUN-TRIBUNE. He was going to tell that goddamn bitch where to get off, but then he realized maybe he should look at a paper first. He took a deep breath and wobbled out of the phone booth. Maybe John had a paper behind the bar.

But it wasn't necessary to ask because Nels Langren, the loud-mouthed lawyer from the North Shore, had already spread an afternoon edition under Karl's nose.

"That damn kid of yours must have one hell of a PR man, Anderson. That's all I can say," Langren said.

Karl had been itching to get back to the Pacific and settle the score with those dirty little Japs when Langren butted in. So he wasn't impressed with the front-page expose that featured a large photo of two shady characters leaving his son's funeral home and the screaming headline: "DEATH MERCHANTS DEAL DENTAL GOLD."

Mark appeared silently behind his father's shoulder and gazed disbelievingly at the SUN-TRIBUNE. Mark closed his eyes tight and massaged them. When he opened them, the incriminating photograph was still there.

"Holy shit!" he said.

"Well, what do you know?" Langren said, turning around. "It's Mr. Publicity himself. John, fix this young man a drink. Whatever he wants. On me."

"Thanks, Mr. Langren," Mark said.

"What's this 'Mr. Langren' stuff? It's Nels to you, my young friend. Who the hell does your PR, anyway? God, this is dynamite, kid. First you get that write-up in the business section, and now you get your funeral home plastered all over the front page. Who're you screwing over there?"

"Nobody, Nels."

Langren slapped Karl's back. "You oughta be damned proud of this kid of yours, Anderson. Front page! Jesus H. Christ! We pay our goddamned PR firm three grand a month, and they can't even get us in the want ads. Jeez. You oughta be damned proud."

Karl glanced at the paper and grunted. He sipped his drink. Then he said: "That's nothing. You should have seen the write-up I got when I was in high school. I was a lifeguard at Foster Avenue Beach and . . ."

As his father blithered on and on, Mark got madder and madder. But instead of confronting dear old Dad, he quietly excused himself and called Diane Roth.

"Mark," she said, glad to hear from him. "It ran a little sooner than I thought, but everything came together yesterday. God, I couldn't believe it when I found out those guys from Imperial are on the police force. I just wrote the second-day story about how they're being suspended and . . ."

"Diane you plastered my funeral home all over the fucking front page! You said you were going to keep me out of the story! You promised you were . . ."

"Mark, I'm sorry. I told layout not to run a picture with your funeral home in it, but somebody goofed. I'm really sorry. But you're not in the story. Just like I promised. Have you read it?"

"I don't have to read it to see that goddamn picture on the front page with 'Anderson Funeral Home' as plain as day. Those guys are already callin' me," Mark said.

"Really? What did they say?"

"I'm afraid it won't make much of a story. Just that they liked the article. But maybe they'll kill me, and take all my fillings and then you'll really have a story."

"Mark, that's not funny, and you know it. Nobody's going to hurt you. Those guys are in so much trouble right now every reporter in Chicago is going to know everytime they sneeze."

"Great, you guys can all beat them over the heads with your notebooks if they come after me. Shit!"

"Mark, what's wrong? Did you talk to your father today?" Mark emptied a gutterful of obscenities into the phone. When he was spent, Diane Roth was long gone.

Chapter Sixteen

Karl Anderson and his youngest boy took their drinks into the oak-trimmed main dining room and settled under a stained glass window emblazoned with the crest of the family's native province, Varmland.

Mark looked longingly at the burgeoning smorgasbord. Christmas in October.

Karl crooked his finger at Ingrid the waitress and ordered two bottles of Pripps Swedish beer. "Nothing like a cold beer and good food," he said.

"Right, Dad."

As practiced Swedish-Americans, they made three trips. They heaped their first plates with anchovies, pickled herring, beet herring, various salads, cheese and hardtack. Then the heavy stuff: Swedish potato salad, smoked salmon, a jellied veal loaf called Sulta, tongue, baked ham, cold cuts, shrimp, jello, fresh fruit and limpa bread.

They filled their third plates with Swedish meat balls, brown beans, potato sausage, turnips with mashed potatoes, barbecued ribs and, of course, more herring.

When they returned to their table, Ingrid had thoughtfully provided them each with a glass of ice-cold Aqua Vit.

Karl lifted the potent liqueur and said, "Skol."

Mark klinked his father's glass and downed the firewater in a gulp. As he hoped, it instantly obliterated any and all remorse over his phone conversation with Diane. Ingrid refilled their glasses, and they toasted again. Another shot of the anis-flavored potato liqueur, and Mark Anderson had no recollection of his phone conversation with Diane Roth. For that matter, he had no recollection of Diane Roth.

They ate in silence, subconsciously racing to clean all three plates first. It took them three Pripps and two Aqua Vits to do it, and Karl outpaced his son by two forkfuls.

He stiffled a belch and motioned for Ingrid to remove his empty plates.

"Are you finished?" she asked Mark.

"I don't think I'll ever eat again. Please. I can't eat another bite."

Ingrid clucked maternally. "I hope you saved room for dessert."

Mark looked guiltily at the plump woman in the silly Swedish costume. "Of course."

"Some coffee with your dessert?" Ingrid said.

Mark groaned and waved his hand.

"I know what you need," Karl said. He winked at Ingrid and she toddled off to the bar.

Karl settled deep in his chair and contemplated the hand-tooled copper lighting fixtures.

Reeling from the flood of food and alcohol, Mark closed his eyes. The room spun madly. He blinked, and it stopped. But it started as soon as he closed his eyes again.

"I think I will have that cup of coffee," Mark said when Ingrid returned from the bar.

She set a crystal glass before each man. "Mr. Anderson? Would you like some coffee too?"

Karl made a face.

Mark looked at his drink. "What is it?"

"I thought you were a man of the world. You mean to tell me you don't recognize a stinger when you see one?"

"A stinger? What's in it?"

"White creme de mint and brandy. Best after-dinner drink you can get. Skol."

Mark klinked his father's glass and took a sip. The old man was right: this was dynamite. Mark took another big sip. Who the hell needs dessert when they're serving this stuff?

"You kids have got to take better care of your mother," Karl said.

"Beg your pardon, Dad."

Karl grabbed Mark's wrist. "I'm not going to be around forever, you know, and . . ."

"Dad, don't talk like that. Those treatments are going to work. You'll be as good as new in no time."

Karl shook his head.

"Well, we'll see. But whatever happens to me, I want you kids to take better care of your mother. That woman works and slaves for you kids. She's picked up after you, nursed you when you were sick, and now she's lucky if she even gets a goddamn Mother's Day card from you.

"Best goddamn mother a kid could have, and you don't even have the goddamn decency to call her. Works and slaves for you goddamn kids, and you don't have the goddamn decency to call her. That woman . . ."

Karl worked variations on this theme for 20 minutes and would have continued indefinitely if Ingrid hadn't interrupted.

"Phone call, Mr. Anderson. It's your wife," she announced.

"Oh shit!" Karl said, looking at his watch. "I told her I was going to be home for dinner. You go talk to her. Tell her I'm on my way."

"She's your wife, Dad," Mark said. "You talk to her."

Chapter Seventeen

"Dad, I'd be happy to give you a ride home."

"I said no," Karl said. "Now if you'd hurry, I can catch the 6:54."

Mark hurried.

"Dad, I don't think I'm going to be able to drive you on Friday. I've got . . ."

Karl struggled out of the car, coughing as he went. "I don't know how the hell you can drive with the seat so far up. And don't worry about Friday. Your mother said Judy can take me."

"Oh, maybe the kids could go along and look at the buffalos. Well, look, Dad, I, ah, thanks for today. I really . . ."

Feeling a coughing attack coming on, Karl grunted and stomped off to catch the train.

Mark watched his father disappear into LaSalle Street Station and wondered if he was going to cry at the funeral.

He exhaled and watched the riffraff roll along Van Buren Street. Van Buren Street was so seedy -- even in broad daylight. Mark pulled into a parking spot, ignored the meter and went into the first available gin mill, THE LAST STOP BEFORE HOME.

It stank of stale beer, urine and sweat. The few patrons were all men and all down on their luck.

Mark bellied up to the bar and ordered a shot and a beer.

He drank three rounds, ignoring everyone but the jerk in the mirror.

Mark swilled the last of his beer and stumbled out without leaving a tip.

He walked three blocks in the wrong direction before he vaguely remembered that the car was the other way. He was startled by a passing elevated train and cursed at it. A pair of black jackrollers sized him up from a doorway, and he glared menacingly at them, hoping they'd try something.

They took him for a crazy honky and decided to wait for easier prey.

Despite the coolness of the evening, Mark was sweating profusely when he reached his car. He fumbled frantically for five minutes before he realized he had left the keys in the ignition. He was about to kick the window in when he tried the door and found that he had forgotten to lock it.

"Shit! Some asshole coulda stolen this fucking car."

He considered taking a cab home then decided he could drive.

He found a bag of pot and some rolling papers. After spilling more than he rolled, Mark got a huge, sloppy joint together and lighted it with a match from the Swedish Athletic Association.

A seed crackled and popped and landed on his white shirt, burning a big hole over his heart. Mark swatted clumsily at the brush fire, cursing and shouting. When the fire was out, he took a series of big hits and found first gear. But he popped the clutch out too fast, and the Dart lunged into the middle of Van Buren. He tried again with the same results.

Blue lights revolved suddenly in his rear mirror, startling him. Mark snuffed the joint in the ashtray and got out of his car.

He straightened his tie, popped a dinner mint in his mouth and walked slowly and steadily to the police car.

"Problem, officer?"

"I was just going to ask you the same question. Let's see your license."

"Oh sure," Mark said, patting himself down. "Here."

"What are you doing on Van Buren at this hour, Mr. Anderson?"

"Actually, my father has cancer, see, and I was dropping him off at the train station. I took him for this new kind of treatment out in the 'burbs, and we just had dinner."

"Looks like you might have had a few drinks with dinner."

"A few. But I'm okay. Really. I just live a mile or two from here -- at 21st and Canal. I'll be all right. Really."

The patrolman looked at Mark's license, at Mark and at Mark's license again.

"You promise you'll go straight home?"

"Scout's honor."

"All right, Mr. Anderson. Here's your license. Remember, straight home."

Mark nodded grimly and replaced his license. "Straight home."

He returned to his car, said a short prayer, and gave his full attention to getting underway. He got it right this time, and joined the patrolman at the next stoplight. Mark waved and nodded.

The officer nodded back and mouthed: "Straight home."

Mark nodded again and gave the OK sign with his right hand.

When the light changed, he turned south on Wells and drove like a responsible citizen until the squad car had disappeared west on Van Buren.

Then Mark found himself along for a wild, lurching ride through the nearly deserted central business district. Coming in and out of a blackout, he wondered who was driving. Not that it really mattered because everything was just fine.

Fine until another one of those damned elevated trains scared the daylights out of him.

"You motherfucker!" Mark screamed, turning left on Lake Street in hot pursuit. He chased the train through three red lights, dimly aware of the blaring horns and startled curses. He overtook the train at Ashland and let out a victory yell.

"I win, asshole. I win!"

But the victory was short-lived for he passed out just as he paralleled the infamous Henry Horner public housing projects. Mark smiled dumbly as the windshield rushed to meet his forehead.

*   *   *

Mark awoke with a hacking cough and a splitting headache.

After Mark passed out, the car had caromed off a pylon and climbed the foot-and-a-half curb. Now it was perched at a steep angle with the two left wheels planted on the street and the right wheels suspended over the sidewalk. Mark was slumped by the door.

"God!" he said.

There was a bloody star in the windshield, directly over the steering wheel.

Realizing he was across the street from a public housing project, Mark was sure he had hit a little black kid.

He got out and looked around. No body. Nobody. Too cold.

He guessed he was lucky, but he was still too drunk to think much of it. Plus, there was that splitting headache.

Where the hell did that come from?

Must have been that Aqua Vit.

Mark rubbed his forehead and found the thick crust of clotted blood.

"Please, God, just get me home. I'll do anything. Anything. I promise."

Mark managed to get his car started, but he wasted ten minutes trying to get it down off the curb. Then, with the muffler hanging half off, he roared west on Lake Street for three miles before he realized he was going the wrong way.

Trailing a shower of sparks and sounding like a dragster, he found an entrance ramp and followed the Eisenhower Expressway east toward the Loop. He rolled down his window and stuck his face in the blast of cold air everytime he felt faint.

A black pimp in an Electra wanted to race him, but Mark just wanted to get home alive.

"Go ahead and kill yourself sucker," he said, slapping his face to stay awake.

Mark weaved and dodged his way through the infamous "Spaghetti Bowl" interchange and was surprised and grateful to finally be gliding down the Canal Street ramp.

He parked on the street alongside his funeral home and switched off the ignition.

"Pffffeeewww," he said, letting his spinning head fall back over the seat.

Mark rubbed his face and took several deep breaths. He snatched the keys out of the ignition and plodded toward his back door. Then he remembered the heavies from Imperial and the SUN-TRIBUNE article.

Certain they were waiting inside, Mark crouched to the front entrance. He was sure the door had been jimmied.

He let himself in as quietly as he could and crept to the corner where he kept his one weapon -- a lead-filled baseball bat. Thus armed, he tiptoed into the darkened parlor. He stumbled, startling someone or something.

Mark swung the bat with all his might.

There was a howl and then silence.

Mark rushed to the wall and fumbled for the light switch. Then he dropped to his knees in horror. He had crushed one of his kittens. He lifted the dying animal and held it against his face.

"I'm so sorry," he said, "I'm so sorry."

The other kitten fled for its life.

"Oh my God. Help me. Please. Please help me."

This time he really meant it.

Chapter Eighteen

Mark was tethered to a stake and Indian squaws were stacking faggots in a circle around him. The chief gestured and the squaws lighted the dried wood. Mark curled into a ball to keep the blistering heat from his face and chest.

Then the thick smoke enveloped him and he awoke coughing. Grateful that it was just a dream, he vowed to stop reading those books about the depredations of the Iroquois.

Mark coughed again and realized the smoke was real. His smoke detector was blaring away just as advertised.

Mark lurched drunkenly out of bed and went to open his bedroom door. The knob seared his hand. Black smoke billowed in around the edges. Then the first of many flames jumped in, trapping him.

He put his pillow over his face and paced frantically. Then he got his wits and threw his chair through the window. He scrambled out on the ledge, cutting his hands and legs on the jagged glass.

"Saltar, señor! Saltar!"

Mark looked down at the crowd forming on Canal Street.

"What?"

"Saltar -- jump!"

He heard sirens rushing toward him and decided to wait, but then a fireball blew into his bedroom nearly knocking him off the ledge. Mark dropped 20 feet, landing too hard on his left ankle.

His neighbors grabbed him and pulled him away from the inferno that had been the Anderson Funeral Home and Cremation Service.

Chapter Nineteen

"You the owner?"

The paramedic was almost finished dressing Mark's hand.

"Yeah, and who might you be?"

"Inspector McCaskey. Bomb and Arson Squad."

"Bomb and Arson?"

"Fire department called us in. Said your place smelled like a kerosene factory. They didn't find the can, but whoever did it wanted to make sure that you knew. You got any enemies ah, Mr., ah . . ."

"Anderson. With an 'o.' Mark Anderson. Enemies?"

"Yeah, you know, dissatisfied customers -- that sort of thing."

Mark stared woodenly at the smoldering shell of his funeral home.

"Well, Mr. Anderson?"

"What?"

"Do you have any enemies? Anyone mad enough at you to have torched your place like this?" McCaskey produced a small spiral notebook and pen.

Mark was about to reply when he spotted her. She had been hovering nearby all along, but now she had stepped under the streetlight and he could see the shock of red hair protruding from the snap-brim cap. She wore a tan raincoat and had her notebook ready too.

"No," Mark said. "No, I can't think of anyone who would do a thing like this."

"You sure," McCaskey said. "What about that story in the SUN-TRIBUNE. You have anything to do with . . ."

"Look, Inspector, I told you: I don't have any enemies. I run an honest business here. I even try my best to get along with the local gangs. In fact I did a funeral for one of their leaders. So to answer your question, no I don't have any enemies, and I don't know who would do a thing like this. Look, I'm sorry to talk like this, but I'm upset, okay?"

"I understand. Just a few more questions, and I'll let you go."

When Inspector McCaskey finished his interrogation, Mark

tried to get around Diane Roth without talking to her.

She cut him off.

"Mark, for God's sake, it's me, Diane."

He gently pushed her aside, saying: "I have nothing to say to the press."

"Mark wait. Please. Mark -- you can stay with me tonight. Mark . . ."

Ignoring her, Mark went to the Salvation Army canteen truck and said to a volunteer: "I'm the guy who owned this mess. You guys got a place I can stay for a night or two?"

"Sure. Why don't you have a cup of coffee, and as soon as we finish serving all these firemen, we'll take care of you."

Mark cupped the coffee under his nose and inhaled the aroma, hoping it would sober him up. It didn't.

"Mark, would you please talk to me?" Diane said, joining him.

"About what? How the power of the press is going to protect me from those guys? Isn't that what you said -- that I shouldn't worry, because your almighty paper was going to protect me? Well, where the hell was your big, bad paper when I almost got burned alive ? Huh? Are you getting this all down?"

Diane put her notebook in her pocket. "Why didn't you tell that cop who did it?"

"I don't know they did it."

"Yes you do."

"No I don't."

Diane sighed. "Mark, would you please come and stay with me tonight. You can take a nice hot bath and sleep in my bed. I know you're upset, but . . ."

"Upset? Me? Shit. No, I'm not upset. I just get my goddamned business burned down around me because of your stupid fucking newspaper, and you think I'm upset. No, Diane, I'm not upset. No way. I just don't ever want to see you again. You understand?"

Diane gasped. "All right. If that's the way you want it. But . . ."

"That's the way I want it."

Chapter Twenty

"Mom, believe me, I'm all right."

"Well, why don't you come down here and stay for a few days. As long as you want. The bed's still in your own room, all I have to do is put some clean sheets on it, and . . ."

"Mom, I'm 27 years old."

"I know, Dear, but I still think you should stay here until things get settled."

"Thanks, Mom, but things are fine here. Really, they are. Look, the reason I was calling was to talk to Dad about the insurance. Is he there?"

"He's in back watching the golf. Just a minute, I'll get him. Mark?"

"Yes?"

"You're sure you won't come and stay here. It would mean so much to your father and I. This has been so hard on him, and, well, I know he'll never say it, but he does miss you."

"I know, Mom. And thanks, but I've really got to get on my own two feet."

"Well, if you change your mind, your . . ."

" . . . bed is always ready. Thanks, Mom."

"I'll get Dad. Hold on."

A muscular, young black man stepped up behind Mark and jiggled the change in his pocket. "How long you gonna be man?"

"Just a second or two." Mark felt his face flush.

"Sign says calls can't go no more than five minutes. You been here at least six."

"Look, I'm almost -- hello, Dad? Hi, Dad. Yeah, yeah, I'm fine. Look, the reason I'm calling is about the insurance money. I was wondering if you . . ."

Karl set down his drink. "You're damned lucky I could find a company to write a policy for a dump like that. Especially in that slum."

"Dad, what about the claim? Are they going to pay me, or aren't they?"

Karl took a swig of scotch. "There was a rider on your policy. Standard stuff."

"Yeah. And?"

"They don't pay in the event of arson."

"But it hasn't been proven yet. They're still investigating."

"Newspapers say it's arson, and that's good enough for the insurance company."

The black dude tapped Mark on the shoulder and said: "Come on, man, this is the only phone. I gots a lots of calls to make."

"Look, Dad, I've got to go. Uh, how are you feeling? How are the treatments going?"

"Lousy."

"Oh. Well, maybe things'll take a turn for the better. Uh, well, I guess . . ."

A voice crackled over the ancient PA system: "Attention in the building; attention in the building: the AA meeting will begin in five minutes in room 202."

"Come on, man," the black dude said. "I gots to get a hold of my old lady before that damn meeting starts."

"I didn't know we had to go to AA meetings here," Mark said to the black dude.

"What?" Karl said. "What are you talking about?"

"Huh? Oh, I was talking to somebody here, Dad. Look, I've really got to go. I'll call you in a day or two. Take care."

"Want to talk to your mother again?"

"No. Tell her I'll call in a day or two when I get settled. Take care, Dad."

Karl grunted and hung up.

"Phone's all yours."

"Lot a good it's gonna do me now."

"Sorry."

"Yeah."

Without thinking, Mark found himself filing into room 202 and signing the attendance sheet. He took a seat in the last row and closed his eyes. When he opened them again, a young man about his age was standing behind the podium and suggesting that they "begin this meeting with a quiet time."

Chapter Twenty-One

"I'm Domingo, and I'm an alcoholic."

Domingo then proceeded to tell a story similar to Mark's. Granted, Domingo was second-generation Mexican-American, but his drinking and drugging habits resembled Mark's.

So much so that Mark moved to the first row during the coffee break. Attendance at this second part of the meeting wasn't required, so it was just Domingo, Mark and a few others.

A black man named Bill said: "I got so wasted when I was workin' up in Alaska that I almost froze to death a coupla times. That booze ain't never done me no good. I just want to stay sober and live a decent life. That's all I want. You think this here AA can do that for me?"

Domingo smiled. "Yeah. All you gotta do is don't drink and go to meetings. It's that simple. Next man."

"Ah, I'm Mark Anderson. Ah, I guess you don't give your last names here."

"You can if you want. My last name's Molina. I don't care who knows I'm an alcoholic as long as I don't forget it. You like to make a comment, Mark?"

"Well, ah, actually I'd like to talk to you after the meeting. If that's okay?"

"Sure."

"But I would like to say that I enjoyed hearing what you had to say. And I have to admit, I'm really surprised to see such a young guy in AA. I thought AA was only for old guys. You know."

"Yeah, you gotta be at least 65 and have spent at least 10 years on skid row before they'll even consider you for membership. That's what I thought too when I first came around. But you'd be surprised at all the young people in AA. Sure surprised me. Keep coming back, Mark. Next man."

When each man had made his comment, Domingo lead them in the Lord's Prayer.

"You mind talking out here," Mark said, leading Domingo toward the hall.

"Why not?"

When they were alone, Mark said: "Look, I'm not here because I'm some drunk or something like these other guys. I had a funeral home at 21st and Canal that got burned down. You might have read about it in the SUN-TRIBUNE."

"Oh yeah. Arson, right?"

"Well, that's what the newspaper says. Anyway, I didn't get any insurance money, and because of that damned newspaper I'm kind of blacklisted in the business right now. I can't even rent a hearse from anybody. I belong to this small association, and they'd like to help me, but they don't have any money. See, I've been talking to these people at Graceland Cemetery about a simple cremation service. All I'd really need is a station wagon and a storefront somewhere. My car was ruined in the fire and the place was a total loss. I just need somebody to loan me a little money 'til I get back on my feet. That's all."

"What about your family?"

"My father's real sick. That's a long story."

"Well, my friend, AA's not a bank or an employment agency. We help each other to stay sober. That's it."

"Well, I'd kind of like to stay sober. I mean, you know, at least get it under control. The booze has been messing me up a little lately."

"You ever have a blackout?"

"A what?"

"You know, you get so drunk you don't even know what you're doing. You know you did something, but you just don't remember. One time, my wife and I had this big fight about my drinking, and I said I was going to start a new life. Next thing I know, I'm in Seattle. I don't even know how I got there. Or why. Seattle, man! I don't even know anybody in Seattle."

Mark laughed. "You're kidding?"

"No, man. At least you think I would have had the sense to go somewhere warm like San Diego or something. But no, I end up in Seattle where it rains all the time."

"I never did anything like that. Well, I did, uh . . ."

"Yeah? Tell me about it."

"I got kind of drunk and ended up chasing this el train. You know -- like that scene in the FRENCH CONNECTION where

Gene Hackman's chasing that guy on the elevated in New York?"

"Oh, yeah, that was crazy."

"Yeah, well, I did something like that not too long ago. And the thing is, I really don't remember much about it. So I guess that's like a blackout, right?"

"That's a blackout all right. Hey, you like to go to another meeting? My home group meets tomorrow night, and I could give you a ride. There's a guy there who's in real estate. He's buying a lot of old buildings in Uptown near Graceland Cemetery. Maybe you could talk to him."

"Really?"

"Yeah, and maybe you could talk to me about a car. I run a garage near DePaul University see, and . . ."

Chapter Twenty-Two

Helen Anderson heard her husband leave his bed, pad into the bathroom and close the door. She listened to his muffled coughs long enough to realize the treatments weren't working. She said a prayer and went to her mate of 32 years.

"Honey, are you all right?"

Karl scowled at the bloody sputum in the toilet. "Go back to bed, Helen. Just a little cough. That's all."

Helen let herself into the bathroom and looked at the evidence.

"Oh, dear! Will you please go see Dr. Tiefenbach. Please."

Karl brushed his wife's hand away, but Helen stood her ground.

"All right. If you don't see Dr. Tiefenbach, I'm leaving. Do you hear me, Karl? I'll leave if you don't see Dr. Tiefenbach."

Karl coughed up some more bloody sputum and flushed the toilet. His throat was raw and sore.

"All right, I'll make an appointment in the morning. But I'm also going to call Casey-O'Day."

"You mean the . . ."

"Yes. The funeral home on 101st Street. I think it's time to start getting my affairs in order. Don't you?"

Helen looked at her husband and realized she was going to lose him.

"Well, what do you think?"

"I, I . . ." Helen lost control and collapsed crying in her husband's arms.

Karl took his wife to bed, but their lovemaking was cut short by another, more savage coughing attack.

*   *   *

Michael J. Tiefenbach, M.D. peered over his bifocals. "I'm a doctor, Karl, not God. But I will say this: if you don't have surgery, and if you don't have it soon, well, I don't have to tell you, do I?"

"You're sure I have to have the whole smear? A hole in my

throat? All that business?"

"Karl, your wife's too young for widowhood. Don't you think?"

Dr. Tiefenbach gathered the tubes and mirrors with which he had examined Karl's throat. He wondered if the man had much of a chance even with surgery.

"Couldn't you just scrape the damn thing off? I was reading somewhere about this new ..."

"Karl, as your doctor, I can say that the only recourse now is a total laryngectomy. It's too late for anything else. Now, when can we schedule the surgery? I'll need to notify the hospital."

Karl turned away from his meddlesome doctor and looked out the window.

"Karl, are you listening? I said: we have to schedule your surgery as soon as possible. When are you available?"

"Why not Monday morning? Might as well start the week off right."

"Good. Now, if you'll excuse me, I've got some other patients to see before I make my rounds. I'll have Dorothy make all the necessary arrangements. I imagine they'll want you to check in Sunday night, but I'll have Dorothy call you. Well, I'll see you then."

Karl nodded and carefully adjusted his tie so as not to irritate his throat, donned his suit jacket and walked heavily out of the examination room.

He didn't remember his son's new number, so he had to call information.

"No, operator, I don't know what damn street it's on. For Christ's sake: 'Anderson Funeral Home' -- in Chicago. That should be enough."

"Just a minute, sir. Let me check again. Well, I do have an 'Anderson Cremation Service' on Broadway."

"That's it. Give me the number."

"Mark, this is Dad. I'm at the Medical Center, and, what the ..."

". . . Cremation Service. We're not here to help you right now, so if you'll please leave your name, number, the time of your call and a short message after the beep, we'll get back to you as soon as we can. Thanks for calling Anderson Cremation Service."

Beep.

"Christ Almighty!"

"Are you finished, sir?" said a nurse who wanted to use the phone.

"Do I look like I'm finished?"

The young woman backed off.

Karl grunted and redialed his son's number. This time he waited for the beep and said: "Mark, this is Dad. I'm at the Medical Center. Nothing important. I thought you might like to join me for lunch at the club. Come if you can make it. Otherwise, call your mother. I think she's planning something for this Saturday. Bye."

Chapter Twenty-Three

Jennifer Adams and the Channel 12 Action Crew were more than a hour late, but Mark assured the cremation attendant that they were coming.

"Look, I can't hold this body much longer," the man said. "I have to shut down this unit at 5."

"Five more minutes, all right?"

"All right, but if they're not here, we're going to have to go ahead without them."

"All right."

Mark looked at his watch and stomped his feet. It was a brilliant November afternoon, but in another half hour it would be too dark for good television.

The white van appeared four-and-a-half minutes later.

"Sorry we're so late. We were out at the County Hospital doing a story and one thing lead to another, and we just couldn't get away," said a striking woman in a sable coat with hair to match. She took Mark's hand and fixed her hazel eyes on his. "I'm Jennifer Adams. Channel 12 News. Pleased to meet you."

"Hi, I'm Mark Anderson. Anderson Cremation Service. I spoke to you on the phone. This is John Davis. He operates the crematorium here."

Jennifer Adams nodded formally at the older man.

"We're ready when you are Miss Adams," Davis said.

"Fine. Just give my crew about five minutes to get their equipment ready."

Jennifer Adams dug her nails in Mark's arm and pulled him aside. She took the SUN-TRIBUNE clippings from her purse and waved them in Mark's face. "All right. Let's have it."

"Let's have what? What are you talking about?"

"What do you think?"

"You mean . . ."

"I mean Diane Roth doesn't write this kind of copy about just anybody." Jennifer Adams released Mark's arm and stepped back to appraise him. "I heard you were a hunk, and you looked pretty good in your picture -- but in person. God!"

"Ready when you are, Jennifer," the mini-camera operator called.

"Half a sec, Frank." Jennifer lowered her voice. "You want a good story, right?"

"Of course. That's why I've been ringing your phone off the hook for the last two weeks."

"You've got it, but under one condition."

"Yes?"

"You give me the same thing you gave Diane Roth."

Mark smiled. "You've got it."

They did an outside interview first to capitalize on the fading light. Mark was nervous at first, but he relaxed by mentally undressing Jennifer Adams.

"Well, just look at this cemetery around us," Mark said, in response to her opening question.

The mini-cam panned the crowded cemetery.

"There's hardly any more room here. And that's true in most cemeteries in the Chicago area. And where are you going to build new cemeteries? In Lincoln Park? No way. That's why I developed my simple cremation plan. People are tired of going to funeral homes and being treated like they're at a used car lot. I think the SUN-TRIBUNE investigation made that pretty clear.

"People want simple, dignified service from the funeral industry, and they're not getting it from a lot of my colleagues."

"Mr. Anderson, do you think your colleagues had anything to do with the fire that destroyed your funeral home?"

Mark swallowed. "It's still under investigation. I can't really comment on that, but I can say that I'm not real popular at the moment with the more traditional funeral directors."

Mark went on to explain how some of his unsavory colleagues steered consumers away from cremation by "talking about sizzling bacon and all kinds of horrible things. But the fact is, simple cremation is a very dignified, sensible means of disposal. We all know the body is about 90 percent water, so it's really a process of evaporation. That's basically what it is."

"Is there a number people can call if they want more information on cremation?"

Mark practically burst a blood vessel. "Ah, as a matter of fact there is. It's . . ."

Then they moved inside and shot scenes of John Davis and Mark wheeling a cardboard casket to the crematorium.

"Is there a body in there?" Jennifer asked.

"Yes," Mark said. "In fact, the man arranged for this himself about a month ago. He was dying of cancer, and all his relatives were dead or lived out of town. He knew they'd have a big fight over what do about the funeral, so he called me and arranged it all ahead of time. We had a real nice talk."

They slid the casket into the unit and shut the door. John went back and ignited the unit as the crew recorded his every movement.

"This is going to be great," Jennifer said. "Just great." She looked lustily at Mark. "That is if . . ."

"I'm a man of my word, Ms. . . ."

"Jennifer."

"Jennifer."

*　*　*

"Let me try my answering machine again. Maybe I can get through this time."

Jennifer Adams stroked the hair on Mark's chest. "All right. But you get right back here when you're through. I'm not done with you yet."

Mark sighed. "God, are you training for the Olympics or what?"

"I told you: I have an insatiable sexual appetite. Now hurry up."

"All right."

Mark finally got through to his answering machine.

"Holy shit," he said. "I think your story really did it. It's rewinding the whole tape."

"I'm not surprised. We ARE the number-one-rated newscast in the Chicago market." Jennifer went naked to the bar by the window with the magnificent view of Lake Shore Drive.

There were ten messages from people who had seen Mark on the 6 o'clock news and wanted more information about cremation. There were three crank calls from kids who had watched the show. And seven people were ready to send him checks sight unseen.

Domingo wanted to go to an AA meeting with him that night.

A Unitarian minister in Evanston wanted him to speak.

TIME Magazine wanted his subscription.

And: "Mark, this is Diane. Nice going. What'd you do to get that bitch to do a story like that? By the way, you won't have to worry about those creeps from Imperial Limited anymore because they're being indicted by a federal grand jury tomorrow morning. You can read all about it in the morning paper. Tell Jennifer Adams to eat her heart out. And, call me sometime. Okay?"

And: "Mark, this is Dad. I'm at the Medical Center. Nothing important. I thought you might like to join me for lunch at the club. Come if you can make it. Otherwise, call your mother. I think she's planning something for this Saturday. Bye."

Jennifer set a scotch and water next to her naked lover and said, "What's wrong? You look like you just saw a ghost."

Mark looked at the hot woman and the cold drink and opted for Domingo's offer of an AA meeting.

Chapter Twenty-Four

When Mark phoned home the next day, his mother told him of his father's impending surgery.

"You were a nurse, Mark, do you think everything is going to be all right?"

Mark looked out the window at the intersection of Broadway and Montrose and watched a drunken American Indian shake his fist at a bus.

"I don't know, Mom. I'm not God. All we can do is pray for him."

"What?"

"Yeah, I guess that does sound funny coming from me. Remember what a hard time you had getting me to go to Sunday School?"

"You did give me some fits. And Jon was such a little angel. Have you found a nice Lutheran church up there, Dear?"

Mark thought of all the church basements he had been sitting in lately and laughed. "Not exactly. Actually, uh, I've been going to AA."

Helen put her hand to her heart. "AA? You mean . . ."

"Yeah: Alcoholics Anonymous. I met this guy while I was staying at the Salvation Army, and, well, one thing led to another and I've been going to AA for -- well it's been two weeks now."

Helen thought of all the times she had begged Karl to go to AA and sighed. "I'm so pleased, Dear."

"Thanks. And things are working out real well with the new location. Business has been good thanks to that story Channel 12 did on me. Did you happen to . . ."

"No. But you were the talk of the grocery store the next morning. How's Darlene?"

"It's Diane, Mom. Actually, we haven't been seeing each other lately."

"Oh. Well, maybe you'll meet a nice Lutheran girl up there. Jon and Judy and the kids are coming over for dinner tonight. I was hoping you could join us."

"Yeah, Dad left a message the other day. That's why I was calling -- to say I could come."

"Oh, good. Six o'clock okay?"

"Fine. Uh, is Dad there?"

"He went downtown to take care of some things. Said he was going to have lunch at the club. Maybe you could surprise him. I know it would mean so much to him. Then you could come out with him. You're welcome to stay the night."

"Thanks, Mom, but I've got a ton of work here."

"All right. But there're fresh sheets on your bed if you change your mind."

"Thanks Mom."

Mark found his father ensconced on his favorite stool at the Swedish Athletic Club.

"So, John, am I right or am I right?"

"Looks like you've got company for lunch, Mr. Anderson," John said.

Karl turned and grimaced. "Better get some of that Irish crap, John."

"Hi, Dad. John."

Karl tried to outgrip his son, but he no longer had the strength. Mark let him win anyway.

"See, there's life in the old boy yet."

"I never doubted it for a minute, Dad."

"Jameson's, Mr. Anderson? With a splash, right?" John said.

"Uh, no. Actually, I'll just have a tonic and lime."

"What?!?" Karl said.

"I just want a tonic and lime today. Anything wrong with that?"

"No, not if you're an old lady with a sore tit. Get him that Irish crap, John. Maybe that'll bring him to his senses."

"No, I really want a tonic and lime."

"Very well, sir. Tonic and lime it will be."

"Mom told me about the surgery, Dad."

"Tonic and lime? What the hell kind of drink is that?"

Mark reddened. "It's what I feel like drinking right now. So what does your doctor say about it? What's his name?"

"Tiefenbach. Dr. Tiefenbach. Tief-en-bach -- it's German, I think."

"Whatever. So what did he say?"

Karl watched John the bartender squeeze a lime wedge into his son's sorry excuse for a drink. "John, put a shot of good gin in that."

John reached for the green bottle.

"No, I just want a tonic and lime."

John's hand hovered over the Tanqueray.

"What the hell's gotten into you?"

"I don't feel like drinking today."

Karl shrugged. "All right, John, give the kid his Shirley Temple. And put a cherry in it."

John did as he was told.

Mark deposited the cherry in an ashtray.

"Well, here's to your health, Dad."

Mark hoisted his glass.

"I only toast real men," Karl said, sipping his martini.

"Here's to your health anyway. So what does Dr. Tiefenbach say?"

Karl looked morosely at the Viking scene over the bar. "Dad, I asked you a question. What's wrong?"

"The bastard's gonna cut my throat out on Monday morning. All right?"

He turned back to his drink and took a long pull.

"Dad, I'm . . ."

"If you're so goddamned concerned," Karl said, "you'll have a real drink and toast me like a man."

John reached for Mark's glass.

"No, thanks. I'm on the wagon."

Karl took his drink and headed for the smorgasbord.

John touched Mark's arm and whispered, "Come on, have a drink with your old man. It would mean the world to him. One drink's not going to kill you. Come on, what do you say?"

Mark looked at the bottles lined up along the bar, ready to help the sons of Sweden harken back to a better time and place. "All right, but just one. You hear?"

"I hear you, Mr. Anderson," John said, happily fetching the green bottle.

*   *   *

Mark smiled grimly as he followed his father up the walk. He had held himself to three drinks. Just three. No more, no less. Maybe I'm not an alcoholic, he thought. Maybe I just needed to dry out for a couple of weeks to get my bearings straight.

Helen rushed from the kitchen to greet them. She wiped her hands on her apron, held Mark's face and kissed him on the cheek. She shuddered when she smelled the liquor on his breath.

"Just had a few, Mom. You know."

"Damn kid tried to tell me he was on the wagon," Karl said, removing his coat. "Can you believe that? Took me the longest time to talk some sense into his head. Well, how about something to wet your whistle?"

Helen held her breath.

"Can I use the phone, Mom?"

"Sure, this is your home too, Sweetie."

"I mean the upstairs phone."

"Fine."

Mark dashed upstairs and called Domingo.

"Hey, Mark, what's up?"

"I fucked up."

"What?"

"I had three drinks today, Domingo. I had lunch with my old man at his club, and I had three drinks. I went in there with no intention of having a drink, and I even held out for a while, but I just gave in."

"Hey, go easy on yourself, man. So you went out and did some more research. Lots of people in AA do that. No problem. You hear me?"

"Yeah."

"So where are you now?"

"At my parents."

"You feel like having a drink now?"

"Kind of. But not really. You know what I mean?"

"Yeah. I know. How about I pick you up and we go to a meeting tomorrow morning? I know a real good one at Ravenswood Hospital."

"I'd like that, Domingo. A lot."

"Me too. I'll see you at 10. Hey, how's that station wagon running?"

"Like a champ."

"What'd I tell you."

Mark went downstairs and asked his mother if she had any coffee.

"I was just going to make a pot."

"Good, I sure could use some."

Helen was delighted. Karl was furious.

Karl made himself a drink and lumbered off to watch college football.

Mark lingered in the warm kitchen enjoying the rich aromas of his mother's cooking.

"So how are you, Mom?"

"You know Mom. Just fine dear." She bit her lip.

"It's been hard on you, hasn't it?"

The tears finally came, and Helen Anderson went to her son's waiting arms.

When Helen regained her composure, she said: "We went to Casey-O'Day this morning."

"You mean the funeral home on 101st Street?"

"Yes," she said, crying again.

Mark patted her shoulder.

"It doesn't look good, does it?"

"No," Helen said, reaching for a Kleenex. "No, I don't think he's going to be with us much longer."

She moved away from her son, and busied herself with the broccoli.

"Your father has decided to be cremated, Mark. I haven't told Jon and Judy yet, but I thought you should know. Especially since you're in the business. He was very impressed with your article in the paper. Said it made a lot of sense to him, so that's what he arranged."

"Yeah, it does make a lot of sense. But let's hope he won't need it for a long time to come."

Helen collapsed against her son and cried some more.

"I'll be all right. Just give me a minute or two. Why don't you walk the dog or something?"

"Mom, the dog's been dead for two years. I'll go set the table."

"I already did."

"I'll go downstairs and get some more ice. Dad always needs

more ice."

"Good idea."

Mark went to the basement and fetched another ice bucket for his father's bar. He saw that his mother had left his Boy Scout patches over the washer and dryer.

He hurried back upstairs and was pouring milk in his coffee when his father appeared and said, "Help your mother."

"I am."

"She's worked and slaved for you kids," Karl said.

"I know, Dad."

Helen emerged from the powder room and took the roast from the oven. "Which one of you handsome gentlemen wants to do the honors?"

"I will," Karl declared.

Karl took his carving knife, sharpened it carefully and proceeded to carve the entire roast while his son looked on.

"There," he said, when he was finished. "That's how you carve a goddamn roast. Now, if you'll excuse me, I'm going to fix myself a real drink."

*   *   *

Jonathan finally finished explaining his new teacher evaluation model. It had gotten an honorable mention at an administrator's convention, and Helen was beside herself with pride. Jon's wife seemed pleased, but Karl didn't care.

He had gone into one of his funks during the first course and was now ready to unload.

But his grandchildren, Kristin and Erika, wanted to see the Charlie Brown Thanksgiving special. That's all they had talked about during dinner. Now that dinner was over, they wanted the payoff.

"Kristin! Erika! Would you two sit still?" Judy said.

"Mommy, we want to watch Charlie Brown," Erika said.

"I told you, it's not on for another 15 minutes," Judy said, nervously eyeing the active volcano at the head of the table. "Now sit up and be still."

"Hey, why don't you two come out to the den with Uncle Mark? I'll read you a story until the show starts. How's that sound to you guys?"

Kristin and Erika giggled.

"I want CURIOUS GEORGE," Kristin said, scrambling off her chair.

Her little sister ran squealing after her.

"Well, if you'll excuse me, I have some nieces to entertain."

"Thanks, Mark," Judy said, smiling.

As Mark settled on the sofa with his nieces and began his reading, he heard his father rev up. Tonight it was going to be Winston Churchill. Usually the old man saved Winston Churchill and the Battle of Britain for Christmas Eve, but then he was going to have his throat cut out in less than 48 hours.

"We shall fight them on the beaches," Karl began, his eyes misting over. "We shall fight them in the hedgerows. We shall ..."

Mark buried himself in CURIOUS GEORGE as best he could, pointing out key words and phrases to the girls. They cuddled close and asked him countless questions.

Mark timed his reading to end just when the Charley Brown special began.

"And that's how Curious George learned the alphabet," he said, closing the book with a clap. "Well, it's time for your show, girls."

In their haste to turn on the television, Kristin and Erika knocked grandpa's wooden Navy ship on the floor. Mark was about to inspect it for damage when his father burst into the room and snatched it off the floor.

Mark instinctively herded his nieces out of harm's way and waited for the inevitable: "Goddamn kids!"

They were the last natural words the Anderson family heard from Karl. He dashed the ship against the floor with all his might and stormed off to one of his gin mills on Western Avenue.

Chapter Twenty-Five

The woman at the front table surveyed the smiling faces and asked: "Is there anyone here this morning at their first AA meeting, or in their first week of sobriety?"

Mark looked at Domingo. Domingo nodded.

Mark raised his hand and everyone applauded, welcoming the newcomer.

"Uh, actually, this isn't my first meeting. I was sober two weeks, and I went out and drank. My name is Mark, and I'm an alcoholic."

Several people said: "Keep comin' back, Mark."

Domingo squeezed Mark's arm, and a woman in the next row whispered: "We all have trouble getting the program, sweetie. Just bring the body, and the mind will follow."

The speaker that morning, a bearded man named Jeffrey, told of how he had gone "back out there" after four years in AA. "When I took that first drink," he said, "it filled every pore in my body, and for five minutes I was on top of the world. I even said 'Where have you been, my old friend?' But within ten minutes all the old shit was back, and worse than ever."

Jeffrey, Domingo and some others took Mark out for breakfast after the meeting, invigorating him with love and understanding.

Then Domingo gave him a ride back to his home/office.

"Holy shit!" Mark said as they came around the corner. "Somebody busted my front window!"

Not only that, somebody or somebodies had ransacked Mark's storefront office, slashed his car tires and left this typed note: "Quit your bitching, or it's going to be worse next time."

Mark kicked a shard of glass and screamed: "Those mother fuckers? Do believe this? I go to an AA meeting, and this is my reward. Shit!"

"Easy, man," Domingo said. "Easy. Just because you sober don't mean everything gonna be peaches and cream, man. Come on, get a hold of yourself and call the police."

Mark laughed. "A lot of good that's going to do. They're still investigating the fire in my other place. Everytime I call, they put me on hold, then I get disconnected."

"Call the police, Mark."

"All right."

Domingo found a broom and started sweeping.

When the police came, Domingo got on the phone and organized an AA work party. Mark told the police that he had no reason to suspect anyone in particular but that he had been saying some rather critical things in the media about his profession.

One of the cops had a brother-in-law in the funeral business. "Yeah, them old-timers don't like nobody rockin' the boat," he said. "Maybe you oughta cool it for a while."

"What?!?"

Domingo put a hand on Mark's shoulder. "Hey, man, I got a bunch of people comin' over to get this place back together again. Everything's going to be okay."

Mark sighed. "Yeah."

The cops left, and they set to work. They were making real progress when they heard the Harleys out front.

"Hey, what kind of people did you call, Domingo?!?"

Domingo was about to reply when two of the biggest, baddest bikers in the world walked into the well-ventilated offices of the Anderson Cremation Service.

"You the guy who was on the news the other night?" the first biker said.

"Yeah," Mark said, wondering what they could use for weapons.

"We liked what you had to say, so we want you to bury Snake," the biker said.

"Snake?" Mark said, trying not to laugh.

"Yeah, I still can't believe it,"the other biker said.

"Dude was in the rack porkin' his old lady, and he just croaked." The biker made a gruesome face. "We had just been partyin' with him 'cause it was his 40th birthday. Then he goes home to pork the old lady, and he croaks. Just like that. Scarey, man, real scarey."

"Yeah," Mark said.

The other biker said: "Hey, where are our manners: I'm Weasel, and this is Rat."

"Glad to meet you. I'm Mark Anderson, and this is my friend Domingo Molina. Sorry about the mess."

"You musta had one hell of a party in here last night," Rat said.

"Well actually there are some people in my business who aren't too happy about what I've been saying about the industry. I think they kind of want to keep things the way they are -- you know, somewhere in the Dark Ages."

"I'll tell you what," Weasel said, peeling fifty $100s from his bulging bill roll, "you do Snake up right and nobody'll ever mess with you again. What do you say to that?"

"I say your friend's going to go out in style," Mark said.

Chapter Twenty-Six

"Sorry I'm late, Mom, any word?"

Helen looked up from her knitting.

"He's just out of surgery. They're taking him to intensive care. We should be able to see him soon."

"Jon. Judy. Where're the kids?"

"With my mother," Judy said, staring at her brother-in -law.

There was nowhere to sit, so Mark went to the window and leaned against the radiator.

"Sorry I couldn't get here sooner, Mom I'm in the middle of the weirdest case of my career. A biker name Snake. Can you believe it. It's going to be some funeral."

Jon whispered in his brother's ear: "Nice goin', stupid. Don't mention funerals again, all right?"

Mark glared at his older brother.

"Jon and Judy have been with me all morning, Dear," Helen said. "I've been in good company."

Jonathan gloated at his little brother.

Mark wanted to punch him.

"Have you talked to the doctor?" Mark said.

"No, but one of his nice, young residents stopped by to see us."

Helen bent back to her knitting, noisily clacking her needles.

"Well, what did he say?"

"If you had been here, little brother, you would have heard," Jonathan said.

"We can't all be perfect, Johnny. What did he say, Mom?"

Helen inspected her knitting against the light. "Oh, darn, I missed a stitch. My eyesight must be going."

"All right," Mark said, "I'll find out myself."

He went to a house phone and had Dr. Tiefenbach paged. An overwrought young resident appeared 15 minutes later. He explained that Dr. Tiefenbach had departed for a conference in Boston and demanded to know what was so important.

"My father." Mark said. "Karl Anderson. He had a laryngectomy this morning. I want to know how he's doing. That's all."

"He should be in intensive care by now. He was in surgery a long time. Almost five hours."

"Five hours?!?"

"Yeah, it was a big tumor."

"Did you get it all?"

"Look, I've got rounds. I'd love to tell you that we got it all, and that your father's going to walk out of here like a new man in a couple of days, but medicine is not an exact science. All right?"

"You think he's going to make it?"

"He's alive, all right? And he's not my only patient. All right?"

Mark shrugged. "Yeah, sure. Thanks for your time and attention."

He watched the resident rush off to the next medical crisis and went to the pay phone.

"Domingo?"

"Un momento."

"Hola. ¿De quien es?"

"Domingo, cut the Espanol. It's me, Mark."

"Mark, how you doin'? How's your Dad?"

"Not so good. I have this bad feeling. Like this is it."

"Yeah. Listen, Mark, you got to remember that you didn't cause your father's problems, and you can't cure them."

"Yeah."

"How's your family?"

"Fine. Mom's knitting up a storm; my brother's being an asshole."

"You feel like drinking?"

"No. It hasn't crossed my mind. I went to a meeting before I came. It's amazing. Something like this happens, and I don't even think about drinking."

Domingo laughed. "Yeah. Amazing."

They were quiet a moment. Mark heard hubcaps dropping in the background. Someone swore in Spanish.

"Look, I gotta go," Domingo said. "Work's piling up here."

"Thanks, Domingo. I appreciate your help yesterday too. God, if you hadn't pinched my arm when those guys said their names, I woulda burst out laughing, and we'd be dead now.

"You've been a real help these last few weeks."

"No problem. Just pass it on. Talk to you later."

Mark found his family at his father's bedside in intensive care.

One look and Mark had to grip the rail. He had seen it all as a nursing student, but this was Dad with all those tubes and wires sticking out of him. And Dad was not looking good.

"We're all here, Honey," Helen said, stroking her husband's forehead. It was the only part of his body she could touch without disrupting some medical device.

"Yeah, Dad," Jonathan said, "we're all here."

Mark moved in close and nodded.

Karl Anderson blinked, seeing his family through a film of fear and pain. But he was glad they were there. And that they were together.

Chapter Twenty-Seven

The Chicago Outlaws Motorcycle Club turned out in force for Snake's funeral, filling Mark's storefront. Despite the considerable police presence outside, everyone proudly displayed his "colors," including a few Hell's Angels who biked in from New York to pay their respects.

"Man, he looks real nice," Weasel said to Mark. "Real nice." He slipped Mark a $100.

"Thanks. I did my best."

Embalming the 305-pound moose had not been as bad as Mark had suspected; the hassle came when he tried to comb out the old biker's matted red hair. He had broken three combs in the process and finally ended up giving Snake a shampoo and rinse for the road.

Now Snake looked terrific lying there in his full colors in his swastika-drapped coffin.

Snake's old lady Linda stood guard. She was a heavy-set woman with raven hair, green eyes and hips that belonged in the National Hockey League. She wore the only dress she owned -- a green polyester number that made her look as big as a barge.

"Come on, who wants to have a drink with Snake?" Linda said, waving a quart bottle of Jack Daniels.

Weasel, Rat and Toad stepped forward and soon there was a line of men with animal names waiting to have their last drink with Snake.

Linda watched alertly as each man took a swig from the bottle, poured some on Snake's mouth and dropped money or some memento in the casket.

"Oh, Rosie, not your stuffed armadillo!"

"Yeah," Rosie said, drying his eyes, "Snake should have Leo in the next world."

A biker named Toad fired up a joint, took a deep hit and fixed it between Snake's lips. "It'll help you in Valhalla, man," Toad said.

Others offered Snake snorts of cocaine and an amazing assortment of pharmaceuticals.

Then they started throwing money in the coffin to settle past debts and to give Snake some spiritual spending power.

"Hey, Dog, no checks," Linda said.

"Sorry," the embarrassed biker said, replacing it with a $10 bill.

All this was accompanied by blaring Janis Joplin music.

Snake was completely covered with money and drugs when Mark finally stepped forward to close the casket.

"Wait," Linda whispered. She opened a cavernous plastic purse and shovelled everything in. "You don't really think he needs it now, do you?"

Mark shrugged.

With the help of three bikers, Mark loaded Snake and his coffin into Mark's gunmetal gray Ford wagon. Domingo and his crew had labored over it half the night, and now it looked positively hot.

Mark nodded at the lieutenant in charge of the police detail, and a three-wheel motorcycle escort was formed at both ends of the funeral procession. As Mark got in his car, 233 Harleys roared into life, waking even the most resolute Uptown drunks. Weasel and Rat put Snake's leather aviator cap on the seat of his bike and balanced it between them.

Linda was climbing in with Mark when a newspaper photographer rushed forward to get her picture. Three bikers were on him in an inkling. It took six burly cops to free the photographer, but even they agreed that taking pictures wasn't such a good idea.

All of Uptown turned out to watch Snake take his last ride down Broadway, Sheffield and then west along Irving Park Road to Graceland Cemetery. A mob of reporters and TV mini-cam trucks were waiting at the entrance, but the police wisely kept them well away from the funeral procession.

Mark spotted Jennifer Adams in the crowd and waved gamely. She waved excitedly, thinking she had an exclusive. But Mark kept driving.

"You know somebody on TV," Linda said, impressed.

"Sort of."

"Wow."

The police escort fell away, and Mark led the procession to a remote corner of the cemetery where John Davis and a crew stood a discreet distance away from a freshly dug grave. The sky was an angry gray and the wind was racing down the lake from the northeast.

Mark parked as close to the grave as possible, got the resiliant Linda into the hands of Weasel and Rat and went to have a quick word with John Davis.

"John, I really appreciate you setting this up for me. Especially after all the . . ."

"Hey, you're one of our best customers, Mark. You think a bunch of sleazy operators are going to push this place around. Come on. And besides, this cemetery has a lot of history to it. Way I look at it, this is just another colorful chapter," Davis said.

"Well, I really appreciate it."

"No problem. You wouldn't believe what happened earlier."

"What?"

"While we were digging the grave this morning I noticed that we had one too many on the crew. Little guy. But we don't have any little guys. Turned out to be this lady from the newspaper. Damned if I know where she got a pair of our coveralls, but she had us all fooled for a while. Boy, she was a real hellcat. Had a devil of a time getting her out of here," Davis said.

"She have red hair by any chance?"

"Sure did. Why, you know her?"

"Sort of."

"Not the type you'd bring home to mother. Had a mouth on her like a truck driver," Davis said.

"I'll bet."

When all the bikes were parked, Mark and the pallbearers unloaded Snake and bore him to his grave. They set the bronze casket on the grave and circled it. The rest of the mourners filled in behind them.

Then Weasel said: "Let's have a moment of silence for Snake."

They had a moment of silence for Snake.

Then Rat said: "Let's join hands and say the Lord's Prayer."

They joined hands and said the Lord's Prayer.

Weasel and Rat nodded, and two Outlaws brought Snake's bike forward.

"Tell them to lower the casket, man," Weasel said.

Mark signaled John Davis, and Snake was lowered into the frozen earth.

Then suddenly everyone had a hacksaw or wrench in his hands, and Snake's Harley was chopped to bits. These were distributed evenly among the mourners, and then each stepped forward, wished that that particular part would serve Snake well in the next world and threw it into the grave.

When they were finished, they had another moment of silence for Snake. Then everyone produced a pistol, held it over his head, and at Weasel's command, fired into the air.

A flock of frightened pigeons flew in frantic circles and the motorman of a passing elevated train on the nearby Howard Line stopped his train and took cover. Having surrounded the cemetery with a sizeable force, the police merely adjusted their stances. The media went into a frenzy, but the police kept them at bay.

Mark grinned thinking of all the bills he could pay.

When the bikers had spent themselves and their ammunition, they returned to their bikes, formed ranks and processed in an orderly fashion to a bar on Broadway.

Before hopping on the back of Weasel's bike, Linda invited Mark to join them, but Mark declined saying he had lots of work to do.

He was exiting the cemetery when Diane Roth raced up to his car and demanded: "Where are they going? Come on, take me along. I can get an exclusive."

Mark rolled up his window and drove away.

Chapter Twenty-Eight

"Hey, Dad. How're you doing?"

Karl lifted a hand.

Mark went to the bedside and kissed his father's forehead. He could feel his father's skull.

"So how are you?"

Karl fumbled with the bed adjustor.

"Here, let me, I'm an old hand. There, now you look like you're ready for business."

Karl said "thanks" by gulping air and burping it back up his esophagus.

"Don't mention it, Dad."

The two men looked at one another and then looked away. There was a long silence punctuated by nurses rushing to and fro in the corridor.

Karl motioned for the bed table.

Mark wheeled it into position.

Karl found his pad and pencil and wrote: "Can't get the hang of esophageal speech."

"I could understand you, Dad."

Karl shook his head and coughed phlegm up through the surgically created hole in his neck, or stoma. Mark handed him tissues.

When his father stopped coughing, Mark asked, "What does Dr. Tiefenbach say?"

Karl wrote: "Says I have to do what spch. therpst wants."

"Well, why don't you try talking some more? I'm not in any hurry."

"Tired," Karl wrote. "Want to sleep. Come back tomorrow. OK?"

Mark looked at his poor, sick father.

"Are you sure?"

Karl nodded.

"Okay." Mark put his hand on his father's forehead and whispered, "I love you, Dad."

Karl nodded.

Chapter Twenty-Nine

The Chicago Outlaws were so pleased with Snake's funeral that they put the word out on the street that anyone who even sneezed in Mark's direction would be beaten with blunt instruments. No one sneezed in Mark's direction.

Mark's fame spread through the North Side, and anyone who had ever had difficulties with funeral directors came to him for honest, affordable service. This group included: the area's growing gay population, Indians and Pakistanis, American Indians, Koreans, Vietnamese, environmentalists, consumer advocates, Mexicans, Puerto Ricans and the occasional wino with $400 in his sock.

When Mark wasn't transporting bodies to the crematorium at Graceland or counselling the bereaved, he was telling groups of Unitarians, lesbians, lakefront liberals and others about the dignity of simple cremation and/or burial.

In addition to helping him stay sober, Domingo tutored Mark in Spanish and one day hanged a "Se habla Español" sign in the window.

"But I'm not ready yet," Mark said. "I might tell somebody his sister looks like a turtle or something."

"Don't worry," Domingo said, "you'll do fine."

And while Mark did just fine, his father had to undergo two debilitating months of radiation therapy to ensure that the cancer had been completely checked. Then he had a problem with his stoma and had to be hospitalized again. A malignant tumor was removed from his mouth before Christmas.

His speech therapist insisted through it all that he master esophageal speech. Karl struggled, but he just couldn't get it. But at least one family member was with Karl every day. And every day consisted of long, awkward silences at his bedside, watching him slowly slip away.

Mark and his mother met in the corridor after one such session the week before Christmas.

"Can your lady friend Darlene come for Christmas, Mark?"

"She's not my lady friend, Mom, and her name is Diane," Mark said impatiently.

"Oh, that's right. You told me that before, didn't you?"

"Yeah. Things didn't work out, and we haven't been seeing each other."

"Well, I'm sure there are plenty of other fish in the sea."

"Mom, I'm sorry I snapped at you like that. I guess this is getting on my nerves."

Helen Anderson patted her son's shoulder. "You've been a great help to us both through all this, Mark. A great help."

Mark kissed his mother on the cheek. "To answer your question: I'd love to come for Christmas. But I'll just come alone if you don't mind?"

"Well, if you meet some nice Lutheran girl you're welcome to bring her."

"Mom!"

"I know. But I just don't see why a big handsome guy like you can't find a nice girl."

Mark took a deep breath. "First I have to get my business off the ground, and then I want to get personal life together. Then I'll worry about finding a woman."

"Are you still going to those meetings, Mark?"

"You mean AA?"

"Yes," Helen said.

"Yeah. I'm still going."

"I wish your father would have gone years ago."

"You can't change the past, Mom."

"I know," she said. She shook her head and faced Mark. "Well, I'm sure the right girl's out there waiting for you. You just haven't met her yet."

"I suppose. Be patient, Mom. Okay?"

"I will. The doctor says Dad can come home for Christmas, and I think it would be nice to have everyone together. Oh, and could you pick up Aunt Selma? She offered to take the bus, but I told her you'd give her a ride. Can you imagine her riding the bus all the way to Beverly from the North Side?"

Mark could well imagine his great-aunt riding the front car of a roller coaster.

"I'd be glad to give her a ride. By the way, have you thought of a Christmas gift for Dad?"

"Well, not really. I thought maybe I'd get him a new bathrobe, but . . ."

"I've got another idea. Something we can all give him. Here, tell me what you think of this . . ."

Chapter Thirty

Selma Anderson was 79, single and sensibly dressed.

"Oh, the house looks lovely, Dear. Just lovely," she said.

"Thanks, Aunt Selma," Helen said. "I wanted the house to look nice for Karl. Mark, why don't you make Aunt Selma and I a drink?"

"Good idea."

Mark went to his father's bar and automatically filled a glass with the good scotch. He had it under his nose when he realized what he was doing.

Mark poured the scotch down the sink. Then he washed his face with cold tap water. He was about to phone Domingo when his mother called: "Mark, could you help your father?"

Karl Anderson was too weak to make it down the stairs himself, but that hadn't stopped him from trying.

"Merry Christmas, Dad," Mark said, meeting him halfway. "How about a hand?"

Karl nodded.

"Here, put your arm around my shoulder. There, that's it. Okay, here we go."

Mark guided his father to the living room couch. Karl coughed and shook his head.

"You want to go to your chair in the den, Dad?"

Karl nodded vigorously.

"Karl, why don't you sit out here. There's no football game on tonight is there?"

"I don't think so, Mom. But if he wants to go to the den, then he should go to the den."

"What do you say, Aunt Selma?"

"Oh for pity's sake, Karl's a big boy now. Let him sit where he wants," Selma said.

Mark helped his father to his favorite chair. Karl motioned with his free hand, but Mark didn't understand what he wanted. Karl attempted esophageal speech.

"Oh, I get it," Mark said, "you want a pillow to sit on."

Karl nodded impatiently.

Mark took one from the couch and put it under his father's boney bottom. Even with the padding, Karl winced in pain as he settled in his wooden chair. Once it had barely held him; now it dwarfed him.

"How's that, Dad?"

Karl grimaced and waved his finger.

"You want the TV on?"

He nodded no.

"Mom? Would you come in here for a second?"

Helen soon appeared and said, "Oh, he wants his pad and pencil and Kleenex. I'll get them, Mark. You two can have a nice visit. Aunt Selma and I are just talking girl talk anyway."

When Karl had his essentials, he wrote: "Join me for a Christmas drink?"

"No. But I'll be happy to fix you one. Martini?"

Karl shook his head and wrote: "You make terrible martinis. sctch & wtr. With twist."

"I'll do my best, Dad."

His best wasn't good enough. Karl took one sip and scowled.

"What's wrong, Dad? Too much scotch?"

Karl struggled to his feet, shuffled to the kitchen and poured the drink down the sink. Clearly, Karl could still walk when he wanted to. He got a fresh glass, made himself a proper scotch and water and returned to his throne.

Mark sipped his ginger ale and stared out the window. Then his father handed him another note that read: "Andy Williams Christmas Special on Channel 7."

"Sure," Mark said.

They watched the cheap sentimentality in silence until Jonathan and his family arrived an hour late, a half-hour later.

* * *

Jonathan, of course, carved the turkey, and Judy helped Helen and Aunt Selma with everything else. Karl stayed tuned to the TV, and Mark read HOW THE GRINCH STOLE CHRISTMAS to his nieces.

When all was ready, Helen asked Mark to light the candles and help Dad to his seat at the head of the table.

Jonathan said the blessing, and they were all reaching for their silverware when Mark said: "Before we start eating, I thought this might be a good time to give Dad his gift."

Mark fetched a small box wrapped in green paper and presented it to his father.

Karl sipped his scotch and water and tried to look pleased.

"Come on, Dear, open it," Helen said.

Karl took another sip and unwrapped an electro-larynx complete with rechargeable batteries. He held it at arm's length and regarded it uncertainly.

Karl pressed the button and his granddaughters giggled at the strange buzzing noise. He leaned over and buzzed Erika on the forehead. She squealed with delight.

"Do it to me, Grandpa," Kristin said.

Grandpa obliged his other granddaughter. Then he pressed the device against his neck. "God bless us everyone," he said, his eyes misting.

"A toast," Mark said, raising his ginger ale. "To Dad and his new voice."

"Here, here," Jonathan said, regarding his little brother with a new respect.

They drank their toasts, and Karl repeated: "God bless us everyone."

Everyone smiled and started eating. Everyone that is but Karl.

"Do you know who wrote that?" he asked.

Enthralled by Grandpa's new voice, Kristin and Erika shook their heads.

"Charles Dickens wrote that," Karl said. He paused and took another sip of scotch and water.

Knowing what was coming, Helen said: "Sweetie, your dinner's going to get cold. Why don't you tell us after dinner?"

But Karl would not be deterred. He had a belly full of scotch and a new voice. And it was Christmas Eve.

"God bless us everyone," he repeated, staring at the Swedish candles.

"You're doing real good, Dad. We can understand every word," Mark said.

"Do you know who said that?"

Judy prompted Kristin to say, "Tiny Tim."

Ignoring her, Karl sipped his drink. "Charles Dickens was the best goddamned writer who ever lived." He pounded his free fist on the table, rattling the dinnerware. "You hear me, the best goddamn writer who ever lived. Not like these punks today who can't tell the difference . . ."

And so it went until he tired and went to bed without wishing anyone a Merry Christmas.

Chapter Thirty-One

When Mark returned to his apartment, he slumped in a chair and watched a freezing rain glaze Broadway Avenue. A northbound bus slid right through the stop light at Montrose. No matter, traffic was light.

But it looked heavy in the Corner Tavern across the street. And inviting.

Mark was heading for the door when he spotted Domingo's number tacked next to the phone.

"!Feliz Navidad!"

"Domingo?"

"Un momento."

Happy Spanish voices filled the phone.

"Hola. Aqui esta Domingo."

"Feliz Navidad and all that good shit. It's Mark."

"Mark, how you doin', man? Merry Christmas!"

"Not so hot. I just got back from my parents. It was a total bust."

Somebody started playing a guitar in the background, and there was singing.

"I'm sorry to hear that."

Mark sighed. "I don't know, man. I just feel really rotten. It's Christmas Eve, and I feel like hell."

"You take a drink today?"

"No. But I sure thought about it."

"Yeah, but did you take one?"

"No, I didn't."

"What you worried about?"

"I shouldn't be worried, should I?"

"No. It's Christmas Eve and we're both sober. What's to worry about?"

"Yeah."

"Hey, why don't you stop by and have some dessert?"

"Naw. I'm kind of tired."

"I know, you just want to sit there and feel sorry for yourself. Come on over. Meet the family. Have a good time."

"Twist my arm."

"Consider it twisted."

There was laughter and clapping in the background as the song ended.

"All right. I'll be right over."

Chapter Thirty-Two

Karl was back in the hospital before New Year's Eve.

On New Year's Day 1979 doctors found another tumor in his esophagus. Dr. Tiefenbach prescribed a regimen of chemotherapy and radiation treatment.

Karl had only had three when he developed pneumonia. His blood count dropped sharply, and there was nothing more for the doctors to do. Karl said he wanted to die at home.

Mark visited every night he didn't have a case and nursed his dying father.

Jonathan and Mark bought Karl a portable television and watched the Super Bowl with him. Karl used his electro-larynx a lot. Although the talk was mostly limited to football, he did tell his boys how much he appreciated their company.

It was his last good day, and he was comatose within a week.

Mark was just walking out the door to go see him when the phone rang. He had turned the answering machine on, but it could be that minister in Evanston who was interested in a prearrangement agreement for his congregation.

"Anderson Funeral Home and Cremation Service. May I help you?"

"Mark, it's me -- Diane Roth."

"Oh -- hi. How've you been?"

"Busy."

"Yeah, me too. Listen, can I call you back later? I've got to get down to my parents's house. My father's not doing so hot, and I'm going to . . ."

"Would you mind a little company?"

"What?"

"I said, I'd like to come along. If you don't mind?" Diane said.

"You sure?"

"Yes, I'm sure. Mark?"

"Yes."

"I'm really sorry."

"Me too. Especially about the way I spoke to you on the phone after that . . ."

"You had every right to talk to me like that."

"No I didn't," Mark said. "And the more I thought about it, the more I realized that it wasn't your fault that my place got burned down. I mean I was using you as much as you were using me. I wanted the free publicity, and I got it."

"We both used each other, Mark. But I'd like to think that there were some healthy things going on too."

"Yeah, I guess. Well . . ."

"I'll be right over, okay?" Diane said.

"I'll be ready."

*   *   *

They were southbound on the Dan Ryan near the Magikist sign that blinked big red lips at motorists.

Diane sidled next to Mark and rubbed his thigh. She kissed him on the cheek and smiled.

"You're sure you don't have a tape recorder hidden in your purse?" Mark said.

"Actually, I've got a bunch of midgets with mini-cams in there. Mark, I'm really sorry. Honest."

"I know. I am too. And I'm glad you called. I almost called you a couple of times. My mother wanted me to bring you down for Christmas Eve, but I knew . . ."

"You knew what?" Diane said.

"I knew you wouldn't want to come. I don't know. I was still pissed at you. When I saw you at Graceland the day of the biker funeral, I figured all you ever cared about was getting some goddamned story."

Diane kissed Mark again and said, "I don't even have a reporter's notebook in my purse. So tell me what's been going on with you. But I don't want to know if you crawled in the sack with that witch Jennifer Adams to get on Channel 12."

Mark smiled and told Diane about his successes in AA and business.

Diane kissed him on the neck.

"Oooh. Do that again."

"Not while we're on the expressway."

They rode in silence for a while, savoring one another.

"How are you holding up, Mark?"

"Okay, I guess. I don't know. You were lucky you weren't there on Christmas Eve. I thought it was going to be really something. You know -- giving him that electro-larynx so he could talk and all. I really thought it was going to be like the Waltons or something."

"But it wasn't, was it?"

"No, it wasn't any different than any other Christmas. Just that it was his last Christmas. That's it."

Diane caressed Mark's neck and said, "I'm here, Mark."

* * *

Mark found his father's pulse much weaker than yesterday. His breathing was labored and raspy, and his eyes were glazed and distant.

"I don't think he even knows we're here," Helen said.

Diane shuddered. "Would you mind if I go downstairs?"

"Not at all, dear. Mark, why don't you go too? There's some coffee ice cream in the freezer."

"Why don't you go, Mom? I'll take care of Dad tonight."

"All right. Come on, dear. I hope you like coffee ice cream."

"I love it," Diane said.

Mark swabbed his father with a sponge and cleaned the phlegm away from his stoma. Then he watched him as long as he could. Finally, he put his hand on his father's forehead and said, "I love you, Dad."

Mark turned out the light and went downstairs to have coffee ice cream.

"I think this is it, don't you?" Helen said.

Mark nodded.

"Would you like us to stay tonight, Mrs. Anderson?"

"That's very kind of you, Dear. I'll be all right. And if anything happens, the funeral home says I can call day or night. And Doris Brown from across the street has been a real trooper. No, you kids go on home. I'll be all right."

"You're sure, Mom?"

"I'm sure."

*   *   *

Mark gently lifted Diane's head off his shoulder and slipped out of bed to answer the phone. It was 6:30 and clear.

"Hi, Mom."

"Mark. How did you know?"

"I just did. When did he go?"

"I got up at 6 like I always do. I went in to check his breathing just the way you showed me. And, and, oh Mark . . . "

Mark listened to his mother sob and bit his lip.

"I was fine until I called you. Doris and Frank Brown are here. I've called the funeral home. I was fine until I called you." She sobbed again.

"We'll be right down, Mom. Have you called Jon yet?"

"No. Would you call your brother?"

"Sure. Mom?"

"What?"

"I'm really sorry."

"He's in a better place."

"Yeah. I'll call Jon, and we'll be right down. Take care." Kristin Anderson giggled when she realized it was her Uncle Mark.

"Kristin, could you please go get your daddy?"

"He's taking a shower, Uncle Mark."

"Well, could you go get him? It's very important, Kristin."

"Why are you calling me so early in the morning?"

"Because it's very important. Could you go get your daddy? Please. I'll read you a story if you do."

"Okay." Kristin dropped the phone, went to the bathroom door and said, "Daddy, Uncle Mark wants to talk to you."

The shower kept running.

"Kristin, can you hear me? Kristin," Mark shouted. "Have him call me when he gets out of the shower."

Too far away from the phone to hear, Kristin repeated: "Daddy, Uncle Mark wants to talk to you. Daddy, Uncle Mark wants to talk to you. Daddy . . ."

The shower kept running.

When it finally stopped, Kristin repeated, "Daddy, Uncle Mark wants to talk to you."

Jonathan rushed to the phone. "Mark, what . . ."

"You know why I'm calling."

"When did it happen?"

"This morning. About six. Mom just called. The Browns are there now, and we're on our way."

"Mark, I've got to call school and take care of some things. We'll see you over there later this morning. Okay?"

"Sure. Take care, Johnny."

"You too, Mark."

Mark was cradling the phone when Diane slid her arm around his shoulder. He turned into her embrace and wept for his Daddy.

Chapter Thirty-Three

The next three days blurred in Mark's mind.

His mother was forever introducing him to some Beverly matron, saying: "Mark, you remember Mrs. So-and-So. You used to play with her little boy Tod."

Women were always trying to get him to eat, and their husbands all wanted to pour him a good, stiff drink.

The Reverend Ernest Gusdahl, pastor of Good Shepherd Lutheran Church, appeared early the first day to attend to his parishoner Helen and couldn't be gotten rid of. He was young, eager and inept. He also loved to eat and complain about his expanding waistline.

Mark accompanied his mother and brother to the funeral home to finalize arrangements. When he suggested that they rent a casket, the fat funeral director laughed.

"Rent a casket?" Jon said, laughing too. "You can't rent a casket."

"Why not?" Mark said. "Dad's going to be cremated, not buried. I rent caskets all the time for cases like this."

"Well," the funeral director said, adjusting his polyester suit coat, "we certainly do not consider ourselves the Hertz of the funeral business. Now then, ma'am, can I show you to the showroom?"

Mark swallowed his tongue as his mother and brother let the funeral director talk them into buying a $3,000 bronze job known as the Centurion. He knew they would put his father in a cardboard cremation casket after the funeral and resell the Centurion, but he also knew that he was not the family conscience.

Domingo brought a carload of AA friends to the funeral. Mark tried to get the good women of Good Shepherd to feed them before the service, but they refused, saying: "We only have enough food for the family."

They had enough food for an army.

Diane held Mark's hand through Pastor Gusdahl's long eulogy. Although Karl was strictly a Christmas and Easter man, Gusdahl gushed over him as though they were lifelong buddies.

When it was finally over, Mark, Jonathan and four of Karl's friends from work bore him down the aisle to the hearse. Mark and Jonathan hugged one another and cried. One of the other pallbearers patted their shoulders and said: "It's tough to lose your dad."

Karl was cremated on the third day. Jonathan couldn't get time off from school, and Helen had had enough, so Mark went alone.

When the attendant was about to close the cast iron door, Mark said, "Wait a minute. Can I put this in there with him?"

"What is it?"

"It's a wooden ship. He was in the Navy. It was real special to him."

"Suit yourself."

Mark placed the broken ship on his father's cardboard casket and stepped back. He nodded, and the attendant committed Karl Anderson and his ship to the flames.

Chapter Thirty-Four

"So what do you think?" Diane asked, spooning the last of her double-fudge sundae.

"Well, I don't think they're in any danger of being discovered by CHICAGO Magazine. But you're absolutely right: they've got the best ice cream in the city. How'd you ever find this place?"

"Oh, I get around."

The owner of the DanDee Ice Cream Shop shouted at her son in Greek, and the fat little boy fetched a broom and began sweeping behind the counter. The classical music complemented the hand-painted fairy tale scenes on the walls above the wooden booths.

Mark finished his banana split.

"Diane, I'm -- you know . . ."

"Me too, Mark," Diane said, taking his hand.

The owner cleared their table, and served more coffee.

"Did you know that your freckles connect when you blush?"

"You're not supposed to notice my freckles," Diane said.

"They're not real obvious. Besides, I think they're cute."

The owner looked up from her romance novel and smiled at the lingering lovers in the last booth. It was past closing time, but who were they hurting? Plus the radio station was playing Mozart. The only thing they needed was some more ice cream, and she had plenty of that.

The End

Commuting Distance

"The man, for the time being, becomes a part of the machine in which he has placed himself, being jarred by the self-same movement, and receiving impressions upon nerves of skin and muscle which are none the less real because they are unconsciously inflicted."

--The Book of Health, 1884

Chapter One

Bonnie Bragg clutched the young man's sleeve and drew him closer.

"Well, if you ask me, I think we should just tell them Jews in Israel where to stuff it and put all our chips with the Aay- rabs. They's the ones with all the oil after all. Goodness, with all the money we spend on Israel, they might as well become the 51st State. But are they grateful? No sir. Instead they spy on us like we was the enemy or some such thing. Why, if y'all ask me . . ."

"I hate to interrupt you, Mrs. Bragg, but there's something I must tell you," Jeffrey Cotter said, backing a half-step away from the heavily perfumed Texan.

"Do what?"

"I'm Jewish."

Bonnie Bragg didn't miss a beat. "Well, our little Howard Novick here is Jewish, and he doesn't mind my criticizin' Israel. Do you now, Howard?"

Howard Novick excused himself from MEDCORP's chief financial officer and humbly approached the CEO's wife. He was a slender, unmuscled man with thinning hair and a loose-fitting black suit. He wore glasses with black plastic frames and a worried look. He chain-smoked Merits and hardly touched the hors d'oeuvres.

"I beg your pardon, Mrs. Bragg," he said, politely.

"Howard I was jus' tellin' this nice Mr. Conners here that you don't mind when I criticize Israel, even though you're Jewish."

"No, Mrs. Bragg, of course not."

"Good," Bonnie Bragg said, smiling broadly. "By the way, have you two been formally introduced?"

"We met at the office," Howard said.

"Well I bet you didn't know each other was Jewish, now did you?"

The two men nodded.

Bonnie Bragg took their shoulders and pushed them together. "Well now that you do, why don't you have a nice little Jewish chat an' all?"

Howard Novick and Jeffrey Cotter watched the chairman's wife mingle off.

"Actually I'm Catholic," Howard said. "My father's mother was Jewish, but I was raised Catholic."

"Abandoned the faith of Moses, eh?" Jeffrey Cotter said, joking.

"I don't look at it that way."

Jeffrey Cotter sipped his scotch and water and eyed the chairman's speechwriter. Cotter was one of three Capitol Hill staff members participating in MEDCORP's third annual Congressional Relations Seminar. MEDCORP reaped legislative benefits every new year by wining and dining aides to key Senators and Congressmen each December. The program was Howard Novick's idea, but William "Big Bill" Bragg characteristically took all the credit.

"How DO you look at it?" Cotter said, accepting a fresh drink from Ruby, the Bragg's black maid.

"My father wasn't religious; my mother was. So we went to Mass on Sunday instead of synagogue on Saturday. Besides, you're only Jewish if your mother was."

"Did your father convert?"

Howard clenched his teeth. "No. He didn't. So, what do you think of MEDCORP so far?"

"Well, I was just telling Senator Smaxton today that MEDCORP is big enough for its own regulatory agency." Senator Floyd Smaxton, D-Ark., was chairman of the crucial Senate Health Regulatory Committee.

In one fluid motion, Howard drew a pack of Merits from his breast pocket, mouthed a cigarette and lit it with his engraved Zippo.

Cotter caught sight of the insignia. "Marines?"

"Yeah." Howard sucked the smoke deep into his lungs and clouded the air between them. "You?"

"Ah, no. Actually, I didn't -- you know."

Howard Novick measured Cotter through the smoke. "So, you think 'prospective payment' has a chance?"

Congress was considering it as a replacement for cost-based reimbursement of hospitals for care they provide under Medicare. Instead, hospitals would be paid according to rates established in advance, meaning that MEDCORP would have to lower its prices. Meaning that MEDCORP would have to back away from the public trough.

"More than that. I'll bet you $10 some system of prospective payment becomes law early in '83," Cotter said.

"Make that a hundred bucks, boy, and you got yerself a bet." It was Big Bill Bragg himself, and he was hootin' and hollerin' drunk.

Jeffrey Cotter took another sip and eyed the former West Texas State fullback and CEO of the world's leading supplier of wound management systems, catheters, penile implants and other hospital stuff.

"You're on, Mr. Bragg. But I want it on the public record that I'm betting personal funds, not government money."

"You heard him, Howie," Bragg said.

"Shall we shake on it, Mr. Bragg?" Jeffrey Cotter said.

"Why sure, good buddy." Bill Bragg extended a side of Texas beef and engulfed Jeffrey Cotter's normal-sized hand. "You better pay up when you lose, or me an' Howie here is gonna send the Marines after you, boy. Ain't that right, Howie?"

"Yes, sir Mr. Bragg."

In freeing his hand, Jeffrey Cotter saw a tattoo partially protruding from Bragg's rolled up sleeve. It read: "Semper Fi, Mack."

"Mr. Bragg, what makes you so sure prospective payment won't pass in 1983?"

Howard Novick shifted his stance and lit another cigarette.

Bill Bragg thunked Howard on the shoulder, and Howard automatically gave his boss one and lit it for him.

"For God's sake, don't either of you boys tell Bonnie I'm havin' me a smoke," Bragg said, scanning the room. Seeing that his wife was on the far side blithering with the chief financial officer's fat wife, Bragg pulled smoke into his enormous chest cavity. When he exhaled, half the room filled with smoke.

"What was the question again?" Bragg said. He spotted Ruby, and she planted a fresh Jack Daniels on-the-rocks in his other paw.

"I said: what makes you so sure prospective payment won't pass in '83?"

"Boy, I'm not only sure, I KNOW prospective payment ain't got a snowball's chance in hell in '83, '84 or any other damn year. I know more people in Washington than you can spit at, boy. And they all tell me that there's no way Congress is gonna pass prospective payment. No way. You jus' start savin' up your pennies, old buddy, so you can pay your bet a year from now."

Bill Bragg gulped his drink, plunked the cold wet glass on the never-played grand piano and lumbered off to intimidate some subordinates.

"Well, Howie, what do you think?"

Howard Novick just blew smoke.

Chapter Two

Howard Novick arose precisely at 5:59, switched off the alarm radio, and padded into the bathroom. He didn't even look at his wife Connie who was sleeping in the next bed. Their children: Helen, 9, and Jennifer, 7, were asleep in their room down the hall.

The routine was the same every morning: first a scalding shower to open the pores and soften the thick black whiskers, then a shave with Foamy and a fresh blade, followed by a well-executed bowel movement. Whoever coined "shit, shower and shave" had it all mixed up.

At precisely 6:15, Howard tiptoed back into the bedroom to dress. He didn't keep it dark in deference to Connie: light was unnecessary to select from a wardrobe that consisted entirely of: seven pairs of black socks, three pairs of burgundy loafers with tassles, and five, white, button-down shirts.

Howard took the first shirt off the rack and tested the crease with his thumb and forefinger.

"Shit," he said, throwing it on the floor. He sampled the next one and found that Connie had somehow managed to get this one right. God, if that woman ever had to go out and get a real job, she'd be in big trouble.

Howard had five suits, one for each day of the week, with the suit of the day foremost on the rack. Today's suit was charcoal gray. Yesterday's suit was charcoal gray. Tomorrow's suit was charcoal gray. So were the other two.

Howard's six ties hung from a clipped hanger and were variations on your basic black and red stripes. Oh yes, there was that tie he had received for five years of loyal service to MEDCORP -- it was blue and with tiny repetitions of the company's logo -- a stethoscope over a globe. Office pundits claimed it was a dead ringer for the female reproductive system.

At 6:25 Howard went to the kitchen and prepared his breakfast -- a bowl of Kellogg's Corn Flakes, a glass of grapefruit juice and a Merit cigarette.

At 6:30, Howard Novick donned his tan London Fog and

slipped soundlessly out the back door. No boots, gloves, or hat --
it was only four blocks to the train station. But it was a black
December morning, and Howard was blowing into his hands
when he tripped over Jennifer's sled. Although Howard caught
himself before he tumbled into the wet snow, he yelled:
"Connie!" A sleepy figure appeared in the window above.

"Tell that damn kid to put her sled in the garage where it
belongs! I almost tripped over it and broke my neck." Howard
kicked the sled out of his way and trudged off down Devine
Drive toward the Regional Transportation Authority's Raven
Heights commuter station.

He arrived there precisely at 6:40, bought a CHICAGO SUN-
TIMES and CHICAGO TRIBUNE and took his customary
position on the platform.

The four-car, bilevel train arrived exactly at 6:45, and Howard
and the conductor exchanged their customary greetings.

"Morning, John."

"Morning, Mr. Novick."

Howard climbed up to the second level on the right side of the
smoker and took the last single seat. He folded and stored his
London Fog on the overhead rack, placed his monthly ticket in
the clip below his seat, and settled down for the second-best part
of his day -- the 25-minute ride to work.

The routine never varied: first a cursory look at the front and
business sections for news of the medical industry. Both papers
carried a wire story about an acquisition by MEDCORP's
archrival, ALLMED. Howard clipped them with his pocket
Swiss Army knife. No big deal, it was just some little company
in Michigan that made petri dishes. ALLMED would have to
buy a hell of a lot of petri dishes before they ever, ever got close
to MEDCORP.

In summer, Howard would flip to the sports sections for news
of the one professional team he cared about -- the Chicago
White Sox, but it was winter. Winter meant more time for what
mattered -- the crossword puzzles.

Oblivious of the snow-clad beauty of the North Shore suburbs
flashing past his window, Howard quickly conquered the SUN-
TIMES crossword, musing: I'm not a racist, but it's pretty
obvious why they make this damn thing so easy. Jeez, pretty

soon they won't even put captions under the pictures.

With 15 minutes remaining, Howard lighted another Merit and tackled the TRIBUNE's morning attempt to befuddle its upscale readers. As usual, the product of a rigorous Catholic education breezed through it and was on the last word when the train slowed for the downtown Evanston stop.

"A nine-letter word meaning 'outstandingly bad.' Hmmm. Hell, that's easy -- 'egregious.'"

Howard completed the puzzle with his corporate Cross mechanical pencil and tossed the TRIBUNE on the SUN-TIMES. Neither were worth keeping, for the big prize would come that afternoon during the ride home.

The train discharged Howard promptly at 7:10, and he walked the two blocks to MEDCORP's towering architectural mishmash in the usual 2.5 minutes. He was in his 11th floor office with his sleeves neatly folded, his IBM-PC cranked up, and a plastic cup of black coffee at 7:20. Work didn't start for another hour and ten minutes, but Howard Novick was ready.

*   *   *

"Morning, Howard."

Howard looked up from the speech he was writing for Bill Bragg. His archrival Judy O'Brien was arriving with the usual one minute to spare. Judy and Howard were vying for Calvin "Cal" Babbington's position as Executive Vice President for Public Affairs. At 66, Babbington could vacate his plush corner office anytime he wanted to, but as husband to the founder's favorite niece, he knew no one could budge him so long as the venerable Henry Matthews lived. And although the octogenarian publically professed a profound Christian faith, he was in no hurry to put it to the ultimate test.

"Morning," Howard said.

Judy O'Brien crossed the threshold into Howard's office and brushed the thin, graying brown hair out of her eyes. At 5'1" and weighing only 100 pounds, it seemed a miracle that she could direct MEDCORP's financial relations, nurture two hyperactive sons and a deadbeat husband who was forever trying to get rich quick care for her dying mother-in-law, and serve as president of

Women Executives of Corporate America, or WECA. But then miracles often happened to good Irish-Catholic girls. Even ones who had become Episcopalians to advance their careers.

"You see that ALLMED acquisition in the paper this morning?" Judy said, trying to keep her briefcase and various plastic bags from falling on Howard's floor.

"Yeah. So?" Howard turned back to his PC and typed a line of corporate speak.

"Well, doesn't it make you nervous?" Judy wanted to sit down and rest her sore feet, but she had her pride.

"No. Like Mr. Bragg says . . ."

"'. . . they're gonna have to buy one hell of a lot of petri dishes before they ever get close to MEDCORP.' OK, if that doesn't make you nervous, then maybe this will." Judy rummaged a magazine out of her overstuffed briefcase and tossed it on Howard's neatness.

It was the January, 1983 issue of the industry's leading trade magazine MODERN HEALTHCARE, and the cover bore an artist's rendering of Mason Davis, ALLMED's daper CEO.

"Holy shit!" Howard said, reaching for a Merit. "Where'd you get this? This isn't due out on the street for another week."

Judy O'Brien allowed herself a little smile. "I have my sources, Howard. I'll give you a few minutes to read it, then let's meet, OK?"

Howard Novick looked up at the woman who reminded him so much of his mother and pursed his lips. "But I've got to . . ."

"Howard, I think it had better wait. Read the article. I'll see you in the conference room in five minutes."

*   *   *

Were his skin a few shades darker, Don Kelly would be a dead ringer for the Chicago Bears' star fullback, Walter Payton. He allowed his black hair to curl naturally, and he defied unwritten corporate grooming standards by sporting a luxurious mustache.

Kelly was mostly Irish and looked it. Black Irish actually, for one of his foremothers had been more than a little friendly with a shipwrecked sailor from the vanquished Spanish Armada. He and his wife Eileen lived in a two-bedroom apartment in Rogers

Park, the Chicago neighborhood adjacent to suburban Evanston. Don and Eileen were childless by choice.

"Morning, Al," Don said to the uniformed lobby attendant.

"You ride your bike today?"

"Sure, Al, why not? It's got fenders, and the roads are pretty clear. Why not?"

"Well, you're a better man than me, Mr. Kelly."

"Naah," Don said, dashing to catch an elevator.

He got to his office a tad tardy -- at 8:35 -- and was hoping to relax with the morning paper and a cup of coffee when he saw the pink slip bearing his boss's painfully precise handwriting. "Meeting in conference room. ASAP!"

As senior writer, Don Kelly reported to Howard Novick.

"Shit!" Don said, grabbing his monogrammed MEDCORP portfolio.

Howard Novick peered over his glasses when his subordinate burst into the conference room. Judy O'Brien and HER senior writer, Meg Sanders, smiled thinly. Judy drove a Volvo station wagon. Meg, who fancied silk designer dresses, drove a black BMW with "HERS" vanity plates. Her husband John had a twin with "HIS" tags.

"Sorry to be late," Don said, radiating wintry freshness.

"Work starts at 8:30," Howard said.

"I know. I had a flat this morning. Would you believe it? So what's up?"

Judy O'Brien pushed MODERN HEALTHCARE across the walnut table. "This."

"Hmmm," Don said, flipping to the cover story. "Wow! 'A visionary voice for the healthcare industry . . . Mason Davis is strategically directing his company into a future full of high profits and technology . .' God, those guys need an editor. Has Big Bill seen this yet?"

"No, Mr. Bragg has not seen this yet," Howard said. "That's why we're having this meeting."

"Gotcha. Judy, I thought you said MODERN HEALTHCARE was going to do a cover on Bragg. You said it was in the bag," Don said, loosening his tartan tie and rolling up his sleeves.

Meg Sanders arched her back and gave Don Kelly her cattiest look.

Don smiled back, thinking: Oooh, I'm scared. And I sure hope you didn't pay whoever did that to your hair.

Meg's washed out brunette hair was swirled high above her sharp-featured face. Every week it was a new hairdresser, and every week it was a disaster. Don wondered why the self-involved little yuppie didn't just spend the money on a health club and do something about her sagging shoulders and drooping ass.

Meg Sanders looked through Don Kelly and said: "Apparently somebody at ALLMED talked them out of it. But whatever happened, we've got to respond proactively."

Proactively, Don thought. Oh yeah, corporate speak for covering your rearend.

"That's right," Judy said, "this story can impact us negatively or it can impact us positively. Our job is to see that it impacts us positively."

All this talk of impacting made Don Kelly suck his molars.

"What do you have in mind, Judy?" Howard said.

Judy and Meg perked up like a couple of teacher's pets. "Well, as a matter of fact," Judy said, opening her portfolio, "I have a plan that . . . "

"Sorry, I'm late." It was Calvin Babbington and he still reeked of the Braggs' booze. "They've got to stop having those little do's on weeknights. I'm getting too old for this kind of thing. Now, what's all this about? Susie said there was a big PR crisis this morning. I don't see how some little petri dish acquisition is going to . . ."

"Read it and weep," Don Kelly said, pushing the magazine under the executive vice president's red nose.

Cal Babbington patted his pockets for his bifocals. Unable to find them, the bantam businessman dashed back to his office. He returned five minutes later in a full state of fluster.

"Must have left them in the car. What's it say?" By car he meant an '83 Lincoln Continental.

No one wanted to announce the bad news. Finally Don Kelly said: "It's a cover story on ALLMED, Cal. Says they're gonna win the ballgame."

Cal Babbington loosened his paisley tie and removed his charcoal gray suit jacket. It sorely needed a good cleaning and pressing in addition to bearing numerous cigarette burns and whiskey stains. Babbington tapped Howard on the shoulder, and Novick automatically gave his boss a Merit and his lighter.

"Does Big Bill know about this?" Babbington said, lighting the cigarette.

As righteous ex-smokers, Judy and Meg winced and wanted to lecture Cal. But maybe the cigarettes would hasten his demise.

"No," Howard said, "Mr. Bragg doesn't know yet." Howard helped himself to a Merit.

Babbington rubbed his temples, got up, paced, sat down, fidgeted with his fingers and finally stubbed out the half-smoked cigarette. His face reddened up to where his auburn "rug" took over, which unfortunately did not match the gray hairs that sprouted from the perimeter of his stout head.

"Well, let's hear some suggestions. I'm not paying you people to sit on your rearends and gather moss," Babbington said. He got up and resumed pacing.

"Cal, I was thinking maybe we should write a letter to the editor, for Mr. Bragg's signature, of course, and send it to MODERN HEALTHCARE. Compliment them for their fine article, but not so subtly suggest that they didn't get the whole story," Judy O'Brien said.

"I think that would be the proactive thing to do," Meg Sanders quickly said.

Cal Babbington turned on his size-six tasseled loafer. "What do you think, Howard?"

Howard blew smoke and shrugged.

"And you, Don?"

"I think we should just ignore it. We're going to look like bush leaguers writing them a letter. If you ask me, the *proactive* thing to do would be to get Bragg's picture on the cover of FORTUNE or FORBES. I told you a long time ago, an old friend of mine from the DAILY NEWS works in the Midwest bureau for . . ."

The conference room phone buzzed.

Cal Babbington jumped and nodded at Howard.

Howard answered it, listened for a long moment, nodded twice and said, "Yes, sir, he's right here." Extending the phone toward Cal Babbington, he added: "It's Mr. Bragg. He wants to talk to you, I believe."

Babbington took the phone. As he listened to the Texan's tirade, the color drained from his face and his knees buckled. Don Kelly got a chair under him before he collapsed on the floor.

When it was finally over, he cradled the phone and said: "He's seen the article. In fact, he's got it on his desk up there, and he wants to see me in 30 minutes. He wants to respond, people. He wants to know why the hell we let this happen, people. He wants to know why he's paying a fortune for you people and getting this kind of stuff. . ."

Cal Babbington's rising outburst was cut short by an acute coughing attack.

The others planned the counterattack while he recovered.

"I've got a printer coming in at 9:15 to talk about the annual report," Judy said.

"And I've got that business communications seminar in the Loop at 11," Meg said. "I'll have to leave in about 10 minutes if I want to get there on time."

And Howard said: "I'm writing the Conference of Healthcare Providers speech for Mr. Bragg. He's got to have a draft before lunch. What are you working on, Don?"

Don wanted to laugh. Everything. Annual report copy. Management newsletter stories -- the entire January issue, in fact. The entire January/February issue of the employee magapaper -- PROBE. A speech for the Chief Financial Officer. Copy for a brochure describing MEDCORP's charitable foundation. All due yesterday.

"I guess I'm elected, huh?"

"You've got that right," Howard Novick said.

Chapter Three

A Merit dangling from his mouth, Howard Novick entered Don Kelly's office without knocking and tossed the copy on his cluttered desk. There were red marks everywhere.

Don glanced at it half expecting an "F" in the upper-right-hand corner.

"What's the difference between 'farther' and 'further'?"

Don rummaged in his drawer and pushed an ashtray toward his boss. "I don't know, Howard, but I'm sure you'll tell me."

" 'Farther' refers to physical distance. For example: He walked *farther* into the woods. 'Further' refers to an extension of time or degree. For example: She will look *further* into the mystery." It was a recitation right out of Howard Novick's bible, THE ASSOCIATED PRESS STYLEBOOK AND LIBEL MANUAL.

"I guess I blew it again, huh, Howard?"

Howard Novick tapped his cigarette against the ashtray. "When I hired you, I told you I didn't have time to be your editor. You told me your copy wouldn't need editing. Yet, I have to waste valuable time correcting your copy. What would have happened if I gave Cal the copy the way your wrote it?"

Don shrugged. "But you've got to admit I've finally got the hang of 'affected' and 'effected'. Of course, it doesn't seem to matter much around here anymore, because everybody's using 'impacted' all the time."

Howard sucked at his cigarette. "Clean this up and have it on my desk in five minutes."

* * *

"Come in," Big Bill Bragg said, peering through his brass telescope.

Howard Novick stepped into the cavernous office overlooking Lake Michigan and awaited further, not farther, orders.

"Where's Babbington?"

Howard cleared his throat. "He took the Congressional aides out to Matthews Industrial Park for the tour."

Bragg adjusted his telescope. "Figures. So what've you got for me, Howie?"

Howard cleared his throat again. "It's a letter to the editor of MODERN HEALTHCARE."

The chairman swivelled his telescope, searching for something. When he found it, he smiled broadly. "You write it, Howie?"

"Yes, sir."

"Then, I'm sure it's fine. Come here, Howie, I want you to take a look at something."

Howard carefully crossed Bragg's Oriental carpet and joined his boss at the window. He had always wondered what Mr. Bragg looked at through his telescope.

"Go ahead, Howie. Give yerself a good look," Bragg said, slapping Howard on the back.

Howard bent at the waist, closed his left eye and looked into the telescope.

The view of Lake Michigan and the Chicago skyline from the 21st floor "Eagle's Nest" executive suites was magnificent, so Howard assumed Bragg had aimed the telescope at the ice forming along the lake or perhaps at that ore boat out there trying to complete one more run before the ice thickened. Wrong on both counts.

Big Bill Bragg had aimed his telescope at a highrise apartment complex three blocks east of MEDCORP headquarters. Specifically, he had targeted an apartment on the tenth floor. Howard peered in past the open curtains and let his eye adjust to the dim light.

"Oh my God!"

There for the Almighty and Howard to see was a naked woman masturbating on a couch.

"Every morning at ten. Jus' like clockwork. Damndest thing I ever seen," Bragg said. "You ask me, Howie, I think that crazy little bitch leaves them curtains open on purpose. What do you think?"

His glasses were getting in the way, so Howard tore them off and made his eye focus. She was a real blonde all right, and what a beauty. Not an ounce of fat anywhere, and those breasts. And her, her . . .

"Speak up, boy."

"I, ah, I don't know."

"Here, let me have another look. Why don't you make us a couple of drinks? The usual for me." Bragg bent back to his telescope, exclaiming, "Oooh eeeee, baby! Hot damn!"

Howard went to the wet bar against the opposite wall and made his boss a Jack Daniels on-the-rocks. He fixed a tonic and lime for himself. Then he grinned slightly and added a dash of Russian vodka.

"Here, Mr. Bragg."

Bragg extended a paw and sipped his bourbon without breaking his concentration. "Go, baby, go! Take another look, Howie, she's really goin' to town now."

Howard removed his glasses and loosened the tie he had tightened for this meeting. The blonde beauty was coming and coming and coming. Howard's throat dried. He took a long sip and another look. His heart beat so fast he feared for his life.

"You like that, don't you, Howie?"

"Well, yeah. Yeah, I do."

"How long you been married, Howie?" Bill Bragg jiggled his ice cubes and took another gulp.

Howard had to think. "Umm, it was ten years this July."

"You ever play around on the little lady, Howie?"

The blonde was really giving herself a hand now. "No, sir," Howard said, trying not to hyperventilate.

"How old are you now, Howie?" Bragg gulped the last of his drink and ambled over to the wet bar.

Howard didn't have to think. "I'll be 40 in less than a month -- on January 6th."

"Ah, the big four oh. And you say you ain't never stepped out on the little lady. Not even one little ol' time."

Howard peered longingly into the telescope. "No sir, not even one little old time."

* * *

"Lunch?"

Don Kelly looked up from his wordprocessor. "Yeah, Howard, as soon as I print up Bragg's letter."

"It can wait. Come on, I'm starving."

"I thought this was the PR crisis of the decade. We had to get this to MODERN HEALTHCARE by this afternoon or the world was going to end."

"Screw Judy."

"What?!?" Don studied his boss. There was a gleam in Howard's eye he had never seen before.

"I said: screw her. You see her running around worrying about this? Come on, I'm hungry."

When they got to the cafeteria on the tenth floor, Don Kelly grabbed his tray and headed for the salad bar.

"You're gonna turn into a rabbit if you keep eating that stuff," Howard said.

Howard, on the other hand, headed straight down line one, collecting a jello salad, french fries, two double cheeseburgers, fried cheese "fingers," the biggest slice of chocolate cake on the counter, a Coke -- and for greenery -- an enormous dill pickle.

They reconnoitered at a table in the smoking section and chowed down.

"Howard, how can you eat like that every day and not gain weight?" Kelly said.

"Because I have the metabolism of an atomic furnance. Come on, eat up, I want to take a walk after lunch."

"Sure."

Howard mowed through his food, grinding it mercilessly between his teeth. Kelly was still munching his veggies when Howard said, "Let's go."

Stuffing a celery stalk in his mouth and two carrot slices in his back pocket, Kelly followed Howard to the trash compactor.

In his haste, he nearly collided with Big Bill Bragg who was bearing a double order of tuna salad and dozens of rye crackers.

"Excuse me, Mr. Bragg."

"Don't mention it, good buddy." Bragg scanned the cafeteria.

"Well, I think I'll go see what them overpriced lawyers been doin' down in legal. Would you look at this sorry-ass meal I gotta eat. Another week on this damn diet, and I think I'll jus' roll over an' die."

Kelly watched the chairman lumber over to a table full of constipated legal types and plop his tuna salad in their midst.

"What the goddamned hell y'all doin' for the good of the cause today?" Bragg said, settling into an undersized chair. "Or am I jus' payin' you boys for legal advice I don't need?"

Don wanted to hear their attempts to respond, but Howard was in a big hurry. And he clearly didn't want to get bogged down with Bragg because he was hiding behind the trash compactor.

"Come on," Howard hissed.

"OK. OK."

They were soon on the streets of downtown Evanston. It was a brilliant but bitterly cold winter afternoon. Chicago's preppiest suburb had adorned itself with real pine and mistletoe, and the boutiques were bustling with wealthy suburban matrons and MEDCORP employees.

"Where to, Howard? The book store? The hobby shop?"

"Nah, let's go this way for a change."

Without waiting, Howard crossed the street and hurried east along Grove Street.

Don jogged to catch up and said, "Howard, there aren't any stores over here. Where're we going?"

"For a walk. Anything wrong with that? "

"No, not at all. Hey, as long as we're heading this way, why not go by the lake?"

Howard grunted but turned left at Chicago Avenue.

Don had to double-step to keep up. "Where're you going, Howard?"

Howard jammed his hands in his pockets and forged ahead. He stopped abruptly in the middle of the block.

"You know somebody who lives here, Howard?"

Howard gazed up at the building he had seen earlier through the telescope.

"Howard, what's up? Who're you looking for? This is a pretty classy joint. You have a girlfriend in here you're not telling me about, Howard?"

"Come on," Howard grunted, "let's go. We've got a lot of work to do this afternoon."

"Sure, Howard, anything you say."

They turned left at the next corner and headed west on Davis past a row of shops.

"Hey, Howard, do mind waiting half a sec? I need a tube for

my bike."

"All right, but make it quick."

Howard rubbed his hands together and stomped his feet. He scanned the passersby but no one looked like her. Not even close. Wondering what the hell was keeping Kelly, he turned and peered into the bike shop.

Howard almost fell over. The woman at the end of the telescope was handing Kelly his inner tube.

"Howard, I didn't think you were interested in cycling," Don said.

"Well," Howard said, smiling at the blonde behind the counter, "it's never too late to learn,is it?"

*   *   *

As usual, Howard caught the 5:25 for home. He exchanged his customary greetings with the conductor, took his regular seat in the smoker, and settled down with the highlight of each working day -- THE NEW YORK TIMES crossword puzzle.

The answers didn't come easy today, for Howard had more than vocabulary on his mind. But he was a product of a good Catholic education, and that meant perfect recitation of the *Confiteor* in the face of Sharon Baker's bulging blouse in the 7th grade at St. Scholastica Grade School.

"Next stop -- Raven Heights," the conductor called.

Howard took a deep breath. One word to go. He had never failed to complete a NEW YORK TIMES crossword in the allotted time.

Never.

But every time he closed his eyes to concentrate, she was there. Giving herself a hand.

Howard exhaled. A 12-letter word meaning "misconduct in public office." He already had the first three letters -- "mal." Obviously a Latin word, and Howard had aced Latin both in high school and at Marquette.

"Come on, Mr. Novick. This is your stop."

Howard rubbed his temples. "Mal, mal, mal, mal -- malversation. That's it -- malversation."

Normally, Howard would keep a successfully completed NEW

YORK TIMES crossword puzzle for future reference, but today he tossed it aside.

Today was the first day of the rest of Howard Novick's life.

Chapter Four

"Hi, honey. Hard day at work?"

Howard closed the door and looked at his wife Connie. She was mashing potatoes the way her mother had taught her in Sheboygan, Wisconsin. Connie still had two years before she faced the big four oh, but her ass had spread prodigiously, and Howard hated her utility mom haircut.

"The usual," Howard said, moving into his den.

His daughters were sprawled in front of the TV watching Andy Griffith reruns.

"Don't I get a kiss?" Howard said.

"Sure, Daddy," Helen said, getting up and pecking her father on the cheek. At seven, she already showed signs of inheriting his lean physique. She certainly had Howard's aloofness and mental toughness. Helen was Daddy's girl.

"What about you, Pumpkin?"

Jennifer rolled on her back and covered her face. She was a shy, pudgy five-year-old who hid behind her mother when company came over.

"You have to kiss me," she said.

"Forget it," Howard said, kicking off his tassled loafers. "What's for dinner other than mashed potatoes?"

Connie wiped her hands on her apron. "Left-over turkey, coleslaw and . . ."

"Great. Call me when it's ready."

Howard went to their bedroom, inserted trees in his shoes, removed his suit coat and tie, donned a pair of slippers and returned to the living room where he contemplated yet another puzzle -- a jigsawed copy of Claude Monet's "Grainstacks, Snow, Sunset, 1891." He was having a devil of a time with the hazy background to the right of the stack in the foreground.

Damn Frogs. Why didn't they use primary colors like everybody else?

Howard stared at the grainstacks until they became the blonde's heaving breasts. He tried to pick up a puzzle piece, but his fingers were too moist to hold it.

"Dinner's ready," Connie called.

Howard had a hard-on.

"Just a minute."

He held his hands in front of his face. They hadn't trembled like that since his first night in Vietnam.

"You want milk with your dinner, Howard?"

"No, I think I'll have a beer."

"A beer?"

"You heard me."

"We don't have any beer."

"I'll go get some."

Howard donned his London Fog and walked four blocks to the convenience store. Despite the numbing cold, he still had a hard-on when he got there. A real diamond cutter.

Howard thought of sand dunes and sewage and the swelling finally subsided. But when he saw that the teenager behind the checkout counter was a blonde, Howard got hard again.

He had to walk two extra blocks to eliminate the second erection.

"I was about to call out the Canadian Mounties," Connie said, when he returned.

"Very funny."

Connie watched her husband open his beer and fretted. "Everything okay at work, Howard?"

"Everything at work is fine," he said, taking his place at the head of the table. He nodded at Helen and bowed his head.

Helen said: "Bless us, oh Lord, and these thy gifts which we are about to receive from thy bounty, through Christ our Lord. Amen."

The Novick family crossed themselves and ate in silence for five minutes before Howard said: "Helen, I bet you can't spell 'egregious.'"

"Can I try, Daddy?" Jennifer said.

"I asked your sister. Besides, you're only five years old."

"What was the word again, Daddy?" Helen asked.

"Egregious. It means 'outstandingly bad,' and I'll give you a clue: it begins with 'e' and it has nine letters."

"Egregious," Helen said, feeling it in her mouth. "E, g, r, e, g, i, o, u, s. Egregious. Is that right, Daddy?"

"Not bad," Howard said, sipping his beer. "Now how about 'malversation.' It means misconduct in public office. It has 12 letters and it comes from the Latin."

"Say it again, Daddy."

"Mal-ver-sa-tion. Malversation. You've got 10 seconds."

Helen took a deep breath and furrowed her brow just the way her father did when he was concentrating. "M, a, l, v, e, r, s, a, t, i, o, n. Malversation. Is that right, Daddy?"

Howard allowed a little smile. "That's right, Princess. Now help your mother with the dishes."

Howard took his beer back to his puzzle and spent the rest of the evening contemplating the heaving grainstacks.

Connie knitted another unnecessary bit of nothing, and after breezing through her homework, Helen joined her sister in front of the television to watch a sitcom about a manically happy black family who acted white enough to live in Raven Heights.

When the show was over, Connie shepherded her girls upstairs.

"I'm going to watch the news," Howard said, opening another beer.

"OK," Connie said, studying him. "Good night."

When the females were finally quiet up there, Howard switched to a cable channel that showed soft porn and let the blonde at the end of the telescope come over him.

Chapter Five

Cal Babbington slugged down the last of his extra-dry martini and grinned as the waiter served his cup of turtle soup.

Cal had told the troops he was going to confer with some division-level colleagues at Matthews Industrial Park in North Chicago. Instead, he had ducked downtown to his favorite Chicago haunt, Banyon's Restaurant. It had the clubby, cigar-scented atmosphere a man in his 60s could really appreciate, and as far as Cal was concerned, Banyon's turtle soup was the best in the world.

"I think I'll switch to beer," he told the waiter. "Heineken."

He happily doused his soup with sherry, tucked the linen napkin in his collar and lifted a spoonful to his mouth. Cal sighed as the wonderous flavor radiated down his throat.

He poured more sherry, stirred it in, and was lifting another spoonful when quite another sensation overcame him.

First, the fingers of his left hand went numb causing him to drop his spoon in the soup. Then the room spun madly and the lights strobed. Cal tried to get up but couldn't. He called for help but only babbled like a baby. Finally, a carotid artery burst unleashing a geyser of blood into Cal's brain.

He groaned and fell face first into his turtle soup.

The foursome at the next table laughed. They were lawyers on a long lunch hour and thought one of their fellows simply couldn't hold his liquor.

A quick-thinking Mexican busboy didn't find Cal's predicament so funny. He set his tray of dirty dishes on the lawyer's table and lifted Cal's head out of the rust-colored soup. Glistening bits of turtle meat clung to Cal's pallid face.

"Meester, can you hear me?"

Cal groaned pitifully.

"Doctor, doctor," the busboy called. "Ees doctor here?"

No doctors in the crowded restaurant but plenty of lawyers and judges. Someone whispered, "I wonder if his will's in order."

Someone else said: "If it was my case, I'd sue the bastards who made the turtle soup."

"Ees no doctor here?" The busboy frantically scanned the room. "Somebody call doctor."

An Iraqi waiter had the presence of mind to call 911, and a Chicago Fire Department paramedic unit was at the scene within 10 minutes. Within another 10 minutes, Cal Babbington was in the emergency room of nearby Northwestern Memorial Hospital surrounded by gadgets bearing the familiar MEDCORP trademark.

*   *   *

"I realize he can't talk, Mrs. Babbington, but could you get him to just shake his head if he thinks the ALLMED file is in his top drawer."

"Really, Mrs. O'Brien, is this necessary?" Clarice Babbington said. The strain on her had been enormous, and she was going to call her uncle if these dreadful people from Cal's office didn't stop calling.

"Yes, Mrs. Babbington, I'm afraid it is quite necessary." Judy O'Brien glanced over her shoulder.

"Well, all right, but I really must insist. This has to be the last time. The doctor says Mr. Babbington's not to get too excited or tired."

"Fine. This will be the last time. But I really have to find that ALLMED file."

"Very well. Just a moment." Clarice cupped the phone and looked at her poor, suffering husband. He was in a wheelchair by the window. He could not talk understandably, and he often drooled, but, according to the doctor, he had coherent thoughts.

Right then, for example, Cal was wondering if the turtle soup had done him in.

"Cal, honey, it's one of those dreadful creatures from your office. She wants to know something about the HAMSTED file -- if it's in your top file drawer. Is it?"

Cal stared at his wife. She had been such a saint. And he so wanted to tell her about the turtle soup. Maybe get a lawsuit going. Had to be a bad batch. Maybe the Banyons were trying to cut a few corners by buying low-grade turtles.

"Dear, that woman from your office wants to know what you

did with the SHAKMED file. Shake your head yes if it's in your
top drawer."

Cal wasn't sure what his wife was talking about, but he was
certain there was something in that turtle soup so he shook his
head up and down.

Clarice uncovered the phone. "He's shaking his head up and
down, so it must be in his top drawer."

"Oh goodie," Judy said. She was about to hang up when she
remembered. "How is Cal doing by the way?"

"Well, dear, I guess as good as can be expected. But . . ."

"That's nice. Bye."

Judy had ransacked Cal's desk when Howard appeared silently
behind her.

"Looking for this?" he said, holding the ALLMED file for her
to see.

"Howard, where did you . . ."

Howard just smiled.

* * *

"Want to go to the bike shop?"

Kelly looked up from his rabbit food. "But Howard, we were
there last week. I thought maybe we'd go over to Crown Books."

"Why don't you go? I'm going over to the bike shop."

"Suit yourself."

Howard detoured slightly enroute to the trash compactor so he
could eavesdrop on Judy O'Brien and Tom Barkley,
MEDCORP's handsome chief financial officer.

". . . prospective payment's got a real good chance of becoming
law this year," Barkley was saying. At 49, he looked more like a
model for SKI Magazine than the CFO of a medical supply
company. Of course, he had just returned from a Christmas ski
vacation in Colorado.

"I think so too," Judy said. "And I think this company better
get its act together if it's going to respond proactively."

Howard smiled inwardly and hastened to the bike shop on
Davis Street.

"Can I help you?"

Howard looked at the skinny Jewish kid behind the counter.

"Uh, actually, I was, uh, is . . ."

"Is what, man?"

"Last time I was here I was talking to another clerk about shoes,and she was . . ."

"We're not clerks, man. We're mechanics. OK?"

"Whatever. Anyway, she was going to get some information for me. I wanted to talk to her. Blonde hair, blue eyes."

"She quit."

Howard gasped.

"I said she quit. You want to look at some shoes, I'll show you some shoes. You want cleats?"

"Huh? No. Forget it."

Howard was freaking out by the time he got to her apartment building.

"Can I help you?" the doorman said. He was a wary young black man who took pride in keeping the riffraff out of his building. And this guy in the raincoat sure had the look of a honky pervert.

"Uh, no," Howard said, wondering how he had wandered into the lobby. "Just came in to warm my hands." Howard glanced at the building directory. No help there, the names were listed alphabetically, not by floor.

"You want to warm your hands, there's a coffee shop down the street."

"Yeah. Thanks."

Howard went directly to a camera store on Davis Street and bought a pair of high-powered Bushnell binoculars with his corporate American Express card. That way Connie would never see the bill.

Sealed in his office, Howard went to the window and trained the binoculars on the blonde's apartment. He was just focusing when his door opened.

"What are you looking at, Howard -- old ladies in their underwear?" Judy said.

"Nothing," Howard said, stuffing his binoculars in a drawer. "Nothing at all."

It was true, the apartment in question was quite empty -- of people and furniture.

"What do you want, Judy?"

"You, Howard."

"What?"

"Did you forget -- it's your 40th birthday today. Come on, we've even got a cake for you."

Chapter Six

Howard lit a Merit and sauntered down to the west end of the floor where the women and a few men were gathered around a butcher block table used by the design department.

There was a chocolate cake from Schmiesing's Bakery with "Happy 40th, Howard" written on it in red icing, balloons and the inevitable card.

"Do you have to smoke?" Meg Sanders said.

Howard glared at her.

Betty Draper, a middle-aged secretary in personnel, got Howard an ashtray. "He's the birthday boy. If he wants to smoke, it's his business. Isn't that right, girls."

The other women, mostly middle-aged secretaries, chorused their agreement.

Howard exhaled in Meg Sanders's general direction.

"Come on, Howard, open the card," said Susie Clarke, the 48-year-old mother of four who served as secretary for the Public Affairs Department. Susie's strength was in organizing birthday parties, not in secretarial work.

Howard took another drag and stubbed his cigarette in the ashtray. Susie had written: "To Howard on his BIG birthday" on the blue envelope.

Howard smiled gamely and opened the envelope. There was a cartoon man on the cover holding a cake with countless candles. His hair was thinning and he wore a worried expression.

Howard read the caption: "There's one good thing about turning 40 . . ."

Howard opened the card and continued: ". . . you get plenty of exercise blowing out all the candles."

Everyone laughed or tried to.

Almost everyone on the 11th floor had signed her or his first name somewhere on the card.

"Thanks, everyone," Howard said.

He wanted to throw up. Especially when they labored through "Happy Birthday."

Instead, he dutifully cut the cake and then turned it over to the moms for the real slicing.

Howard had his mouth full when Judy sidled up next to him and said, "Well, Howard, how does it feel to be half way to 80? You know the average life expectancy of males in this country is only 72, so that means the game's more than half over for you, old boy."

It was then that Howard Novick knew there was no God.

* * *

A six-letter word meaning "a nonbeliever; especially, a Christian."

Howard already had the first three letters -- "gia" -- so the rest should be easy. And he had a good ten minutes before Raven Heights, but it wasn't happening today.

Howard looked out the window and was surprised to see so much beauty. The setting sun had painted an orange band across the bottom of the jet sky, silhouetting the oak trees lining the tracks. Women in expensive foreign station wagons waited at the stations for their husbands. Howard wondered if his blonde goddess was out there somewhere waiting for some empty suit in a London Fog.

"Raven Heights, next stop," the conductor called.

Howard looked at the crossword. Definitely not a Latin word, he thought, tossing it on the luggage rack. As he got up, he realized he had a hard-on.

A real diamond-cutter.

Despite a chilling three-block detour, Howard was still hard when he climbed his doorstep.

He instinctively turned the knob and pushed. He nearly dislocated his shoulder. The door was locked. And the lights were out.

Howard tried to think. Thursday night -- Helen's dance lessons, Jennifer's tumbling class, the mother and daughter dinner at church, obedience school for the cat. He couldn't remember. Connie had shouted something at him that morning, but he just didn't remember.

Howard fumbled with half-frozen fingers for his keys. When he finally got the door open, he pulled off his London Fog and threw it on the couch.

Then the lights went on and his parents, who were supposed to be in Sarasota, Florida, stepped out of the kitchen along with Connie, the kids and Howard's sister Madelynn and her boyfriend of the moment.

Stan Novick moved toward his only son as if to embrace him. Then he caught sight of the protrusion in Howard's pants and said: "Howie, is that a banana in your pocket, or are you just glad to see your old man?"

Chapter Seven

"Would you take that stupid look off your mug and give your old man a hug?"

Howard looked dumbly at his family. He had been half-expecting to walk in and find the blonde specter jacking off on his couch.

"Mom, Dad. Madelynn. I, this is . . ."

"Hello, dear," Theresa Fitzpatrick Novick said.

Madelynn waved demurely at her big brother and introduced her date, Libardo Barbosa. Libardo had a pronounced Columbian accent; thick, black hair over a Hispanically handsome face and an incredible physique.

Howard stepped forward and let his father give him a hug and a kiss on the cheek. As always, the old guy reeked of Aqua Velva, and there was less hair on top, but he looked fine for a man of 68.

Theresa stepped in and gave her son a quick hug and a kiss.

"What are you two doing here? I thought you never came north of the Mason-Dixon line between October and May."

"It's not every day my kid turns 40," Stan said, slapping his son on the back. "Where's that package, Doll Baby?"

Theresa handed Howard a box wrapped with paper flamingos, alligators and palm trees. "Your father picked these out," she said.

There was nothing Howard particularly wanted for his 40th birthday, and his parents had always managed to misread his interests by about 100 miles, but he hoped this time would be different.

"Golf balls," he said, trying to mask his crushing disappointment. Howard hated golf.

"Yeah, Howie, but not just any golf balls." Stan took one out and showed everyone. "Snow-Bird golf balls. See -- half-orange for when you play up here in the tundra, and white for when you come down and play with your mom and me in Florida. Plus, there're 40 of 'em. You don't need to count 'em, your old man wouldn't gyp you."

"I don't know what to say. I, ah . . ."

"Can I give you my gift now, Daddy?" Helen said.

"Me too, Daddy," Jennifer said.

Helen gave her father a coffee mug emblazoned with: "World's Greatest Dad."

Howard smiled and gave her a great big kiss.

Jennifer presented him a ceramic ashtray she had made in school. "Sister says it's as good as one you could buy at a store," she said.

Howard held the crudely formed object for all to admire. "She's absolutely right," he said.

"When you quit smoking, Sweetie, you can use it as a coaster for your new coffee mug," Theresa said. "You are going to quit, aren't you?"

Connie took a deep breath. "I've been after him."

"I'm sure you have, dear. Well, what did you get our little Howie for his big birthday?"

Connie blushed and handed Howard a brightly wrapped box. "I made it myself," she said.

Howard bussed her on the cheek and opened it. Connie had knitted him a red scarf with green reindeer. Green except for the squared antlers which were brown. Howard was amazed that anyone could work so hard to make something that looked so bad.

"Thanks," he said, bussing Connie again on the cheek. "Now, I'm all set for work -- a scarf, an ashtray and a coffee cup. Who could ask for anything more?"

Madelynn shrugged. "Sorry, big brother, I didn't get a chance to get to the store. Next time you're downtown, I'll buy you lunch, okay?"

Howard smiled at his 36-year-old sister. "Sure, kid," he said.

Connie clapped her hands. "Well, let's go eat, everybody. I've made Howard's favorite -- baked ham with pineapple rings."

"Oy vey," Stan said, "baked ham. If my old grandfather the rabbi could see me now."

*   *   *

"Hey, Howie, who the hell runs your Florida operation?" Stan said, helping himself to another slice of ham.

Howard felt his throat constrict. "Actually, we have several divisions down in Florida. Why?"

"Well, whoever's in charge down there must have calluses on his rearend, because every time you blink, you see a package or a truck with ALLMED on it. Those guys are all over Florida like flies on you know what.

"You better tell that big Texan of yours to get his rearend in gear, or he's gonna miss a golden opportunity. You know how many old geezers there are down in Wrinkle City?"

"A lot, I'm sure. Dad, I don't mean to disagree with you, but you're talking about home healthcare. That's a soft market."

"Soft, schmoft. What's soft about some old duck buying a couple hundred bucks worth of, um, well you know -- adult diapers every year. You multiply that by a coupla million, kiddo, and that's anything but soft. Of course, what's in them diapers might be . . ."

"Stanley," Theresa said, elbowing her husband. "Not in front of your grandchildren."

They were an odd physical match -- he the dark-complected second-generation Russian Jew and she the red and gray-haired Irish Catholic colleen -- but they retained the emotional closeness that had prompted them to defy their cultures 41 years ago.

"Sorry, kids. But do you catch my drift, Howie? You guys are missin' out on a golden opportunity down in Florida."

Howard stabbed a sweet potato and stuffed it in his mouth. He chewed for a while. "We're geared for the big delivery, Dad. ALLMED can have the home healthcare market. They can compete all they want with Walgreens and Osco and the other drugstores. We're leaders in supplying hospitals, and we're going to remain so."

Stan clapped. "Spoken like a true speechwriter. Well, listen son of mine, things are changing fast in your business. Real fast, and those guys from ALLMED are right in the middle of it, and I don't see as how your gang is doin' much about it."

Howard swallowed hard and turned to Libardo who was seated on his right. "So what do you do, ah . . ."

"Libardo. That's okay, everybody always forget my name. I'm

a bike racer."

"Yeah," Madelynn said, "you should see him in his bike shorts. In fact, he was wearing them the first time we met. We were doing this ad for a yoghurt company, and they wanted to use real bike racers. So the modelling agency sent Libardo and these other hunks in their skin-tight racing outfits. God, every woman in the agency practically -- well, it was quite a day."

Connie coughed uncomfortably, and Theresa glared at her over-sexed, unmarried daughter.

"You can make a living riding bicycles?" Howard said.

Libardo flashed an amazing set of teeth. "Well, during the winter, I work as a bike mechanic, but I do all right. The prize money isn't enough to live on, but my team has a sponsor. That's how you do it. The sponsor makes up the difference. We do okay."

Howard cleared his throat. "There, ah, many women bike racers?"

Everyone stared at the birthday boy.

"Sure, and more all the time."

Howard wondered if there was any safe way of asking if Libardo knew the blonde of his daydreams, but Connie was staring at him.

"How do you keep in shape during winter?"

"As long as the roads are clear, we ride all winter. But if it snows too much, we ride the rollers."

"The rollers?"

"They're steel cylinders connected with a pulley. You put your bike on them and ride. No scenery, but you get a real good workout. Hey, maybe in spring you like to come out and ride with us. We ride right near here on Sheridan Road."

"I don't think so," Howard said. "I'm too old for bike riding. Besides, I don't even have a bike."

*   *   *

Howard dropped his toothbrush in its slot, turned off the light and went to bed.

"Aren't you going to kiss me goodnight?" Connie said.

"What?!?"

"Aren't you going to give me a goodnight kiss?"

"Oh. Okay."

Howard rolled over on his elbow and was about to kiss Connie when he realized she was stark naked.

"I thought I'd give you a little something extra for your birthday, Howard."

"But my parents -- they'll hear . . ."

"They won't hear a thing. And who cares if they do. Come on, Howard, you're always complaining that we don't make love enough. Now's your chance."

"But it's not the right time of the month."

"I know." Connie rummaged in the dark and handed Howard something.

"Is this . . ."

"Mm huh. Come on, put it on. The Pope'll never know."

Howard wasn't sure he could go through with it until the blonde on the couch came to mind.

Chapter Eight

It was a brilliant Sunday morning in March with more than a hint of spring in the air.

Howard was driving Connie and the girls home from Mass at Saints Timothy & Thomas Catholic Church. Howard was still bristling because Father Dan had told one of his happy little homilies about how all God's children should love one another.

"I can't believe it takes that guy all week to come up with something as stupid as that. 'I'm going to tell you a little stowey.' God, if that guy had to go out and get a real job, he'd be in big trouble."

Connie set her jaw. "Howard, if church bothers you so much, why go?"

"Because you nagged me half to death last time I stopped going."

Howard turned left and headed south on Sheridan Road. The sun was warming the inside of their 1980 Chevy Caprice, so he cracked his window slightly and sniffed at the scent of spring. A woman in a white Mercedes convertible passed them.

"We should get a new car," Howard said.

"What's wrong with this car?" Connie said.

"Yeah, Daddy," Helen said, "what's wrong with this car? There's plenty of room back here."

"I just think it's time we got a new car. That's all."

"Howard, we've been through this before. We can't afford a new car, unless you want Helen to give up her piano lessons and Jennifer to stop tumbling class."

"Right. Stupid idea. Sorry I brought it up."

Howard drove in silence, lusting after the mansions that were set back from the road. Any one would do. Any one at all.

Then the pack appeared around a curve. There were more than 50 of them. Each riding a custom-made Italian racing bike, and each wearing a skin-tight racing suit.

"What are you doing, Howard? Howard, what are you doing?"

"I want to watch."

Howard pulled his old clunker off on the shoulder and rolled down his window.

The bike racers buzzed by in a cascade of color and efficient effort. Howard wanted to be among them. Especially when he picked out the blonde beauty who had eluded him since December.

She wore a red and white jersey over her blue lycra tights and was moving forward in the pack. It was her all right. No doubt about it.

"Good God," Howard said, hyperventilating.

"Howard, are you all right?"

Howard blinked and took a deep breath. "Yeah, I think so. Yeah, I'm okay. Come on, let's go home and eat some pancakes."

* * *

The next morning, Howard couldn't finish even the SUN-TIMES crossword. The warm weather seemed to be holding, so he stared out the window hoping she might ride by on her bike.

"Evanston -- Davis Street, next stop."

Howard bounded off the train and ran east on Davis to the bike shop. The store didn't open for another four hours, but that didn't discourage Howard from lusting after the Italian racing bike in the window. He put his hand in his pocket and fondled his American Express card.

"Oh baby," he said.

He was still muttering that expression an hour later when Judy O'Brien appeared suddenly in his office. .

"Cute coffee cup, Howard. 'World's Greatest Dad,' huh?"

"Yeah," Howard said, turning the mug so Judy couldn't see the lettering. "So what do you want?"

"What are we going to do about this, Howard?"

"What are we going to do about what, Judy?"

"Didn't you read the paper this morning?"

"Uh, no. I had some errands I had to run. What's wrong?"

"What's wrong is that Congress passed prospective payment over the weekend. This company just got caught with its pants down. If you want my opinion, I think Bragg better give one hell of a speech next week at the hospital administrators' convention. Here, read it and weep."

Howard scanned the clippings. Judy was right. Congress had snuck prospective payment in at the last minute. Both papers quoted Senator Floyd Smaxton of Arkansas as saying that passage was assured all along because "the American people have had a belly-full of skyrocketing health-care costs."

Howard had intended to quit smoking that day, but this was too much. He rummaged in his drawers until he found a match, a Merit and Jennifer's ashtray.

"Cute ashtray, Howard."

Howard glared at his rival.

"Have you talked to Bragg yet?"

Howard looked at his wordprocessor and realized he hadn't even turned the damn thing on.

"No."

"Well, you'd better. . . Good morning, Mr. Bragg."

Big Bill bulldozed past Judy and settled heavily in one of Howard's undersized guest chairs. "Close the door on yer way out," he said.

Judy flushed and left.

"What the goddamned hell are we gonna do about this, Howie?"

Howard gestured at the clippings and moved his lips. Only smoke and dry reedy whispers came out.

"No, I mean this," Big Bill said, handing Howard a telex.

It had just come in 15 minutes ago and read: "Recalling our little wager of December 19, Mr. Bragg, I do believe you owe me $100. I shall be glad to accept your check at your earliest convenience. Warm Regards, Jeffrey Cotter."

"Pay him, I guess," Howard said.

"Hell no!" Big Bill thundered. "Hell no!"

"As I recall, Mr. Bragg, the wager was that some system of prospective payment would pass in 1983. Now, as I understand this new system, it's nothing at all like the one Cotter's boss Senator Smaxton was pushing. So it seems to me you have him on a technicality."

Big Bill brightened. "I knew you'd come up with something, Howie. Damn, I jus' knew it. Now write that little Jewboy a letter and tell him why I ain't payin'."

Big Bill blustered off to see what the rest of the troops were doing for the good of the cause, and Howard weakly wished his boss wouldn't talk that way in front of him.

Chapter Nine

"An' when I say we ain't gonna climb in bed with our customers, I mean we ain't gonna climb in bed with our customers."

Big Bill stepped back from the podium and smiled at Henry Matthews. MEDCORP's founder and honorary chairman was seated in the front row of the plush Henry Matthews auditorium that May morning for MEDCORP's annual meeting.

"When Henry Matthews founded this great company 60 years ago with a suitcase and a prayer, he promised that Matthews Medical Supply, as it was then known, would forever remain a supplier to hospitals. Mr. Matthews pledged that his company would never compete with its hospital customers.

"We're known as MEDCORP now, but we still make that same promise. In fact, when Mr. Matthews asked me to succeed him, he made me promise that I'd never enter MEDCORP into any kind of business agreement with our customers other than to serve as their faithful supplier. He feels that our forte is in supplying hospitals, not in operating them.

"He said to do both would be unfair. Those rascals in legal would describe it as restraint of trade. I'm just a poor little Texas boy, so I'd call it just plain ole monopolizin'," Big Bill said. He paused for the audience's laughter.

Henry Matthews smiled and waved a boney hand. The 84-year-old turned down his hearing aid and settled back for the rest of the chairman's report to shareholders. He was certain that all was fundamentally well with the company he had founded with a suitcase and a one-way train ticket to Des Moines.

Thus Old Henry was deep in his memories when his hand-picked successor concluded with these words: ". . . of course, that doesn't mean that MEDCORP is going to sit still while the marketplace changes. No, sir. I tell you, ladies and gentlemen, this corporation is on the move. We didn't get to be the world's leading supplier to hospitals by sitting on our brains. No, sir. We're prepared for whatever comes down the pike, and we'll always come out on top. No matter what it takes. That's my promise. That's my commitment. Thank you for your time."

Big Bill removed his bifocals and exchanged winks with his speechwriter who was waiting discreetly in the wings.

*   *   *

"Well, what do you think?"

Connie looked up from her knitting. This time it was a blue shawl for her mother. A blue shawl with red lady bugs.

"Good heavens! Howard, what in the . . ."

"Bike clothes. They're bike clothes," Howard said, stepping all the way into the family room.

Jennifer and Helen turned away from the boob tube and squealed at the sight of their father wearing what looked like cut-off leotards.

"What's that say on your shirt, Daddy?" Helen said.

"Campagnolo. It's an Italian bike manufacturer. In fact," Howard said, heading for the basement, "there's a reason why I bought a jersey with 'Campagnolo' on it."

He returned a moment later with a gleaming red Campagnolo racing bike.

"Look," Howard said, lifting it with two fingers, "lighter than a feather."

"Can I ride it, Daddy?" Helen said.

Howard's expression hardened. "No. This isn't a toy. This is a precision machine. No one except for me rides this bike. Is that understood?"

"Yes, Daddy," the girls chorused.

Connie put down her knitting. "Howard, how much did all this cost?"

Howard shrugged. "Don't worry, I've already paid for it."

"What? The only check you write is for your monthly ticket. How could you have . . ."

"I opened an account at the credit union at work. I charged it all on my company American Express card and paid the bill with my credit-union checking account. It's all paid for, Connie. Don't worry. Besides, you've been after me to quit smoking. I figure this'll help."

"How long have you had this, Howard?"

"Since March. I wanted to wait for spring to really arrive before I took it out for its inaugural run."

Connie stared open-mouthed at her husband. "Oh my God, Howard, your legs!"

Howard glanced down at his nobby knees. "It's what all the racers do. Hair creates drag, so you shave it off. Plus, if you do go down, you stand less of a chance of getting infections from all that dirty hair. Well, I'm off. Ciao."

"Howard, wait."

"What?"

"Shouldn't you wear a helmet?"

"Helmets are for sissies. See you later."

Howard had to balance himself and the bike against the house to get his "cleats" fixed to the pedals. Then, as instructed, he tightened the straps and pushed off down the driveway with visions of the beautiful blonde bicyclist fixed in his head.

Air rushed against his face as he accelerated down the driveway and turned north on Devine Drive. Already Howard could see why she liked cycling so much. It was wonderful. Better than anything he had done for a long, long time.

Howard waved merrily at a startled neighbor and started pedaling.

Whoops, wrong gear. What had that kid said about shifting -- oh shit, a stop sign . . .

It wasn't a bad spill. No damage to the $1,500 custom-made bike, and only a few nicks and scrapes for the greenhorn who was trying to ride it. The worst part was that Howard had been unable to free his feet from the toeclips and had gone down strapped to the bike.

It took him a while to sort things out.

"Need help, Mister?" said a kid passing by on a street bike.

"No, I'm all right."

After convincing himself that his bike was undamaged, Howard carefully continued on his way. There was so much to do and remember, he wondered if he would ever get it right. The blonde angel and her friends made it seem so easy, but it pained his back to bend over the handlebars. And how come that damn kid didn't say what that skinny little seat (he called it a "saddle" didn't he?) would do to a guy's gonads?

But Howard persisted. After all, he knew he looked cool. He somehow managed to get through downtown Raven Heights without incident and soon was pedaling south on Sheridan Road in search of a certain blonde racer.

He didn't find her, but a pack of junior-high-school students on crumby ten-speeds caught him halfway up a hill. Howard was hacking so hard he thought his lungs would come out his mouth any moment.

"That as fast as you can go, man?" one of the kids said.

Howard swiped at the sweat running down his forehead and doubled his efforts.

The kids easily eluded him and were blocks away by the time he finally crested the hill. Howard ached everywhere, especially in his soul. At the next intersection, he turned for home, and when he got there, he took his bike straight to his corner of the basement and covered it with a sheet of plastic.

"How was your big ride, dear?"

Howard ignored his wife and went straight to the bathroom where he took the longest and hottest shower of his life.

Chapter Ten

"Well, Howie, what'd you think?"

Howard looked out his window and watched New York become small and distant.

"You were superb, Mr. Bragg. Just superb. Especially with that reporter from the NEW YORK TIMES."

"Yeah," Big Bill said, jiggling his ice cubes, "I guess I showed that little kike a thing or two. Thinkin' he could get the best of this ole Texas boy. Well, how do you think them financial analysts liked the speech?"

"From what I could hear, they loved it. Just loved it. Although, I'm not so sure they believe us when we say we're not going to climb in bed with our customers."

Big Bill leaned over and poured more bourbon in his glass. He took a big gulp and smiled broadly. "Funny, you should mention that, Howie, because I had a little conversation with Bob Adams before we left for the airport, and it looks like we're gonna do exactly that."

"Bob Adams? You mean TEHA?"

Also known as "YEE-HA," TEHA stood for Texas Episcopal Hospitals of America, a rapidly expanding chain of for-profit regional hospitals with an eye to becoming a nationwide operation. Bob Adams was TEHA chairman and a teammate of Big Bill's at West Texas State.

"I mean that together, MEDCORP and TEHA is gonna wrap up this damn market. And there ain't a goddamned thing them sons-a-bitches at ALLMED is gonna be able to do about it. We'll have complete control of health care in this country -- from manufacturin' and deliverin' to slappin' on band-aids and sendin' you the bill. You either play ball with us, or you don't play ball at all."

Howard waited for the Lear jet to complete its ascent. "But what about what you just told the analysts? What about our shareholders? What about Mr. Matthews?"

Big Bill pawed Howard's knee. "What the hell do you think I keep you around for, Howie? You jus' write one of them fancy ole' speeches of yours an' ole Henry an' them damn shareholders won't know what hit 'em.

"Which reminds me -- since I need you so much as a speechwriter, me and Tom Barkley thought it'd be best if Judy O'Brien took Cal's job. That little gal's real good with numbers an' the like, and that's what we're gonna be needin' -- somebody who can talk numbers to reporters and analysts."

Although he had been trying to quit smoking, Howard kept a pack in his pocket for emergencies. He smiled gamely and filled his lungs with smoke.

*   *   *

"Help me, Howie," Big Bill said, settling behind his mammoth desk.

Howard paced past the brass telescope and thought ruefully of the blonde who used to be on the other end. He turned on his toe and faced the honorary chairman and founder.

"What Mr. Bragg is saying, Mr. Matthews, is that MEDCORP isn't really going into the hospital business with Texas Episcopal Hospitals of America. You may also have heard it referred to as TEHA. At any event, if approved by shareholders of both companies, the agreement would simply mean that we serve as TEHA's exclusive supplier. We would be free to continue supplying our other customers and . . ."

"Now just you wait a minute, young man." Henry climbed out of Big Bill's overstuffed couch and grabbed Howard by the lapels. He was a flinty old man who walked five miles a day. "What's all this about providing them with management consulting?"

"Merely a form of hospital supply. Value added. No different really from dressings and gauze, Mr. Matthews," Howard said, avoiding the old man's gaze.

"Are you a Christian, young man?" Henry said, holding his grip.

"I beg your pardon."

"Have you accepted Jesus Christ as your Lord and Savior? Are you a Christian?"

Howard wished he had a cigarette, but not even Big Bill

smoked in the founder's presence. "Yes, sir. I take my family to church every Sunday."

Henry released Howard and let a smile crease his weathered face. "Then you know how important a man's word is. When I was a little boy, my father took my family to Africa where he did missionary work for the Presbyterian Church. In those days, Presbyterians believed in missionary work. Are you a Presbyterian?"

Howard cleared his throat. "Actually, I'm, ah, a Catholic."

"A Catholic! Did you know that, William?"

"Well, yeah, Mr. Matthews. I knew that, but . . ."

"You let a pope-loving Catholic write your speeches?"

"Yes, sir."

Henry Matthews folded his hands and looked at the two of them. "I don't know what this company is coming to, and I don't really want to know. Now if you gentlemen'll excuse me, I must be about the Lord's work. There are still some real Christians left in this world, believe it or not."

*   *   *

Without Henry Matthews' support, Big Bill Bragg couldn't sell the TEHA deal to shareholders at a meeting he convened on July 15.

Furthermore, the possibility of the deal going through upset a number of MEDCORP's major customers. Big Bill's biggest coup had been to implement a computerized order-entry system that enabled a hospital to order anything it wanted with the touch of a keypad. But it also meant that MEDCORP could keep careful records on a given hospital's activities. Records of great interest to an ambitious chain like TEHA.

Despite Big Bill's repeated promises that "MEDCORP would never even consider sharin' such sensitive information with TEHA," MEDCORP lost 20 percent of its customers in two weeks to ALLMED.

By the end of July, MEDCORP's stock had dropped $15 a share to a post-Depression low of $28. Shareholders were furious, and raiders were lurking in the shadows. Judy O'Brien was forever on the phone with financial reporters or in meetings with a harried Tom Bradley. Howard remained huddled over his wordprocessor with one Merit after another in his mouth.

Then Mason Davis and ALLMED came out of the blue with an offer to buy MEDCORP -- lock, stock, and penile implants.

Big Bill was bright red when he came down to the cafeteria that day for his massive mound of tuna salad. All were silent as he bulldozed through the line. Everyone prayed for the gift of invisibility as the chagrined chairman searched for an empty seat.

Howard and Don Kelly were chosen.

"You boys mind if I join ya?"

Kelly was about to shake his head no, when Howard grabbed his forearm.

"Not at all, Mr. Bragg," Howard said.

Big Bill was soon plowing crackers through the tuna mountain. He ate in loud silence for a moment and then exploded.

"That goddamned, son-of-a-bitch ain't gonna buy this company! Not next week, not the week after, not never! Who the hell does he think he is, comin' in the back door like this? Goddamn him! Goddamn him and the day he was born! He ain't gonna touch this company. No way in hell! You hear me, Howie?"

"Yes, sir," Howard said, discreetly brushing Big Bill's tuna and crackers off his shirt.

Chapter Eleven

"You wanted to see me, Mr. Bragg?"

Big Bill remained hunched over his telescope. "Get a look at this, Howie."

Howard's heart hurried. She was back! The blonde angel was back. He quickly crossed the Oriental carpet.

"Go on, have a look."

Howard was bending to see when he realized the telescope was directed at the Quality Inn Motor Lodge, not at the blonde's former apartment.

"Son-of-a-bitch didn't even take his goddamned socks off," Big Bill said, slapping Howard's back.

Howard swallowed and watched the pale man with the pot belly mount the young black woman. His face reddened as he rode her; her expression grew blanker. Howard was disappointed and disgusted.

"You'd think they'd close the curtains," Howard said, backing away.

"Hell no, Howie," Big Bill said, taking another peep. "What would I do for entertainment all day? Whoo-weeee! Pork her, boy, pork her!"

Howard grimaced and gazed longingly at the building where the blonde had lived.

"You talkin' to yourself, Howie?"

"No, sir."

"That's good, boy." Big Bill turned away from his telescope and padded over to his wet bar. "That's real good, 'cause I need you to write the best damn speech you got in you."

Howard had seldom seen his boss so serene. In the two weeks since the ALLMED offer, the man had been the most brutal bear in the woods. Now he was the son of Bambi.

"Want a drink?"

"No thanks, Mr. Bragg."

Big Bill poured himself a generous measure of bourbon and turned to his speechwriter.

"Ain't you gonna ask why I got this shit-eating grin on my face right now?"

"Well, actually, I was kind of curious, Mr. Bragg."

"Howie, remember when I said we ain't never gonna get in bed with our customers?"

"Sure."

"Well, I wasn't lyin'. We ain't gonna get in bed with our customers. No, sir. But we sure as hell IS gettin' in bed with ALLMED. And there ain't nobody that's gonna stop us now."

*   *   *

"Well, look at it this way -- it's within commuting distance, and even though I'll have to start a half-hour earlier, I'll get home a half-hour earlier."

Connie looked up from her frozen peas and instant mashed potatoes. "But Howard, they're cutting your salary by more than $5,000, and what are the girls and I going to do without a car?"

Howard speared a piece of ham steak and plopped it in his mouth. He washed it down with a gulp of whole milk. "Connie, I'm lucky to have a job. A lot of people have been or are about to be riffed."

"Howard, talk English. Please."

"Reduction in force -- it means . . ."

". . . they were fired."

"Something like that."

"Daddy, did you fire anyone?" Helen asked.

Howard smiled thinly and wondered how long Don Kelly would hate him. Mr. Bragg expected everyone to make sacrifices for the good of the new cause, and Kelly was expendable.

"Eat your peas, Princess."

"Yes, Daddy."

The Novicks finished their meal in silence. The girls cleared the table and raced to the television to watch recycled sitcoms about women with magical powers.

Howard had a Merit while his wife did the dishes.

"Howard?"

"What?"

"Do you think I should get a job?"

"What are you talking about?!?"

"Well, I've been thinking it over, and I just don't see how we're going to manage. There's Helen's piano lessons, and Jennifer's tumbling classes, tuition for both girls, the dentist, the . . ."

"Back up."

"What?"

"I said, back up. Back up to tuition for both girls. Let's talk about tuition. Let's talk about taking those kids out of that stupid Catholic school and putting them in a public school where they belong. We're paying taxes for the public schools, for Christ's sake, so we might as well get our money's worth."

"Howard, I wish you wouldn't take the Lord's name in vain. Especially when the girls can hear." Connie concentrated on a piece of fat that had bonded to the frying pan.

Howard stubbed his cigarette and lighted another. "Sorry. It's just that. . . "

"It's just what, Howard?" Connie stole a glance at her husband. He had been so testy since all this business at work started. A visit with Father Dan would do him a world of good, but she knew how that would go over.

"Nothing. I'm gonna go for a walk."

"Wear your jacket, it looks like it's getting chilly out there."

"Yes, Mommy," Howard said, slamming the door.

Chapter Twelve

Nobody told the people who first planned Chicago's suburbs that by October 1983 everybody and his brother would live and work in suburbia.

And nobody told Howard Novick just how much he would hate sitting in slow-moving suburban traffic every morning and night.

Howard lighted another Merit and punched at the portable cassette player Connie had gotten him. That "Love Doctor" from public television started blithering about "how we have to give one another a big hug and . . ."

Punch.

Howard smoked in silence and watched the traffic creep westbound along Lake-Cook Road. He had been underway for 45 minutes now and could just barely see ALLMED's architecturally insignificant headquarters looming in the smog.

God, I'd give my right arm for a crossword -- any crossword. Even the SUN-TIMES. Howard hadn't had time to work one crossword since he started working at ALLMED's headquarters in Foxfield. It was only 12 miles from his house, but the traffic was so horrible, he seldom covered the distance in under an hour.

Howard had smoked two more Merits by the time he entered the ALLMED gate.

He slowed at the guard station and waved perfunctorily.

"Just a moment, sir."

Howard braked. "Yes?"

"Who are you here to see, sir?"

Howard didn't recognize this guard. There seemed to be a new one every morning. "I work here. Howard Novick. I work for Mr. Bragg."

The guard consulted his clipboard. "Spell that last name, sir."

Howard looked at the line of cars crowding his rearview mirror. "For Christ's sake, I've been working here almost two months now. Howard Novick. I work for Mr. Bragg."

"Well, sir, I don't see anything like that on my list. You'll have to clear it up at the control station."

Howard ground his teeth and did as he was told. As he was walking to the security building, he watched first Meg Sanders and then Judy O'Brien breeze through the gate without a hitch.

"Bitches," he muttered, wondering how long they would keep landing on their feet.

It took him 15 minutes to get a temporary pass.

"I've had to do this every day," Howard told the young woman behind the counter. "This is ridiculous."

"Well, I'm sorry, sir, but for some reason, your name has never appeared on our list of new employees. Maybe you should talk to your . . ."

". . . boss about it. I know. Believe me, I will."

Howard searched the vast lot for a spot. He found one a half-mile from Building B where he worked.

Still, he managed to get to his cubicle two minutes before 8 a.m., the official starting time.

Howard glanced around. As usual, the ALLMED people all appeared to have been at their desks for at least a half an hour. Or more. Maybe they had stayed all night. That seemed to be the style in this drab, boring, awful place with no windows and buzzing fluorescent lights.

Howard reached for his Merits. He had just inhaled the first puff when the woman in the adjoining cubicle started coughing. Others joined the chorus. Howard fidgeted and took another puff. The coughing grew louder.

"All right," he said, much louder than he meant to. "I'll quit! But first I'm going to finish this cigarette in peace."

"Why wait? Quit now," one of his anonymous ALLMED colleagues suggested.

Howard fought the urge to tell them all to get fucked. He finished his cigarette and stubbed it in the ashtray he had brought from home. Then he tried to decide what to do first: rearrange his paper clips or clean his typewriter. Cryptic memos promised the advent of wordprocessors, but Howard knew he wouldn't see one for a long time.

He had just settled on the paper clip option, when somebody called: "Hey, get a load of this."

Everyone in ALLMED's public affairs department left their

cubicles and went to the one tiny window that faced the parking lot.

Big Bill was trying to back his '84 Mercedes 380SEL into his assigned parking place. Big Bill's titular role of chairman did not include limousine service. That was the exclusive privilege of ALLMED's president and chief executive, Mason Davis.

"Where did that guy learn to drive?" someone said.

Howard elbowed his way to the window and watched his boss struggle with the manual transmission. Poor guy. At MEDCORP, he had been chauffeured to his desk.

Big Bill let the clutch out too fast and the German car went kaput. He ranted and raved and tried again. This time he gave it too much gas and the black car slammed into the building with a force that spilled coffee.

"God," somebody said, "that guy's dangerous. The sooner we dump him, the better."

"I heard we're paying him an arm and a leg to sit around all day and twiddle his thumbs," someone else said.

Howard held his breath and watched Big Bill stumble up the walk.

"Look at that. He's drunk. Do you believe it? He's drunk," a co-worker said, tugging at Howard's sleeve.

Howard tore loose and walked briskly back to his desk to await the call. It came 10 minutes later.

"Howie, what the hell are you doin' for the good of the cause this mornin'?"

"Well, Mr. Bragg, I ah . . ."

"Don't sound too good to me, little buddy. Why don't y'all come on up here an' have an eye opener."

"Be right there, Mr. Bragg."

Howard made certain that his picture I.D. was clipped to the right side of his jacket, loaded up his Merits and matches and hurried through the rat maze to Big Bill's spacious new digs.

"Morning, Jane," Howard said.

Big Bill's new secretary smiled professionally. "Good morning, Mr. Novick. He's expecting you."

"Good. Oh, by the way, could you see about a pass for my car. I seem to have been overlooked."

"I'll try. But I can't promise you anything. Would you like

coffee this morning?"

"No thanks."

Howard opened the particle-board door and stepped into what looked more like a bowling alley than an executive office. The corporate art consisted of overblown color photographs of ALLMED's product line. The one over Big Bill's desk showed some poor wretch being hitched up to an ALLMED Digitron Dialysis Maintenance Monitor.

Big Bill stood by his one window looking at the fall colors. "Son-of-a-bitch says he wants to put some kind of shoppin' center over there. Now why the Sam Hill would he want to do that?"

Howard shrugged. "I don't know, sir."

"That makes two of us. Come on, Howie, let's me and you have a drink." Big Bill went to his fully stocked bar. "What'll you have? I'm buyin'."

Howard wanted to say something cautionary, but he knew how that would go over. Especially when Mr. Bragg was already loaded.

"I'll have a bloody Mary. But easy on the vodka."

"Suit yourself, Howie."

Big Bill made the drinks and toasted his speechwriter. "Semper Fi, Marine."

"Semper Fi," Howard said, clinking Big Bill's glass.

"Sure do miss that view," Big Bill said, settling on a leather couch. "You know, I gave that telescope away when we moved over here. Not a damn thing worth lookin' at out here but a bunch of crows. Hell, for two cents, I'd go get me a .22 and start plinkin' at 'em."

Howard stood at the chairman's right hand and sipped his drink.

"They treatin' you all right down there, Howie?"

"Yes, sir. Just fine."

"Good. Good. Well, how you comin' on my speech for the nurse's association?"

"You approved it last week."

"That's right. Yeah. Well, I guess we're all caught up then, ain't we?"

"Yes, sir. It would appear so."

Their eyes met for a moment and then focused elsewhere. A wall clock made the only sound for a long moment. Then Big Bill's phone rang.

"Want me to get it, Mr. Bragg?"

"No, Howie, I'll get it. What they're payin' me, I ought to answer my own damn phone. Yeah Jane. What?!? Yeah, yeah. Send him in. No, wait. Give me five minutes. Five minutes, you hear?"

"Something wrong, Mr. Bragg?"

"Somethin' wrong? Howie, Old Man Matthews is out there. Old bastard wants the grand tour."

"I thought he washed his hands of this whole thing."

"Guess his curiosity got the better of him. Come on, help me hide all this booze. An' see if you can find that pack of Lifesavers I bought the other day."

*   *   *

Henry Matthews wore a carnation and a look of disapproval.

"That's all well and good, William, but what do you do all day?"

Big Bill opened a brochure and pointed. "Well, for starters, Mr. Matthews, all the management consulting services report to me. And . . ."

"Fiddlesticks, William. Fiddlesticks. You don't do a gall-darned thing do you?"

Big Bill got up from his desk and walked to the window. "Howie, tell Mr. Matthews about all the things we do around here."

Howard was seated opposite Mr. Matthews so he had to look the founder in the face and lie. He couldn't do it.

"Just as I thought. Then at least answer my next question, William. Why did you do it? Why did you let them ruin my fine company?"

Big Bill turned away from the window and looked imploringly at his speechwriter. Howard shrugged, thinking, yeah, I'd like to know too.

Big Bill's face reddened. "Well, it seemed like the proactive thing to do, Mr. Matthews. The marketplace was changing, and we thought that. . ."

"Oh, cut the crap, Billy. I may be an old man, but I'm not an old fool. What was your price?"

"I beg your pardon, sir."

"I said: how much did these people have to pay you to get you to give them my company lock, stock and barrel?"

"Howie, tell Mr. Matthews how we . . ."

"I'd like to know too, Mr. Bragg."

Big Bill settled heavily behind his desk. "Mr. Matthews, it's not what you think. Let me show you around, have you meet some of the people who report to me and . . ."

"I'm not a Cub Scout, Billy. I don't need a tour. I just want to know how many pieces of silver it took to buy your soul."

Big Bill looked at his speechwriter and begged for help. Howard coldly turned his attention to the fall foliage beyond the window.

*   *   *

Later that day, Howard sat alone in the cafeteria overlooking the Illinois Tollway and had his usual double-death burger, fries, whole milk and chocolate cake.

Although it was against the unwritten rules, he went outside for a walk after lunch. It was a magnificent fall day, and he was drawn to the trees at the edge of the ALLMED property. He reached for a smoke and realized he was out. Howard took a deep breath of crisp October air. What better time to quit.

He walked across the broad lawn, scuffing his tasseled loafers. A uniformed man from security intercepted him halfway to the trees.

"Where are you going, sir?"

"For a walk."

"That's not really allowed."

Howard stopped. "Why not?"

"Because it's not."

"I see."

Howard turned around and walked back to Building B. When he got inside, he went straight through the lobby and out into the parking lot.

Howard managed to find a station that played a fair amount of rock. He rolled down the window, snapped his fingers in time to the music, and rolled out on the frontage road.

He wasn't quit sure where he was going until he spotted her.

Yes, it was her. Well, wait a minute.

Howard cut around an old lady in a Valiant and got closer.

Yes! Yes! It was the blonde angel!

The blonde angel on a beautiful red racing bike!

Howard clocked her at 25 m.p.h. before the red light caught him. She ran it and disappeared north on Sheridan Road.

Connie and two of of her fat friends from church were knitting an enormous orange blanket with black pumpkins when Howard dashed in the door.

"Howard, what are you . . ."

"Hi, Dear. Ladies," Howard said, rushing down to the basement.

Connie got up from the knitting and went to the head of the stairs. "Honey, are you all right?"

"Couldn't be better. Could you get me my bike clothes? In the closet -- on the top shelf."

"Howard, you didn't get fired, did you?"

"Don't bother; I'll get them myself."

The ladies of the Saints Timothy and Thomas sewing circle were soon confronted by a middle-aged man in skin-tight lycra bike clothing.

"Howard, are you all right? What . . ."

"I'm fine, Connie. Just fine. Decided to take an afternoon off -- that's all. Everybody's entitled to an afternoon off once in a while, aren't they?"

"Yes, but . . ."

Howard and his Italian racing bike were northbound on Devine Drive before Connie could finish her sentence. Howard was in tenth gear and riding hard by the time he hit Sheridan Road.

He figured she had a good 15 miles on him, but he had the rest of his life to catch her.

The End

Chicagoland owes its existence to a
unique assortment of computers, as
unique as the characters featured in
the novel. Written on a Compaq
Deskpro™ with WordStar™ software.
Produced on an Apple® Macintosh SE.™
Designed with Quark EXpress™
software. Printed on a Qume®
ScripTen™ laser printer. Typeface
selection: Adobe's Post Script® fonts:
Times Roman/Times Roman Italic for
text ; and Times Roman Bold for
heads. Copies from the ScripTen™
were shot as camera-ready art by the
printer.

Written and Published by:
Charles McKelvy
The Dunery Press
P.O. Box 116
Harbert Michigan
49115-0116
Phone: 616 469-1278

Designed and Illustrated by:
David Bates
David Bates Design
1312 Cleveland
Evanston, Illinios 60202
Phone: 312 328-5392

Printed by:
Jerry Weber
Patterson Printing
1550 Territorial Road
Benton Harbor, Michigan 49022
Phone: 616 925-2127

Order Form

The Dunery Press
P.O. Box 116
Harbert, Michigan
49115-0116
USA

Telephone 616 469-1278

Please send me the following books from The Dunery Press:

___**Chicagoland**
  by Charles McKelvy
  @ $7.95 each.

___ **My California Friends and Other Stories** *
  by Natalie McKelvy
  @ $8.95 each.
  *Available in December 1988

Name_____

Address _____

City _____

State _____Zip _____

Michigan residents:
Please add 4% sales tax

Shipping:
$2 for the first book and 75 cents for each additional book.

___ Please send me a FREE copy of The Dunery Press catalog

Notes

Notes

Notes

Notes

Notes

Notes

Notes

Notes